HIS UNEXPECTED LEGACY

BY
CHANTELLE SHAW

Chantelle Shaw lives on the Kent coast, five minutes from the sea, and does much of her thinking about the characters in her books while walking on the beach. An avid reader from an early age, her school friends used to hide their books when she visited, but Chantelle would retreat into her own world, and still writes 'stories' in her head all the time.

Chantelle has been blissfully married to her own tall, dark and very patient hero for over twenty years, and has six children. She began to read Mills & Boon as a teenager, and throughout the years of being a stay-at-home mum to her brood found romantic fiction helped her to stay sane!

Her aim is to write books that provide an element of escapism, fun, and of course romance for the countless women who juggle work and home life and who need their precious moments of 'me' time. She enjoys reading and writing about strong-willed, feisty women and even stronger-willed sexy heroes. Chantelle is at her happiest when writing. She is particularly inspired while cooking dinner, which unfortunately results in a lot of culinary disasters! She also loves gardening, taking her very badly behaved terrier for walks and eating chocolate (followed by more walking—at least the dog is slim!).

CHAPTER ONE

Earl's Daughter bags Sicilian Billionaire!

The lurid tabloid headline caught Kristen's attention as she hurried past the newspaper kiosk at Camden Town tube station. Maybe it was the word *Sicilian* that made her stop and buy a copy of the paper, although it did not cross her mind that the headline could be referring to Sergio. It was only when she had jammed herself into a packed train carriage and managed to unfold the paper that she saw his photograph—and for a few seconds her heart stopped beating. Conflicting emotions surged through her as she stared at the image of her son's father. She had not expected Nico to bear such a strong resemblance to Sergio but the likeness between the three-year-old boy and the swarthy Sicilian was uncanny.

Kristen's first instinct was to tear her eyes from the page but curiosity compelled her to study the photograph and the caption beneath it:

> *Lady Felicity Denholm was spotted with her new fiancé, Italian business tycoon Sergio Castellano, when the couple visited the London Palladium earlier this week.*

The text beside the picture continued:

Earl Denholm is reported to be delighted that his youngest daughter is to marry one of Italy's richest men. The Castellano Group owns a chain of luxury hotel and leisure complexes around the world. Sergio heads the property development side of the business, while his twin brother Salvatore runs the family's world-famous vineyards at the Castellano estate in Sicily.

Wedged between a businessman wielding a large briefcase and a teenager wearing an enormous backpack, Kristen gripped the support rail as the train picked up speed. It was becoming something of a habit to learn of Sergio's marriage plans in the press, she thought bitterly. She remembered how shocked and hurt she had felt four years ago when she had read about his engagement to a beautiful Sicilian woman, barely two months after their relationship had ended. Presumably his first marriage had not lasted long if he was now about to marry a member of the English aristocracy.

In the photograph Felicity Denholm was clinging to Sergio's arm and wore the triumphant smile of a cat that had drunk all the cream, Kristen noted sourly. Sergio was even more stunningly good-looking than he had been four years ago. His black tuxedo moulded his broad shoulders and emphasised his powerful physique. But it was his face that trapped Kristen's attention. Blessed with a perfectly chiselled bone-structure, his features were leaner than she remembered. Harder. And, although in the picture he was smiling, nothing could detract from the implacable resoluteness of his jaw.

He was a man who knew his own mind and who pursued his goals with ruthless determination, proclaimed his dark, curiously expressionless eyes. They appeared to be black, but Kristen knew that his eyes were actually the colour of bitter chocolate and could, on rare occasions, soften and invite you to drown in their depths.

Memories flooded her mind of the golden summer she had spent in Sicily four years ago. She had met Sergio soon after she had arrived and the attraction between them had been instant and electrifying. She remembered the first time he had kissed her. They had been talking and laughing together, when he had suddenly dipped his head and brushed his mouth across hers. Even now, the memory was so intense that her stomach clenched. The kiss had been so beautiful and she had realised at that moment that she was in love. Foolishly, she had believed that Sergio shared the sentiment, but for him she had simply been a fleeting diversion from his jet-setting lifestyle.

It was a relief when the train pulled into Tottenham Court Road station and she shoved the newspaper into her bag as she was swept along with the throng of commuters towards the escalator. But the leaden sensation in Kristen's chest remained when she reached the street, and a few minutes later she walked through the doors of Fast-track Sports Physiotherapy Clinic and was greeted with a concerned look from her boss, Stephanie Bower.

'I take it from your expression that Nico didn't want to go to day-care again?' Steph's eyes narrowed on Kristen's tense face. 'Or are you ill? You look like you've seen a ghost.'

'Actually, I've seen Nico's father.' The words spilled from Kristen before she could prevent them, the sense of shock that still gripped her causing her to abandon her usual reticence about her private life.

Steph emitted a low whistle. 'No way? I thought you'd

had no contact with him since Nico was born. Where did you see him?' She stared at the newspaper Kristen handed her.

'That's him, Nico's father,' Kristen said flatly, pointing to the photo on the front page.

'Sergio Castellano! You're kidding, right?' Steph's eyebrows disappeared beneath her fringe when Kristen shook her head. 'Jeez—you're not kidding. But how on earth did you ever get mixed up with a drop-dead sexy, hotshot playboy? Not that I'm surprised,' she added hastily. 'Let's face it, you're a gorgeous blonde and you were bound to catch his attention. But you are a physiotherapist living in Camden and he's a billionaire who likes to cruise around the Med on a luxury yacht the size of the QE2. Where did you meet him?'

'In Sicily,' Kristen sighed. 'I'd taken a gap year from university to concentrate on trying to win a gold medal at the gymnastics world championships, but I had a bad bout of flu and fell behind with my training. My GP suggested I should go somewhere warm for a while to recuperate. My stepfather, who was also my coach, had a friend who owned a villa in Sicily which happened to have a gym. Alan rented the villa for six months, and he, Mum and I flew out there. But soon after we arrived my mum and stepdad had to return to England because Alan's father had died unexpectedly.

'I remained in Sicily.' Kristen gave a rueful smile. 'It was the first time I'd ever lived on my own. Even though I was studying at university, I still lived at home so that I could follow Alan's strict training schedule. I loved gymnastics, but I had started to feel that it had taken over my life. I'd never even had a proper boyfriend. I guess that's why I was swept off my feet by Sergio,' she said heavily. 'The Castellano estate was close to the villa where I was staying. I quite literally ran into Sergio one day on the beach and he was so sexy and charming that I was blown away by him. I couldn't believe my luck that he seemed to be attracted to me.'

She grimaced. 'I was very naïve. My stepfather was a dominant figure in my life and he was determined that I would be a top gymnast. I'd had a sheltered upbringing, but suddenly I was free from Alan's influence and I rushed headlong into an affair with Sergio.'

Steph gave her a speculative look. 'But at the end of the summer I suppose you had to return to England, and you came home with more than just a suntan,' she murmured. 'I assume you fell pregnant with Nico while you were in Sicily? Didn't Castellano offer to support you when you told him you were expecting his baby? What a bastard, especially when he's loaded...'

'I didn't tell him.' Kristen interrupted Steph before she could launch into one of her feminist diatribes against the male species. Fresh from an acrimonious divorce after discovering that her husband who she had adored was a serial adulterer, Steph's opinion of men was that they should all be boiled in oil.

'Sergio doesn't know about Nico. He made it very clear during our affair that he wasn't looking for a committed relationship of any kind, and I knew when I found out I was pregnant that he wouldn't be interested in his child.'

The full truth of what had happened four years ago was too complicated to explain, and too painful for Kristen to want to dwell on. Often when she looked at Nico she thought about the other baby she had lost and felt an ache of sadness. Forcing her mind from the past, she saw that Steph was concentrating on the newspaper article.

'So Nico's filthy-rich father is getting married to a spoiled socialite, and it says here that the couple will share their time between his home in Sicily, a luxury apartment in Rome and the multi-million pound house that Sergio is currently buying on Park Lane. That's when he and the lovely Lady Felicity aren't aboard his yacht or travelling on his private jet,' Steph said sardonically. 'Meanwhile you are struggling to bring up Castellano's son alone, with no financial help. It's outrageously unfair.'

Kristen shrugged. 'I'm not struggling,' she murmured, unaware of the weariness in her voice. The salary she earned as a physiotherapist covered her mortgage and bills, and although it was true that the cost of living seemed to have rocketed recently she was still able to provide Nico with everything he needed. 'It's true I can't go mad with money, but who can at the moment?'

Steph dropped the newspaper onto her desk and gave Kristen a rueful look. 'I know you're finding things more difficult now that you have to pay childcare costs since your mum died. But I'm not just talking about the fact that you are struggling financially. You're still grieving for Kathleen, and so is Nico. It's the reason he's been so clingy lately and why he cries every time you leave him at nursery.'

'His nursery worker says he stops crying after I've gone,' Kristen muttered tightly. She knew Steph was simply showing friendly concern, but she felt guilty enough about leaving Nico, and the sound of his sobs as she had walked out of the day-care centre this morning had made her feel as if her heart was being ripped out. 'What do you suggest I do? I would love to stay at home with Nico like my mum did, but I'm a single mother and I have no choice but to go to work.'

'I think you need to take a sabbatical,' Steph said firmly. 'I wouldn't be saying this if I wasn't so worried about you. Heaven knows, you're a valuable member of staff.

But I can see you're close to the edge. You need to take a couple of months off while you try and come to terms with losing your mum, and so that you can be a full-time mum to Nico.'

Tears filled Kristen's eyes as she thought of her mother. Kathleen had moved in with her when she'd given birth to Nico and had looked after him when Kristen had returned to work. The accident five months ago had been such a terrible shock. Kathleen had popped to the shops because they had run out of milk and been hit by a speeding car as she had crossed the road. She had been killed instantly, the policewoman who had broken the news had explained. Kristen was thankful that her mum hadn't suffered, but Steph was right, she hadn't come to terms with the tragedy and her grief was made worse because she knew that Nico desperately missed his beloved Nana.

She sighed. 'It's a nice idea, but I can't give up work. I'd have to win the Lottery first.'

'Here's your ticket.' Steph picked up the newspaper and jabbed her finger at Sergio's handsome face. 'It's only fair that Nico's father should take some responsibility for his son.'

'No!' Kristen said so fiercely that Steph gave her a curious look. 'I told you, Sergio is unaware of Nico's existence. And if he knew he had a child he wouldn't want anything to do with him. I'm certainly not going to ask him for money.'

'I'm not suggesting you demand a massive maintenance agreement,' Steph argued. 'You simply want a bit of financial help for a couple of months so that you can give Nico the care and attention he needs right now.'

'My son is my responsibility,' Kristen said in a tone that warned her friend to drop the subject. But she had to admit that Steph had made a valid point when she'd said that Nico was in need of extra care to help him deal with the loss of his grandmother. He might only be three years old, but Kristen didn't underestimate his grief. Over the past few months he had grown pale and listless and his lack of appetite was worrying.

'Give him time,' Kristen's GP had advised. 'Nico gets upset when you leave him at nursery because he's afraid, quite naturally under the circumstances, that you won't come back. Gradually he will come to accept the death of his grandmother. All you can do is to give him plenty of love and reassurance.'

She would love to rent a cottage by the sea for the summer and take Nico away for a holiday, Kristen thought wistfully. But it was impossible. The mortgage on her house would not pay itself. She pushed thoughts of the past away and forced herself to concentrate on her appointments. In her job she treated patients with a wide variety of sport-related injuries and usually she found the work absorbing. But today the clinic dragged, and even during the Pilates class she ran later in the day her mind was distracted and for once she was glad when the session was over.

The Tube was as busy at the height of the evening rush-hour as it had been in the morning but luckily there were no delays on her line and she was on time to collect Nico. He was waiting with the other children, his eyes fixed on the door as the parents filed into the nursery, and the moment he caught sight of Kristen his face lit up with a smile that tugged on her heart.

'Mummy!' He hurtled across the room and into her arms.

'Hello, Tiger. Have you had a nice day?'

Nico did not reply, but as Kristen lifted him up he linked his arms around her neck and pressed his face into her shoulder. His hair smelled of baby shampoo and felt like silk against her cheek. He was the most precious thing in her life and the intensity of her love for him brought a lump to her throat.

'I missed you.' Eyes as round and dark as chocolate buttons looked at her from beneath long, curling lashes. Nico's eyes were the exact same shade as his father's. The thought slid into Kristen's mind as she recalled the photo in the paper of Sergio and she felt a knife blade pierce her heart.

'I missed you too. But I bet you had a lovely time with all your friends,' she said encouragingly. 'Did you play in the sandpit with Sam?'

Nico stared at her solemnly. 'Can we go home now?'

Kristen set him back on his feet. 'Go and get your coat. We'll stop off at the park, as long as you promise not to climb to the top of the climbing frame.' A shudder ran through her at the memory of how he had fallen and been badly hurt on their last trip to the park. Sometimes she struggled to cope with Nico's exuberance.

As he shot off across the room, she turned to speak to his play-worker, Lizzie. 'How was he today?'

'He's been very withdrawn,' the young woman admitted. 'I tried to persuade him to join in with the activities but it's obvious he's missing his nana.' She gave Kristen a sympathetic look. 'This must be a difficult time for you and Nico. Perhaps, with the summer coming, you could take a holiday. I'm sure it would do you both good.'

There was only one way Kristen could take Nico on holiday, and that was to ask for financial help from his father. Back home at her tiny terraced house, she reread the newspaper article about Sergio's engagement while she was cooking dinner.

It is expected that the couple will celebrate their engagement at a lavish party to be held tonight at the

Hotel Royale in Bayswater, which was purchased by the Castellano Group a year ago and has undergone a one-hundred-million pound refurbishment.

If only there was a way she could speak to Sergio before the party. Kristen's heart lurched at the prospect of revealing to him that he had a son. She glanced into the living room, expecting to find Nico watching TV, but he had picked up a framed photograph of Kathleen and was staring at it with a wistful expression on his face that made Kristen's heart ache.

'Come and have your dinner,' she said softly.

'I don't want any, Mummy.'

If Nico's appetite didn't pick up soon she would have to take him back to the doctor, Kristen thought worriedly. She forced a smile. 'Try and eat a little bit, and then I'll tell you something exciting.'

She was rewarded with a flicker of interest in Nico's chocolate button eyes as he ran into the kitchen and took his place at the table. 'What's ic-citing?'

'Well, I've been thinking that it would be nice if I took some time off work so that we could have a holiday by the seaside. Would you like that?'

Nico's wide smile was all the answer she needed. It brought home to Kristen that she hadn't seen his cheeky grin for weeks and her heart broke at the thought of her little boy's sadness. She would make Nico happy again, she vowed. She would do whatever it took to see him return to his usual sunny nature, and if that meant swallowing her pride and asking his billionaire playboy father for financial help it would be a small price to pay.

'Honestly, I've no idea why the newspaper printed an article about us being engaged.' Felicity Denholm met Sergio's frown with a guileless smile. 'I admit I told a journalist that you're in London to finalise a business deal with my father, and I may have mentioned that you're planning to host a party tonight, but that's all I said.'

She perched on the edge of Sergio's desk so that her skirt rode up her thighs and gave a tinkling laugh that grated on his nerves. 'I can't imagine where the story about us planning to get married came from, but you know how the paparazzi like to stretch the truth.'

'In this instance there is not a shred of truth to stretch,' Sergio bit out. His jaw hardened as he struggled to control his impatience. He disliked the media's fascination with his private life and he fiercely resented the publication of a story that was pure fiction.

Felicity shook her glossy chestnut curls over her shoulders. 'Well, we've moved in the same social circles while you have been in London, and we were photographed together the other night when we bumped into one another at the theatre. I suppose it's understandable that the press believe there's something going on between us.' She shifted position so that her skirt rode higher up her thighs and leaned towards Sergio, an artful smile on her red-glossed lips. 'It almost seems a pity to disappoint them, doesn't it?' she murmured.

Sergio's eyes narrowed. Denholm's daughter was an attractive package and he had briefly considered accepting her not very discreet offer to take her to bed. But he had a golden rule never to mix business with pleasure and he had been far more interested in persuading the Earl to sell a property portfolio that included several prime sites in central London than to satisfy his libido with the lovely but, he suspected, utterly self-centred Felicity.

He was sure it had not been purely coincidence that she had appeared at every party he had attended in recent weeks. Her topics of conversation might be limited to fashion and celebrity gossip but she had stalked him with extraordinary determination. It was even possible that Felicity had been following her father's instructions, Sergio mused. The Earl was a wily character who had been forced to sell his property portfolio to pay for the costly upkeep of the family's stately home. Perhaps Charles Denholm had hoped to regain control of his assets by promoting a marriage between his daughter and the Sicilian usurper to his crown.

Sergio was infuriated that he had no way of proving who had planted the engagement story in the paper. All day his temper had simmered while he had dealt with the speculation caused by the article, and the last straw had been a terse telephone conversation with his father, who had demanded to know why he had learned of his son's plan to marry from a newspaper.

'The story is just that—a figment of a journalist's imagination,' he told Tito. 'If I ever decide to marry, you will be the first to know. But don't hold your breath,' he added sardonically.

His father immediately launched into a tirade about it being time Sergio packed in his playboy lifestyle, settled down with a nice Italian girl and, most importantly, produced an heir to continue the Castellano family line.

'You already have an heir in your granddaughter.' Sergio reminded his father of his brother Salvatore's little daughter, Rosa.

'Of course, but she cannot shoulder the responsibility of the company alone,' Tito growled. 'Salvatore is a widower and unlikely to have more children, and so I have to put all my hopes on you, Sergio.'

Sergio was aware of the unspoken message that he was a disappointment to Tito. But he would not pick a bride in the hope of winning the old man's approval. It would be pointless anyway. They both knew he was not the favoured son. And he had no wish to marry. It amazed him that his father did not understand his attitude when Tito's own marriage to Sergio's mother had been a disaster that had ended in bitterness and hatred that had had lifelong consequences for him and his brother.

Dragging his mind from the dark place of his childhood, he jerked to his feet and moved away from the desk where Felicity was still artfully sprawled. He wondered why, despite her obvious charms, he didn't feel a spark of interest in her. In truth, he was becoming bored of meaningless sex. But what other kind of sex was there? he brooded. He had no interest in relationships that demanded his emotional involvement. Work was his driving force, although deep down he acknowledged that his ruthless ambition was partly fuelled by a desire to prove to his father that he was as worthy a son as his twin brother.

In his leisure time, all he required from the women who shared his bed was physical gratification. So why had he been feeling restless lately? What was he searching for when he had everything he could possibly want?

'I have demanded the paper prints an admission that the story is entirely untrue,' he told Felicity. 'I can only apologise for any embarrassment the article may have caused you. As you know, I am giving a party tonight to celebrate the completion of the business deal with your father. Members of the press have been invited, and I intend to make a statement to set the record straight about us.'

Felicity tilted her head and gave him a kittenish smile. 'Or you could ravish me on your desk,' she invited boldly. 'And then, who knows—maybe it won't be necessary for the newspaper to retract the story.'

Maybe he was old-fashioned but he preferred to do the

chasing, Sergio thought as he strode across the room and held open the door. 'An interesting proposition, but I'm afraid I must decline,' he drawled.

The young Englishwoman flushed at his rejection and slid off the desk. 'No wonder you're known as the Ice-man,' she muttered sulkily. 'Everyone says you have a frozen heart.'

Sergio gave her a coolly amused smile that did not reach his eyes. 'Everyone is right. But I have no intention of discussing my emotions, or lack of them, with you.' He glanced at his watch and ushered Felicity out of his office. 'And now, if you'll excuse me, I have some work to do.'

The décor of the Hotel Royale was unashamedly opulent. Clearly the new owners, the Castellano Group, had spared no expense on the refurbishments and it was easy to see why the hotel had been awarded five-star status. The clientele were as glamorous as the surroundings, and as Kristen walked through the marble lobby she was conscious that her businesslike black skirt and white blouse were definitely not haute couture. It didn't help that her feet were killing her. She was ruing her decision to wear a pair of three-inch stilettos that had been an impulse buy and had sat unworn at the back of her wardrobe for months.

Having made the decision to try and speak to Sergio, she had arranged for her neighbour to babysit Nico before she had caught the Tube to Bayswater. She half-expected the concierge to ask the reason for her visit but the reception area was busy and she walked past the front desk without anyone seeming to notice her. There was a good chance that Sergio would refuse to see her and so it seemed better to surprise him. The newspaper article had mentioned that he was staying in his private penthouse suite. As the lift whisked Kristen smoothly towards the top floor she could feel her heart beating painfully fast beneath her ribs.

It was a crazy idea to have come here, whispered a voice inside her head. Even if she managed to find Sergio, the prospect of telling him he had a son was daunting. She felt sick with nerves and when the lift doors opened she was tempted to remain inside and press the button for the ground floor. Only the memory of Nico's excitement when she had promised to take him on holiday hardened her resolve to ask for financial help from Sergio.

She walked along numerous grey-carpeted corridors with a growing sense of despair that she did not have a clue where his private suite might be. Turning down another corridor, she was confronted with a set of double doors and a sign on the wall announced that she was outside the Princess Elizabeth Function Room.

A waiter emerged from a side door and, catching sight of Kristen, he thrust a tray filled with glasses into her hands. 'Don't just stand there,' he said, sounding harassed. 'They're about to make a toast and some of the guests are still waiting for champagne.'

'Oh, I'm not…' she began to explain, but the waiter wasn't listening as he opened the doors and practically pushed her into the room.

'Hurry up. Mr Castellano is not happy that the party is running late.'

'But…' Kristen's voice trailed off as the waiter hurried away. Glancing around the enormous function room, she realised that her outfit was almost identical to the waitresses' uniform and it was easy to understand how she had been mistaken for a member of staff.

But at least she had found Sergio.

Her heart lurched as her eyes were drawn to the man at the far end of the room. His almost-black hair gleamed like raw silk beneath the blazing lights of the chandeliers. Taller than everyone circled around him and a hundred times more devastatingly handsome than the photo in the newspaper, it was not just his physical attributes that made him stand out from the crowd. Even from a distance, Kristen was conscious of his aura of power and charisma that made all other men seem diminished.

With his stunning looks, huge fortune and blatant virility, Sergio Castellano captured the attention of every woman in the room. But, although he smiled and exuded effortless charm, Kristen sensed a restless air about him. His dark eyes flicked around the room as if he was searching for someone. She caught her breath. He could not possibly know she was here, she reminded herself. And yet in Sicily their awareness of each other had been so acute that they had sensed each other's presence across a crowded room, she remembered.

She watched a woman walk up to him and recognised her as the woman from the paper, Lady Felicity something-or-other. The woman he was planning to marry. The sensation of a knife-blade being thrust between her ribs made Kristen catch her breath. Four years ago Sergio had broken her heart but after all this time she had not anticipated that seeing him again would be so agonising.

He stepped onto a raised platform where a microphone had been set up. Kristen guessed he was about to announce his engagement to Felicity and she was unprepared for the violent feeling of possessiveness that swept through her. For years she had tried to forget Sergio because she had believed he was married to his Sicilian bride. But here he was, about to reveal his plans to marry another woman, while *she* was struggling to bring up his son on her own.

'Ladies and gentlemen—' Sergio's gravelly voice filled the room, and an expectant hush descended over the guests

'—as you are aware, tonight's party is to celebrate the Castellano Group's acquisition of an extensive portfolio of properties from Earl Denholm. Following an article in a certain daily newspaper, there is another matter I would like to address regarding Lady Felicity Denholm and myself…'

'No! You can't marry her!'

The words tumbled from Kristen's mouth before she could stop them. Her voice sounded deafeningly loud in the silent room and she felt her face burn as the party guests all turned to look at her. She swallowed as Sergio jerked his head in her direction. Even across the distance of the room, she sensed his shock as he recognised her.

'Kristen?'

The husky way he spoke her name, the slight accent on the first syllable, touched something deep inside her. Her eyes locked with his and she felt the same inexplicable connection she had felt the very first time she had seen him. But when they had met on a Sicilian beach Sergio had smiled at her. Now, his shocked expression was rapidly changing to anger—which was hardly surprising when she had just ruined his engagement party, Kristen thought ruefully.

Dear heaven, what had she done? But it was too late to backtrack now.

'It…it isn't right,' she faltered. 'You have responsibilities…you have…' Her nerve failed her. She could not reveal to Sergio that he had a son when he was staring at her with a coldly arrogant expression that froze her blood.

'What are you doing here?' His voice sounded like the crack of a whip and jerked Kristen from her state of stunned immobility. She became aware of the startled faces of the guests around her and felt sick as the magnitude of what she had done hit her. She shouldn't have come and she had to leave, immediately.

She thrust the tray of drinks into the hands of one of the guests and ran across to the double doors just as they opened to allow several waiters bearing trays of canapés to file into the room.

'Stop her!'

The harsh command filled Kristen with panic. A security guard stepped in front of her, blocking her path, and she gave a startled cry as a hand settled heavily on her shoulder and spun her around. She stumbled in her high heeled shoes and fell against Sergio's broad chest.

He stared down at her, his dark eyes blazing with fury. 'What the hell is going on?'

As she stared at his handsome face, the words of apology died on Kristen's lips and her brain stopped functioning. But her senses went into overdrive. The feel of his hand on her shoulder seemed to burn through her thin blouse and the close proximity of their bodies caused her heart to slam against her ribcage. For timeless moments the voices of the guests faded and there was just her and Sergio alone in the universe.

The anger in his eyes turned to curiosity and something else that made the hairs on the back of her neck stand on end. An electrical current seemed to arc between them and Kristen felt heat surge through her body. But then a flashlight flared, half-blinding her, and when Sergio came back into focus his expression was once more furious.

His fingers gripped her shoulder so tightly that she winced. '*Dio*, the press are going to love this,' he said bitterly.

The press! The flashbulbs suddenly made sense. Kristen stared wildly at the flank of photographers who were circling her and Sergio. No doubt the journalists were eager to know why she had interrupted him just as he had been about to announce his engagement. 'Oh, God,' she muttered and, with a strength born of desperation, she tore free from Sergio's hold and shot past the security guard, out into the corridor.

With one of their quarry gone, the journalists crowded around Sergio. 'Mr Castellano, do you want to make a statement?'

'No, I damned well don't,' Sergio growled savagely. What he wanted to do was race after Kristen and find out what she was playing at. He had hardly been able to believe his eyes when he had looked across the ballroom and seen her, and one part of his mind had instantly registered that she was even lovelier than his memory of her.

Enzo, his PR man, appeared beside him and for once the usually unflappable manager looked shaken.

'I think you should say something and explain the situation,' Enzo advised in an undertone meant for Sergio's hearing only. 'Earl Denholm seems to think that you have humiliated his daughter by ending your engagement to her in public, and he's threatening to call off the deal.'

'*Santa Madonna!* There was *no* damned engagement. I assumed Felicity had made that clear to her father.' Sergio's nostrils flared as he struggled to control his temper. He had no wish to talk to the press, but if the deal with Denholm was about to blow up in his face he realised he had no choice.

He spun back round to the journalists, his face now expressionless as he controlled his anger. 'There has been a misunderstanding. Miss Denholm and I are not engaged…'

A microphone was shoved at him. 'Has she called it off because she found out about your mistress?'

'Who is the mystery blonde who just left?'

'Are you planning to marry the waitress?'

Sergio's patience snapped. 'I'm not planning to marry anyone—ever.' He glanced at his PR man. 'Enzo, I'll leave you to deal with this—while I deal with the "mystery blonde",' he said with grim irony, and strode out of the function room.

CHAPTER TWO

WHERE THE HELL was she? Sergio stared up and down the empty corridor before turning left out of the function room. His instincts proved correct as he walked swiftly and turned a corner to see a petite blonde-haired figure at the far end of the passageway.

He was rarely surprised by anything, but tonight he had received a shock that was still causing his heart to thud unevenly. He had seen a ghost from his past, although Kristen Russell—for all her ethereal beauty—was no spectre from the spirit world. She was very real, albeit a woman now rather than the innocent girl he had known four years ago.

An unbidden memory came to him of the first time he had made love to her. It had been a new experience for both of them, he thought wryly. He had been shocked to discover she was a virgin. Before he had met her, and after their relationship had ended, his numerous affairs had been with women whose sexual experience matched his own. It was true that his affair with Kristen had been different from any of his previous relationships, but ultimately it had ended for the same reason his affairs always ended—she had wanted more from him than he could give. When she had left him, he had let her go, knowing there was no point trying to explain his bone-deep mistrust of emotional commitment.

Psychologists would no doubt blame his childhood and in particular his mother as a reason for his inability to connect with women on a deep level. Sergio's mouth curved into a derisive smile. Maybe the shrinks were right. As a child he had taught himself to block out pain—both mental and physical—until nothing could hurt him. It was a trait he had continued as an adult and his freedom from emotional distractions gave him an edge over his business rivals and had earned him a reputation for ruthlessness in the boardroom.

Yet he admitted that he had missed Kristen, and for a while after she had returned to England he had been tempted to follow her and re-ignite the fiery passion that he had never felt so intensely for any other woman. He had resisted because nothing had changed. He could not be the man she wanted. And then there had been Annamaria, and for the only time ever in his life his actions had been driven by love. The cruelty of her untimely death had served as a reminder that even he could not freeze his emotions completely.

Sergio forced his mind from the past and continued his pursuit of Kristen along the corridor which led only to his private suite. She was clearly finding it difficult to keep up a fast pace in her high-heeled shoes and her hips swayed, causing her tightly clad *derrière* to bob tantalisingly in front of his eyes.

His footsteps were muffled by the thick carpet, but Kristen must have sensed someone was behind her because she glanced over her shoulder and gave an audible gasp when she saw him.

'If you're looking for the way out, you won't find it along here,' he told her curtly.

Kristen froze and, realising the futility of continuing along the corridor that appeared to be a dead end, she slowly turned to face the man who had haunted her dreams for so long. Sergio had caught up with her and was standing so close that she breathed in the sensual musk of his cologne. He towered above her, a darkly beautiful fallen angel in black tailored trousers and matching silk shirt. Her eyes darted to his face, and she caught her breath as she felt a kick of sexual awareness in the pit of her stomach. The faint shadow of black stubble on his jaw accentuated his raw masculinity and the curve of his wide mouth promised heaven. But it was his eyes that trapped her gaze, as dark and sensuous as molten chocolate, framed by lush black lashes.

Once, a long time ago, his eyes had held warmth, desire. But now his expression was cold and she sensed his anger was tightly controlled.

'Besides, it's pointless to look for the exit,' he said in a dangerously soft voice. 'You won't be going anywhere until you've explained what in God's name is going on.'

'I'm sorry I interrupted your party,' she said frantically. 'It was a stupid thing to do.' She hesitated, feeling guilty for the trouble she must have caused. 'I...I hope Miss Denholm isn't too upset.'

He gave a dismissive shrug. 'She is not important.'

Kristen was shocked by his careless dismissal of his fiancée. 'How can you regard announcing your intention to marry as unimportant?' She gave him a disgusted look. 'Although it's not the first time you've got engaged so I suppose it might seem boring.'

Sergio's eyes narrowed at her sarcastic tone. 'What do you mean?'

Four years of hurt and anger exploded from Kristen. 'You didn't waste much time replacing me in your bed, did you?' she said bitterly. 'I heard that you'd got engaged to a Sicilian woman soon after we broke up. That's why I didn't…'

'Didn't what?' he prompted when she broke off abruptly.

'It…it doesn't matter.'

She tore her eyes from his face. The reason she had not contacted him to tell him she was pregnant after she had left Sicily was not only because she had learned of his intention to marry another woman. She had been certain he would not be interested in the child she had conceived by him, and now she questioned why she had considered asking him for financial support for his son.

But surely it was fair that Sergio should take some responsibility for Nico? The voice of reason inside her head refused to be ignored. She had made the decision to ask him for financial help for Nico, and now that they were alone she had the perfect opportunity. Taking a deep breath, she said quickly, 'I was wondering if I could speak to you?'

'Certainly,' he drawled sardonically. 'I'm fascinated to hear why you gatecrashed my party. And after you've explained yourself to me, you can give a statement to the press.

'Dio!' His tenuous control over his temper cracked. 'Have you any idea of the furore you've caused? Because of you, my business deal is about to go down the pan.'

So he regarded his engagement to Lady Felicity as a business deal! Kristen shook her head. She had known that Sergio was hard but, even so, she was shocked by the proof of his complete lack of emotion. She must have been mad to think he would agree to give financial assistance for Nico.

'Actually, forget it,' she muttered. 'There's no point in me talking to you.' She tried to walk past him but his hand shot out and gripped her shoulder. Panic sharpened her voice. 'Will you please let me go?'

'You must be joking,' Sergio said grimly. 'Our conversation hasn't even started. Come into my suite so that we can be assured of privacy.'

It was an order rather than an invitation and, before Kristen could argue, he opened the door and steered her into an elegant sitting room. But she barely noticed the décor. The feeling that she had walked into a trap intensified when Sergio closed the door and her vivid imagination pictured her as a fly caught in a spider's web, with no chance of escape.

'Take a seat,' he commanded, waving his hand towards the large sofa in the centre of the room.

Kristen remained standing just inside the door, tension emanating from every pore. Sergio frowned as it occurred to him that she looked nervous. Hell, he had every right to be angry with her, he assured himself as he recalled the scene in the function room. But the possibility that she was afraid of him made him uncomfortable. He raked his hand through his hair. As he stared at her, an image flashed into his mind of her ravaged, tear-stained face at the hospital in Sicily. She had been devastated by what had happened, but soon afterwards she had returned to England and he didn't know if she had coped okay. He should have phoned her to see how she was, his conscience pricked. But at the time it had seemed better to make a clean break, and if he was honest his pride had been hurt by her decision to leave him.

'How are you?' he asked gruffly.

She looked surprised by his softer tone. 'I'm fine… thank you.'

'It's been a long time since we last saw one another.' Irritated with himself for his uncharacteristic lack of savoir faire, Sergio stalked over to the bar. 'Would you like a drink?'

There was a bottle of champagne in an ice bucket and, without waiting for her to reply, he popped the cork, filled two tall flutes and held one out to her. With obvious reluctance, she crossed the room and took the glass from him.

'To old acquaintances, or perhaps I should make that to unexpected visitors,' he said drily. 'Why did you interrupt my party, Kristen?'

Kristen took a gulp of champagne and felt the sensation of bubbles bursting on her tongue. 'I've already told you that I wanted to talk to you…about something important.' She bit her lip, finding it impossible to utter the statement, *By the way, you have a three-year-old child who you've never met.*

Sergio nodded towards the sofa. 'In that case, you had better sit down.'

Sitting seemed the safest option when her legs felt like jelly. Kristen sat, and immediately sank into the soft cushions. She tensed when he sat down next to her and stretched his long legs out in front of him. He extended his arm along the back of the sofa and she couldn't restrain the little quiver that ran down her spine as she imagined his long, tanned fingers stroking her exposed nape where her hair was swept up into a chignon.

An awkward silence fell until he said abruptly, 'So, what did you want to talk to me about?'

Kristen's heart missed a beat and, to steady her nerves, she took another gulp of champagne.

'I…' While she was searching for the right words she made the mistake of looking at him, and whatever she had been about to say died on her tongue when she discovered that he was looking at her in a way that convinced her he was remembering her naked. The bold glitter in his eyes was inappropriate and outrageous, but the damning heat in her breasts as they swelled and strained against her suddenly too-tight bra was even more shocking.

'As you probably know, the Castellano Group owns many hotels around the world,' Sergio was saying. 'Staff issues would normally be dealt with by the Hotel Royale's manager, but I will try to be of help.' He frowned. 'I admit I am puzzled to find you working as a waitress, Kristen. As I recall, you left me to return to university and finish your studies.'

For a few seconds Kristen stared at him blankly, before realisation dawned that he had mistaken her for a waitress. She glanced down at the plain black skirt she had bought to wear to her mother's funeral. As far as Sergio was aware, there was no other reason why she would have been at his private party.

He made the past sound so black and white, she thought bitterly. It was true she had left him to go back to university, but only because he had made it clear that in the long-term there was no place for her in his life. His offer for her to be his temporary mistress had not been enough to persuade her to give up everything she had worked for.

She darted a glance at his hard-boned face. There was no point in raking over the cold embers of their relationship. Everything had been said four years ago. Sergio had wanted her, but only on his terms. As much as she had loved him, she had been angry at his refusal to make compromises and ultimately his intransigence had been proof that he had not cared about her.

Sitting beside Kristen, Sergio inhaled the light floral fragrance of her perfume and he felt a sharp stab of desire. He tried to remind himself of the reason he had brought her to his suite. She owed him an explanation for the fiasco in the function room and he was determined to discover the reason she had interrupted the party. But, as he glanced at her and their eyes met, he was finding it hard to think about anything other than the fact that she was even more desirable than she had been four years ago.

Kristen stiffened when Sergio stretched out his hand and brushed a stray tendril of hair off her cheek.

'You are even more beautiful than I remember.' His deep voice caressed her senses like rough velvet. 'Your eyes are the bright blue of a summer sky and your hair is the colour of ripe corn.'

From any other man the statement would have sounded corny, but Sergio's sexy accent turned the words to poetry. It would be too easy to drown in the molten warmth of his eyes, to fall beneath his spell. Kristen trembled with anger, yet she could not deny the savage, shameful excitement that shot through her. At the party Sergio had been about to announce his engagement to another woman. How dared he now turn his effortless charm on her?

Determined to appear composed, even though she felt anything but, she finished her champagne and hoped he didn't notice her hand was shaking as she placed her glass on the coffee table. 'I should leave,' she said curtly. 'I'm sure Miss Denholm would be devastated if she knew you had invited me into your suite to…to…'

'To what, *cara*?' he drawled. 'You asked to speak to me and I simply agreed to your request.'

'You were flirting with me,' she snapped, stung by the amusement in his voice. 'You had no right to call me beautiful.'

'Why not, when it's the truth?'

Sergio stared at the pulse jerking at the base of Kristen's throat before returning to linger on her mouth, and watched as she moistened her lower lip with the tip of her tongue. The anger he had felt earlier had been replaced with a primitive desire he could not control. She was as tightly wound as a coiled spring and he could almost taste the sexual awareness in the air. Four years was a long time and he had had plenty of other women since Kristen. But none had made his gut twist with raw need like she had done. Like she still did.

His senses were so finely tuned to her that he knew she was going to jump up from the sofa and, before she had time to move, he caught hold of her wrist and forced her to remain seated.

'Let go of me!' She was breathing hard, drawing his eyes to the thrust of her breasts beneath her high-necked blouse. There was something very tantalising about the row of tiny buttons that were fastened right up to her throat. He would never have the patience to unfasten each one, Sergio thought, sexual hunger corkscrewing through him as a memory came into his mind of her small, pale breasts with their rosy tips.

'You are despicable,' Kristen told him hotly. 'You're meant to be hosting a party to celebrate your engagement to a beautiful debutante.'

In truth, Kristen had forgotten about the party, but now guilt joined the gamut of emotions churning inside her. She knew full well that Sergio's emotions were a barren wasteland, but presumably Felicity Denholm was under the illusion that he cared for her. 'That poor woman…'

'I'd save your sympathy if I were you,' Sergio said drily. 'Don't believe everything you read in the gutter press. The engagement story was pure fabrication.'

Kristen swallowed. 'You mean you're not going to marry Lady Felicity?'

'You know my feelings about marriage, *cara*.'

Oh yes, Kristen knew. He had voiced his opinion of marriage loud and clear when they had been together, which had made his decision to marry a Sicilian woman with almost indecent haste after they had broken up all the more hurtful. She closed her eyes against the image in her mind of Sergio and his beautiful dark-haired fiancée. When she had seen the photograph of them in a magazine a few months after she had left Sicily, she had felt sick to her stomach.

Something fluttered against her cheek and she lifted her lashes to find Sergio's face so close to her that she could see the tiny lines fanning around his eyes. The brush of his fingertips across her skin was as soft as gossamer yet she felt as though his touch had branded her.

'What is the real reason you sought my attention tonight?'

Sergio was aware that his voice was not quite steady, but the shock of Kristen's appearance was having a strong effect on him. In the ballroom he had been conscious of a prickling sensation on the back of his neck as he'd been about to address the party guests. He had felt an inexplicable sense of anticipation as he had scanned the room, but he hadn't noticed Kristen until she had spoken.

'First you interrupted the party and then you ran away from me, knowing, I am sure, that I would follow.'

This was the moment to tell him about Nico. Only the words were trapped in her throat, as if some primitive instinct she did not understand warned her to keep her son's existence a secret. It was not a conscious decision. At that moment Kristen was incapable of logical thought. She felt light-headed, and it belatedly occurred to her that she had been too on edge about meeting Sergio to eat any dinner. Drinking a glass of champagne on an empty stomach had been foolish. It must be the effect of the alcohol that was making her heart race, she told herself. The dizzy sensation had nothing to do with the fact that Sergio had lowered his head so that she could feel his warm breath whisper across her lips.

'Was *this* the reason you wanted to see me, *mia bella*?' he demanded.

Her denial died on her lips, or rather it was crushed beneath Sergio's lips as he slanted his mouth over hers and claimed her with the arrogance of a tribal chieftain intent on proving his dominance.

The kiss was hot and hungry, demanding a response from Kristen that, heaven help her, she could not deny, although at first she tried. Her common sense made a last ditch attempt to pull her back from the brink of insanity and gave her the strength of will to clamp her lips together while she tried to push him away. But he was too strong for her to fight him when the ache in her heart was so desperate to be healed.

Sergio traced the determined line of her lips with his tongue, tempting her, teasing her until her lips were no longer firm but soft and pliant. Her breath escaped on a soft gasp as she opened her mouth for him, and he made a gruff sound of pleasure that tugged on her heart. She had never been able to resist him, Kristen acknowledged ruefully. Four years ago she had sensed the loneliness inside him that he took such care to hide and she had responded to it as she did now, with tenderness as well as passion.

Sensing Kristen's capitulation, Sergio gave a growl of triumph. But suddenly they were no longer locked in a battle of wills as the tenor of the kiss subtly altered and became deeper and more intense. The empty years melted away, leaving a scorching desire that had never been doused. When he finally lifted his head, he stared down at her lips—crushed like rose petals after a rain storm—and his eyes glittered.

'For four years you have been in my blood.'

His words sounded almost like an accusation and snapped Kristen back to reality.

'Even while you were married?' she said bitterly. 'If so, then you betrayed your wife as well as me.' A sickening thought struck her. 'Are you still married?'

His expression was unreadable. 'No.'

He offered no explanation of why his first marriage had ended. It was none of her business, Kristen reminded herself. It had been over between her and Sergio a long time ago and it was time to let go of the past. She bitterly regretted coming to his hotel and she had changed her mind about asking him for financial help. Nico was her responsibility.

'You look tired,' he murmured. 'I hope you are not working too hard at the hotel?'

The unexpected softness of Sergio's tone caught Kristen unprepared, and her eyes flew to his face. She flushed when she realised that he still believed she was employed as a waitress at his hotel, but the truth was impossible to explain when she was drowning in his midnight-dark gaze.

She snatched a shallow breath as he lifted his hand and released the clasp that secured her chignon so that her heavy mass of hair uncoiled to midway down her back.

'I'm glad you did not cut it,' Sergio murmured, threading his fingers through the curtain of gold silk.

No way would she admit that she had kept her long hair because he had loved it. It had been easier for Kristen to assure herself that she eschewed having a more complicated style because she could not afford expensive trips to a hair salon.

She tore her eyes from him. 'I should go.' Her composure was balanced on a knife-edge. So why didn't she stand up and walk over to the door? He was still holding her wrist, not tightly, but the rhythmic brush of his thumb pad over her pulse point was seductive, heating her skin, her blood, her desire.

'It's still there, isn't it, *cara*?' His husky voice scraped across her sensitive nerve-endings. 'All it took was one look across a crowded room and the fire burned for both of us.'

It had been the same the very first time he had seen her on the private beach belonging to the Castellano estate, Sergio remembered. He had been furious when he had spotted a trespasser, but when he had caught up with the young woman his anger had died. With her peaches and cream complexion, corn-gold hair and eyes as blue as the sky, she had reminded him of an exquisite doll. But then she had smiled and he had seen that she was a living, breathing, beautiful woman.

She was even more beautiful now, he acknowledged. But the faint purple smudges beneath her eyes gave her a vulnerable air that filled him with irrational anger. If she had remained as his mistress in Sicily he would have ensured that she was financially secure when he had tired of her. Instead she had chosen her independence, but it had not got her far if her cheaply made clothes were anything to go by. She would look stunning in beautifully designed clothes that flattered her slender figure. In his mind he pictured her wearing silk dresses and lace negligees that would glide over her satiny skin as he undressed her.

Why not rekindle the flame? he asked himself. It was not his usual practice to revisit the past. In his experience, by the time an affair ended it was as stale as old toast and nothing could revive his interest. But his interest in Kristen had never completely faded. The sizzling chemistry between them was so hot it was in danger of combusting and proved that there was unfinished business between them.

Kristen was perched on the very edge of the sofa, as

tense and watchful as a nervous gazelle poised to flee. But she had not pulled her wrist from his grasp, and when he glanced at her she swept her long lashes down a fraction too late to hide the hunger in her eyes.

'Tesoro...' he murmured.

'Don't!' The endearment felt like an arrow through Kristen's heart. She jerked to her feet but stumbled on her high heels and fell against Sergio as he leapt up and caught her in his arms. *'Let me go.'* It was a cry from her soul, but he ignored the husky plea and swept her against him, tangling one hand in her hair as he lowered his head and captured her soft, tremulous mouth.

His second kiss was deeper and sweeter than the first, drugging Kristen's senses and breaking through her defences so that she sagged against him while he worked his magic. She could hear her blood thundering in her ears, and when she laid her hands on his chest she could feel his heart beating with the same frantic rhythm as her own. The realisation that she had such a strong effect on him was somehow comforting, and with a low moan she slid her hands to his shoulders and kissed him with all the wild passion that had been locked inside her since they had parted.

This was madness. Kristen's mind whirled as the walls of the room spun when Sergio lifted her into his arms. She knew she should stop him, especially when she opened her eyes and discovered that he had carried her into his bedroom. The sight of a vast bed draped with a black satin bedspread should have rung alarm bells in her head. But when he sank down onto the mattress, still cradling her in his arms, and sought her mouth once more, it seemed so right and so natural to part her lips and allow his tongue to probe between them in an erotic exploration that stole her breath.

How many nights had she dreamed of Sergio making

love to her? Kristen wasn't sure if this was really happening. It seemed impossible that her most intimate fantasies were coming true, but as his mouth plundered her lips, demanding her ever more passionate response, everything faded and there was just this man and this moment in time when the universe stopped.

CHAPTER THREE

'La mia bella Kristen!' Sergio murmured huskily.

The unexpected tenderness in his voice drove the lingering doubts from Kristen's mind. He had called her his beautiful Kristen and the fire in his eyes, the hard glitter of sexual need that he made no attempt to hide, made her feel beautiful. Caught up in a dream world, he was the only reality and she clung to him, curling her arms around his neck to prevent him from lifting his mouth from hers. His dark hair felt like silk as she shaped his skull with her fingertips, and when she moved her hand to his jaw the faint shadow of growth felt abrasive against her palm.

His hands were equally busy tracing restlessly over her arms, shoulders, the length of her spine, as if he was reacquainting himself with her body by touch. When he stroked his fingertips lightly across her breasts the sensation was so intense that she could not hold back a soft cry of pleasure. It had been so long since she had felt the sweet stirring of sexual desire but now it coursed through her veins, heating her blood so that her cheeks grew flushed and she felt boneless and utterly wanton.

Somehow, without realising that they had moved, Kristen found herself lying flat on her back and Sergio was tugging at the buttons on her blouse.

He cursed. 'The patience of a saint is required to undo

these damned things. And I have never professed to piety,' he growled as he gripped the hem of her blouse and pushed it up to her neck.

Her bra was made of sheer, stretchy material that offered no resistance when Sergio tugged the cups down to expose her naked breasts. As far as Kristen was concerned her small breasts had never been her best feature, but his breath hissed between his teeth as he stared down at her. 'Your body is *perfetto*,' he said thickly. He touched her nipples delicately, almost reverently, creating starbursts of pleasure that grew stronger as he rolled the tight nubs between his fingers until they were as hard as pebbles.

A fiery path shot down Kristen's body and unerringly found the heart of her femininity. She felt the moistness between her legs and squeezed her thighs together to try to ease the ache of need that throbbed insistently there. Her nipples felt hot and swollen from Sergio's ministrations, and when he replaced his fingers with his mouth and laved each rosy peak with his tongue she gasped in delight at the magic he was creating, and felt herself sinking deeper into a swirling black vortex of pleasure.

He kissed her mouth again, a hard, fierce kiss that lacked his earlier tenderness as raw, primitive need took over and set its own urgent demands. Kristen recognised Sergio's hunger and shared it. He was her man, her master, and her body was impatient to feel him inside her. Her fingers scrabbled with his shirt buttons and a tremor ran through her when she parted the silk and skimmed her hands over his naked torso, revelling in the feel of his satiny skin that gleamed olive-gold in the lamplight.

His chest was covered in whorls of dark hair that arrowed over his flat abdomen and disappeared beneath the waistband of his trousers. She trailed her fingertips down his body and caught her breath when she felt the swollen length of his arousal. A memory of his powerful manhood driving into her was almost enough to make her come before he had even touched her intimately, and he must have sensed her desperation for he groaned something in a harsh tone as he caught hold of the hem of her skirt and shoved it up to her waist.

Kristen wished she was wearing prettier underwear rather than a pair of plain white briefs and nude-coloured tights that were surely a passion-killer. But of course she hadn't dressed for her meeting with Sergio with seduction in mind. Reality made an unwelcome reappearance into her dream world, and she froze. *Was she mad?* For the past four years she had schooled herself to believe that she was over Sergio and he meant nothing to her, but within an hour of meeting him again she was lying half-naked on his bed and he was about to…

What he was about to do became very clear as he knelt above her and undid his zip. Kristen's heart lodged in her throat as she watched him drag his trousers and boxers down his thighs to reveal his massive erection. His body was magnificent, a powerhouse of muscle and sinew that at this moment was primed to give and receive sexual pleasure.

Apprehension and doubt faded as she sank back into her dream world. Reality had no place here tonight. This was one stolen night of pleasure to repay her for all the lonely nights when she had huddled in bed, dry-eyed because the ache inside her went too deep for tears. Sergio's desire for her, the proof of which was jabbing impatiently between her legs, made her feel like the carefree girl she had been when she had met him. Making love with him then had been uncomplicated—passion in its purest form—without the baggage of hopes and expectations that had come later.

'*Cara*, it has to be now,' Sergio groaned. Dull colour

seared along his razor-edge cheekbones. 'You unman me,' he said harshly. 'You are the only woman to ever make me lose control.'

Good, Kristen wanted to tell him. You are the only man, full stop. She did not want to think of him having sex with other women. It was easier not to think at all, just to feel, to touch and taste him and absorb the essence of his raw masculinity. When he peeled her tights and knickers down she lifted her hips to aid him and opened her legs as he stroked his finger over her opening before slipping it into her slick warmth. She was on fire instantly and gave a little moan as he moved his hand rhythmically and brought her swiftly to the brink.

'Sergio…' She whispered his name like a prayer, a plea, unable to deny her need. She wondered why he hesitated until she saw him slide a condom over his arousal, and then he moved over her and pushed her legs wider apart as he positioned himself and eased slowly forward so that the tip of his shaft pushed into her silken folds.

The sensation of him possessing her inch by incredible inch, and pausing to allow her unused muscles to stretch and accommodate him, was almost too good to bear. Kristen's heart was pounding, not only with the pleasure he was inducing but with a fierce joy that went beyond the physical experience of making love with him. Her breath left her on a soft sigh that brought a smile to Sergio's lips.

'Do you like that, *cara*?' He thrust deeply and gave an unsteady laugh when she gasped. 'The best is yet to come, *mia belleza*.'

And so he proved as he slid his hands beneath her bottom and established a fast rhythm that drove her wild as each powerful thrust of his body took her inexorably higher towards the peak. She clung to him, digging her fingertips into his shoulders as the ride became faster and more urgent. Caught up in the maelstrom, her body moving in perfect accord with Sergio's, Kristen lost the sense of them being two individual people, for they had become one unity, one body, one soul.

What was it about this woman that made having sex with her such an intensely sensual experience? Sergio wondered. He had had many mistresses, but only Kristen had ever answered a need deep inside him that he could not explain or define. One thing he did know was that she tested his self-control to its limits. This was not going to be his finest performance, he acknowledged ruefully. He could already feel the pressure building inside him, and he could hear his blood thundering in his ears as he fought against the tide of pleasure that threatened to drag him under.

He wanted it to be good for her. And somehow concentrating on her pleasure lessened the urgency of his own desire so that he was able to pace his strokes and maintain a steady rhythm of hard thrusts deep into her. Her breathless moans told him her orgasm was close and he clenched his jaw as he felt the first spasms rack her body. Suddenly she tensed and arched her hips and the soft cry she gave decimated his restraint. She was so beautiful with her rose-flushed face and her gold hair spread like a halo across the pillows. For a few seconds he glimpsed an unguarded expression in her eyes that shook him, but before he could question what he had seen her lashes drifted down as her body trembled in the throes of a shattering climax.

His own release was almost instantaneous and the power of his orgasm stunned him. His body shook as his seed pumped from him and his lungs burned as he dragged in oxygen. His limbs felt heavy as a delicious lassitude swept through him. Sergio could not remember ever feeling so relaxed. Kristen felt so warm and soft beneath him and he was reluctant to break the spell that held him captive.

The strident ringtone of his phone was a violent intrusion that shattered the peace. With a curse Sergio reached for his phone on the bedside table, intending to cut the call, but he frowned when he glanced at the caller display and saw that his brother was on the line. A call from home was unexpected and he could not ignore it.

'Excuse me, *cara*. I have to take this,' he murmured as with one hand he hauled his trousers back up and climbed off the bed.

Kristen watched Sergio walk out of the room, and only when he had closed the door behind him did she release her breath on a shuddering groan. The sleepy contentment that had swept through her in the aftermath of making love with him had disappeared and her limbs trembled uncontrollably as reaction set in.

Sickening shame churned in her stomach. She must have been out of her mind, she thought grimly. There was no excuse for her behaviour and no use blaming one glass of champagne for her loss of inhibition. The unpalatable truth was that she had been swept away on a tide of lust. But now she felt like a cheap tart and she couldn't blame Sergio if he thought she was an easy lay. Her humiliation was compounded when she glanced down at her dishevelled clothes. Her skirt was bunched up around her waist to reveal her naked thighs.

Sitting up, she tugged her bra back into place and pulled her blouse down. Her breasts felt tender and when she slid off the bed the slight soreness between her legs was another cringing reminder of her stupidity. Her knickers and tights were lying on the carpet where Sergio had dropped them. Their passion had been so intense that he had not even taken the time to undress himself or her, and the sight of her discarded underwear emphasised how grubby the whole unedifying event now seemed.

Glancing at her watch, she was shocked to find that only an hour had passed since she had run away from the party. When Sergio had taken her to bed she had lost all sense of time, but the reality was that they had had a quickie, and now, in a situation that was painfully familiar, he had abandoned her and was on his phone, no doubt discussing business.

Sergio's insistence on putting work before everything else, including their relationship, had come between them four years ago and was one reason why Kristen had walked away from him. Nothing had changed, she thought, choking back a bitter laugh that was dangerously close to a sob. Did he expect her to simply lie here and wait for him to come back to the bedroom? If so, then he was going to be disappointed.

Her shoes were at the end of the bed where she had kicked them off. She hurriedly pulled on her knickers but shoved her tights into her handbag, not wanting to waste a second putting them on. To her huge relief, the sitting room was empty and Sergio's voice came from another room which she guessed was a study. She glimpsed him through the half-open door, but he had his back to her and didn't turn his head as she walked noiselessly across the thick carpet and let herself out of the suite.

'I can't say how much longer I'll be staying in London. I'm not certain of my plans,' Sergio told his brother, aware as he spoke that his meticulously organised schedule had just altered radically. 'I'm sorry to hear that Tito is unwell, but it sounds like the situation is under control.'

'This latest lung infection is an indication that age is catching up with Papà, and he is becoming frailer. But he is responding to the antibiotics and there is no need for you to rush back. Whoever this woman is, she must be quite something for you to have interrupted your schedule for her,' Salvatore commented drily.

The image of Kristen spread half-naked across his bed slid into Sergio's mind and he felt a tightening in his groin. But he had no intention of confiding to Salvatore that he'd just had the best sex of his life. 'What makes you think it's a woman?'

A sardonic laugh sounded down the phone. 'With you it's always a woman, Sergio.'

He would be the first to admit that he was no angel, Sergio acknowledged as he ended the call. He had a high sex drive and a low boredom threshold. Only one woman had warmed the coldness inside him but he was pretty sure that the reason Kristen had lingered in his mind for the past four years was because he had never found the same intense sexual compatibility with anyone else. Having sex with her again had proved that theory. *Dio*, he had been so hot for her that he had behaved like a rutting bull tonight, he thought grimly. There had been no finesse in the way he had made love to her, but next time he would take things slower and satisfy all her needs as well as his own.

He was not unduly surprised to find the bedroom was empty when he strolled in. He assumed that Kristen was in the bathroom, but when she did not reappear after five minutes and there were no sounds to indicate she was running a shower or bath he tried the door and discovered it was unlocked.

Where the hell was she? His stomach gave a sickening lurch of disappointment as it became clear that she had gone. His earlier good mood gave way to frustration. He couldn't understand why she would take off without a word. Sergio raked his hand through his hair and dismissed an uncharacteristic flash of self-doubt. The sex had been as good for her as it had for him, of that he was certain. Just thinking about the little moans of pleasure she had made when she had come was having a predictable effect on his body.

But maybe, inconceivable though it was to him, she was shy and felt embarrassed that they had fallen into bed within minutes of seeing each other again. It hadn't been something he had planned when he had invited her into his hotel suite, Sergio thought ruefully. But it wasn't surprising when their passion for each other four years ago had been as scorching as a Sicilian summer. Now that Kristen had reappeared in his life he did not intend to let her go until his desire for her was utterly sated. And fortunately he would easily be able to find her. She was an employee at the hotel and her details would be on file.

Reassured that she could not slip away from him, he poured himself another glass of champagne and put a call through to the Hotel Royale's manager requesting information on a waitress named Kristen Russell. Half an hour later, when it became clear that there had never been a woman of that name employed at the hotel, his ice-cold anger made the hapless manager more nervous than if he had given vent to his temper. And, after he had dismissed the man and was alone again, Sergio stared out at the London night sky with eyes that were hard and empty of emotion.

Monday morning brought rain and grey skies that ended the previous week's promise that summer was on the way. The postman delivered a pile of bills which Kristen opened while she simultaneously ate a piece of toast, loaded the washing machine and packed Nico's lunch box.

'Do you want to take an apple or a banana to nursery?'

She sighed when he made no response. 'Please choose, sweetheart. We must get going or I'll be late for work.'

'Don't want to go to nursery.' Nico's bottom lip trembled ominously. 'We can stay home today, Mummy.'

Kristen glanced at the clock and took a deep breath, determined to remain patient. It didn't help matters that she was tired and the house was a mess after Steph and a few other friends had come over on Sunday evening and stayed until late. Steph had needed cheering up after she'd received her decree absolute, and had brought several bottles of wine with her—which had all been drunk.

She would have to take a trip to the bottle bank after work, Kristen thought ruefully. At least trying to help her friend had kept her mind from dwelling on what had happened when she had met Sergio on Friday evening. But memories of making love with him had kept her awake for most of last night and consequently she had a thumping headache.

'Today is a work day for me and a nursery day for you,' she explained gently to Nico. 'You'd better put your Wellingtons on as it's raining.'

It took another five minutes to persuade Nico into his coat and locate keys, her handbag and his backpack. The rain was falling harder, bouncing off the pavement and drumming loudly onto her umbrella as she clasped Nico's hand and tried to hurry him along the street, but they had only gone a few paces when he stopped dead.

'I don't want to go.' Two fat tears slid down Nico's cheeks and as Kristen looked at his unhappy face she felt a clenching pain deep in her stomach that reminded her of the contractions she had felt when she had given birth to him. More than anything in the world she wished she could spend the day with him, but she couldn't rely on a fairy godmother to pay the gas bill and the council tax demand.

'Sweetheart, you know you have to go to nursery while I'm at work. I've got an early appointment and I can't be late.'

Out of the corner of her eye Kristen caught sight of a sleek black saloon car driving past. It was noticeable because of the slow speed it was travelling and, for some inexplicable reason, she felt a tiny flicker of unease when she realised that the car's heavily tinted windows hid the occupants from view. Her sense of trepidation increased as the car pulled into a parking space a little further up the road. Stop being paranoid, she ordered herself angrily. After her desperate flight from the Hotel Royale on Friday night her nerves had been on edge all weekend, but her fear that Sergio would find her had faded when she had reminded herself that he had no idea where she lived.

She was jerked from her thoughts as Nico tugged his hand free and ran back up the street. 'Hey…where are you going?' Kristen hurried after him and caught hold of him as he reached the garden gate.

'I don't want to go to nursery,' he said mutinously.

Sensing a tantrum brewing, Kristen knew she had to regain control. 'Well, I'm sorry but you are going,' she told him firmly.

Nico began to cry loudly, his chest heaving with the force of his sobs, and as Kristen stood in the pouring rain, knowing that she was going to miss her train and would have to reschedule all her morning's appointments, she felt like howling too. 'That's enough, Nico.' Her voice sounded sharper than she had intended and guilt swamped her when he wept harder.

'Kristen, what the hell is going on?'

Dear heaven! Her heart slammed against her ribs. She had believed she was safe, felt sure that she would never see

Sergio again. But against the odds he had found her. Squaring her shoulders, she spun round to face her nemesis.

'Why did you run away the other night?'

She could almost believe he sounded hurt, but she must have imagined it, Kristen told herself. She, better than anyone, knew that Sergio did not waste his time and energy on emotions. She tore her eyes from his, shaken and confused by the intensity of his gaze. It did not help her equilibrium that he looked gorgeous in a pale grey suit and navy silk shirt. Dark patches were forming on his jacket as he stood in the rain, and his hair was already soaked and fell forwards onto his brow.

'How did you find me?'

His eyes narrowed at her cool tone and he raked a hand impatiently through his wet hair.

'With considerable difficulty,' he said tersely. 'You lied to me, Kristen. You don't work at the hotel.'

'I never said I did. You just jumped to the conclusion that I was an employee.' She flushed at his derisive look. Despite the protection of the umbrella, her long braided hair was damp and stray tendrils were stuck to her face. She shot Sergio a glance and quickly looked away again, hating her body's involuntary response to him. 'Look, I can't stop. I'm late.'

'You can't stop! *Dio*, I haven't come here for a chat!' he exploded, and Kristen suddenly realised that beneath his icy control he was furious. 'I take it you haven't seen this morning's headlines?'

She gave him a puzzled look. 'No, I haven't. Why?'

Instead of replying, he unbuttoned his jacket, pulled out a newspaper and thrust it at her. The headline, in bold print, seemed to leap off the page.

Billionaire Dumps Debutante for Domestic!

Kristen stared in horror at the photograph beneath the

headline, which showed her leaning against Sergio, clinging to his shirt front and staring up at him like a love-sick idiot.

'What on earth…?' The picture had been taken when Sergio had chased after her to stop her fleeing from his party, she realised. She had stumbled on her stupid high heels and grabbed hold of him for support. Frantically she skimmed the newspaper article.

Sicilian love-rat Sergio Castellano has certainly lived up to his reputation as a serial playboy. Feathers flew when his fiancée and mistress both turned up at a party at the Hotel Royale. Felicity Denholm was said to be distraught when Sergio left the party to chase after the mystery blonde who is believed to be a waitress at the hotel.

'Oh, heavens,' she said faintly.

'Is that all you can say?' he demanded savagely. 'Thanks to your little escapade on Friday evening, my business deal with Earl Denholm is threatened, my personal reputation is on the line and the price of the Castellano Group's shares has plummeted.'

Kristen bit her lip. 'I'm sorry. I don't know what else to say.'

'My PR manager is frantically putting a damage limitation plan into action and has written a statement for you to make to journalists.' Sergio glanced at his watch. 'I've arranged a press conference for nine o'clock. If we go now we should make it on time. My car is over there.' He swung round and took a few steps but, realising that Kristen was not following him, he glanced back at her, impatience etched onto his hard features. 'Come along. What are you waiting for?'

'I can't go with you. I have to take Nic...' She broke off and watched tensely as Sergio walked back to her. He seemed to realise for the first time that she wasn't alone and glanced over her shoulder to the child standing behind her. Kristen was thankful that Nico's baseball cap hid his face but, as Sergio continued to stare, she gripped her son's hand.

'Is he your child?' There was a curious note in his voice she could not define.

Kristen swallowed. 'Yes.' She tried to step past Sergio and her tension escalated when he did not move out of her way. 'Please excuse us. I need to get him to nursery.'

'So are you married? You have a different surname, which is one reason why it took me forty-eight hours to find you,' he revealed with an edge of impatience. 'I was searching for Kristen Russell, but your name now is Lloyd. Is that the name of your child's father?'

Nico had been standing silently, his gaze fixed curiously on the stranger. But, perhaps conscious of Sergio's scrutiny, he suddenly pulled off his cap and held it out to him. 'My hat's got Bertie Bear on it—see?' he said innocently.

The ensuing silence only lasted for a few seconds, but to Kristen it seemed as though time was suspended and it was a lifetime before Sergio reacted.

'Santa Madonna!' His breath hissed between his teeth and he jerked his head back as if he had been slapped. He flicked his eyes to Kristen's white face and then back to the child by her side. 'It's not possible,' he said hoarsely. 'You lost the baby. I was with you at the hospital when you had the miscarriage.'

CHAPTER FOUR

KRISTEN DID NOT reply—could not, when there was no oxygen in her lungs—but she held Nico's hand tighter as Sergio crouched down so that he could study the little boy's face.

'He is my son.'

It was a statement, not a question, and there was a note of awed wonder in his voice that made Kristen's stomach clench. She had felt the same sense of amazement when she had looked at her son for the first time minutes after she had given birth to him. But she was startled by the raw emotion when Sergio spoke. She did not understand his reaction. It had been obvious when she had suffered the miscarriage that he had not shared her devastation, and in fact had been relieved that she was no longer carrying his child.

There was no point in denying the truth, yet Kristen hesitated. Three days ago she had made the decision to tell Sergio he had a child, so why did she now feel such trepidation and an urge to snatch Nico into her arms? She forced her throat to work and whispered, 'Yes, he's yours.'

Sergio straightened up and growled something ugly in a low tone meant for Kristen's ears only. 'I don't understand. You were bleeding when I rushed you to the hospital.'

His words brought back painful memories of that terrible day. She had felt so scared, Kristen remembered. She had not known she was pregnant until a doctor at the hospital explained that she had lost the baby, but she had been overwhelmed with sadness and guilt that perhaps the miscarriage had somehow been her fault.

She bit her lip. 'When I had the miscarriage I lost Nico's twin. But at the time I was unaware that I was carrying two babies,' she explained shakily. 'I only found out I was still pregnant after I returned to England.'

'But you didn't think to tell me?' Sergio's expression was coldly contemptuous. His barely controlled anger sparked Kristen's temper and helped to lessen the feeling of guilt churning inside her.

'I did think of letting you know but, before I could contact you, I saw the announcement of your engagement to a woman in Sicily. I read about your engagement in a magazine at my doctor's surgery, but the magazine was a few weeks out of date,' she explained shakily. 'By the time I read the article I realised that you must already be married and…and I guessed you would not welcome the news that I was expecting your illegitimate child.'

Sergio's jaw clenched. His skin was drawn so tight over the bones of his face that his cheekbones were sharply prominent.

'He is my child,' he said hoarsely. 'What right did you have to keep him a secret from me?'

'You had married someone else!'

Kristen felt Nico give a start at the sound of her raised voice and she silently cursed herself. She gave him a reassuring smile and replaced his cap on his head to protect him from the rain.

'I can't talk now,' she muttered to Sergio. 'Nico is getting soaked, and I don't want him to spend all day at nursery school in damp clothes.'

Nico's bottom lip trembled. 'Mummy, I don't want to go.'

Somehow she managed to keep her voice calm. 'Sweetheart, we've been through this and I've explained that you have to go today.' Her heart sank when Nico started to cry again, and she tensed when Sergio stepped closer to prevent her from walking away from him.

'Surely he's too young to go to school? He can only be a couple of months over three years old.'

'He was three in March. He doesn't go to school yet, but he attends a day-care nursery.'

'Which he clearly doesn't enjoy,' Sergio said tautly. 'Does he cry like this every day?'

Kristen stiffened at the note of censure in his voice. 'He loves it once he's there,' she said defensively. 'It's just the thought of going that upsets him.'

'Then why send him?'

'Because I have to work.' She lifted her chin and met Sergio's unreadable gaze, her own faintly challenging. 'Bringing up a child is expensive.'

'If I had known you were pregnant, naturally I would have supported you and my son.'

'How would you have done? Would you have told your wife about your illegitimate child?'

Kristen could not hide the bitterness in her voice. They were going round and round in circles, she thought wearily. 'This is a pointless conversation. In case you hadn't noticed, you're soaked to the skin.' She tore her eyes from the front of his shirt, which was now so wet that she could clearly see the delineation of his six-pack beneath the navy silk. 'I'm late for work, and Nico should be at nursery, so please move out of the way and allow us to pass.'

Sergio's cold eyes flashed with sudden fire as his hand shot out and fastened like a band of steel around her wrist.

'Don't you dare dismiss me,' he said savagely. 'This conversation is far from over.'

He glanced at Nico and must have realised that his aggression was scaring the little boy for he said in a softer voice, 'I'll drive you to his nursery and then to your workplace. Where do you work, anyway? Your name wasn't on the list of staff at the Hotel Royale, so why were you working as a waitress there the other night?'

Kristen flushed. 'It was a misunderstanding. I'm not a waitress…I'm a physiotherapist.'

His eyes narrowed. 'Then what were you doing at my party?'

'Can we talk about it another time?' she said desperately. Now was not the moment to admit that she had intended to ask him for a financial contribution for Nico.

'You can be sure we will talk later,' Sergio promised grimly. He turned his head from her as if the sight of her disgusted him and crouched down in front of Nico once more.

'Hello, Nico.' A faint tremor shook his voice and his expression softened as he studied the little boy. 'Would you like to have a ride in my car?'

Kristen bit her lip. The man she had known four years ago had been so adept at hiding his feelings that she had believed him to be emotionless, but Sergio was clearly struggling for self-control.

Nico was sufficiently intrigued to cease crying. 'What's your car?'

'It's that big black one just along the road.'

'I don't have a child seat for him,' Kristen muttered.

'I believe there is an integrated booster seat in the rear of the car.' Sergio dismissed her objection without sparing her a glance and focused his attention on his son.

'What do you say, Nico? Will you stop crying if I take

you to your nursery school in my car? *Bene*,' he murmured when the little boy nodded. 'Come on then, let's get out of this rain, shall we?'

Kristen could not define the feeling that swept through her as she watched her son trustingly put his small hand into Sergio's larger one. Nico was usually shy with people he didn't know and the only male contact he'd had in his life was with elderly Mr Parker who lived next door. Yet he was happily walking off with Sergio and seemed to have forgotten about *her*, Kristen thought with a pang.

'You shouldn't encourage him to go off with a stranger,' she said sharply as she walked quickly along the pavement to the waiting car. 'He doesn't know you. I don't want him to think it is okay to get into a stranger's car.'

Sergio's eyes glittered. 'It is not my fault he doesn't know me. But that unfortunate situation will not continue and he will soon know me very well.'

Something in his tone caused a hard knot of dread to settle in Kristen's chest. 'What do you mean?'

'I mean that I want to be involved in my son's life. *Dio*,' he growled when she made a choked sound, 'I have just discovered that I am his father. Did you expect me to simply walk away from him? Boys need their fathers,' he added in a curiously driven voice.

'At his age, Nico needs his mother more than anyone else,' Kristen said desperately.

'A mother who dumps him in a nursery all day.' Sergio's tone was scathing. 'A three-year-old child requires more parental attention than you are giving him.'

Kristen reeled as if he had physically struck her. 'Nico is my world and I would willingly give my life for him. How dare you say that I don't give him enough attention?' Her voice trembled with anger at the accusation. Yet it was true that only three days ago she had decided she needed to spend more time with her little boy to help him get over the death of his grandmother, her conscience reminded her.

Nico's voice dragged her from her thoughts. Sergio's driver had lifted him onto the booster seat in the back of the car and secured the seat belt around him, but now there was a tiny quiver of uncertainty in Nico's voice as he said, 'Are you coming, Mummy?'

'Of course I'm coming with you.' Tearing her eyes from Sergio's impenetrable gaze, Kristen handed his driver her umbrella and climbed into the car. To her dismay, Sergio slid in next to her instead of walking round to the other passenger door. His wet clothes were moulded to his body and Kristen could feel his hard thighs pressed against her through his rain-soaked trousers. He smelled of rain and expensive cologne, and the combination was so intensely sensual that her heart-rate quickened.

Heat pooled low in her pelvis and she instinctively lifted her hand to her throat to hide the urgent thud of her pulse just as Sergio turned his head towards her. His brows lifted mockingly and she flushed, aware that he had understood the reason for her betraying gesture. She had never been able to disguise her fierce awareness of him, she acknowledged bleakly.

Four years ago she had fallen for him so hard that nothing else had seemed important, not even her gymnastics training and the goal of winning a world championship title that had been her dream since childhood. When she had met Sergio she had dreamed instead of marriage, children, the whole happy-ever-after scenario. But the dream had ended when she had lost their child.

'Perhaps it is for the best.' Even now the memory of Sergio's words had the power to hurt her. After she had lost their baby, she had been distraught. But he had paced around the hospital room and avoided making eye contact

with her. His words had ripped her emotions to shreds as much as the agonising stomach cramps that had torn through her body during the miscarriage. The knowledge that he had not wanted their child had made her realise what a fool she had been to believe in fairy tales.

While Kristen gave the driver directions to the nursery, Sergio leaned his head against the back of the seat, conscious that his wet clothes were sticking to the car's leather upholstery. But he did not give a damn that he could wring the water from his bespoke silk shirt or that his hand-stitched leather shoes made by the finest Italian craftsmen were probably ruined. Everything else faded to insignificance compared to the discovery that he had a son.

He looked over at Nico and felt a curious sensation as if his heart was being squeezed in a vice. His child—his little boy! It still hadn't completely sunk in that the angelic-looking *bambino* was his flesh and blood. But the evidence spoke for itself. Nico bore all the markings of his Sicilian ancestry with his almost-black hair that, unlike Sergio's own cropped style, was a mass of baby curls and his dark brown eyes. His complexion was olive-toned, although he was worryingly pale, which was not surprising when he had spent the first three years of his life in England's unpredictable climate, Sergio thought bitterly. He was sure the child would thrive in Sicily's warm sunshine, and the sooner he could take him home to the Castellano estate the better.

Nico…he silently sounded his son's name. He was glad Kristen had given him an Italian name but it was a small consolation when she had stolen the first precious years of the little boy's life from him. Anger burned like a branding-iron in his gut as his eyes were drawn to the woman sitting stiffly beside him. How could someone so goddamn beautiful be such a treacherous bitch?

He swallowed the bile that had risen in his throat. Three nights ago he had decided that he wanted her back in his life. Now he wanted… Slowly he unfurled his clenched fist and sought to control his rage. He knew what he was capable of if he lost his temper—and so did his mother's lover who, when Sergio had been fifteen, had made the mistake of hitting him.

Dio! It had been twenty years ago, but the memory was still vivid in his mind and the shame he felt at what he had done still scourged his soul. It was no excuse that, after years of suffering physical abuse from his unpredictable, alcoholic mother, he had snapped, no excuse that for the first time in his life he had been driven to defend himself and hit back.

It had taken two security guards who had worked at the apartment block where his mother lived to pull him off her lover, while she had screamed hysterically. She had accused him of being a savage, he remembered grimly. After everything she had put him through—the misery of his childhood and the cruelty he had suffered almost daily—the irony had not been lost on him. The punk she had been sleeping with had deserved every blow Sergio had inflicted on him, but afterwards he had felt ashamed that he had sunk so low. He hated to admit that for a few seconds he had felt empowered by fighting back, and shockingly there had been a moment when he had imagined it was his mother he was hitting rather than her lover.

He had felt sickened with self-disgust. He wasn't an animal, and he had vowed that day never to lose his temper again. He was almost afraid of his physical strength, afraid of what he was capable of. His anger had to be controlled, and the only way to do that was to cut off all his emotions. And so he had taught himself to bury his feelings and use his brain rather than his fists. Don't get mad, get even, was his rule in life.

He stared unseeingly out of the car window, his mind locked in the past. A memory slid into his mind of watching Patti—his mother had insisted that he use her name instead of calling her Mamma—opening a letter and reacting furiously when she learned that she had been turned down for a film role. His heart had sunk when she had reached for the gin bottle, knowing that her drinking would be a prelude to violence. Sure enough, she had punished him for some misdemeanour; he couldn't remember what he was supposed to have done to warrant the sting of the cane across the backs of his legs.

He had been six years old, a lonely little boy in New York, desperately missing his home in Sicily and unable to understand why Papa did not come for him. His mother had told him it was because Papa did not love him.

Sergio dragged his mind back to the present. He sensed Kristen's tension and the realisation that she was nervous of him left a bitter taste in his mouth. He would never lay a finger on her in anger. The idea was abhorrent to him. But he hated her for what she had done, and he hated even more the swift, hot surge of desire that arrowed through him as he stared at her delicate features.

'How long does Nico stay at nursery every day?' he asked abruptly.

'He stays there all day while I'm at work. I usually drop him off at eight-thirty and collect him at five-thirty.'

'Aren't you concerned that being away from you for so long could be detrimental for him?'

'I admit it's not a perfect situation,' Kristen replied sharply, bristling at the criticism in his voice, 'but I have no choice. I have a career…'

'Ah, yes...your career.'

She frowned. 'Why did you say it in such a sneering tone? Yes, I have a career. I studied hard at university to qualify as a physiotherapist, and I'm proud of what I've achieved. I have no choice but to work...'

'You had a choice,' Sergio said harshly. 'You could have told me about my son when he was born and I would have made sure that you did not have to dump him in day-care while you pursued your precious career.'

Kristen was prevented from replying as the car pulled up outside the nursery building and Sergio immediately stepped out onto the pavement. But inwardly she was seething at the way he had made her out to be an uncaring mother. The only reason she worked long hours was to keep a roof over their heads and she missed Nico desperately while she was away from him. She unfastened the little boy's seat belt and lifted him out of the car, but when she tried to set him on his feet he clung tightly to her.

'Mummy, I want to stay with you.'

Nico's play-worker had advised that it was best to ignore his tears and say goodbye quickly and cheerfully. 'The minute you've gone he's no longer upset, and he's quite happy to play with his friends,' Lizzie had assured her. With that in mind, Kristen prised his arms from around her neck and walked him briskly into the nursery. She was conscious of Sergio following close behind her but she did her best to ignore his unsettling presence.

The play-worker met them in the hallway. 'Hello, Nico, have you come to have fun with us today?' Lizzie said brightly.

Kristen saw the curious look she gave Sergio and realised she would have to introduce him. 'Why don't you go and find Sam?' she asked Nico. She waited until he had gone into the play-room and then turned to Lizzie.

'This is Sergio Castellano…' she hesitated '…Nico's father.' Glancing at Sergio, she explained, 'Miss Morris is the senior play-worker at Little Acorns Nursery.'

'I'm delighted to meet you, Miss Morris,' Sergio murmured in his sexy accent that brought Kristen's skin out in goose-bumps. And clearly she was not the only woman to be bowled over by his mega-watt charm, she thought ruefully as she noticed Lizzie's cheeks turn pink.

'Please call me Lizzie, Mr Castellano,' the play-worker said rather breathlessly. 'May I say it's so nice to finally meet Nico's father. Would you like to come into the office while Kristen makes sure Nico is settled?'

'Thank you—Lizzie. And do please call me Sergio.'

'Oh, yes…certainly.'

Leaving the flustered play-worker with Sergio, Kristen went to find Nico. He was sitting on a bean-bag and looked so disconsolate that her heart ached. 'How about playing with the train set?' she suggested.

He shook his head, and the sight of tears sliding down his cheeks evoked the usual feeling of guilt that she was leaving him. But, remembering Lizzie's advice to keep goodbyes brief, she leaned down and dropped a kiss onto his cheek. 'Have a lovely day and I'll come back very soon.'

His sobs followed her as she hurried out of the playroom and into the corridor. Lizzie emerged from the office, followed by Sergio, who frowned when he heard Nico crying. 'Are you sure he isn't being bullied?' he asked tersely.

Lizzie looked shocked. 'Oh, no! He just gets upset when he's separated from his mother, but his tears don't last for long. It's a fairly common reaction with children of his age,' she explained. 'And Nico is particularly sensitive at the moment. But don't worry. I'll take good care of him.'

It was a pity that Kristen didn't seem to feel the same

concern for her son that the play-worker did, Sergio thought darkly as they left the nursery and walked back to the car. The sound of his son's sobs affected him deeply and brought back memories of how as a little boy he had often wept silently into his pillow at night, afraid that if he made a noise he would anger his mother. He had cried because he missed his father.

'As soon as my lawyers can arrange a custody hearing I intend to claim my legal rights to my son,' he informed Kristen abruptly. 'Nico belongs in Sicily with me.'

Shock caused the colour to drain from Kristen's face. 'Don't be ridiculous. He's just a baby. No court would allow you to take him away from his mother.' She bit her lip. 'We must put Nico's welfare first. I don't want him upset in any way.'

'I saw when you walked away from him while he was crying how concerned you are for his emotional welfare,' Sergio said with icy sarcasm. Hearing Nico crying had aroused his protective instincts and he was tempted to stride back into the nursery and snatch his little son into his arms. It was a father's duty to protect his child—a duty his own father had failed to do. But he would not fail his son, Sergio vowed grimly. Kristen did not seem to care overmuch about Nico and he was sure the boy would be far happier living with him.

In the car Kristen gave directions to the driver on how to reach her work while Sergio called his PR manager.

'Enzo will give a statement to the press and explain that we have no personal involvement,' he told her when he ended the call. 'It's rather ironic, considering that we have a child, but I want to keep Nico out of the media spotlight for as long as possible.'

'I understand if you want a relationship with Nico,'

Kristen said huskily. 'But surely it would be better for him if we come to an amicable arrangement about when you can visit him rather than arguing over who should have custody of him.'

'I don't want to visit him.' Sergio turned his gaze from the rain lashing the car window and looked into Kristen's bright blue eyes. 'I want my son to live with me so that I can be a proper father to him.' There was a curious fervency in his voice as he continued, 'I want to tuck Nico into bed every night and eat breakfast with him every morning. I want to kick a football with him and take him swimming.' He shot her a glance. 'Have you taught him to swim?'

'Not yet,' Kristen admitted. 'There isn't a public pool near to where we live, and weekends go so quickly. He's only three, for goodness' sake,' she said tersely when Sergio frowned.

'My niece is only a year older than Nico, but Rosa has been able to swim virtually since she learned to walk.'

His criticism of her mothering skills rankled. 'If I could afford for Nico to live in a house with its own private pool, I've no doubt he would be able to swim like a fish,' she snapped.

'If I had known I had a son, he would have grown up from birth at my house on the Castallano estate and I would have taught him to swim in my pool.'

Kristen's angry gaze clashed with Sergio's furious glare. 'You keep saying you would have supported him, but I don't understand how you would have done. You were married when Nico was born. How could he have lived with you in Sicily? Why did your marriage end, anyway?' She could not deny her curiosity. 'Did your wife leave you or…'

'She died.'

'I…I'm sorry,' she whispered, shocked as much by the

revelation as by the complete lack of emotion in Sergio's voice. She wanted to ask him: when? How? For the past four years she had been haunted by the photo she had seen in a magazine of the beautiful woman Sergio had married. She had been jealous, Kristen admitted to herself.

'Did you love her?' She could not hold back the question that had burned inside her for four years.

'It's none of your business.'

His reply was polite but dismissive and she flushed, hating herself for her curiosity and him for his arrogance. Determined not to risk another put-down, she stared out of the window and willed the traffic jam to clear before she was any later for work.

'I'm surprised that I have never seen your name mentioned by the media.'

Puzzled by the statement, she glanced at him. 'Why on earth should I be of interest to anyone?'

'Four years ago you were regarded as one of the best gymnasts in the UK and were tipped to win a gold medal at the world championships. But after you left Sicily and returned to England you seemed to disappear from the sport.' Sergio's jaw hardened. 'I realise now that you must have taken a break from training and competitions while you were pregnant. But didn't you return to gymnastics after Nico was born?'

Kristen shook her head. 'I never competed again after I had him. I gave up gymnastics completely. It wasn't possible to combine the hours of training necessary to compete at world-class level with being a mother,' she explained when she saw the surprise in Sergio's eyes.

'But gymnastics meant the world to you.'

'Nico is my world now,' she said simply. 'Being his mother is more important to me than anything.'

She turned her head to the window to watch the traffic crawling along Tottenham Court Road, and missed the sharp look Sergio gave her. 'It will be quicker for me to walk the rest of the way to work. The clinic isn't far from here.'

Sergio asked the driver to pull over, but as Kristen was about to step out of the car he put his hand on her arm. 'Here's my phone number in case you need to get hold of me. I'll meet you at Nico's nursery at five-thirty to drive you both home.'

She took the business card he handed her and shoved it into her pocket. 'There's no need for you to come to the nursery. I usually take Nico to the park on the way home.'

'Then I'll bring a football and we will stop off at the park. I'm looking forward to being able to play with my son.'

'Fine.' She looked away from the challenge in his eyes, determined not to let him see how scared she felt that he might truly try to win custody of Nico. Sergio could easily afford the best lawyers, but heaven knew how she would afford to pay legal costs if there was a lengthy court case. The possibility that she could be forced to give up her son filled Kristen with dread.

CHAPTER FIVE

THE DAY HAD begun badly and grew steadily worse. Arriving late for work meant that Kristen missed her first appointment and spent all day playing catch-up and trying to rearrange physiotherapy sessions.

After work she hurried to the station and squashed herself into a packed carriage. But a few minutes into the journey the Tube train ground to a halt in the tunnel and the lights flickered off, plunging the carriages into darkness. Breakdowns on the underground system happened rarely and when the train did not move after five minutes a few passengers started to become agitated. Kristen checked her phone, knowing it was unlikely she would pick up a network connection deep underground. There was nothing anyone could do except wait in the darkness but, as the minutes stretched to ten, fifteen, twenty, her tension grew as it became clear that she would be late to pick Nico up from nursery.

At five twenty-five that afternoon, Sergio parked outside Little Acorns Nursery and studied the group of parents already gathered outside the door of the building. Kristen had not arrived yet, but he was early. Five minutes later when the nursery door opened and the parents filed in she still had not shown up. Knowing that Nico was waiting, Sergio walked inside and was greeted by Lizzie Morris.

'Hi! Kristen isn't here yet, but she comes straight from work and sometimes she is a few minutes late.' Lizzie smiled. 'You can wait with Nico if you want. I'm sure he'll be pleased to see you.'

Nico was sitting in the book corner, his eyes focused intently on the door. A flash of instant recognition crossed his face when he saw Sergio and he gave a tentative smile that tugged on Sergio's heart.

'Mummy's not here.' The smile faded and Nico's bottom lip trembled.

'She will be here soon,' Sergio reassured him gently. 'While we wait for her shall I read you a story?'

He was rewarded with another smile that stole his breath. *Dio*, his son was beautiful. He couldn't take his eyes from the little boy's face. Nico's features were like his own in miniature, although he had his mother's nose, Sergio noted. He opened the book that Nico had handed him and began to read in a voice that wasn't quite steady.

Trapped on the Tube train, Kristen's tension escalated with every passing minute. The staff would look after Nico until she arrived, she reassured herself. Lizzie would realise there must be a good reason why she was unable to phone and explain why she was delayed. But imagining Nico's disappointed face when she didn't walk through the door with the other parents brought tears to her eyes and she felt sick with worry.

Eventually the fault on the underground line was repaired, but by the time she raced out of the station and was able to phone the nursery she was forty-five minutes late and frantic.

'Is Nico okay? Tell him I'll be there in a couple of minutes,' she said to Lizzie, panting as she ran along the street.

'Kristen, calm down. Nico's fine. His father took him.'

'W...what?' By now Kristen had arrived at the nursery but, on hearing Lizzie's shocking news, she slowed her pace and walked into the building, feeling as though her heart was about to explode out of her chest. 'What do you mean his father took him?'

'Sergio arrived just before five-thirty and he waited around for a while, but we both realised that you must have got held up at work. I explained that it had happened on a couple of previous occasions,' Lizzie said guilelessly. 'Luckily he said he would take Nico with him.' Lizzie seemed unaware of Kristen's tension and smiled cheerfully. 'Sergio filled out a parent/guardian form when he came in with you this morning. If he hadn't, of course, I wouldn't have been able to allow him to take Nico. But he was fine about it, and Nico was really excited to go in Sergio's car. Mind you, I'd be pretty excited about travelling in a Jaguar XJ. It's a gorgeous car.'

Lizzie stopped short of saying that Sergio was equally gorgeous, but Kristen guessed from the nursery assistant's pink cheeks that she had been bowled over by a surfeit of Sicilian charm. Hurrying out of the nursery, she pulled Sergio's business card from her jacket pocket and entered his number into her phone with shaking fingers. *Pick up, pick up...* Her imagination went into overdrive and she felt sick with terror that Sergio might have taken Nico out of the country on his private plane. She had read about so-called tug-of-love cases where children had been taken abroad by one parent without the other parent's consent. *What if Sergio disappeared with Nico and she never saw her little boy again?*

'Castellano.' Sergio finally answered the call and at

the sound of his deep voice Kristen's knees almost gave way with relief.

'What have you done with Nico? Where is he…?'

Sergio's reply was terse. 'I haven't *done* anything with him. I simply collected him from nursery when you failed to show up and brought him back to my hotel. He's perfectly okay, although he was upset that you weren't there to pick him up,' he told her coldly. 'I understand from Lizzie Morris that today is not the first time you have been late.'

'There have only been two other occasions,' Kristen defended herself. 'And, like today, they were not my fault. The train broke down in the tunnel and I couldn't phone…'

'I really think you should have tried harder to get to Nico on time,' Sergio interrupted her. 'Have you any idea what it's like to be the only child left waiting to be collected? The fear he must have felt that you weren't coming for him?'

His words scraped Kristen's already raw feeling of guilt. She had a strange sense that Sergio was speaking from personal experience—as if knew what it felt like to be a scared little boy waiting for his mother to show up. But she told herself she must be imagining things. The Castellano family was hugely wealthy and he must have enjoyed a privileged childhood. He certainly didn't know what it was like to be a single working mother with all the responsibility that entailed, she thought grimly. His complete lack of understanding of her situation made her want to scream.

'You're a bloody expert in child psychology, I suppose,' she said grittily. 'Of course I feel terrible that I let Nico down.' Tears suddenly filled her eyes and her throat closed up. 'Thank you for being there for him,' she choked. 'I'll come to the Hotel Royale to collect him, but it might take me a while because the trains are busy during the rush-hour.'

'Stay where you are and I'll send the car for you.'

Sergio cut the call before Kristen could argue. He always had to be in control of every situation, she thought grimly. His wealth gave him power, but it was more than money; his supreme confidence and arrogant self-assurance made him a commanding and authoritative figure—and his steely control over his emotions would make him a dangerous enemy.

The penthouse suite of the Hotel Royale looked very different from the last time Kristen had visited. On Friday evening the elegant sitting room had been immaculately tidy, but now it resembled a toy shop. Numerous boxes and torn wrapping paper littered the carpet; there was a train track complete with model trains in one corner, an enormous tractor, a robot figure and a model garage filled with toy cars.

Nico was sitting on the floor, pushing cars along a plastic roadway and making an engine sound. He barely looked up when Kristen walked in, before he returned to his game sending cars along the track to Sergio, who was pushing them back to him.

The biggest surprise for Kristen was to see Sergio stretched out on the floor, apparently absorbed in playing with the little boy. His tie was draped over the arm of a chair and his shirtsleeves were rolled up, revealing his tanned forearms covered with a mass of dark hairs. He looked so big next to Nico, yet Kristen noted with a pang the close physical resemblance between the man and the child.

She paused in the doorway, feeling strangely awkward and excluded. Usually when she met Nico at nursery he would hurtle into her arms and she would cuddle him. But, although he glanced at her again, he remained on the floor with Sergio.

'Mummy, I've got lots of cars.'

'So I see.' Telling herself to stop being so stupid, she smiled and walked over to kneel down next to him. Immediately she was conscious of Sergio's cool scrutiny. 'Anyone would think it's Christmas,' she murmured drily. 'You must have bought an entire toy shop.'

'I have three Christmases to make up for.' He didn't try to hide the bitterness in his voice. Kristen flushed and quickly focused her attention on Nico.

'It looks like you're having fun.'

'You didn't come.' Nico lifted his chocolate button eyes to her. 'I looked and looked for you, Mummy.'

Kristen swallowed. 'I'm sorry, sweetheart. The train broke down and got stuck in a tunnel. It wasn't very nice.' Her voice shook. She felt claustrophobic on the Tube at the best of times, and she had felt panicky and terrified while she had been trapped underground.

'My daddy came.'

Sweet heaven! She shot Sergio a startled look and met his bland gaze. Forcing a smile for Nico, she said lightly, 'Yes, it was very kind of him to collect you from nursery, wasn't it?'

Nico nodded. 'I went in my daddy's big car.'

Kristen knew she shouldn't be surprised by Nico's uncomplicated acceptance of the situation. He was aware that his friends at nursery had daddies and he was bound to be fascinated by Sergio. But she was angry that Sergio had revealed his identity without checking with her first.

Leaving Nico to his game, she walked across the room and sank down on the sofa before her legs gave way. Today had been one unpleasant shock after another.

Sergio followed her and gave an impatient frown as he correctly read her mind. 'What did you expect me to do?

Surely it's better for him to know that I'm his father rather than a stranger?'

She bit her lip. 'I guess so.'

'*Santa Madre!* It would be nice if you could help to make this easier for his sake.'

Sergio's jaw clenched as he sought to control his temper. He had been furious when Kristen had failed to show up to collect Nico, and also disappointed. She had sounded so genuine when she had told him that Nico meant the world to her. He had almost been taken in by her and believed that she was more caring than his own mother had been.

At the nursery he had watched Nico become increasingly upset as he had waited for Kristen, and Sergio's heart had ached for the little boy. It had brought back memories of how his mother had regularly been late to pick him up from the after-school club she had sent him to every day. On several occasions she had forgotten him completely, until one of the staff had phoned her to remind her about her son. Sergio remembered the cramping fear in his gut that one day his mother simply would not show up. What would happen to him then? he had wondered. Who would take care of him? He had given up hoping that his father would come and take him back to Sicily.

He had brought Nico back to the hotel, convinced that Kristen was irresponsible and did not deserve to have custody of their son. But, glancing at her pale face, he recalled how her voice had trembled when she had explained how she had been trapped on a Tube train, and his anger lessened. Her physiotherapist's uniform of navy trousers and white jacket gave her a professional air but she still looked heartbreakingly young with her long golden hair falling around her shoulders. The purple smudges beneath her eyes indicated that she had slept as badly as he had for the past three nights.

Had memories of making love with him kept her awake until the early hours? Perhaps, like him, she could not forget the intense passion that had blazed between them three nights ago. He had never wanted any woman as badly as he had wanted Kristen. And he still desired her, Sergio acknowledged grimly. Much as he might resent the fact, he could not deny the truth.

When she moved her head her hair shimmered like a silk curtain and he could smell the lemony scent of shampoo. A button on her uniform had popped open so that he could glimpse the curve of her breasts beneath her semi-transparent bra. Heat flared in his groin and he shifted his position to try and ease the throb of his arousal.

Just then she glanced at him from beneath her long lashes and as their eyes met and held, something unspoken passed between them. If they had been alone he would have carried her into the bedroom—and she would have let him. It was the one thing he was certain of.

But they were not alone. He jerked his gaze from her and focused on his son—the child she had kept secret from him. Nico was still playing with the toy cars, his expression utterly absorbed as he chatted to himself in his sweet childish voice. A shaft of golden evening sunshine slanted through the window and fingered the little boy's dark curls.

'Dio!' Sergio exhaled raggedly as he felt an arrow pierce his heart. 'How could you have hidden him from me?' he asked Kristen in a tortured voice. 'He is my child. My blood runs through his veins. You must have known I would want to be part of his life.'

She shook her head, genuinely shocked by the raw emotion in his voice.

'You didn't give me that impression in the hospital. After I'd had the miscarriage, you said it was for the best that I had lost the baby…and I took that to mean you didn't want a child.' Her voice shook. 'I thought you were relieved that I was no longer pregnant. And so when I discovered weeks later that I was still carrying your child, I assumed that you wouldn't welcome the news.'

Sergio had stiffened and he looked almost grey beneath his tan. 'I certainly did not feel relieved that you had lost our child. That day at the hospital…' He swallowed convulsively. 'You misunderstood me. One of the nurses had told me that miscarriages often occurred if the baby was not developing properly. She also said that women sometimes blamed themselves when they lost a child, and it was important I should reassure you that you could not have prevented what had happened.

'That was why I said that perhaps it had been for the best. You were so upset, and I didn't know how else to try and comfort you. You were crying and you needed me to be strong…not to cry too,' he said raggedly.

'I was so shocked when the doctor told me I was pregnant, and then in the same sentence that I had miscarried the baby,' Kristen whispered. She stared at Sergio. 'I had no idea that you were sad about it. Did you really feel like crying?' It was hard to believe that he could have been as deeply affected by the loss of their baby as she had.

'The knowledge that we had lost something so precious and irreplaceable felt like a body blow. At first I couldn't take it in. We had created a new life, but tragically our child was not destined to live.'

Sergio watched Nico playing. 'But we did create a new life after all,' he said so softly that Kristen only just caught his words. 'I still can't quite believe that this beautiful little boy is my son.'

She bit her lip. 'I often think about the other baby, and I wonder what Nico's brother or sister would have been like. I feel so lucky to have him, but I mourn for his twin and, although it's selfish, I wish I could have had them both.' She glanced at Sergio. 'I've heard that the bond between twins is unique. Do you feel especially close to your twin brother?'

He shrugged. 'I did not grow up with Salvatore, and when we met again after being separated for many years we did not have a close relationship.'

She gave him a startled look. 'Why didn't you grow up together?'

'My parents split up when Salvatore and I were five years old. My mother returned to her native New York and she took me with her.'

Kristen frowned. 'It seems a strange decision to have separated you from your brother. You told me that your parents had divorced when you were young, but I assumed that you and Salvatore grew up in Sicily with your father.'

'I did not discover until I was much older that my father had been awarded custody of both of us,' he told her emotionlessly. 'My mother snatched me and took me to America. My father tried to get me back but…' He broke off and shrugged.

How hard had Tito really fought for his return? Sergio brooded. Surely in the ten years that he had lived in the US his father could have done more to force his mother to allow him to return to Sicily? The thought was a poison that continually festered in his mind. The only answer as far as he could see was that Tito had not loved him as much as he had loved Salvatore.

'I suppose she couldn't bear to lose both of her children.' Privately, Kristen wondered how Sergio's mother could have taken him away from his brother and broken the special bond between the twin boys.

Sergio's expression became sardonic. 'The only reason she took me was to get at my father. Their relationship was a constant power struggle both before and after they divorced. Patti didn't actually want me. She was busy pursuing an acting career and having a child around was hugely inconvenient.'

Kristen was startled by the bitterness in his voice. 'I'm sure she didn't think that,' she murmured, not knowing what else to say. The coldness in his eyes sent a shiver through her. Four years ago she had thought she had known him, but clearly there were secrets in his past that might explain why he kept such a tight rein on his emotions.

She glanced at her watch and jumped to her feet. 'I must take Nico home. He needs his dinner and a bath before bed.'

'He's already eaten. I asked the chef to prepare him grilled chicken and vegetables and he ate most of his dinner.' Sergio gave her a piercing glance. 'He looks too thin and I am concerned that he is underweight. I think he should be checked over by a doctor.'

'He has been off his food recently,' Kristen admitted, 'but he's perfectly healthy.'

'Nevertheless, I have made an appointment for him to see a top paediatrician in Harley Street tomorrow morning.'

'There's no need.' Her temper simmered at his implication that she didn't take enough care of her son but, faced with Sergio's implacable expression, Kristen swallowed her irritation. It was pointless to argue over a minor issue when the vital question of who would have custody of Nico was yet to be resolved.

'As for tonight,' Sergio continued, 'he can stay here at the hotel. I have already had the second bedroom in my suite prepared for him.'

A tight knot of tension formed in Kristen's stomach

when she realised that she was not included in the invitation. 'I'm not going to leave Nico with you.'

'Why not? I am his father.' His eyes glittered. '*Dio*, is one night, when you have had him to yourself for the past three years, too much to ask for?'

'Mummy, where's Hippo?'

Nico's voice cut through the simmering atmosphere and Kristen tore her eyes from Sergio's angry face and focused on her son.

'He's at home, sweetheart. Would you like to go and find him?'

Relief washed over her when Nico nodded. She could tell that he was tired, and when he climbed onto her lap and put his head on her shoulder she cuddled him. He was her baby and she would fight to the death for him. She glanced at Sergio and flushed at the sardonic expression in his eyes.

'Hippo is his favourite toy,' she explained. 'He takes it to bed with him every night.'

'In that case I'd better drive you both home,' he said coolly. 'I don't want to upset Nico. But I warn you, *cara*,' he added in a dangerously soft voice, 'don't try to play games with me.'

When Sergio parked outside Kristen's small terraced house she noticed, as he no doubt did, that the front door badly needed a coat of paint. It was one of many jobs that she never had time to do, she thought with a sigh. Walking into the house, she was horribly conscious that the wallpaper in the hallway was peeling. Decorating was another job on the to-do list that lack of time and her tight budget did not stretch to. Since her mum had died she had been getting by, surviving, but not really living, she acknowledged. Grief had sapped her energy and dulled her spirit and it was a bitter irony that seeing Sergio again had made her feel more alive than she had done in months.

Sergio followed her into the kitchen and she saw him frown at the sight of the empty wine bottles on the table. The clothes rack was draped with her underwear and the sink was full of dirty dishes that she hadn't had time to wash up in the rush to get out that morning. Fortunately the living room was reasonably tidy, although shabby, Kristen acknowledged. It was funny how she had never noticed how worn the carpet was until now, and the red wine stain—courtesy of Steph spilling her drink the previous evening—added to the room's neglected air.

Sergio had carried Nico in from the car, and Kristen felt a tug of possessiveness at the sight of the little boy resting his dark curls on his father's shoulder. He was *her* baby.

'I'll take him straight up for his bath. I expect you want to get back to the hotel.'

'I'm not in any rush.' Sergio's jaw tightened at her unsubtle attempt to dismiss him. 'We need to talk.'

Had four words ever sounded so ominous? Kristen watched Sergio glance disparagingly around the room. It was on the tip of her tongue to point out that, unlike him, she could not afford to buy a luxury mansion in Mayfair, which the newspaper had reported he was currently purchasing, but she thought better of it and led Nico up the stairs.

Left alone in the dismal sitting room, Sergio recalled the empty wine bottles in the kitchen and almost gave in to the urge to chase after his son, snatch him into his arms and take him to Sicily immediately. The house was in dire need of renovation, and it was apparent that Kristen had had a party recently—unless she had drunk several bottles of wine herself.

He grimaced. His mother had preferred gin and, even

though it was years since his childhood, he couldn't bear the smell of it. Patti's temperament had been unpredictable at the best of times and alcohol had made her either maudlin or cruel. Unfortunately there had been no way of telling what mood she would be in and, as a small boy not much older than Nico, Sergio had felt constantly on edge, fearful of angering his mother and provoking her violent temper.

A loud scream dragged him from his thoughts. The sound of a child's hysterical sobs chilled Sergio's blood and he took the stairs two at a time and burst into the bathroom to find Nico—not being beaten, as he had wildly imagined—but in the throes of a full-blown tantrum while Kristen endeavoured to wash his hair.

She was drenched, and one part of Sergio's mind registered that her white tunic top was virtually see-through and he could clearly make out the firm swell of her breasts beneath her uniform.

'He hates having his hair washed,' she explained somewhat unnecessarily as Nico wriggled out of her grasp and covered his head with his hands.

'*No,* Mummy,' the little boy yelled furiously.

Sergio struggled to prevent his lips from twitching when he recognised that his son had inherited his hot temper. 'Does he always react like this?' he murmured.

'Every bath-time,' Kristen told him wearily. She was unaware that Sergio had frowned because he had glimpsed the shimmer of tears in her eyes. Her shoulders slumped as she waited for him to criticize her once again. He clearly thought she was a useless mother, and maybe he was right, she thought miserably. Nico was adorable, but he was also a strong-willed little boy and she was worried that if she didn't learn how to deal with his tantrums he would become wilful. If only her mum was still here, she thought, swallowing the lump in her throat. Kathleen had been brilliant with Nico and Kristen missed her advice and guidance.

She stiffened when Sergio knelt down beside her in front of the bath. He seemed unconcerned that the floor was wet and, to her surprise, he rolled up his shirtsleeves. But his next comment surprised her even more.

'It must be tough working full-time as well as bringing up Nico on your own without any help,' he said quietly.

Kristen almost believed that he understood how tired and overwhelmed she felt sometimes, but then she remembered his threat to seek custody of Nico. No doubt he would seize on an admission that she found being a single mother challenging.

'I manage okay,' she told him shortly. 'I don't need anyone's help.'

Studying Nico's mutinous expression, Sergio was inclined to disagree with her, but he sensed she was on edge and refrained from pointing out that once he had gained custody of his son she would be free to concentrate on her career.

He smiled at Nico. 'I'll make a deal with you. If I let you wash my hair, will you let me wash yours?'

Intrigued, the little boy nodded. Sergio bent his head over the bath and, with a squeal of laughter, Nico filled a plastic jug with water and tipped it over his father's hair. Within seconds Sergio's shirt was soaked through, but Kristen could not help but be impressed with his patience with Nico and, to her astonishment, the little boy didn't make a fuss when it was his turn to have his hair washed.

'He's really taken to you,' she said gruffly as she lifted Nico out of the bath and wrapped a towel around him.

'Why are you surprised? He is my son and as much a part of me as he is of you.' Sergio watched Nico scamper along the hallway to his bedroom and felt an almost painful surge of love for his child. He had missed so much. The precious first days, weeks and months of his son's life were gone for ever and he wanted to weep for what he had lost. But there was no point in looking backwards. The future was what mattered, and he was determined that he would not be denied another day of Nico's life.

To Kristen's consternation, Sergio unbuttoned his wet shirt and slipped it off, revealing his tanned torso and the hard ridges of his abdominal muscles.

'I'm afraid I don't have a tumble dryer,' she mumbled, knowing she should look away, but her eyes were locked on the mouth-watering view of his gorgeous half-naked body.

'No matter, I always keep spare clothes in the car.' He picked up a towel and blotted the moisture from the whorls of dark hairs covering his chest. Kristen drew a sharp breath when she saw several red scratch marks on his shoulders.

Following her gaze, Sergio's mouth curved into an amused smile. 'You were a wild-cat the other night, *cara*.'

'That wasn't me…' She came to an abrupt halt, colour scalding her cheeks as a memory of clinging to his sweat-slicked shoulders and raking her nails over his skin when he had brought her to a mind-blowing orgasm flooded her mind. Dear heaven, she had behaved like a wanton creature in his arms.

The sultry gleam in his eyes warned her that he had a total recall of making love to her three nights ago. Her pulse leapt and involuntarily she swayed towards him. Her senses were swamped by his maleness—a mixture of aftershave and the indefinable scent of pheromones. Sexual awareness crackled in the tiny bathroom. She watched his eyes darken and held her breath as he dipped his head towards her.

'Mummy...'

Kristen assured herself that she was relieved by Nico's timely interruption. 'I'd better go and see to him,' she said jerkily and shot out of the bathroom, followed by Sergio's mocking laughter.

CHAPTER SIX

WHEN KRISTEN WENT downstairs after she had tucked Nico into bed there was no sign of Sergio and she assumed he had gone back to his hotel. She couldn't understand why she felt deflated. A reprieve from his threatened talk could only be a good thing. But as she filled the sink with water to begin the washing-up he strolled into the kitchen, still bare-chested, and carrying a holdall that she guessed he had collected from his car. Heaven knew what her neighbours must think! She tried to ignore the urgent thud of her heart as he opened the bag and took out a T-shirt, which he pulled over his head.

Unfortunately he looked no less sexy in the tight-fitting black shirt that emphasised his muscular physique. He would look good wearing a bin bag, Kristen thought ruefully. He unsettled her and she wished he would go away and give her some space.

'I realise we have things to discuss, but I'm tired tonight. It's been a difficult day,' she muttered, not sure whether to laugh or cry at the understatement. 'Do you want to come over tomorrow evening instead?'

Sergio gave her a piercing glance and noted that the shadows beneath her eyes had darkened to purple bruises. Her delicate features were drawn and she looked fragile and barely any older than she had done four years ago. The first time he had seen her, she had been dancing on the beach, he remembered. Actually, she had been practising her gymnastics floor routine, she had explained, blushing with embarrassment when she had realised she'd had an audience. Sergio had been entranced by her slender, graceful body and her fey beauty. She had touched his soul in a way no other woman had ever done. But he had no intention of succumbing to her magic again, certainly not now he had discovered that she had kept his son from him.

'You seem to be under the misapprehension that I am going somewhere, but I'm not leaving,' he said curtly. 'I want to see my son first thing in the morning.' Sensing that she was about to argue, his expression hardened. 'The other reason I'm going to spend the night here is to make sure you don't disappear with Nico.'

'I wouldn't do that,' Kristen said sharply, stung by his scathing tone.

'You hid him from me for three years,' he reminded her coldly.

She shook her head, despairing that she would ever make him understand why she had acted as she had. 'I truly believed you would not want him. When we were together you constantly told me you didn't want a committed relationship, and having a child is a massive commitment.' Faced with his implacable expression, she sighed and gave up. 'Anyway, there's nowhere for you to sleep. The house only has two bedrooms, and Nico's room is too small for you to share with him.'

'Then I guess I'll have to share with you.'

Unexpectedly, Sergio smiled, revealing his gleaming white teeth. Kristen caught her breath as she was instantly transported back to the first time she had met him on the beach in Sicily. He had been wearing running shorts and a vest top that had shown off his tanned, athletic body.

With his dark hair falling into his chocolate-brown eyes, he had been the sexiest man she had ever laid eyes on, and when he had smiled she had been utterly blown away by him. They had become lovers within days of that first encounter, she remembered. Four years on, the attraction between them was still potent and three nights ago it had blazed into an inferno. But Kristen knew she couldn't risk her emotional security by sleeping with him again.

'I'd rather share my bed with the devil,' she said tartly, desperate to disguise the ache of tears in her voice as she was overwhelmed by memories of the past.

His brows rose. 'I didn't get that impression on Friday night.'

She flushed. 'That was a mistake. The champagne went to my head.'

'You only had one glass.' He gave her a speculative look. 'I take it you haven't been drinking champagne today?'

'Of course not. I was at work, and then trapped on a Tube train for nearly an hour,' she reminded him drily.

'In that case, my experiment should reveal the truth.'

Kristen had not been aware of Sergio moving, but suddenly he was far too close for comfort and, as he reached behind her and cupped her nape, she realised too late that she had walked into a trap.

'Don't...' Her voice faltered as his head swooped and his warm breath feathered her lips.

'I am about to prove that you are a little liar, *cara*,' he threatened softly, before he stifled her protest by slanting his mouth over hers.

It was no gentle seduction. His lips were firm and demanding, taking without mercy as he twined his fingers in her hair and hauled her against him, trapping her with his arms, which felt like bands of steel while he ravished her tender mouth.

Kristen's determination to resist him was dissolving in the honeyed sweetness of his kiss. It felt so good when she had been starved of him for so long. It would be so easy to sink into him and give in to his sensual mastery. Summoning her willpower, she attempted to push against his rock-hard chest, but it was futile. She couldn't escape him, nor could she deny the hot tide of desire that poured through her veins and pooled between her thighs.

With a soft moan, she opened her mouth for him and trembled when he slid his tongue between her lips. Reality faded, just as it had done three nights ago at the hotel. But suddenly, shockingly, he lifted his head and stared down at her, and the triumphant gleam in his eyes acted like an ice-cold shower on her heated flesh.

'Don't ever lie to me again, Kristen. Next time I won't stop at kissing you,' he warned. His mouth curled in self-disgust as he stepped away from her and raked a hand through his hair. 'Believe me, I resent the wildfire attraction between us as much as you do, but it's there and we will have to deal with it because I'm not going to go away. Nico is a part of both of us and we will be forever linked by him.'

His emotive words shook Kristen and tears filled her eyes. Sergio gave her a piercing look but, when she made no response, he said, 'I'll sleep on the sofa tonight, and tomorrow we'll discuss the best way we can bring up our son.' He glanced around the untidy kitchen and his jaw hardened. 'This place is far from ideal,' he said disparagingly.

Kristen felt a stab of fear. Surely he wouldn't be able to state that she was an unfit mother just because she hadn't had time to do the washing-up?

'I'll go and find some bedding,' she mumbled, seizing the excuse to get away from him while thoughts whirled around her head. She ran upstairs and paused on the landing to peep into Nico's room. He had flung back the covers as he usually did and was cuddling Hippo. He looked utterly adorable with his halo of dark curls framing his face and his long eyelashes fanned out on his cheeks. Intense love surged up inside her. She would never give her little boy up, she vowed fiercely. She was deeply suspicious of Sergio's insistence that he wanted to be involved with his son. The man she had known four years ago had been the ultimate commitment-phobe and it would take a lot to convince her that he had changed. Her biggest fear was that he would form a bond with Nico and then walk away when the novelty of fatherhood had faded.

She took a blanket and spare pillow from the hall cupboard, and then went into her bedroom to change out of her uniform, which felt uncomfortably damp after her attempts to wash Nico's hair. Furious with herself for being tempted to wear her new lilac silky top that clung in all the right places, she pulled on jeans and an old T-shirt and quickly brushed her hair, but resisted the urge to put on a bit of make-up. It wasn't as if she wanted to make herself look attractive for Sergio, she reminded herself firmly.

A tantalising aroma of spicy food met her as she walked into the kitchen, reminding her that she had been too busy to eat lunch. Sergio was opening cartons of take-away food. He had found plates and cutlery, and she saw that he had washed up the breakfast bowls.

'I ordered Thai,' he said, glancing at her. 'I remembered you like it and I'm guessing you haven't eaten tonight. There's nothing in the fridge except for a couple of out-of-date yoghurts. What had you planned to give Nico for dinner?'

She prickled at the implied criticism in his voice. 'I was going to call in at the supermarket on the way home from nursery. Here's your bedding,' she murmured, handing him the pillow and blanket.

He gave her a sardonic look when he felt the coarse woollen blanket. 'I've heard of monks wearing hair shirts. Have you decided that I should serve some sort of penance?' he queried drily.

She flushed. 'You could always go back to your hotel.'

'And give you an opportunity to steal Nico away?' He gave a bitter laugh. 'Not a chance, Krissie.'

His use of the nickname that only he had ever called her by twisted a knife in Kristen's heart, but somehow she managed to give a shrug as she sat down and began to help herself to food. Sergio opened a bottle of red wine that she assumed had been delivered with the meal, but when he went to fill her glass she shook her head.

'Not for me, thanks. I rarely drink wine.'

His brows rose. 'Then how do you explain the half a dozen empty bottles that I put in the recycling bin?'

'A few of my girlfriends came over last night. One of them has just gone through an acrimonious divorce and she wanted to celebrate being free and single again.'

'And where was Nico while this drunken party was going on?'

'It wasn't a drunken party!' She glared at him. 'The girls just had a few drinks. Nico was tucked up safely in bed, and I didn't touch any alcohol. I am a responsible parent.'

'What about on Friday evening?' Sergio pressed. 'Where was Nico while you were in my bed?'

Kristen choked on a prawn ball. 'I certainly didn't leave him on his own, if that's what you're implying. My neighbour babysat. Nico was in bed asleep before I left, but he knows Sally very well, and she adores him.'

'You still haven't explained why you were pretending to be a waitress at the party.'

'The waitress bit was a misunderstanding.' Kristen's appetite suddenly disappeared. Sergio had finished his meal and she collected up the plates and carried them over to the sink. 'Do you want to go into the sitting room while I make some coffee? There are a few photo albums with pictures of Nico in the bureau. Feel free to take a look at them.'

She could tell he was curious to know why she was determined to change the subject of her visit to the Hotel Royale, but to her relief he made no comment as he strolled out of the kitchen.

Five minutes later, when Kristen carried a tray into the sitting room, she found Sergio inspecting her huge array of gymnastics medals and trophies that she kept in a glass cabinet.

He turned to her and took the cup of coffee she handed him. 'Do you ever resent that you gave up your sport for Nico?'

'Not at all, although I can't deny that I sometimes wonder whether I would have been good enough to win a world championship title,' Kristen replied honestly.

'So when you returned to England and discovered you were still expecting, it didn't cross your mind to end the pregnancy?'

She drew a sharp breath, 'Of course not. I was devastated when I had a miscarriage, and to be told that I was going to have a baby after all was wonderful—it felt like a miracle. How could you think I might not have wanted our child?' She couldn't disguise the tremor of hurt in her voice.

It probably had something to do with the fact that when

he had been a child his mother had frequently told him she had not planned to fall pregnant with him and his twin brother and wished she'd had a termination, Sergio thought to himself. He shrugged. 'When we met, your pursuit of a gymnastics career bordered on obsessive. You might have considered sacrificing an unplanned pregnancy. After all, you put gymnastics before our relationship.'

'That's not true!' Kristen was stung by the unfairness of his accusation.

'You left me to devote yourself to achieving your dream of sporting glory.'

'I left because you wanted our relationship, such as it was, to be solely on your terms. You demanded that I should give up my life—my gymnastics training, my university studies—to be your mistress, but you refused to make any compromises,' Kristen said hotly. 'The only thing that was important to you was your career. You travelled the world in pursuit of the next deal, the next million pounds to add to your fortune, but you refused to acknowledge that my dreams were important to me.'

She bit her lip. 'Our *relationship* was just about sex as far as you were concerned, wasn't it, Sergio?' Her anger faded as quickly as it had flared and left her with a dull ache in her chest. There was no point in opening up old wounds. 'You asked me to be your mistress, but in the same breath you told me that you were not interested in commitment. What did you expect me to do,' she asked bitterly, 'give up everything I'd worked so hard for, for an affair that might last a few months at most?'

'I couldn't give you what you wanted.' Sergio's voice was emotionless, but Kristen was shocked to see a pained, almost tortured look in his eyes before he brought himself under control and his face became its usual expressionless mask. 'I knew you hoped for more from me—women invariably do,' he said sardonically. 'When you returned to England I realised it was for the best.'

'And so you married someone else.' Kristen felt hurt that he had lumped her with his countless other mistresses and had regarded her as needy just because she had hoped for a more meaningful relationship with him than simply sharing his bed. 'Your Sicilian woman must have been very special for you to have overcome your objection to commitment.'

For a fleeting moment she sensed that he was tempted to talk about his first marriage, but he gave a non-committal shrug.

'Yes, she was.'

He picked up the photo album that he had been looking at earlier and stared at a picture of Nico as a newborn baby. 'He looked so tiny when he was born. What did he weigh?'

'He was a few weeks early and he was just over two kilograms, but I fed him myself and he quickly gained weight.'

Sergio studied the photo, which had clearly been taken in the hospital soon after Kristen had given birth to Nico. She looked very young and scared as she clutched the tiny baby in her arms. Anger burned inside him—anger at her for robbing him of the first years of his son's life, but a greater anger with himself because he had not followed his instincts four years ago and gone after her. She had dented his pride when she had refused to be his mistress, he acknowledged. If he was honest, her rejection had hurt him and it had been the realisation that she made him feel vulnerable that had stopped him from following her to England.

'How did you manage?' he asked harshly. 'Did you have to leave university when you realised you were pregnant?'

'No, I was able to finish my degree before Nico was

born, and afterwards I was lucky to get my current job at the sports injury clinic.'

'It must have been a struggle, though.'

'It hasn't been easy...especially financially,' Kristen admitted.

Sergio wondered why she suddenly seemed nervous. His eyes narrowed on her tense face. 'Why did you come to the Hotel Royale on Friday night?'

Her tongue darted out to lick her dry lips. 'I...came to tell you about Nico.'

'Why now, when you had hidden him from me all this time?'

'I was going to...to ask you for help...a financial contribution for him. You have no idea how expensive bringing up a child is.' Kristen faltered when Sergio's eyes darkened with anger. But when he spoke his voice was tightly controlled.

'You're right. I don't know what it's like to bring up a child, but I wish more than anything that I could have shared the experience of caring for our son from the moment he was born. As it is, I would not have discovered his existence if you had not decided to cash in your most valuable asset. Nico,' he explained when she looked puzzled. 'The knowledge that your child's father is a billionaire must have been too tempting to ignore.' His lip curled. 'How much money did you hope to get from me? Did you plan to demand cash in exchange for allowing me to see my son?'

'No!' Kristen was appalled by Sergio's accusation. 'All this time I believed you had a wife in Sicily. But then I saw your picture in a newspaper and read that you were going to marry an Earl's daughter, and I decided to ask you for a small contribution towards Nico's upbringing.'

'So your decision had nothing to do with the fact that you have debts amounting to several thousand pounds, mainly in the form of store credit cards?' Sergio said coldly. 'I saw the pile of letters and final demands for payment from debt-collecting agencies.'

Kristen swallowed. She had forgotten that the folder containing dozens of letters from creditors was in the bureau where she kept the photo albums. 'You had no right to look at my private mail.'

He ignored her and said savagely, 'Suddenly it all makes an obscene kind of sense. You've maxed out on your credit cards buying designer clothes and handbags, and so you've decided to use me as a cash cow to bail you out and assumed you could use Nico as leverage.'

'The situation is not what it seems,' Kristen said huskily.

'Then what is it?'

'It's complicated.'

'No, it's very simple,' Sergio said grimly. 'You want money and I want my son. Name your price and the amount will be transferred into your account within twenty-four hours—with the proviso that you allow me to take Nico to Sicily.'

'Don't be ridiculous…' Kristen broke off when she realised he was deadly serious. 'I'm not going to *sell* him to you. The suggestion is disgusting. The only reason I was going to ask you for money was to spend on him, not for anything else. But I've managed on my own for three years and I'll carry on managing.'

'You call this managing?' Sergio's expression was arrogantly derisive as he glanced around the shabby sitting room. 'I can provide my son with a far better lifestyle than he currently has with you. My lawyer has already started the legal process for me to file for custody of Nico, but it would be better for his sake if we settled out of court and, to that end, I am prepared to make you a generous financial offer.'

'You know what you can do with your offer!' Kristen snapped. Inside, she was shaking, but she refused to let Sergio see how scared she felt. He was not a man to make vain threats and she did not doubt that he had already begun his legal claim for Nico. 'You think you can buy anything you want,' she said bitterly. 'But nothing would persuade me to give Nico up.'

'Everything has a price, *cara*.' Sergio sounded strangely weary. He gave a harsh laugh. 'Was that what Friday night was about? Did you use your delectable body as a sweetener, and once I had succumbed to your magic you intended to offer my son to me in return for hard cash?'

Incensed by his taunt, Kristen reacted instinctively and raised her hand but, before she could make contact with his cheek, he captured her wrist in a vice-like grip.

'I wouldn't,' Sergio advised in a dangerously soft voice. He flung her arm from him and raked his fingers through his hair, feeling disgusted with himself when he saw her white face. He had not intended to frighten her, but for a few seconds blind rage had swept through him. 'We both need to cool down,' he muttered. 'Why don't you go to bed and get some sleep. You look all in. We'll talk again in the morning.'

Not trusting herself to remain in the same room as Sergio when she was tempted to murder him, Kristen swung round and walked out of the room. Sleep! She laughed hollowly as she marched up the stairs. She felt as limp as a wrung-out dishcloth and with the threat of losing her little boy hanging over her she doubted she would ever sleep again. But when she slid between the sheets her brain mercifully decided that it had had enough for one day, and her last thought was that she must set the alarm on the bedside clock.

Sergio woke to the sensation of his eyelids being prised open. After spending a hellish night on the most uncomfortable sofa he had ever encountered, he craved a couple of hours more sleep, especially when he glanced blearily at his watch and saw that it was five-thirty in the morning. He blinked and refocused on the angelic face hovering above him. Nico was staring at him with his big brown eyes framed by unbelievably long lashes. When he saw that Sergio was awake, he grinned.

'Daddy...'

Sergio felt his gut twist. *'Papà,'* he said softly. 'I am your *papà*.' And you are *il mio bel ragazzo*. My beautiful boy, he thought to himself. Propping himself up on one elbow, he watched Nico line up his toy cars on the carpet. 'Is Mummy still asleep?'

Nico nodded. 'I got dressed,' he said proudly, patting his shorts.

That would explain why his T-shirt was on back to front, Sergio mused. He smiled. 'Clever boy.'

Nico lay on his stomach so that he could push his cars along the floor and Sergio suddenly froze. His eyes were drawn to the black bruises on the backs of the little boy's legs. Bile rose in his throat. *Santa Madre di Dio!* The marks were sickeningly familiar. When he had been a child, his legs had often been covered in bruises after a beating.

Swallowing hard, Sergio noticed another mark on Nico's body where his T-shirt had ridden up.

'Hey, little guy, let me turn your shirt around for you,' he murmured.

Nico obediently stood up and, as Sergio drew the shirt over his head, his breath hissed between his teeth at the sight of several more bruises on the child's ribs.

'How did you get hurt?' He somehow managed to keep his tone light.

'I was very naughty,' Nico told him with an innocence that tore Sergio's heart to shreds.

His head spun. He didn't know what was happening here. Everything inside him rejected the idea that Kristen could have inflicted the bruises on Nico. It was true she hadn't convinced him that she was an overly caring parent and he was deeply suspicious of her motive for finally deciding to tell him that he had a son, but it was hard to imagine that she would hurt her child.

But no one would ever have believed that his charming, beautiful mother had been capable of mental and physical cruelty, Sergio thought grimly. Patti had been the patron of a children's charity, but to her own child she had been a confusing figure—at times overly loving so that he had felt swamped, but she had been prone to violence when she had succumbed to her personal demon, alcohol, and at those times he had been afraid of her. He remembered the sick feeling in his stomach whenever she had summoned him to her study to be punished for the most minor misdemeanour. No one had heard his cries, and no one had come to his rescue—including his father.

Deep within Sergio's soul the scared, unhappy little boy he had once been took over his logical thought processes. A fundamental instinct to protect his child surged through him and he stood up and lifted Nico into his arms. 'How would you like to fly on an aeroplane, *piccolo*?' he murmured.

His heart turned over when Nico looked at him with his big, brown, *trusting* eyes. 'I will always protect you,' he promised his son gruffly, and was rewarded with a smile that somehow eased the loneliness that had haunted him since he had been a small boy who had longed to be with his own father.

CHAPTER SEVEN

WHEN KRISTEN OPENED her eyes she was puzzled to see a stream of bright sunlight filtering through the chink in the curtains. The house was quiet and, unusually, she was alone. Nico had a habit of climbing into her bed in the early hours and he would prod her awake and insist that she read him a story. He must still be asleep, she thought as she stretched, making the most of having the bed to herself.

She looked at the clock and her heart did a painful somersault. *It could not be half past nine!*

A frantic glance at her watch confirmed the worst. She leapt out of bed and cursed as she stubbed her toe on the bedside cabinet. Pulling on her dressing gown, she hurried along the hall and discovered that Nico's room was empty. It was unlike him to go downstairs on his own, but maybe he'd grown bored of waiting for her to wake up, she thought guiltily. Hell, she would have to phone Steph and apologise for being late for work for the second day in a row. With a dozen thoughts running around her head, Kristen pushed open the sitting room door and felt a flicker of unease when she saw that no one was there.

The blanket and pillow Sergio had used to make up a bed on the sofa were neatly folded, and Nico's toy cars were scattered across the carpet. Trying to control her panic, she continued into the kitchen. The half-drunk mug of coffee on the table indicated that Sergio must have left in a hurry. In the silence, the ticking of the clock seemed unnaturally loud. Fear cramped in Kristen's stomach. There had to be a reasonable explanation for Sergio and Nico's disappearance, she told herself.

Catching sight of the empty space where Nico's Wellington boots were kept by the back door, she felt weak with relief. Maybe Sergio had taken him for a walk or to the park.

The doorbell rang and she hurried to answer it, determined to impress on Sergio that he must not take Nico out without informing her first. But the man on the doorstep was a stranger—a short, swarthy man dressed in a suit, who introduced himself as Bernardo Valdi, Sergio's lawyer.

'Signor Castellano asked me to visit you.' The lawyer spoke in English but with a strong Italian accent. 'It might be better if we continue our discussion inside the house,' he added gently when Kristen gasped.

She stepped back to allow him to enter the hallway, suddenly finding that her legs felt like jelly. 'Where *is* Sergio? And, more importantly, where is my son?' she demanded in a trembling voice. Her fear returned, making her stomach churn as a terrible truth slowly dawned. 'He's taken him, hasn't he? Sergio has taken Nico.' Her voice rose. 'He won't get away with it. He has no right. I suppose he's gone back to the Hotel Royale. I'm going to call the police.'

'Calm yourself, *signorina*,' the lawyer said in a quietly authoritative voice. 'Signor Castellano has been granted an emergency custody order of his son.'

'Emergency…' Kristen stared at the lawyer dazedly, wondering, hoping that this was all a horrible nightmare. 'On what grounds?' she whispered.

'The *signor* was concerned for the child's welfare after he saw bruises on him.'

'Dear God! He thinks I hurt Nico?' Nausea threatened to overwhelm her. 'I have to see Sergio and explain.' She stumbled down the hall. 'I'll get dressed and go straight to the hotel.'

'They are not there, *signorina*. Signor Castellano flew to Sicily on his private jet an hour ago, and he has taken his son with him.' Bernardo Valdi gave an exclamation as he reached Kristen's side just in time to catch her as her knees sagged.

The taxi had turned off the main highway running from the airport at Catania to the coastal town of Taormina, and was now heading along narrow roads leading to the Castellano estate. Kristen stared out of the window at the breathtaking Sicilian countryside and felt an ache in her heart. Everywhere was unchanged and familiar, as if time had stood still for the past four years. Farmhouses and small villages dotted the landscape. In early summer the fields were still green but would turn to gold as the crops ripened, and on the far horizon Mount Etna's peak still wore a snowy mantle. The great volcano was sleeping today and only a thin stream of white smoke drifted from its summit into the blue sky.

As they passed a vast olive grove, Kristen's tension increased. She recognised the area and knew that the gates of the Castellano estate were around the next bend. She also knew that the gatehouse was manned by security guards twenty-four hours a day and visitors were strictly vetted before being allowed to enter.

Bernardo Valdi's visit had left her distraught and utterly determined to find her son. It had been easy enough to book a seat on the first available flight to Sicily, but as the taxi drew nearer to the estate she had no plan of action in the likely event that Sergio would refuse to allow her to see Nico. Her nerves jangled as the taxi stopped in front of a set of huge iron gates and a security guard approached. She fully expected to be turned away when the guard spoke on his mobile phone and relayed her name to someone at the house but, to her surprise and relief, he stepped back and waved the car through the electronic gates as they swung open.

The gravel driveway continued for a quarter of a mile before it forked into three separate roads. One led to the main house, La Casa Bianca, where Kristen assumed Sergio's father Tito still lived. Another road disappeared into a pine forest, and in the distance the turrets of a castle—which had been built in the thirteenth century by a Sicilian nobleman and ancestor of the current Castellano family—were just visible above the tree tops. Four years ago, Sergio's brother Salvatore and his beautiful wife Adriana had lived at the castle with their daughter, Kristen recalled.

The taxi took the third road, which wound through an orange grove and skirted a turquoise lake before the terracotta-coloured walls of a large, elegant villa came into view. Casa Camelia held so many memories. Her mind flew back to the first time Sergio had invited her to his home. They had eaten dinner on the terrace overlooking the garden and later he had carried her upstairs to his bedroom and made love to her. It had been her first time, and she had sensed that Sergio had been shocked when he'd discovered she was a virgin. But he had been so gentle, Kristen remembered. The pain of his possession had been fleeting, and the pleasure that had come afterwards when he had brought her to orgasm with his skill and patience had taken her heart prisoner.

How could their relationship have gone so spectacularly wrong that they were now enemies fighting over their son? she thought emotionally. The simple answer was that Sergio had not loved her, while she had loved him too much. She had left him before he could break her heart, but she had been too late.

The taxi drew up in front of the villa and Kristen dismissed her memories of the past as she focused on the battle she knew she faced to reclaim her little boy. Her heart slammed against her ribs as she ran up the stone steps. Someone must have watched her arrive because the front door opened and an elderly man wearing a butler's uniform ushered her inside. A lightning glance around the large entrance hall revealed that it had not changed since she had last been there. The white walls reflected the sunlight streaming through the mullioned windows and sunbeams danced across the black marble floor.

Kristen's eyes flew to the two men standing in the hall. Sergio and his twin brother were strikingly similar in appearance, but she noted with a flare of shock that Salvatore Castellano had changed dramatically since she had last seen him. His once-handsome face was thinner, almost haggard, and his mouth was set in a stern line as if he had not smiled for a long time. His black hair fell to his shoulders and was as unkempt as the stubble that shaded his jaw, and his eyes were dull and hard as lava spewed from Etna that had solidified into black rock.

Salvatore walked towards her with a pronounced limp, and Kristen wondered what had happened to him. 'Kristen, it's good to see you again,' he murmured. Like Sergio, his hard features rarely showed any emotion and she had no idea if he was surprised by her visit. He headed out of the front door, but Kristen was barely aware of him leaving as she stared at Sergio.

Dressed in beige chinos and a cream shirt that contrasted with his olive skin, he looked gorgeous and so relaxed that Kristen's tenuous hold on her composure snapped. How dared he appear as if he did not have a care in the world when she had just spent the worst few hours of her life? Anger swept through her. She resented his powerful physical presence and resented even more her fierce sexual awareness of him.

'Where is Nico? I was so worried when I woke up and found you had gone. When your lawyer said you had taken him...' Her voice cracked as she relived the sheer terror she had felt when she'd feared she might never see Nico again.

Suddenly she was crying, great tearing sobs that wracked her slender frame. 'You bastard!' she choked. Tears streamed down her face, and the need to hurt him as much as he had hurt her made her lift her hand and connect it sharply with his cheek. The sound of the slap echoed around the vast hall and the moment she had done it she felt sick. Physical violence was completely alien to her, yet twice in two days she had lashed out at Sergio. How could she blame him for believing that she was responsible for the terrible bruises on Nico's legs after the way she had behaved?

Sergio had not reacted to the slap, even though he could easily have grabbed her wrist and prevented her from striking him. His expression was unreadable, but for an instant some indefinable emotion flared in his eyes as he watched her fall apart.

Kristen could not stop crying. It was as if a dam had burst inside her, and as she dashed her tears away more came in an unstoppable river. 'I didn't hurt Nico, I swear. I would never lay a finger on him. He fell from the top of the climbing frame at the park. I had told him not to climb too high, but he's such a daredevil and sometimes he can be quite naughty and disobedient. When he slipped I was scared he would hit the ground and break every bone in his body.' She shuddered at the memory of Nico's scream as he had plummeted from the climbing frame. 'Thankfully, I managed to catch him, but during the fall he slammed against the metal bars and was bruised all over his body and legs.'

Recalling the terrifying incident, Kristen couldn't regain control of her emotions. Her chest heaved and she searched desperately in her handbag for a tissue. 'How could you think I would have inflicted those bruises on him? I'm not a bad mother. I love Nico with all my heart and I would never harm him.'

Sergio studied Kristen dispassionately. Her face was blotchy and tear-stained and her eyes were red-rimmed. She had obviously dressed in a hurry and not checked her appearance in a mirror, because if she had she would have seen that her orange T-shirt and pink cardigan clashed horribly. Continuing his inspection, he glanced down and saw that she was wearing mismatched shoes—on one foot a navy blue trainer and on the other a white plimsoll.

Following his gaze, she flushed. 'I left the house in a rush. Which is understandable when you had snatched my son,' she added defensively.

She must have been frantic about Nico not to have noticed that she had put on odd shoes!

As Sergio watched Kristen scrub her hand over her wet face the tight knot of tension in his gut slowly unravelled. The doctor who he had called to the villa to check over Nico had said that the bruises on his legs were probably the result of an accident, and in his opinion were not signs that he had been mistreated. Kristen's explanation about Nico falling from the climbing frame was believable. Her distress was real and painful to witness, he acknowledged uncomfortably. Was it possible he had misjudged her? Doubt crept into Sergio's mind. When he had seen the bruises on Nico his emotions had taken over from his usual cool logic and he had been tormented by memories of how his mother had treated him when he had been a child. His only thought had been to rescue Nico and bring him to Sicily. But perhaps he had overreacted?

'Kristen, you have to stop crying,' he said roughly. 'Nico is ill and he needs you.'

Her eyes widened. 'What's wrong with him?'

'He's running a high temperature and he's been sick. The doctor thinks he has picked up a gastric virus.'

'There's been a vomiting bug going around at nursery.' Kristen drew a ragged breath and finally managed to stop crying. She knew she did not cry prettily and she probably looked a mess, she thought ruefully. But the news that Nico was unwell drove all other considerations from her mind. 'Where is he? Why aren't you with him?'

'The nanny who looks after Salvatore's daughter has been helping to care for him. I'll take you straight to him. Did you ask the taxi driver to bring in your luggage?'

'I don't have any luggage. I'm not planning on staying. I'm here to collect Nico and take him home.'

Sergio's eyes narrowed on her determined face and he seemed about to argue, but thought better of it. 'We will discuss what is best for him later. You certainly won't be taking him anywhere while he's throwing up.'

Kristen hurried after Sergio up the sweeping staircase. On the first-floor landing they walked past the master bedroom. The door was open and she could not resist peeping in. The wallpaper and soft furnishings had been updated and were a soft blue rather than gold as she remembered, but the huge four-poster bed still dominated the room and the sight of it evoked memories she wished she could forget. Now was not a good time to recall in vivid detail

Sergio's naked, muscular body, or to remember the firestorm passion they had once shared and his unexpected tenderness when he made love to her.

There was no hint of tenderness about him now, she noted as she caught up with him. He was waiting outside the door next to his room. His unreadable expression became speculative when his glance travelled from her flushed face to his bedroom but he made no comment other than to say, 'Nico has been asking for you.'

'I'm not surprised. He was probably frightened when you whisked him away from everything that is familiar to him and brought him to a place he has never seen before. What were you thinking of?' Kristen asked him curtly. 'You told me that when you were a young child your mother snatched you and took you to another country. How could you do the same thing to Nico?'

His jaw tightened. 'I had my reasons.'

'Or maybe you were trying to score a point over me and prove how powerful you are?' she said cynically. 'This isn't one of your boardroom battles.' Kristen broke off at the sound of Nico crying. Her fight with Sergio could wait until later.

Pushing open the door, she entered an elegant bedroom which had a pale carpet and silk covers on the bed that were hardly suitable for a pre-school child, especially one with a stomach upset. Nico looked feverish; his cheeks were flushed and his curls clustered damply on his brow. A woman was leaning over him, trying to persuade him to take a sip of water, but he pushed her away and his sobs grew louder until he looked across the room and saw Kristen.

'Mummy...' His lip quivered, and his distress tore Kristen's heart. She dashed over to the bed and gathered him in her arms.

'It's all right, sweetheart. I'm here.' She frowned at Sergio. 'He feels very hot. Have you given him anything to bring his temperature down?'

'He brought up the medicine the doctor left for him,' Sergio started to explain, but at that moment Nico was sick again—all over Kristen. '*Santa Madre!* I can't believe he's got anything left in his stomach,' Sergio muttered as he sprang forward to lift the little boy off her lap. But Nico clung to her and wouldn't let go.

'Leave him,' Kristen said quietly. 'I'll get cleaned up later.'

'But you're covered...'

'It doesn't matter. Pass me a towel so that I can mop him up.' She gave Sergio a fierce look. 'This is what parenting is. It's not about buying expensive toys—it's about being there for your child when he needs you.' She glanced towards the woman who she guessed was the nanny Sergio had mentioned. 'Please leave me alone with him. He's confused and upset, and having people around him that he doesn't know isn't helping.'

It was the early hours of the following morning before Nico showed signs that the worst of the vomiting virus was over. His temperature dropped back to normal and he fell into a comfortable sleep.

'He'll probably be absolutely fine and full of energy when he wakes up,' Kristen told Sergio, who had remained to help nurse the little boy, although he had sent the nanny away. She tucked the sheet around Nico and moved away from the bed so that her voice did not disturb him. 'You'll be amazed at how resilient children are.' As she spoke she was hit by a wave of exhaustion and collapsed onto the sofa.

'He already looks a whole lot better than you do,' Sergio

murmured drily, comparing Nico's healthy colour with Kristen's white face. He quickly looked away from her, unable to meet her gaze. During the past few hours she had proved beyond doubt her devotion to her son. Her patience as she had attended to Nico when he had been sick and comforted him with loving care had shown Sergio how wrong he had been about her, and he felt guilty that he had misjudged her so badly. She was nothing like his mother, thank God. He knew he owed her an explanation of why he had snatched Nico, but he did not find it easy to talk about his childhood experiences.

He sat down next to her on the sofa and felt her instantly become tense. Was she afraid of him? He couldn't blame her after the way he had behaved, he thought grimly. The worry he had put her through when he had disappeared with Nico was evident in her drawn features. She looked infinitely fragile, and when he brushed a stray tendril of hair back from her cheek she jerked away from him as if he had struck her.

But it was not fear he saw in her eyes, although her expression was wary and mistrustful. He deserved that, Sergio accepted. He had done nothing to earn her trust. What he found more intriguing was the fact that her pupils had dilated and her chest was rising and falling unevenly. Sexual awareness could not be denied or disguised, however hard she might try to hide her feelings. His analytical brain acknowledged that her attraction to him was the ace up his sleeve. The first rule of business was to discover your opponent's weakness, and it was useful to know that Kristen was vulnerable where he was concerned.

'Why do you and Nico have the surname Lloyd?' he asked her. 'When I knew you four years ago your name was Russell, so why did you change it?' His jaw tightened as an unwelcome thought occurred to him. 'Did you marry some guy who then became a stepfather to Nico?'

'No, of course not. There hasn't been anyone…' She broke off abruptly, making Sergio wonder if she had been about to say that she had not dated anyone since him. He hoped that was the case, but only because he hated the idea that she might have introduced a boyfriend to Nico, not because the thought of her having sex with another guy made his insides burn as if he had swallowed acid, he assured himself.

'Russell was my stepfather's name,' Kristen explained. 'My real father, David Lloyd, died when I was a baby. When I was eight my mother married my gymnastics coach, Alan Russell, and I took his name.'

'I remember your stepfather. He made it clear that he did not approve of me.' Sergio frowned. 'I only met him once when I came to see you at your rented villa, and he warned me to stay away from you.'

'He didn't approve of anything that distracted me from my training. And you were a major distraction.' Kristen sighed. 'Four years ago I came to Sicily with my mum and Alan, but they were called home and while they were in England I met you. When Alan came back to Sicily he was furious when he discovered I was having an affair with you instead of focusing on my gymnastics training.

'While I was growing up I was very close to Alan. He was a top coach and he spotted my potential early on. It was his dream as much as mine that I should become a champion gymnast. Sometimes…' she hesitated '…I've wondered if he married Mum so that he could have control over me and my career. He was a very domineering man, but the attention he gave me made me feel special and I wanted to do well and please him. But as I grew older I started to resent the fact that I had no other life outside of gymnastics. Alan insisted I followed a rigorous training schedule and I never had time for anything else, including boyfriends.'

'I discovered just how innocent you were,' Sergio said drily. 'Why didn't you tell me you were a virgin?'

Kristen blushed. 'I was scared you wouldn't make love to me if you knew it was my first time…and I desperately wanted you to,' she admitted.

He gave a harsh laugh. 'You were not the only desperate one, *cara*. I'd like to think that if I had known of your innocence I would have held back, but the truth is I wanted you so badly that I could not resist you.'

The possessive gleam in his eyes sent a quiver through Kristen. She recognised the sexual chemistry between them was as intense as it had been four years ago, but her instincts told her to fight the damnable desire that made her body tremble. He had hurt her once before, and she must not forget his threat that he wanted to take Nico from her.

'What was your mother and stepfather's reaction when you told them you were pregnant?'

'Mum was fine about it. But Alan was furious. He knew that if I had a baby it would probably end my gymnastics career. He pushed me hard because my achievements at competitions enhanced his reputation as a top coach, but I suppose I'd always believed that he actually cared about me as a person.' She swallowed. 'He had been my dad since I was eight and I…I loved him. But he tried to persuade me to have an abortion and, when I refused, he threw me out and wouldn't even let me stay at home until after the baby had been born.'

Her stepfather's rejection, coming on top of what she had taken as Sergio's rejection when she had lost Nico's twin and she had felt that he had not wanted their baby, had had a deep impact on Kristen. She had felt betrayed and abandoned by the two men she loved. Both had only been interested in what she could give them; Alan had lavished attention on her because he had hoped she would win sporting glory and enhance his coaching reputation, and Sergio had wanted her for sex. Four years on, the hurt hadn't faded, and she wondered if she could ever trust a man again. She had developed a fierce sense of independence. As a single mother totally responsible for her son, she could not afford to let her guard down.

She forced her mind from the past as Sergio said harshly, 'You mean you were homeless when you had Nico but you still did not tell me you had given birth to my child? *Dio*, did you hate me so much that you preferred to struggle alone rather than come to me for help?'

'I didn't hate you. But when I left Sicily our relationship was over. I've explained that because of what you said at the hospital I believed you would not have been interested in my pregnancy. I lived in my student digs until just before Nico was born, and on my twenty-first birthday I inherited some money from my real father which I used for a deposit to buy a house. That's when I changed my name back from Russell to Lloyd.' Kristen had wanted to end all links with her stepfather. 'I had to work full-time to pay the mortgage. Alan had thrown Mum out too because she supported my decision to have the baby, which made me wonder if he had ever truly loved her,' she said heavily. 'Anyway, Mum moved in with me and she looked after Nico during the day.

'He has only been going to day care for a few months, since…' she swallowed '…since Mum was killed in an accident. That's why he hasn't settled at nursery. He misses his nana. And that is why I decided to tell you about him. I wanted to be a full-time mum to Nico for a few months.

But I couldn't afford not to work and so I was going to ask you for financial help, just temporarily.'

The tremor in Kristen's voice had a profound effect on Sergio. 'I'm sorry about your mother. I remember you were very close to her.'

'Yeah,' Kristen said gruffly. His gentleness was unexpected and she quickly looked away from him, willing herself not to cry. 'It's Nico I'm worried about. I want to do what's best for him.'

'And you have,' Sergio assured her. 'I'm glad you came to me for help, and I'm glad that you are both here at Casa Camelia.'

'You didn't leave me much choice after you brought Nico here without my consent.' Kristen shot him a sharp look. 'As soon as he is better I want to take him home.'

'This is his home.' He met her gaze levelly and although he spoke quietly Kristen heard the implacable determination in his voice, which filled her with despair.

'You saw tonight how much he needs me,' she said urgently.

'I agree. But our son deserves to grow up with his father as well as his mother.'

For most of his childhood, after his mother had taken him to America, Sergio had longed to be with his father. But for ten years he'd had no contact with Tito and when they had finally met again it had been too late to establish the bond that should exist between a father and his son. *A bond that Sergio was determined to forge with his own son.*

Somehow he needed to convince Kristen that Nico would benefit from growing up with his father. But she mistrusted him, and he was beginning to understand how deeply she had been affected by the way he had responded when she had miscarried Nico's twin. He had tried to reassure her that the miscarriage had in no way been her fault, but she had misunderstood his words and thought that he had not wanted their child. It was little wonder that she had kept Nico a secret, Sergio thought grimly. She was a fantastic mother, but it was obvious that she had been struggling to bring Nico up on her own, and the truth was the little boy needed both his parents.

Fear cramped in Kristen's stomach. 'So you still intend to fight for custody of him?'

'I hope we can come to an arrangement by which we can both be involved in Nico's upbringing. You told me you wanted to take a break from work to spend time with him,' Sergio reminded her. 'What I am suggesting is that you and Nico stay here at Casa Camelia for a few weeks while we discuss his future.'

'And if I don't want to stay?'

His eyes met hers, and for a split second Kristen thought she saw a plea for understanding in his gaze. But she heard the determination in his voice when he said, 'You are not a prisoner, *cara*. You can leave whenever you like—but Nico will remain here with me.'

CHAPTER EIGHT

THE WARM, SCENTED bath water was having a soporific effect on Kristen. Her eyelids felt as though they were weighted down and she was having trouble keeping them open. Would Sergio find it convenient if she drowned in his bath? she wondered. It would mean he would gain custody of Nico without a court battle.

The thought of Nico being motherless made her haul herself upright. She would fight to her last breath to stay with him, but there was no escaping the fact that Sergio had the upper hand now that he had brought Nico to Sicily. He had told her she was not his prisoner, but she was trapped at Casa Camelia by her love for her son.

She was too tired to think any more. When Sergio had offered to run her a bath she had agreed without argument, especially when he had remarked in an amused voice that she didn't smell too good after Nico had been sick on her. At least her hair was now clean and rather more fragrant, and when she stepped out of the bath she discovered that Sergio had left one of his shirts for her to wear.

After blasting her hair with a drier, she emerged from the en suite bathroom and was relieved to find he was not in his bedroom. On her way out of the room she noticed a photograph of a beautiful raven-haired woman on the desk, and her heart gave a lurch when she recognised it was the woman she had seen four years ago in a magazine—Sergio's first wife, who he had loved but was now dead. She studied the photo. For so long she had felt jealous of the woman Sergio had married, but now she felt sad for her. She must have been tragically young when she had died. Her mind reeling with confused thoughts, Kristen walked through the connecting door into the adjoining bedroom where Nico was sleeping soundly.

He looked angelic with his dark curls spread on the white pillow, and his cheeks had lost their feverish flush and were a healthy pink. He was cuddling Hippo. Thank goodness Sergio had remembered to bring his favourite toy.

He would be a good father. The thought slid into her head, and she bit her lip as she remembered how gentle he had been with Nico when he had been ill. Sergio had stated that their son deserved to grow up with both his parents and she was finding it hard to disagree, but her life was in London and he based himself in Sicily and travelled around the world for his job.

How could they share custody of Nico and give him the stable and secure upbringing that every child needed? She certainly wouldn't allow him to be passed between them like a parcel, Kristen thought fiercely. The future suddenly seemed frighteningly uncertain. Maybe things would be clearer after a few hours' sleep. It was four o'clock in the morning and after the tension of the last few days she was bone-weary, she acknowledged as she curled up on the bed.

When Sergio walked into the room fifteen minutes later he found Kristen fast asleep, one arm draped protectively across Nico. The sight of mother and child snuggled up together brought a lump to his throat. He couldn't remember Patti ever showing him affection, and he was fiercely glad that his son had a mother who clearly adored him.

But he loved Nico too. His son had captured his heart instantly. How could he not love his own flesh and blood, the gorgeous little boy whose angelic looks were enhanced by his impish smile? How could his own mother not have loved *him*? Sergio wondered bleakly. Had there been something about him that had made him unlovable? Was that the reason his father had not tried harder to regain custody of him?

Nico would never have reason to doubt that his parents loved him, Sergio vowed. He accepted that Kristen had believed she'd had good reasons for choosing to bring up Nico on her own, but he was determined to convince her that cooperation between them would be far better for their son than a custody battle. When they had met at the Hotel Royale he had known he wanted to resume their affair, but now the stakes were higher.

Four years ago he had guessed that she had been in love with him and, although he had no expectation that she still was, he was convinced that she had not slept with him the other night simply because the sex was good. More than good, he amended. She was the only woman who had ever made him lose control. During their affair he had fought the feelings she stirred in him, but now the only battle he planned to fight with Kristen was to persuade her to allow him to have a presence in her life as well as Nico's. And, for Sergio, losing was not an option.

Kristen rolled over on the mattress and came into contact with something warm and solid. Her brain fuzzily realised that the object was too hard to be a pillow and too large to be Nico, and when she opened her eyes her first thought was that she was not in the room where she had fallen asleep. She turned her head and her heart practically leapt out of her chest.

'What are you doing in my bed?' she demanded, uncaring that Sergio appeared to be asleep.

He opened his eyes and gave her a lazy, sexy smile that did nothing to help slow her racing pulse. 'Actually, you are in my bed.'

'Not from choice,' she assured him grittily. His amused expression fuelled her temper and she welcomed her anger as a much-needed distraction from her awareness of his virile body. The disturbing thought struck her that he could very well be naked beneath the sheet draped across his hips. And not only naked! Her gaze slid down his body and the sight of his obvious arousal straining against the silk sheet made her catch her breath.

She needed to take control of the situation. Folding her arms across her chest made her feel more authoritative and hid her pebble-hard nipples. 'How did I get here?'

'I brought you to my room because I heard you crying in your sleep and I didn't want you to disturb Nico. You spoke your mother's name,' Sergio added gently.

She swallowed. 'I dream about her sometimes.' She looked away from him, feeling incredibly vulnerable. She had a vague recollection of being upset and feeling comforted by strong arms that had held her. Another memory, of running her hands over a broad, hair-roughened chest made her blush and hope fervently that it had all been part of a dream.

'I was glad I was able to comfort you.' Sergio confirmed the worst and Kristen winced with embarrassment to know that she had actually stroked her hands over him while she had been asleep.

'I'm sorry if I disturbed you,' she said stiffly.

'Having your gorgeous body cuddled up close to me was no hardship, *cara*.'

Beneath his softly teasing tone, Kristen heard something deeper and darker that evoked a coiling sensation in the pit of her stomach. Desire throbbed between them, but she could not, would not fall into its delicious embrace.

Panic sharpened her voice. 'I did not cuddle up to you.'

'Oh yes, you did.' He moved so fast that before she had realised what was happening she was lying flat on her back and his hard body was covering hers so that she could feel every muscle and sinew of his thighs pressed against her. Even more shocking was the feel of his rock-solid arousal jabbing into her belly, and she couldn't prevent her body's instinctive response as molten heat pooled between her legs.

'You clung to me like a limpet,' he taunted. 'And you cried out my name. Perhaps returning to Casa Camelia brought back memories of all that we shared four years ago?'

'All we *shared* was sex.' Somehow Kristen managed to sound scathing; refusing to let him see how much his words affected her. She pushed against his chest and tried to slide out from beneath him, but he had pinned her to the bed and every slight movement she made resulted in his burgeoning arousal nudging deeper between her thighs. 'You didn't share anything else with me, least of all yourself. You kept a barrier between us and I never knew what you were thinking…or feeling.'

'I gave you more than I've ever given to any other woman,' he told her intently.

'Am I supposed to feel flattered by that? Was I supposed to feel grateful that you fitted me into your busy work schedule?'

'I asked you to stay in Sicily with me. You were the one who chose to leave.'

'Because I knew that if I had stayed as your mistress our relationship would have been all on your terms. You expected me to give up everything that was important to me, even though you knew that gymnastics was a big part of my life.'

'My position as head of a division of the Castellano Group necessitated me travelling extensively and working long hours. But you needed to be in England to train with the gymnastics team. I couldn't see how we could continue our affair if we were rarely together or even in the same country.' Sergio exhaled heavily. 'The reason my parents divorced was because my mother was determined to pursue an acting career in America and she and my father never spent any time together.'

'We could have tried to work something out. But you refused to make compromises. You made me feel that I was unimportant and that my feelings didn't count.' Kristen bit her lip. 'You did the same at the hotel in London. You were in such a hurry to have sex that we still had our clothes on, and as soon as it was over you were on your phone, no doubt discussing business. You made me feel cheap,' she muttered.

'I answered the call because I knew it was from my brother. He is the only person who has the number of my private phone so that he can contact me if there is a problem with our father. Tito's health is not good, and Salvatore rang to tell me he was unwell. I would have explained why I had left you so abruptly...but you had already gone.'

Sergio smoothed her hair back from her brow and looked deeply into her eyes. 'I'm sorry you felt that I did not show you the proper respect you deserve. It's no excuse that my impatience was because I was desperate to make love to you, but I had hoped you would spend the night with me and I intended to act with a little more finesse the next time we had sex.' He shifted his position so that his pelvis ground against Kristen's, and she caught her breath as he whispered in her ear, 'But, instead of telling you what I'd planned, let me demonstrate.'

'I don't need you to demonstrate anything.' She gritted her teeth as she fought the insidious heat of sexual longing that surged through her veins. 'Let me go, Sergio. I need to check on Nico.'

'I went to see him just before you woke up. He's sound asleep, and I have asked the nanny, Luisa, to sit with him while you get some rest.'

She swallowed as he began to undo the buttons running down the front of the shirt she had worn to sleep in. 'Why are you doing this?' she asked desperately. 'What we had was over a long time ago.'

'Was it, Krissie?' He worked his way down the shirt until he reached the last button. 'Can you honestly say that you never thought of me in the last four years, that you never lay awake at night, remembering the touch of my hands on your skin?'

His glittering gaze held her captive as he spread the shirt open and curled his hands possessively around her breasts. 'I remember everything. Making love to you again at the hotel reminded me of just how good it was between us, and now that you have come back into my life I am in no hurry to let you go.'

There were a hundred reasons why she should not allow herself to be seduced by Sergio's velvet-soft voice and the sensual promise in his eyes. She would be mad to respond to the brush of his lips across hers. But her willpower had always been non-existent where he was concerned, Kristen acknowledged dismally. She had spent too many nights tormented by memories of him and her resistance was melting faster than candle wax in a flame as he skimmed his hands over her naked body, making her skin tingle everywhere he touched.

Her heart leapt when he teased her lips apart with his tongue and when he kissed her, slow and sweet, as if he had missed her as much as she had missed him, she responded to him helplessly, her misgivings swept away by the tidal wave of desire that obliterated all rational thought.

Their previous encounter at the hotel had been fast and frantic, but now Sergio took his time to explore her body and rediscover the pleasure points that made her tremble and gasp when he caressed her.

'I love that your breasts are so sensitive,' he murmured as he flicked his tongue over one rosy peak and then its twin until they hardened. He closed his mouth around her nipple and sucked until she whimpered with pleasure.

Sergio still knew her body so well, even though it was so long since they had been in a relationship. Kristen felt a sharp stab of jealousy that he must have made love to other women in the last four years. Don't think, her brain urged, just feel. She was no longer the naïve girl who had fallen in love with him. She understood that her desire for him was just sexual chemistry, and after four years of celibacy it was not surprising that she was impatient to experience the pleasure of his possession.

Her stomach muscles contracted when he trailed his fingertips over her abdomen and explored the dip of her navel, before moving lower. He eased his hand beneath her knickers and slowly, so slowly that she wanted to scream, he inched towards the place where she was desperate for him to touch her. She was embarrassingly wet so that when he gently parted her and slid his fingers between her silken folds her body accepted him willingly and her excitement increased as he teased her clitoris until she gasped and tensed.

'Not yet, *cara*,' he murmured against her mouth before he kissed her deeply. 'This time I promised we would take things slowly.' This time Sergio wanted her to be reassured that he was not seeking quick satisfaction. She had accused him of withholding himself from her during their affair, and he acknowledged the truth of that. His habit of keeping his emotions locked away was too deeply ingrained, but at least he could show her how much he desired her.

His heart kicked in his chest as he pulled her panties off and she spread her legs invitingly. He found her eagerness touching and the realisation that she wanted him as badly as he wanted her gave him hope that he had not lost her. It took all his willpower not to plunge his painfully hard erection into her slick heat, but he resisted the ache in his gut and lowered his head to inhale the sweet scent of her arousal.

Kristen gave a startled gasp when Sergio ran his tongue up and down her moist opening, parting her so that he could bestow the most intimate caress of all. She knew he was fiercely aroused and she had assumed he was impatient to satisfy his own needs, but he was showing her with his clever fingers and wickedly invasive tongue that he was focused entirely on giving her pleasure.

He had a magician's skill, she thought dazedly. Her limbs trembled as he took her to the edge and held her there. The dedication he applied to arousing her made her feel cherished, and when he claimed her mouth once more and kissed her with tenderness as well as passion she knew with an ache in her heart that she was slipping under his spell and there was nothing she could do about it.

Her breath caught in her throat as he positioned himself over her and deftly donned a protective sheath. His golden-skinned body gleamed like satin and the faint abrasion of his chest hairs against her breasts was intensely erotic. Memories of the many times he had made love to her in this room, in this bed, danced through her mind and it seemed the most natural thing in the world to lift her hips towards him as he plunged forward and drove his powerful arousal deep inside her.

'Krissie...' His voice shook, as if he recognised that the connection between them was more than the physical joining of their bodies. But as he began to move, thrusting into her with strong, measured strokes, Kristen stopped thinking and her sensory perception took over. She could hear her blood thundering in her ears, echoing the ragged sound of his quickened breathing. Faster, faster, every devastating thrust increased her excitement. She clung to his sweat-slicked shoulders while he rode her, possessed her, and just when she was sure she could not take any more, he tipped her over the edge and into the most intense orgasm of her life.

'Open your eyes.' Sergio's voice was rough and when Kristen obeyed his command she was startled by the blazing intensity of his gaze. 'I want you to know that it's me you're making love with, me who is giving you pleasure—not some other lover.' Jealousy was a new emotion to him and it burned like acid in his gut.

'I haven't had any other lovers.' She knew as she said the words that she had revealed too much of herself, but strangely she did not care that she had made herself even more vulnerable. She could not lie, and she was glad she had been truthful when he breathed her name like a prayer and kissed her mouth with aching sweetness.

'Tesoro...' Sergio's iron control finally snapped and he climaxed violently, his head thrown back and his throat moving convulsively as he pumped his seed into her and his big body shuddered.

In the aftermath of their passion he lay on top of her, his dark head resting on her breasts. Kristen's heartbeat gradually slowed and she became conscious of her surroundings once more. The bright sunlight streaming through the slatted blinds made her realise that she had no idea of the time. Her frantic journey to Sicily and the hours that she had spent taking care of Nico while he had been ill had played havoc with her body clock.

The strident peal of the phone was an unwelcome intrusion, and as Sergio rolled off her and answered it she was hit by a cold blast of reality. Nothing had changed. They had had mind-blowing sex, but now it was business as usual. His commitment to the Castellano Group was total, and he had probably already forgotten her and was focused on the next big deal.

To her surprise, he cut the call after a brief conversation in Italian. 'That was Luisa, to say that Nico is awake.'

Nico! Guilt swept through Kristen that she had forgotten about him while she had been in Sergio's bed. It was ridiculous to feel shy with Sergio after she had made love with him but she couldn't meet his gaze as she slid out of bed and quickly pulled on the shirt he had lent her, wincing as the material grazed her sensitised nipples.

'I must go to him,' she muttered. 'I hope he hasn't been sick again.'

'Luisa assured me that he woke up full of beans, ate all his breakfast and now he's playing with his train set. But I agree we ought to get up. We're due to have lunch with my father in an hour, which means, regrettably, that we can't spend the rest of the day in bed like we used to do.' Sergio studied her pink cheeks speculatively. 'Do you remember, *cara*, how sometimes we would make love for hours and only leave the bedroom when we needed food?'

'Four years is a long time, and I don't remember much about our affair,' Kristen lied. Anxious to change the subject, she asked, 'Do you know what happened to my clothes?'

'The maid took them to be washed after Nico was sick over you. But in the wardrobe you will find a few outfits that I ordered for you from a friend who owns a boutique in Palermo.'

'A few outfits' turned out to be a whole range of clothes, from formal evening dresses to casual-wear that bore designer labels, which Kristen knew were completely out of her price range. 'I don't need all these clothes, and I can't afford them,' she said as she flicked through the rail. 'You suggested that Nico and I should stay here for a couple of weeks so that he can have a holiday, but I'll have to go back to my job in London…and I'll be taking him with me.'

'We have a lot to discuss,' Sergio said non-committally. 'Perhaps you can solve a puzzle for me. I sent a member of my staff to your house in Camden to bring back some of your clothes, but all Marco could find were a few items that look frankly as though they belong in a charity shop.'

Kristen shrugged. 'That's where I buy most of my clothes. You can find some real bargains if you look carefully.'

'I'll take your word for it. But if you buy second-hand clothes, why do you have thousands of pounds' worth of credit card debts and bills for designer goods?'

Realising that she had no option but to tell him the truth, she sighed heavily. 'I'm not in debt…but Mum owed a fortune when she died. The letters you saw from debt collecting agencies are trying to claim money from her estate. But Mum only had a few hundred pounds in savings, and that has already gone to her creditors.

'Don't think badly of her,' she told Sergio fiercely, even though he'd not said a word. 'I had no idea that she was so unhappy being married to my stepfather. She admitted that she only stayed with Alan because he was my gymnastics coach and she didn't want to ruin my chances of success.

But he was a very controlling man and he destroyed her confidence. She used to go shopping to make herself feel better, but it became a compulsion. It was a form of depression. She never even wore the things she bought; she just hid them at the back of the wardrobe.

'When Alan found out that she had run up huge debts he refused to help her sort things out. The worry of it made her ill, and so I took charge of her finances and I've been trying to repay the money she owed. Even after Mum died, the debt agencies have still been hounding me.'

She glanced at Sergio, wishing she knew what he was thinking, but his expression gave nothing away.

'Your mother was lucky to have such a loyal daughter,' he said gently.

Kristen bit her lip. 'She sacrificed her happiness for me and my gymnastics career. My stepfather always demanded his own way. Who does that remind me of?' she said sarcastically. 'You snatched Nico and brought him to Sicily because it was what you wanted.'

'I acted in his best interests.' Even though he had been wrong to think that Kristen had been responsible for the bruises on Nico, Sergio still believed it was better for the little boy to be in Sicily rather than living in a tiny, shabby house in Camden and spending all day at nursery. Somehow he had to convince Kristen of that.

He threw back the sheet and gave her a sardonic look when she blushed at the sight of his naked body. 'If you keep staring at me like you're doing, we definitely won't make it to lunch,' he drawled.

But, although her flush deepened at his taunt, she kept her eyes fixed on him as he strolled across the room. Her desire for him was his secret weapon and he had no compunction about using it mercilessly, Sergio thought. Sex was the one way he could connect with her and he slid his hand beneath her chin and slanted his mouth over hers to kiss her with passion and a possessiveness that he had never felt for any other woman.

Her response tested his resolve and he felt a pang of regret when he eventually ended the kiss and traced his thumb over her swollen bottom lip. 'My father is looking forward to meeting his grandson,' he said roughly, 'so I'd better leave you to get dressed.'

CHAPTER NINE

NICO WAS WEARING a new pair of jeans and a T-shirt and looked the picture of health when Sergio lifted him into the car. Kristen was relieved that he had completely recovered from the vomiting virus. He seemed to have settled into his new surroundings at Casa Camelia, but she was not sure whether it was a good thing. She didn't want him to be upset when she took him back home to London. Sergio had said that Sicily was Nico's home and perhaps a judge would agree and award custody of him to his father, she thought worriedly.

With Nico safely strapped into the child seat in the rear of the car, Sergio slid into the driver's seat and Kristen felt her stomach dip as her eyes were drawn to his darkly tanned hands on the steering wheel, remembering how he had explored every inch of her body when he had made love to her.

He turned his head towards her. 'You look beautiful. The dress is a perfect fit and the colour suits you.'

Kristen tore her gaze from the glint of sexual awareness in his. She had chosen to wear a sky-blue silk jersey wrap dress to lunch with Sergio's father. Teamed with nude-coloured stiletto heels and matching bag, the outfit was elegant and yet the feel of the silk against her skin was incredibly sensual. 'It was kind of you to order the clothes,' she said stiltedly. 'When I go back to London I will, of course, reimburse you for them.' It would be another debt to add to the bureau where she kept her mother's outstanding bills, she thought ruefully.

Sergio put the car into gear and drove away from the villa. 'You don't owe me anything. It was my fault that you left London in a rush and didn't have time to pack your own clothes.'

It was the first reference he had made to the way he had taken Nico while Kristen had been asleep, and she thought she heard a faint apology in his voice.

'Will anyone else be at lunch besides your father?'

'Salvatore will be there with his daughter.'

'Rosa was only a few months old when I last saw her.' Kristen recalled his brother's pretty baby girl and beautiful wife, Adriana. 'What about Rosa's mother? Is Adriana away? I know she often went to Rome for modelling assignments.'

Sergio shot her a glance. 'Adriana is dead. She was killed in a car accident when Rosa was a year old.'

'Oh…how terrible! No wonder Salvatore looks so haggard.' What a cruel twist of fate that both the brothers' wives had died tragically young, Kristen mused. 'I noticed that he walks with a limp. Was he in the car when the accident happened?'

'Salvatore was driving them home from a dinner party. No one knows why he lost control of the car but it plunged over the edge of the mountain road they were travelling on. Adriana died instantly and Salvatore was seriously injured. My brother has no memory of the accident.' Sergio hesitated. 'He is wracked with guilt that it was his fault Adriana died, but I can't help wondering if his amnesia is an emotional response to the accident and the events leading up to it.'

'What do you mean?' Kristen asked curiously.

Sergio shrugged. 'I suspect that Salvatore's marriage was not as happy as everyone believed. He did not confide in me, but I sensed tension between him and Adriana, mainly over her decision to return to modelling and the fact that she left Rosa behind when she went to Rome for work. Perhaps they argued in the car that night and Salvatore was distracted. He is usually a careful driver. But he can't remember what happened and he blames himself that because of him his daughter is growing up without her mother.

'To make matters worse, it was confirmed when Rosa was eighteen months old that she is profoundly deaf.' Sergio sighed. 'I know Salvatore loves his little girl, but he seems unable to connect with Rosa, and I fear that she is becoming more and more introverted.'

He glanced over his shoulder to Nico, who was loudly singing one of his nursery songs. 'It will be good for Rosa to play with Nico. Salvatore rarely leaves his castle, and Rosa has few chances to meet other children.'

When they arrived at La Casa Bianca, a butler escorted them to the dining room where Tito was waiting. Kristen was shocked when she met Sergio's father, although she managed to hide her reaction. Four years ago Tito Castellano had been a formidable man, but a series of strokes had left him looking older and frail. His black eyes were still sharply assessing, though, and Kristen let out her pent-up breath when he finally turned his gaze from her to his son.

'Sergio, I cannot deny I was shocked when Salvatore told me I have a grandson. I understand that the boy is three years old, so why did I not learn about him until today?'

'It is a private matter between me and Kristen,' Sergio explained in a cool voice.

The slight frostiness between the two men that Kristen had noticed four years ago was still there, she realised. There was no expression in Sergio's eyes, but she was so attuned to him that she could sense his tension. Perhaps the fact that he had spent most of his childhood in America with his mother had made it hard for him to bond with his father. The thought made her wonder if the reason Sergio was determined to keep Nico in Sicily was so that he would have a closer relationship with his son than he had with Tito.

Tito's frown cleared as Nico stepped out from behind Kristen. 'So this is the boy. There is no doubt he is your son, Sergio—he is the image of you.' The old man's eyes gleamed. 'I had almost given up hope that you would do your duty to the family and the company—but finally you have pleased me by providing the next Castellano heir.' His gaze darted to Kristen. 'Now, all that is to be done is to organise the wedding.'

Struggling to hide her shock, Kristen waited for Sergio to tell his father that they had absolutely no plans to marry, but to her confusion he made no response to Tito's statement and instead held out a chair for her to sit down at the dining table.

Anger flared inside her. Well, if he wouldn't say something, she would! Sergio had lifted Nico onto a chair that had been fitted with an additional cushion so that the little boy could reach the table. Now, as Sergio sat down next to Kristen, she glared at him.

'I think you should make it clear that we…' she began, but the rest of her words were lost as Sergio's head swooped towards her and he dropped a hard kiss on her lips that stole her breath.

'I agree we should reassure my father that although there were problems in our relationship which led to you and Nico living in England, we are now both committed to putting our son's interests first and doing what is best for him. Isn't that so, *cara*?'

'Yes...but...' She broke off as, out of the corner of her eye, she saw Nico reach for the water jug. 'Wait, Nico, let me help you...' She spoke too late and watched resignedly as he knocked the jug over and water quickly soaked through the tablecloth.

'It doesn't matter. Let him come and sit here next to me.' Tito was clearly captivated by his grandson. 'Do you know who I am?' he asked the little boy. 'I am your *nonno*.'

'Nonno,' Nico repeated, and grinned at his grandfather.

Tito looked over at the pretty dark-haired little girl sitting beside Salvatore. 'It is good to hear a child talk. You should do more to help Rosa, Salvatore. She may be unable to hear, but she should learn to speak.'

'I am looking for a speech therapist to work on her language skills,' Salvatore replied curtly. His dark eyes showed no expression when he glanced at his daughter and Kristen felt a tug of compassion for the little girl who was growing up without her mother and clearly needed more support from her father.

For the rest of the lunch she concentrated on reminding Nico of his table manners, and when he had had enough to eat she took him to play in the garden and offered to take Rosa too. Nico seemed completely unconcerned that Rosa did not speak, and within a short time the two children had worked out a way of communicating with each other.

Kristen did not have an opportunity to talk to Sergio privately until they were in the car driving back to Casa Camelia. 'Why didn't you explain to your father that we are not in a relationship?' she demanded. 'He seems to have the crazy idea that we are going to get married. Why on earth didn't you deny it?'

Sergio parked outside the villa and immediately jumped out and went to help Nico out of the car. 'We'll discuss it later,' he said coolly. 'I'm going to take Nico swimming this afternoon.'

'That's not a good idea so soon after he was ill,' Kristen said immediately. 'I think he should take things easy for the rest of today.'

'I'd like to see you persuade him to slow down,' he murmured drily as they both watched Nico running up and down the driveway, pretending to be an aeroplane. Sergio gave her an intent look. 'You're going to have to get used to sharing him with me because I'm not going to walk out of his life, however much you might wish me to,' he added perceptively.

'Can you give me your word on that, Sergio? I'm scared you'll let him down.' Kristen admitted her greatest fear. 'Fatherhood is a big commitment, and you need to decide whether you want to be part of Nico's life for the long haul, or not at all.' She could not bear for Nico to grow close to Sergio and then be rejected by him, like she had been rejected by her stepfather.

He had hurt Kristen badly four years ago, Sergio recognised. He had not found it easy to share his feelings, let alone examine what those feelings were. But the situation was different now. They had a child together and, for Nico's sake, Sergio realised that he had to face the demons in his past so that he could build a future with his son and perhaps with Kristen too.

'You don't need to doubt my commitment to him,' he said quietly. 'I will be a devoted father to Nico.' He hesitated. 'I promise I will do nothing to make you regret that we met again, Kristen.'

Sergio's serious tone touched a chord inside Kristen and she blinked to dispel the tears that filled her eyes. 'I hope you're right,' she said gruffly. But as she followed him into the villa she wondered how they were going to resolve the issue of sharing custody of Nico when they lived in different countries—and different worlds—she thought with a rueful glance around the luxurious villa. Sergio had said that Casa Camelia was Nico's home, but it wasn't hers. She would only ever be a visitor here, her presence tolerated by Sergio because she was the mother of his son. The prospect seemed unbearable and she avoided his gaze, desperate to hide the fact that she was falling apart.

'Are you going to come swimming with us?' Sergio asked Kristen as he swung Nico into his arms and the little boy laughed delightedly. 'I'll take him to get changed and meet you by the pool in five minutes.'

'Actually, I won't come. I've got a headache and sitting out in the sun probably won't help it.' The excuse was not completely untrue. Kristen had a slight headache, but what hurt more was Nico's utter fascination with Sergio and the fact that he didn't seem to need her any more.

Sergio gave her a searching look. 'Well, if you change your mind you know where to find us. I'm sure Nico will want you to watch his first swimming lesson. I appreciate that you are finding it hard to share him with me,' he said heavily. 'But you have memories of him from the moment he was born, while I was deprived of being part of his life and I have to build my relationship with him starting from now. I don't want us to fight over him. For his sake we must find a way to put the past behind us and move forward.'

He was right, of course, and his words left Kristen feeling ashamed. She reminded herself that she had only kept Nico a secret because she had believed that Sergio was married, but the real truth was she had been devastated that he had not chased after her when she had left him four years ago.

Had she kept his son from him to hurt him as he had hurt her? The thought made her feel uncomfortable but she forced herself to be honest. Had she denied him his child because he hadn't loved her? He had every right to be angry, she acknowledged. But in fact Sergio had shown remarkable restraint and, rather than playing the blame game, he was more concerned with working out how they could both be parents to Nico.

She could not blame Sergio if he thought she was behaving like a spoilt child, Kristen decided fifteen minutes later as she walked across the patio on her way to the pool. Nico's high-pitched voice and Sergio's deeper tones drifted over the screen of tall shrubs that gave the pool area privacy from the rest of the garden. The sweet scent of jasmine and honeysuckle hung thick in the air and the sun warmed Kristen's skin so that the prospect of a swim was inviting.

'Mummy…' Nico was sitting on the steps at the shallow end of the pool and when he saw Kristen he jumped up and hurtled towards her, a wide smile on his face. 'I want you to come swimming with me and Papà, Mummy.'

Kristen caught his wriggling, damp body close and laughed a little unsteadily as she felt a familiar ache of love for her little boy. 'Okay, I will. Have you been having fun with Papà?' When Nico nodded fervently, she smiled and looked over at Sergio. 'Good,' she said softly, 'I'm glad.'

His answering smile lifted her heart. She felt her pulse race at the sight of him wearing a pair of black swim shorts. Droplets of water glistened on his broad, tanned shoulders and as she watched he ducked beneath the surface of the pool and came up again, pushing his wet hair back from his brow.

'Is the water cold?'

'Not cold enough, unfortunately,' he drawled. His dark eyes glinted. 'Not when you look so gorgeous and incredibly tempting in that bikini.'

Kristen blushed and glanced down at the bikini which she had found with the other clothes he had bought for her. It consisted of two tiny pieces of jade-green Lycra and was far more daring than anything she would have chosen.

'You chose it,' she reminded him.

'And now I'm going to have to swim at least forty lengths to try and get rid of my frustration,' he said ruefully. 'Why don't you stay with Nico and let him show you how well he can swim with armbands?'

It was all about compromise, Kristen mused as she played in the shallow end with Nico while Sergio thrashed up and down the pool. She appreciated that he had given her time to be alone with Nico to prove that he didn't want to monopolize the little boy's attention. For the first time since she had arrived in Sicily, determined to snatch back her son, a sense of calm settled over her and she was even able to fool herself that everything would be all right.

The fragile feeling of hope lasted for the rest of the afternoon. Nico clearly loved having the attention of both his parents and Kristen discovered that sharing responsibility with another adult gave her a chance to relax and enjoy herself. Eventually Sergio carried their tired son back to the house and, after he'd had his tea and a bath, Nico was ready for bed.

Luisa, Rosa's nanny, arrived just as Kristen had finished reading him a story. 'Salvatore offered to put Rosa to bed tonight, and suggested that I should come and see if you need any help with Nico,' she explained, speaking in fluent English. 'It is good that he is feeling better today and was able to meet his grandfather.'

'Yes, Tito seemed much taken with him,' Kristen said, remembering how Sergio's father had not taken his eyes off Nico during lunch.

'Of course! Signor Castellano is delighted. For many years he has hoped that Sergio would provide an heir who will one day inherit the company with Salvatore's daughter.' Luisa shrugged. 'My cousin works as Tito's cook, and she heard rumours among the household staff that Tito had delayed giving Sergio the permanent role of joint CEO of the Castellano Group with his twin brother, and chose instead to name only Salvatore as his successor. But that is to change now that Sergio has a son. Tito has instructed the company's lawyers to upgrade Sergio's status to CEO, the same as Salvatore, and I understand that Tito is impatient for the two of you to marry so that Nico becomes a legitimate heir.'

Luisa smiled, unaware that Kristen's lack of response was because she was too shocked to speak. Her mind was reeling, but everything Luisa had told her made horrible sense. 'I was going to offer to sit with Nico,' the nanny said, 'but he has already fallen asleep.'

'It's not necessary for you to stay, thank you.' Somehow Kristen managed to keep a lid on her anger until the nanny had gone, but as she marched next door into Sergio's room her temper reached boiling point.

'Did Nico settle okay?' He strolled over to meet her, looking unfairly sexy in tailored black trousers and a white silk shirt that contrasted with his bronzed complexion. With his silky hair falling forward onto his brow and his mouth curved into a sensual smile, he looked every inch a billionaire playboy, and jealousy stabbed Kristen through her heart as she wondered how many women must have shared his bed.

'I thought we would have dinner on the terrace…like we used to do,' he said softly. 'But I'm feeling a little overdressed.'

His eyes glinted with amusement and something else that made Kristen catch her breath as his gaze roamed over her bikini-clad body. Despite the fact that she had slipped on a chiffon shirt which matched the bikini, she felt at a disadvantage when he was fully dressed, especially when a quick glance downwards revealed that her nipples were clearly visible, jutting beneath the clingy Lycra bra top.

She pulled the edges of the gauzy shirt together in an attempt to hide her treacherous body from him. 'Why have you not told your father the truth about us? He is still under the illusion that we intend to marry. But I suppose it suits you not to clarify the misunderstanding,' she ploughed on without giving him the opportunity to speak, 'just as it suited you to bring Nico here. I understand now why you were so determined to bring him to Sicily.'

'Do you?' Sergio's face was enigmatic but his voice was cool as he drawled, 'Why don't you enlighten me?'

'Luisa told me that your father refused to name you as his successor jointly with Salvatore until you produced an heir. How convenient for you that you discovered your son, especially when Tito's health is failing. Luisa said she has heard that Tito is now preparing to upgrade you to CEO of the Castellano Group, the same as your brother.' She gave a bitter laugh. 'And to think you convinced me that you wanted to be a proper father to Nico. I should have remembered that you usually avoid commitment like the plague. Thank goodness he hasn't had time to form a close bond with you. I'm going to take him back to England before you have a chance to hurt him.'

She swung away from Sergio but, before she could take a step, he gripped her shoulder and spun her back round to face him. 'What nonsense is this?' he grated. 'I would never harm a hair on Nico's head.'

'No, but you could break his heart. He has really taken to you and doesn't stop talking about his daddy. He won't understand that he comes second in your life, and that the company is the only thing you care about. You brought Nico to Sicily because your father wouldn't name you as his successor until you produced an heir.'

'And you know this because Luisa told you? You believe the word of a member of staff who does not even work at my father's house, and who is well known for her habit of spreading gossip, which in this case is completely unfounded.'

Sergio had not raised his voice, but somehow his quiet tone was infinitely more dangerous. His jaw was rigid with tension and Kristen realised he was furious.

She bit her lip as it belatedly occurred to her that she might have been too ready to jump to conclusions. 'Do you deny it?'

'Of course I damn well deny it. My father stipulated years ago that when he dies, or when bad health prevents him from carrying out his role as head of the company, Salvatore and I will take over from him and we will have equal responsibility. It is true that Tito made some minor alterations to his will recently, and perhaps that is where the rumours have arisen from. But it is *not* true that my position within the company is dependent on me having an heir.'

His dark eyes glimmered with anger as he stared at Kristen's startled face. 'I brought Nico to Sicily because I want the chance to get to know my son. I know what it's like to grow up without a father. It might suit you to deny it, but Nico will benefit from having a male role model. He needs his father, and I...' he swallowed convulsively '...I love him already,' he said roughly. 'I will *never* let him down the way you seem to think I will.'

Shaken by the fervency of Sergio's words, Kristen found that she believed him and felt guilty for accusing him without first checking the facts. 'I'm sorry,' she said huskily. 'I just wanted to protect Nico. I was stunned when your father mentioned a wedding. But I suppose it's understandable that he assumes we are going to get married.'

'He didn't make an assumption. I told him that I intend to marry you.'

Shock caused her heart to jolt painfully against her ribs. 'What...*why*? Why on earth did you do that?'

Sergio's brows lifted in an arrogant expression that made Kristen itch to slap him.

'Do you have a better idea for how we can both be parents to our son and spare him the uncertainty of a custody battle?'

'I can think of a dozen ideas that do not involve marriage between two people who don't...'

'Don't what, *mia bella*?' Sergio tightened his grip on her shoulder and pulled her towards him, crushing her slender frame against his hard body. 'Don't desire one another? Don't hunger for one another night and day? Because if that were the case, I agree the marriage would be doomed to failure. But I dare you to deny the passion that ignites between us with one look, one touch...one kiss.'

His dark head swooped and he captured her mouth, forcing her lips apart with the bold thrust of his tongue and kissing her with fiery passion that lit a flame inside Kristen. Her body responded to its master, but some tiny part of her sanity still lingered, and when he pushed her shirt over her shoulders she tore her mouth from his.

'What you are talking about is just sex. It's not the basis of a marriage…Sergio…put me down!' She beat her hands on his chest as he lifted her as easily as though she were a rag doll and dropped her onto the bed.

'It's a start,' he said, and the quiet intensity of his voice sent a tremor through her. 'Desire seems a very good reason why I should make you my wife.'

CHAPTER TEN

SERGIO'S PROPOSAL WAS four years too late, Kristen thought bitterly. Not that he had actually proposed. He had told his father he intended to marry her, and as a secondary thought he had casually let her know what he planned. Her anger brimmed over. Four years ago she would have leapt at the chance to be his wife, but his arrogant assumption that she was still the silly, love-struck girl she had been then fuelled her resentment and hurt. Because the real reason, the only reason, he had decided to marry her was for Nico's sake. And, much as Kristen adored her son, she would not endure a loveless marriage that would be all the worse because in her heart she acknowledged that she had never stopped loving Sergio.

What kind of a fool did that make her? She hated herself for loving him. Hated the way her body was so utterly enslaved by him that one kiss was all it took to make her melt in his arms. She realised with a flash of insight that he was always in control because she allowed him to be. Four years ago she had been too young and awed by him to make her own demands and fight for what she wanted in their relationship. But no more. She was a strong and independent woman now; she'd had to be as a single mother trying to hold down a career and bring up a child. She had no intention of marrying Sergio simply because he would find it convenient. But at the same time she could not deny her desire for him. Her breasts felt heavy and she could feel the warm flood of her arousal between her legs. She wanted to make love with him, but on her terms, not his.

He knelt over her, his dark eyes raging with a primitive hunger to possess his woman.

'I desired you from the first time I watched you dancing on the sand. You felt the attraction between us that day too, and it has never faded. You want me as much as I want you,' he said harshly, and with one swift movement he unfastened her bikini top and tugged it away from her breasts.

Kristen's anger exploded. She pushed against his chest, taking him by surprise so that he was momentarily unbalanced, giving her the chance to roll away from him. With the grace and surprising strength gained from years of gymnastics training, she pushed him onto his back and straddled his hips.

'I'm sick of being manipulated by you,' she said fiercely. 'You always want everything to be your way. You snatched Nico and forced me to leave my job and life in London and come to Sicily. But you won't force me to marry you.'

She shook her tumbling mane of blonde hair over her shoulders and sat back a little so that her breasts thrust provocatively forward. Sergio inhaled sharply and the sensation of his arousal stirring beneath her made her feel triumphant that she had power over him. 'You fall far short of what I want from a husband,' she told him. 'But as a lover you are first class.'

Sergio's eyes narrowed. 'Is that so? Are you saying you want to have sex with me but nothing else?'

'How does it feel, Sergio?' she taunted. 'Does it make you feel good to know that the only part of you I'm interested in is your body? That's how you made me feel during our affair.' Her voice shook betrayingly. 'I was good enough for sex but not for you to share your feelings with.'

To her surprise, he did not refute her accusation but sighed deeply. 'I'm sorry I made you feel like that and I'm sorry I hurt you.'

He could not change the past, Sergio thought heavily. He had not met Kristen's emotional needs and he could understand why she was afraid that he would fail Nico in the same way that he had failed her. Somehow he had to show her that *he* could change. He would not find it easy to open up when he had kept his emotions locked away for most of his life, but everything was at stake here and he was willing to try.

He looked into her bright blue eyes and felt an inexplicable ache in his chest. She was so beautiful. His gaze dropped to her small, firm breasts with their puckered nipples and a white-hot shaft of desire ripped through him but, instead of taking control and flipping her onto her back, he relaxed against the pillows and spread his arms wide like an indolent sultan waiting to be pleasured by his favourite concubine.

'If sex is what you want, then take me, Krissie. I'm all yours.'

Sergio's soft words stabbed Kristen through the heart. He had never been hers, not in the way she longed for. His heart and soul belonged solely to himself, and perhaps, she thought with a pang, to his dead wife. Passion was all he had ever given her. So why not accept what he offered and take her pleasure with his virile body, if that was all she could have of him?

The hard glitter in his eyes betrayed his hunger, but amazingly he seemed prepared to allow her to take the lead. A heady sense of power swept through her and a desire to tease and torment him as he had done so often to her. She held his gaze as she unfastened his shirt buttons and pushed the material aside to expose his darkly tanned chest, and leaned forward so that the tips of her breasts brushed across his wiry chest hairs.

The sensation made her nipples tingle and harden. The contrast between her milky-pale breasts and his bronzed skin was incredibly erotic. Colour flared on his cheekbones and his breath hissed between his teeth as her hair fell forward and brushed lightly over his naked torso.

'Witch,' he said raggedly as she moved lower so that her soft hair and her pebble-hard nipples stroked a path over his abdomen. With nimble fingers she deftly undid the zip of his trousers and when her hands slid beneath his boxers and closed around his throbbing arousal Sergio gave a low groan. He knew he was close to the edge and almost gave in to the temptation to roll over and drag her beneath him so that he could find the relief he craved, but he managed to hold back. It was true that when they had made love previously it had always been on his terms, and he had never given himself completely. But if he was ever going to win Kristen's trust he must prove that he did not want to dominate her.

The flick of her tongue over the sensitive tip of his manhood made him clench his muscles to stop himself from falling apart. His body shook as he fought the waves of pleasure that rolled over him when she took his swollen shaft into the moist cavern of her mouth.

'What does it feel like to know that this is all that exists between us?' she murmured.

If it was true, it would hurt him maybe more deeply than any pain he had known in his life, Sergio acknowledged. But he had heard the tremor in her voice and recognised the inherent tenderness of her caresses, and he was certain that she felt more for him than simply sexual desire. It was in her kiss when she arched above him and claimed his mouth with heart-shaking passion. He glimpsed it briefly in her eyes when she guided herself down onto him and took his rigid length inside her, inch by inch, pausing while her internal muscles stretched to accommodate him. Her lashes lowered and hid her expression. But he thought he had seen love there. He wasn't sure. But it gave him hope that perhaps there was a chance he could win her back.

Desire took over wild and wanton as she rode him, her slender body moving with instinctive grace while he cupped her breasts and played with her nipples, increasing her pleasure, escalating her excitement so that she threw her head back and made love to him with an abandonment that touched his soul. They climaxed simultaneously, breathing hard and fast in those moments of sheer physical ecstasy, their hearts thundering in unison when she collapsed on top of him and Sergio wrapped his arms around her and threaded his fingers in her hair.

Eventually the world righted itself and Kristen lifted herself off Sergio and moved away from him. It was ridiculous to feel shy, but she couldn't bring herself to meet his gaze. Making love with him had been heaven, but now the gates of hell beckoned as she wondered if she had given herself away. Had he guessed that desire was only one part of what she felt for him? She had taunted him that sex was all she wanted from him, but she had a horrible feeling that he knew she had been lying.

He confirmed her fears when he propped himself on one elbow and gave her a lazy smile. 'I think it's fair to say we have proved irrefutably that desire is an excellent reason for us to get married.' He paused for a heartbeat before adding softly, 'Another reason is that we forgot to use protection, so unless you are on the Pill there's a chance you could have conceived my child.' He met her stunned gaze with an enigmatic expression. 'I'll start to organise the wedding immediately.'

Dear God! How could she have been so stupid? Feeling numb, Kristen slid off the bed and wrapped Sergio's shirt around her. Without saying a word, she walked into the adjoining sitting room and stood by the window, which looked out over the lake. The setting sun had turned the water to gold and beyond the lake the Sicilian countryside was bathed in mellow light while in the distance tall pine trees were silhouetted against the pink sky. The beauty of the scene, the feeling of being insignificant in the vastness of the universe, intensified the ache in Kristen's heart.

She heard Sergio come up behind her and when he placed a hand on her shoulder she spun round to face him. 'How can we get married when a day ago you believed I was responsible for the bruises on Nico's legs?' she said shakily. 'We are virtually strangers. If you knew me at all you would have realised that I would cut my heart out rather than hurt him.' She swallowed. 'Do you have any idea how I felt when I realised you had taken him? What kind of relationship would we have when there is no trust between us?'

The shadows in her eyes warned Sergio that she deserved to hear the truth, even though that meant finally opening himself up and revealing the grim secrets of his childhood.

'I trust you,' he said intently. 'But I admit that when I saw the bruises on Nico my reactions were purely instinctive. My only thought was to rescue him.'

'You believed he needed to be rescued from me?' Kristen blinked back the hot tears burning her eyes. 'Do you really think I am such a terrible mother?'

'No. Not now that I have watched you with him and seen how deeply you care for him. But in London…'

Sergio hesitated and took a swift breath '…I wondered if you were like my mother.'

'I…I don't understand.' Looking into Sergio's dark eyes, Kristen had the strange feeling that she was hovering on the edge of a precipice and for some reason her heart was thumping.

'My mother used to beat me when I was a child.'

The words circled around Kristen but she could not grasp them or make sense of them. Sergio seemed to realise that she was too shocked to respond and continued in a flat voice, 'The bruises on Nico's legs reminded me of the marks my mother used to leave when she caned me. When I was just a few years older than Nico I used to hope that my father would come and take me home to Sicily. I was desperate for his protection…but he never came.' His throat worked as he fought to retain his iron self-control.

'I guess I went a little mad. I had just discovered my son, and the possibility that he might be physically and emotionally at risk brought back memories of my childhood that, unfortunately, I can never forget. I wasn't thinking straight,' he admitted. 'I have spent my life wondering if my father did not love me and that was why he failed to protect me. I was determined to protect Nico so that he would never have reason to doubt my love for him.'

It was strange to hear Sergio talk of love. Kristen had often wondered why he apparently lacked the normal range of emotions that most people had, and she had longed to break through his air of detachment and discover if he really was the empty shell he gave the impression of being. Now she knew. And the truth was utterly heartbreaking. The lines of strain on his face revealed a man who was struggling to control his emotions—and who could blame him? she thought sadly.

'Why did your mother…?' She could not go on, feeling physically sick as she imagined Sergio as a young boy, being beaten by the person who should have cared for him the most. It made her want to run to Nico's bedroom and hug him tight. She would give her life to protect her little boy and she was able to sympathise with how Sergio must have felt when he had seen bruises on Nico's legs. It was understandable that after his experiences as a child he had wanted to protect his son, but it still hurt that he had believed Nico had needed protection from her.

'I don't know why she did it,' Sergio said heavily. 'I think she was frustrated by her lack of success as an actress, and she had an issue with alcohol. She could be very loving, but I always felt I was walking on a knife-edge and the slightest thing could send her into a violent rage. She told me once that her father used to beat her and her mother after he had been drinking. While she was married to my father she seemed to be a caring mother to me and my brother. But when she took me to America she started to drink heavily. I used to think she beat me because she hated me. She seemed to enjoy making me cry, and so I learned to keep my emotions bottled up. It became a matter of pride not to show my feelings...and as I grew older the habit of hiding what I felt became second nature.'

Kristen felt a lump in her throat. It was no wonder that, after years of suffering physical abuse, Sergio had erected defences as a means of self-protection from being hurt emotionally.

'Why didn't your father help you? Surely, if you had told him what was happening, he would have tried to get you back?'

'I had no contact with him from the age of five. My mother told me that it was my father's choice. Years later, when I returned to Sicily, Tito insisted that he had tried to keep in touch and my mother had prevented him.'

Sergio's jaw clenched. 'Frankly, I suspect that he didn't try very hard.'

'So why did your mother allow you to go back to your father when you were a teenager?'

He hesitated, and Kristen sensed that he was struggling to talk about his past. 'I beat up her boyfriend.' Sergio grimaced when he heard Kristen gasp. 'The guy hit me, and I snapped and hit him back, breaking his nose in the process. For a few seconds I was overcome by sheer rage and I wanted to kill the guy…' he swallowed convulsively '…and my mother too. But afterwards I was ashamed that I had allowed my emotions to get the better of me. I must have scared my mother because she decided she couldn't cope with my anger issues and sent me back to Sicily. But it was too late to build a relationship with Tito, and even with my twin brother. We had been apart for ten years, and I was jealous of Salvatore's closeness to our father. In my mind, Salvatore was the favoured son. I felt I had to prove myself to Tito, especially in business, and show him that I deserved to be his successor just as much as my brother.'

'So you worked obsessively,' Kristen said, gaining sudden insight into why the Castellano Group had been more important to him than anything else, including his relationship with her. Did he still feel the need to prove his worth to his father? she wondered. If so, where would Nico come in his priorities?

He must have read her thoughts because he said quickly, 'Nothing is more important to me than building a relationship with my son. Fortunately, he is young enough that he will hopefully not remember that I wasn't around for his baby years. It is not too late for me and Nico—as it was with me and my father. I will work hard to make up for the time I lost with him.'

The accusation that the lost years were her fault hung

between them and Kristen felt even guiltier now that Sergio had told her about his childhood. 'I did what I thought was best,' she said stiffly. 'You were so distant at the hospital after I'd had the miscarriage, and I truly believed you did not want a child with me.'

'The fault was mine, not yours,' he assured her. 'I was so well-practised at hiding my emotions and it didn't occur to me that you needed to see that I was grieving for our baby too.'

Kristen bit her lip as a dozen 'if onlys' ran through her mind. If only Sergio had confided in her during their affair then she might have understood why he seemed so coldly unemotional. If only she had remained in Sicily with him, instead of going back to England in high dudgeon because he had only asked her to be his mistress, then she would have told him she was still pregnant with her dead baby's twin, and maybe he would have married her rather than the beautiful Sicilian woman whose photo he kept in his bedroom.

She turned away to the window and saw that the sun had sunk below the horizon while they had been talking and a few faint stars were appearing in the purple sky. Somehow the beauty of the heavens seemed tainted by the ugliness of Sergio's revelations and she felt an aching sadness for him, for her and for the course of events that had led them to be on opposite sides, each fighting to be full-time parents to their son.

'When you came to live with your father, did you tell him how your mother had treated you?'

'No.' He shrugged. 'I have explained that we are not close...and there was a part of me that wondered if Patti's mistreatment of me was somehow my fault. It was not something I wanted to talk about with Tito. And I couldn't say anything to Salvatore. He was already angry that our mother had abandoned him when he was a young child. In many ways Salvatore's childhood was as unhappy as mine. He told me that our father was very bitter after Patti left. Tito focused all his time and energy on the company and shut off his emotions. It must be a family trait,' Sergio said grimly. 'I couldn't tell Salvatore that the mother he had missed so desperately when he was a child was a spiteful, unpleasant woman.

'Patti died a year after I returned to Sicily—she drowned in the bath after a heavy drinking session. My brother and I didn't have the chance to ask her why she had treated us the way she did. I was an angry and confused young man, but thankfully one person understood me. I confided in Annamaria and she helped me come to terms with my past.'

Kristen had never heard Sergio speak in such a gentle tone, and she felt a stab of jealousy. 'Who is Annamaria?' The photograph of the dark-haired woman in Sergio's bedroom leapt into her mind, and she knew the answer to her question before he could answer. 'She was your wife, wasn't she?'

'Yes.' Sergio hesitated. 'I think I should explain about Annamaria.'

'There's no need.' Kristen stalled him quickly. The green-eyed demon inside her couldn't bear to hear details of the woman he had married soon after their own relationship had ended. She swung around to the window and crossed her arms in front of her, subconsciously retreating from him as he had done to her in the past.

He must have loved Annamaria to have told her about his childhood. In stark contrast, he had never spoken about personal matters to *her* during their affair, she thought bleakly. Admittedly, he had confided in her now, but only because he needed to explain why he had snatched Nico. He had also asked her to marry him, but not because he loved her. He wanted security for Nico, and she couldn't blame him for that after hearing about his desperately sad childhood.

But sexual compatibility was not a firm basis for marriage. What would happen if Sergio's desire for her faded? She couldn't bear the prospect of being his wife in name only while he had affairs with other women. Oh, she was sure he would be discreet, but she would be so unhappy, like her mother had been with her stepfather.

'I know I hurt you four years ago,' he said quietly. 'I did not realise how much until you told me that you believed I did not want the baby you miscarried.'

He placed his hands on her shoulders and turned her towards him, his jaw tightening when he felt how stiffly she was holding herself. She had put up barriers between them and he could hardly blame her when he had done the same during their affair, Sergio acknowledged heavily. But although she was wary of him she adored Nico and surely she must see that for his sake they had to put the past behind them.

'I promise I can change from the person you knew four years ago,' he said intently. 'I have changed already. I no longer feel the need to prove myself to my father. Being Nico's father is more important to me than any business deal.'

The rigidity of her shoulders told him she was not reassured, and there was a wary expression in her bright blue eyes that warned him he must curb his impatience. He had sprung the idea of marriage on her and, although to him it was the obvious solution that would allow Nico to live with both his parents, Kristen clearly had reservations. He could hardly blame her after he had revealed the abuse he had suffered as a child, he acknowledged bleakly.

'There is evidence which seems to show that in some

cases a person who was badly treated during childhood can go on to mistreat their own children,' he said quietly. 'But I swear I would never harm Nico in any way. If I believed there was even the slightest chance that I could lose my temper with him I would give up my right to be his father.'

Kristen was unbearably moved by the pain she heard in his voice. 'You have already shown yourself to be a brilliant dad and I trust absolutely that you will always take care of him.'

'Then why are you hesitating about accepting my proposal? The quicker we get married the quicker Nico will settle into his new life here at Casa Camelia.'

Sergio's statement set off alarm bells in Kristen. 'That's a very big assumption you have made. Why would we have to live in Sicily? I have a life in London, a career that I enjoy and a wide circle of friends, many of whom have children who are Nico's playmates.'

He shrugged. 'He would make friends here.'

'Probably, but that's not the point.' Frustration surged through Kristen. 'You told me you've changed from the man you were four years ago, but I can't see much evidence of that. You still want everything to be your way. If we were to marry, why couldn't we live in England?'

'I need to live here because the Castellano Group is based in Sicily.'

As soon as the words left his mouth Sergio knew he had made a mistake. The flash of anger in Kristen's eyes warned him he was in danger of losing any headway he had made with her.

'So, just as it did four years ago, the company comes first in your list of priorities, and if I agreed to marry you I would have to change my whole life to fit in with yours.'

Her scathing tone riled him. 'You make it sound as though Casa Camelia is a hovel, and moving here would be a terrible hardship. But it's a hell of a lot better than the rabbit hutch you call home in London. As for your job—you would not need to work and you could spend more time with Nico. Perhaps you could even take up gymnastics again.'

Sergio had played his trump card, Kristen acknowledged. Much as she enjoyed her job, she would love to be a full-time mum to Nico, at least until he started school. And she had often thought she would like to become a gymnastics coach, but she had never had time to attend the training courses while she worked full-time.

But marriage was such a massive step.

'I'm not convinced that a marriage of convenience would be right for us or for Nico. What if we were to divorce in a few years' time? That would be more painful for him than if we organise how we can both be a part of his life while leading separate lives of our own.'

The conversation was not heading in the direction Sergio wanted. It struck him forcibly that he hated the idea of Kristen living a separate life from him in London. She was so beautiful that she would undoubtedly attract a lot of male attention, and there would be nothing to stop her having lovers, maybe even marrying some other guy. Jealousy burned like acid in his gut. He was tempted to seize her in his arms and kiss her until she was mindless with desire, prove that the blazing passion they shared was special—just as she was special to him. But the determined tilt of her chin reminded him that she was not a pushover, and so he dropped his hands from her shoulders and looked deeply into her eyes.

'Nico's well-being is not the only reason I want to marry you, Krissie. And I am not contemplating us getting divorced. I'm talking about making a long-term commitment to you and to the future that I very much hope we will share. I would also like us to have more children. It would be good for Nico to grow up with siblings.'

Her sharp intake of breath warned him that he was going too fast. 'But I understand your concerns,' he said quickly, 'and I think we should put the idea of marriage on hold for a while and spend time getting to know each other again.'

Sergio smiled suddenly, breaking the tension and causing Kristen's heart to perform a somersault as he worked his sensual magic on her. 'What do you say, *cara*? Will you give me a chance?'

What could she say? she thought ruefully. She was still reeling from his statement that Nico was not the only reason he had suggested they get married. What on earth had he meant? With a helpless shrug she said huskily, 'I guess so. Yes.'

CHAPTER ELEVEN

SPENDING A DAY on Sergio's luxury yacht, which boasted a swimming pool, a Jacuzzi and cinema on its list of amenities, promised to be a relaxing experience. Spending a day on Sergio's yacht accompanied by an inquisitive, daredevil three-year-old boy was rather less relaxing, but it had still been a wonderful day, Kristen mused as the *Dolphin* dropped anchor in a small bay close to a private beach belonging to the Castellano estate.

'This is as close to the shore as we can go,' Sergio said as he strode across the deck. Wearing cut-off denim shorts and a fine cotton shirt left open to reveal his darkly tanned torso, he was one gorgeous sexy male and Kristen felt a delicious coiling sensation in the pit of her stomach at the thought that tonight he would make love to her. He had been away on a business trip the previous week and after five nights of aching frustration she was impatient to feel him inside her. Just the thought of his hard arousal nudging between her thighs was enough to make her breasts grow heavy, and she was glad that the sarong she had wrapped around her hid her pebble-hard nipples.

'We'll have to take the motor launch across to the beach. I'll hang on to Nico because he's as wriggly as an eel.' Sergio grinned as he swung his son into his arms. 'I want you to promise me that you will sit still when we go in the little boat, *piccolo*.'

'I will, Papà,' Nico said earnestly.

'Good boy.'

Watching her son rest his head on his father's shoulder, Kristen acknowledged that the bond between them grew stronger with every day. Nico hero-worshipped his daddy, and Sergio's love for his little boy shone in his eyes and was evident in the tenderness of his voice. It was wonderful to hear Nico laughing again, she thought. He was no longer the sad little boy he had been in London, and his grief over his nana's death had been forgotten in the excitement of getting to know his father.

Nico obediently sat still on Sergio's lap as the motor launch skimmed towards the shore and only once did he lean over the edge to try to catch the spray, causing his parents a few moments panic.

'He's utterly fearless,' Sergio said with rueful pride in his voice when they reached the beach and he set Nico down on the sand. 'I think we'll have to postpone another trip on the *Dolphin* until my nerves have recovered.' He smiled at Kristen as they strolled along the beach after Nico, who had shot off in front. 'What did the two of you get up to while I was away?'

'I took him swimming in the pool every day. He's only been learning for a few weeks since we arrived here, but he's almost ready to try without his armbands.' She gave him a quick glance. 'He really missed you.'

'The business trip to Hong Kong was booked months ago and I couldn't get out of going,' he said quickly. 'But I won't go away again or, if I do, I'll take Nico and you with me. I missed both of you.'

Sergio caught hold of her hand and wrapped his fingers around hers as they continued to walk towards the beach hut. Kristen let out a soft sigh. The day had been perfect so far, but then every day that she spent with Sergio was wonderful. The easy companionship that had developed between them reminded her of the early days of their affair. When they had first met he had been recovering from a sports injury which had meant that he'd had to take time off work. They had quickly become lovers, and she remembered they had spent lazy days on the beach and nights of incredible passion back at Casa Camelia. His commitment to the Castellano Group had not been a problem at first, but once he'd returned to his role as head of the property development side of the company their time together had been limited to nights of wild sex, and Kristen had felt hurt that his only interest seemed to be in her body.

Would the same thing happen again if she agreed to marry him? The evidence so far was that he had changed from the man he had been four years ago, she acknowledged. He only went to his office for a few hours a day, and was always home by mid-afternoon to play with Nico. She had come to love the hours that the three of them spent together almost as much as the nights when Sergio made love to her so beautifully that sometimes she had to blink back her tears before he saw them.

She suddenly realised that he was talking to her, and quickly dragged her mind back to the present.

'Did Rosa come over to play with Nico?'

'Yes, Salvatore brought her so that she could swim. He says Rosa has come out of her shell a little since she has had Nico as a playmate.'

Sergio frowned. 'I'm surprised my brother brought her, rather than the nanny. Perhaps Salvatore enjoyed being with you while the children played.'

Something in his tone made Kristen stop walking, and she turned to face him. 'I like your brother, and it was nice to chat to him. He is frustrated that he is still suffering from amnesia and can't remember anything of the accident. He blames himself for Adriana's death.' She watched Sergio's frown deepen and shook her head. 'Surely you can't be jealous of my friendship with Salvatore?'

'I am jealous of any man who looks at you,' he growled. While she was digesting this statement he jerked her against him and tangled his fingers in her long hair. 'I guard my possessions fiercely, *cara*.'

He brought his mouth down on hers and kissed her with a savage hunger that triggered an instant reaction in Kristen. She had long ago given up trying to resist him, and wound her arms around his neck while she kissed him back with all the pent-up passion that had built to an intolerable level during the five nights that he had been away.

'*Dio!* If we were alone I would take you right here on the sand,' he muttered when he eventually lifted his head and dragged oxygen into his lungs. 'I wish we weren't hosting a dinner party tonight. Maybe we could cancel it?'

Kristen wasn't sure how she felt about Sergio regarding her as one of his possessions. There was something very primitive about the idea of being owned by him. But, for all his effort to be a 'new man', he was at heart a hot-blooded Sicilian male, she thought ruefully, and she could not deny a little thrill of pleasure when he wrapped his arms around her and crushed her against his chest so that she could feel the strong beat of his heart.

'Of course we can't cancel. I'm looking forward to meeting your friends, Benito and Lia, and I really liked Gerardo and Flavia when we had dinner with them last week.' Kristen gave an impish smile that made Sergio catch his breath. 'I promise the anticipation will be worthwhile,' she murmured, trailing her fingertips down his chest and abdomen and stopping at the waistband of his shorts.

'Witch,' he groaned, and kissed her again. From along the beach they heard Nico calling for his *papà*. 'I have to go,' Sergio said regretfully.

'Go away on another business trip, do you mean?'

'No. Go and build my son a sandcastle like I promised him.'

She laughed. 'You'd better hurry up then.'

As she watched father and son digging in the sand Kristen's thoughts returned to the phone call she had had that morning from Steph, her boss at the physiotherapy clinic in London. Steph had asked when she planned to return to work.

'I'm not sure yet. I'll let you know in a couple of days,' Kristen had replied. She appreciated that over the last few weeks Sergio had made a lot of effort to allay her concerns about marrying him. Steph's question had been lurking in the back of her mind all day, and the conclusion she had reached was frightening and yet glaringly obvious.

It was almost midnight before the dinner party guests departed. The evening had been fun, Kristen mused as she walked into the master bedroom that she had shared with Sergio for the past weeks. The two married couples they had dined with had young children, and Kristen had arranged play-dates so that Nico could make new friends. He had settled at Casa Camelia amazingly quickly and, although she seemed to spend her life chasing after him to cover him in sun-cream, his arms and legs were already nut-brown and he looked much more Sicilian than English.

Returning to their old life in London was not an option. It wouldn't be fair to uproot Nico and it wasn't what she wanted either, Kristen acknowledged. She walked over to the dressing table and stared at the reflection of the slender, elegant woman wearing a stunning designer gown of black taffeta that was a perfect foil for her blonde hair, which was caught up in a loose chignon on top of her head. The dress was strapless, floor-length and showed off her tiny waist, while the low-cut neckline revealed the pale upper slopes of her breasts.

Sergio had brought the dress back from his trip especially for her to wear tonight. With it he had given her a diamond necklace, and she had caught her breath when he had fastened the single strand of exquisite glittering stones around her neck. But her heart had raced faster still when he had stared into her eyes and told her how beautiful she looked. There had been something in his expression that she could not define, but it gave her hope that the decision she had made was the right one.

Perhaps it was natural that she felt nervous, she thought, as she wandered restlessly around the room. She wished he would hurry up and come to bed. Unlike four years ago, it was unusual for him to take a business call late at night, but an urgent problem had needed his attention.

Her gaze fell on the photograph of the dark-haired young woman on Sergio's desk. He had loved Annamaria and, recalling the soft tone of his voice when he had spoken about her, it seemed very likely that he still did. Biting her lip, Kristen did a reality check. Sergio had asked her to marry him for various reasons, number one being that he believed it would be best for Nico and number two because he desired her, but he had never mentioned love.

She sighed. After the way his mother had treated him as a child, it was understandable that he found it hard to show his feelings and perhaps it was unrealistic to hope that he would fall in love with her. She couldn't blame him for guarding his emotions. But she had sensed over the past few weeks that he did care for her, and maybe in time his feelings would develop into love.

Maybe, if she told him how she felt about him…? Kristen's heart lurched at the prospect of opening herself up to being rejected once again. Sergio had ripped her heart out four years ago, and she was still haunted by how her stepfather had let her down when she had needed his support.

She had two choices, Kristen realised. She could be a coward and carry on hiding her feelings for Sergio, or she could take charge of her own destiny and find the courage to tell him she loved him. Yes, she risked being hurt, but she had been hurt before and survived. Honesty was the best policy, but did she have the nerve to offer her heart to Sergio?

'You look very pensive. What are you thinking about?'

She turned her head at the sound of his voice and watched him close the bedroom door. He looked incredibly sexy in black tailored trousers and a black silk shirt, and she was reminded of when she had seen him at the Hotel Royale in London. It seemed so long ago, but it was only a matter of weeks since she had gatecrashed his party and he had crashed back into her life.

'I have something to tell you. I found out while you were away that there are no repercussions from our carelessness a couple of weeks ago. I'm not pregnant.'

'I see.' Sergio's tone gave nothing away and Kristen had no idea if he was as disappointed by the news as she was.

He strolled over to her and she saw a familiar glint in his gaze as his eyes roamed over the sexy black dress. 'Did I tell you how stunning you look tonight, *mia bella*?'

'Several times.' She knew she couldn't allow herself to be seduced by the sensual promise in his voice, at least, not yet. 'Sergio—I…I have decided to marry you.'

Sergio smiled widely, revealing his white teeth. 'Fantastic!' He felt elated. He had spent the past few weeks trying to win Kristen's trust without putting her under pressure, and it seemed that his patience had paid off. 'I'm glad that you want to be my wife, *cara*.'

He wanted to sweep her into his arms and carry her off to bed so that they could celebrate by making love. He had missed her like hell while he had been away and the news that she was ready to commit herself to him suggested that she had missed him too. Although she had not actually said so. Sergio's elation dimmed a little as doubt crept into his mind. Kristen had said that Nico had missed him when he had gone to Hong Kong, but she had made no reference to *her* feelings.

'It will be good for Nico to grow up with both his parents,' he murmured. 'I'm glad we have been able to resolve matters without a judge having to decide who should have custody of him.'

'Y...yes,' she agreed faintly. Sergio's words were an unwelcome reminder that he had been prepared to fight her for custody of Nico, an unwelcome reminder that the only reason he had asked her to marry him was because he wanted his son. Kristen's determination to admit her love for him faltered. 'Of course our marriage will be for Nico's sake,' she said quickly. 'He adores you, and he is so happy living here in Sicily. I've realised that it would be unfair of me to take him back to London. Also...' a soft flush stained her cheeks '...I think it would be nice for him to have a brother or sister. He's three, and already there will be a big age gap between him and another child, even if I fell pregnant straight away.'

A lead weight settled in the pit of Sergio's stomach. Why did he feel so damnably disappointed that Kristen's reasons for deciding to marry him were sensible and coldly logical? he asked himself irritably. Four years ago he had sensed that she had been falling in love with him, and he had hoped over the past weeks that he might have revived her feelings for him. The realisation that she regarded him as a stud was bitterly hurtful.

He lifted his hand and released the mother-of-pearl clip that secured her chignon so that her hair fell like a curtain of gold silk around her shoulders. 'It would make sense for us to get married as soon as possible. What kind of wedding would you like?'

Taken aback by his cool, almost indifferent tone, Kristen shrugged helplessly. 'Nothing fancy. After all, we're not marrying for conventional reasons so it would be silly to go to a lot of fuss. Maybe we could just slip off to a register office.'

Sergio's brows rose. 'Can you clarify what you mean by "conventional reasons"?'

'Well, it's not as though we are in love with each other like most couples are when they decide to marry…is it?' she said huskily. 'It's just a sensible arrangement.'

'Indeed it is,' Sergio agreed pleasantly. His eyes were hooded, but Kristen sensed that for some inexplicable reason, he was angry with her. 'So, following on the sensible theme, I assume you hope to fall pregnant quickly so that Nico can have a little playmate?'

She bit her lip. 'Well…yes.'

'In that case, we'd better have sex.'

Kristen caught her breath as he swung her round and briskly ran the zip of her dress down her spine. With no straps to hold it up, the taffeta gown slithered to the floor and for some silly reason she was tempted to cover her breasts with her hands when he spun her back to face him. She couldn't explain why she felt so vulnerable. He was the same man who had made love to her with tender passion these past weeks, yet tonight his smile did not reach his eyes and his calculating expression chilled her.

'You had better get into bed—unless you want me to take you here on the carpet?'

'Sergio…?' She couldn't disguise the tremor in her voice but, before she could ask him why he was acting this way, his head swooped and he slanted his mouth over hers, kissing her with searing passion that lit a flame inside her so that she wound her arms around his neck as he lifted her and carried her over to the bed. He placed her on the silk bedspread and she watched dry-mouthed while he stripped down to his underwear. His boxers followed his trousers to the floor and, as usual, the sight of his jutting arousal turned her insides to marshmallow. But, instead of stretching out next to her and taking her in his arms as she hoped he would do, he tugged her knickers off and pushed her legs apart.

Anticipation licked through her as he cupped her breasts and rolled her nipples between his fingers until they hardened and tingled. She was on fire for him, but the faintly speculative expression in his eyes disturbed her.

'Sergio, is something wrong?'

'What could possibly be wrong, *cara*?' he drawled. 'We've both got what we want, especially if you conceive a child tonight.'

If all she wanted was a stud, that was what she would get, Sergio thought grimly. He didn't want to admit that she had hurt more than his pride. His heart was hurting, and that made him angry because he didn't want to feel vulnerable. He didn't want to feel anything, certainly not this hollow ache of loneliness.

He slid his hands beneath her bottom, tilted her hips and unhesitatingly drove his hard shaft into her. Kristen had been fantasising about him making love to her all evening and her body was eager and receptive. But Sergio stilled.

'Did I hurt you?' He cursed roughly. 'I should have taken more care.'

He began to withdraw, but Kristen wrapped her arms around his neck and pulled him back down. 'You didn't hurt me.' Casting aside her pride, she whispered, 'Make love to me, Sergio, please…'

Her husky plea breached Sergio's defences and, with a low groan, he thrust into her and felt the sweet embrace of her body as her vaginal muscles tightened around him. Something was happening to him. He no longer felt in control of himself, but after a lifetime of controlling his emotions he was afraid to let go. Instead he concentrated on giving Kristen physical pleasure. He knew how to please her, knew every secret of her body, and he made love to her with all his skill while he desperately tried to keep his mind, his soul detached from her.

Kristen sensed that something was different. There was no tenderness in the way Sergio made love to her, but her body did not care and simply responded to his mastery so that too soon she felt the first spasms of her orgasm and she gave a soft cry as indescribable pleasure overwhelmed her and enslaved her in its sensual embrace.

Sergio must have been deliberately pacing himself until he felt her come and before the ripples of her climax had faded he gave a powerful thrust and spilled his seed into her, but his harsh groan seemed to have been torn from his throat and almost immediately he rolled off her.

She lay beside him, stunned by the swift, almost emotionless coupling they had just shared. She didn't know what to say to him, especially when he murmured, 'I hope I satisfied you, *cara*?' The endearment sounded faintly mocking and her hurt turned to anger. She wanted to demand what the hell was wrong with him, but he had already got up from the bed and was pulling on his trousers and his grim expression warned her that a confrontation between them now would be explosive.

'I need to read through some paperwork in connection with the phone call I took earlier. I'll go downstairs to my study and leave you to get some sleep.' He hesitated, and for a second she glimpsed a look of pain in his eyes that tugged on her heart. But he blinked, and she wondered if she had imagined it as he said in a curiously husky voice, 'It was a tiring day.'

It had been a perfect day that had been ruined by Sergio's sudden change of mood. Hours later, Kristen was still awake, trying to understand what had gone wrong that had turned him into a cold stranger. Maybe he had changed his mind and no longer wanted to marry her? But he wanted Nico, and so had decided he would have to go through with a wedding to gain custody of his son.

She had promised herself she would not cry, but alone in the bed they usually shared she couldn't hold back her tears. When Sergio stood beside the bed a little before dawn and watched her while she slept, the sight of her tear-streaked face made his gut twist. He reached down and touched her hair. He longed to slide between the sheets and draw her into his arms, but he couldn't tonight after the cold way he had made love to her. It was not her fault that she did not love him. *Dio*, his own mother had not loved him, so why should anyone else? he thought despairingly. He despised himself for upsetting Kristen tonight. She had been right to be wary of him and he couldn't blame her if tomorrow she told him she had changed her mind about marrying him.

His throat ached, and he dashed his hand across his eyes. Big boys don't cry, he reminded himself derisively. He had learned that lesson when he had been only a few years older than Nico, but as he stumbled into the sitting room and sank down onto a chair his shoulders shook with the storm force of his emotions.

Sergio wasn't lying next to her in bed when Kristen woke up. She hadn't really expected him to be, but the sight of the empty space on the pillow instead of his silky, sleep-rumpled hair intensified the empty feeling inside her. Fortunately Nico hurtled into the room like a small tornado and, by focusing on getting him washed and dressed and ready for breakfast, she was able to put her misery in a box, to be dealt with later. It was something she'd had plenty of practice doing after she had left Sicily four years ago, she thought ruefully. But this time around running away wasn't an option. She had to put Nico's best interests first, and that undoubtedly meant remaining at Casa Camelia.

When she went downstairs the butler informed her that Sergio had gone to Rome and would not be back until late that evening. Kristen knew that the Castellano Group's head office was located in the capital city. She understood that Sergio held an important position in the company but, while she could cope with her own disappointment that he would be away all day, it was not fair on Nico. Her old fear that he would become bored of fatherhood and return to his old workaholic ways was still on her mind that afternoon when she took Nico up to La Casa Bianca to visit his grandfather.

Tito was in the garden, resting beneath the shade of a pergola. Age and poor health had etched deep lines on his face, but his eyes lit up as he watched Nico kicking a football across the lawn.

'My grandson is a fine boy and a true Castellano. He reminds me of his father when he was a child.' His voice became husky. 'But I do not have many memories of Sergio. He was very young when my wife took him away, and when I saw him again he was almost a man.'

Kristen bit her lip, startled by the emotion she had heard in Tito's voice. 'Did you miss him during the ten years that he was living in America?'

'With all my heart.' Tito sighed deeply. 'I desperately wanted to bring him home to Sicily, but his mother told me that he was happy living with her and didn't want to come back to me. I feared that Patti had poisoned his mind against me. But what could I do? If I had snatched him back he might have hated being here, and hated me. And so I waited and hoped that one day he would return. But every time I looked at his twin brother it was a painful reminder that I had two sons, and when Sergio did finally come home there was a distance between us that I have never been able to breach.'

'Have you ever told him what you have just told me?' Kristen said in a choked voice. 'Because, if not, I think you should as soon as possible. Sergio's childhood growing up with his mother was…difficult,' she said carefully, not sure how much Tito knew about the abuse Sergio had suffered as a little boy. 'He believes that you didn't love him, and that was why you didn't try to regain custody of him.' She stared at the elderly man, her eyes bright with tears. 'Please talk to him and let him know that you did—and do—care about him. It…it could make all the difference to how he feels about himself.'

Tito nodded slowly. 'Castellano men are not good at showing their emotions.' He darted a keen glance at her. 'But perhaps you have discovered this?' He sighed again. 'I am old, and I would like to set the record straight with my son while I still have time.'

'Thank you,' Kristen whispered fervently.

'You love him, don't you?' Tito smiled gently at her

startled expression. 'I saw your love for him in your eyes the first day when you introduced me to my grandson. And I also saw that Sergio loves you.'

Kristen's heart jolted beneath her ribs. She was tempted to tell Tito he was mistaken, but what was the point in shattering an old man's dreams? Instead, she called to Nico, who had kicked his football into a flower bed. 'I think I had better take your grandson home before he completely wrecks the garden,' she said to Tito. She hesitated, hoping he would keep his promise to share his feelings with Sergio. 'Remember what I told you.'

His tired eyes suddenly twinkled. 'And you remember what I told you, my dear.'

CHAPTER TWELVE

KRISTEN WAS LOST in her thoughts as she walked down the front steps of La Casa Bianca and almost collided with a tall, dark figure. For a split second she thought it was Sergio and her pulse quickened, but it slowed again when she saw it was Salvatore.

'Your disappointed expression is not good for my ego,' he teased in the faintly sardonic tone Kristen had come to expect from him. There was an air of remoteness about Sergio's twin brother that she had initially found off-putting. But as she had got to know Salvatore a little better over the past weeks she sensed that he was haunted by the accident three years ago in which his wife had died, and she recognised the same loneliness in him that she sensed in Sergio.

'You took me by surprise. Sergio has gone to Rome for the day,' she said, unaware of the wistful note in her voice.

Salvatore nodded. 'The company's Chief Financial Officer, who is an old family friend, has suffered a suspected heart attack and Sergio has gone to the hospital.' His eyes narrowed on Kristen's pale face. 'I understand that congratulations are in order. My brother told me that the two of you have decided to get married. I expect you are busy planning the wedding?'

Kristen gave a listless shrug. 'It will only be a small

event. After all, it is Sergio's second wedding.' The demon jealousy inside her prompted her to ask, 'Was his wedding to Annamaria an extravagant affair?'

Salvatore looked puzzled. 'Certainly a great event was planned, and Annamaria was thoroughly involved in the preparations. But by the time of the wedding…' He broke off and gave Kristen an intent look. 'I assumed Sergio had told you about Annamaria.'

'He tried,' Kristen admitted. 'But I didn't want to talk about her.' She flushed beneath Salvatore's speculative gaze.

'Take my advice and ask him about her,' he said in an unexpectedly gentle voice that played havoc with Kristen's already raw emotions. The sound of a helicopter overhead caused them both to look towards the sky. 'Sergio is back earlier than expected.' He glanced over to where Nico was playing on the front lawn with Rosa. 'The children are having fun together. Let me take Nico back to the castle so that they can carry on with their game. It will leave you free to have a conversation with my brother, who, by the way, is a damned idiot,' Salvatore muttered. 'I would very much like you to be my sister-in-law, Kristen, and I am looking forward to the wedding.'

The memory of how Sergio had made love to her with such cold detachment the previous night made Kristen feel reluctant to face him and, instead of heading straight back to the villa, she took the path that circled the lake and watched two white swans drifting gracefully on the water. She had read somewhere that swans mated for life. Presumably their lives were less complicated than humans'—but perhaps she was making things complicated when actually the situation was very simple. She sighed. The truth was she loved Sergio and she wanted to spend the rest of her life with him. So why hadn't she told him? If only she had been honest about her feelings for him four years ago; Nico might have grown up with his father from birth. But back then she had been too unsure of herself to fight for what she wanted. Was she going to make the same mistake again? Kristen asked herself impatiently. She didn't have to think about the answer, and she half ran back to Casa Camelia.

The helicopter was on the helipad at the front of the house but there was no sign of Sergio. She raced through the front door and up the stairs, but when she burst into their bedroom she stopped dead when she saw him sitting on the end of the bed. His shoulders were hunched and he was holding his head in his hands, but he lowered them when he heard her and jerked his eyes to her face.

'Where the hell have you been?' he demanded hoarsely. 'You left my father's house nearly an hour ago. I thought…' He swallowed convulsively and, to Kristen's shock, he dashed his hand across his eyes—but not before she had seen the betraying glimmer of moisture on his lashes.

'What did you think?' she asked faintly.

'That you had gone. That I had driven you away.'

Understanding dawned. 'Salvatore took Nico to the castle to play with Rosa. There was no need for you to worry. I wouldn't take Nico away from you,' she told him urgently.

'I wasn't worried about that. I was scared that I had lost *you*.' Sergio stood up and, as he walked towards her, Kristen was shaken by the terrible bleakness in his eyes.

'Would you care if you had lost me?'

'*Dio*, how can you ask that?' His voice shook. 'Of course I would care.' He raked a hand through his hair. 'Perhaps these will explain better than words.'

Only then did Kristen notice the exquisite bouquet of

red roses on her dressing table. *What on earth?* She bit her lip as Sergio handed the bouquet to her. The sensual fragrance of the roses filled her senses and her fingers trembled as she stroked the velvet-soft petals. There was a note attached to the bouquet. She ripped it open and stared at Sergio's distinctive bold handwriting:

'Can you ever forgive me?'

He had written one short line, yet she sensed powerful emotion behind the words and it was as if a fog around her brain had suddenly cleared.

What was he asking her to forgive him for? Her throat ached with tears. For finding it hard to show his feelings, or for hiding his emotions, as he had learned to do when he was a child and his mother had beaten him? Dear heaven, she had been so selfish to hide how she felt about him while she waited for him to tell her that he loved her. Maybe he didn't, but he cared about her enough to buy her roses.

'When I arrived home I came to find you to give you the flowers,' he said in a curiously strained voice, 'but one of the staff told me you were visiting my father.'

'I saw the helicopter. Salvatore told me you had gone to the hospital in Rome to visit a friend, but you are back earlier than expected.'

'Fortunately, Gilberto's health scare turned out not to be a heart attack.'

Kristen breathed in the roses' rich perfume. 'These are beautiful. Thank you.'

'*Can* you forgive me for the way I behaved last night, Krissie?'

This was a Sergio she did not recognise. A man clearly wracked with emotion. But what did it mean? What had he meant when he had said he had been afraid he had lost her?

'Sergio...you once offered to tell me about your first

marriage.' She took a deep breath. 'Will you tell me about Annamaria now?'

He frowned, clearly surprised by her request.

'I was desperately hurt when I discovered that you had married so soon after I left Sicily,' Kristen confessed.

'You don't have to remind me that I failed you badly four years ago,' he said harshly. 'It's pathetic, I know, but the truth is I couldn't face up to how I felt about you. It was easier to keep my emotions locked away. I missed you like hell when you left me, but then I heard the news about Annamaria and she became the focus of my attention.

'Annamaria was my best friend,' Sergio continued. 'When I returned to Sicily as a teenager I was full of anger and resentment against my mother, my father and the whole world. Annamaria's father was a close friend of Tito's, and we spent a lot of time together. She saw past my anger, and she was the only person I was able to talk to about how my mother had mistreated me.

'When she was in her early twenties, Annamaria was diagnosed with leukaemia. For eight years she fought the disease, but each time she appeared to be cured it returned. She was in Switzerland to try a new form of treatment during the summer that you came to Sicily. She came home soon after you had left, having learned that her illness was terminal.'

Kristen drew a sharp breath. 'How terrible that must have been for her and her family—and for you.'

'Her father broke the news to me. He also confided that Annamaria's deepest regret was that she would never be a bride and her father would never have the chance to give his only daughter away in a traditional wedding service.'

'I loved Annamaria as a friend.' Sergio sought Kristen's gaze and she saw a plea for understanding in his dark eyes. 'After all the help she had given me, I wanted to make her last months of life as happy as possible, and so I asked her to marry me.'

A gentle smile crossed his face. 'Planning her wedding day gave her something to think about other than her illness. There was the dress, the bridesmaids' outfits, the flowers to organise. We had planned to marry in the village church, with a huge reception afterwards. But Annamaria's health suddenly deteriorated and she was admitted to a hospice. We held the service at her bedside, and she still managed to wear her bridal gown.' He glanced over at the photograph on the desk. 'She looked beautiful. She was so happy that her hair had grown back once she had stopped the chemotherapy. Annamaria was my dear friend and an incredibly brave person,' Sergio said quietly. 'She died five days after our wedding.'

Kristen swallowed hard. 'I'm so sorry. At least you helped her realise her dream.' She wanted to put her arms around Sergio and hug him tight, but she felt ashamed of the jealousy she had felt for Annamaria and she could not meet his gaze.

Where did they go from here? she wondered as the silence lengthened between them. Where was her courage when she needed it? She cleared her throat. 'Sergio, I…'

'Don't,' he interrupted her in a tortured voice. 'Please don't tell me that you have decided not to marry me. I know I deserve it after last night, but will you give me a chance to explain why I behaved like a complete boor?'

When she did not reply, Sergio took a deep breath. 'I never thought I would marry again after Annamaria. I was sure I did not want a wife or a family of my own. Children need to be loved, but I had buried my emotions for so long that I assumed I would not be able to love a child.

'I was wrong,' he said huskily. 'From the moment I met my son I was overwhelmed with love for him. Nico unlocked the key to my heart and showed me that I was capable of love. It was a revelation, but still I was afraid to admit how I felt about you.'

Kristen's heart skittered when he reached out and touched her hair. His hand was unsteady as he slid it beneath her chin and tilted her face to his, and when she looked into his eyes she was stunned by the fierce emotion that he did not try to hide.

'Four years ago I should have listened to my heart, which insisted that you loved me,' he said deeply. 'Instead, I was swayed by the ugly voice inside my head which taunted that if my own mother had not loved me, why should you. Full of bitterness, I remained in Sicily and concentrated on the only thing I seemed to be good at, which was brokering business deals and making money.'

His eyes grew bleak. 'If I had not been in London on a business trip and you had not come to the Hotel Royale, I would never have known about my son. I don't blame you for hiding him from me and I understand why you did. I had shut you out and never shared my emotions with you, and you were scared I would hurt Nico like I had hurt you.'

No one could accuse Sergio of not sharing his emotions now, Kristen thought. Her heart ached as she stared at his haggard face. But she still could not quite believe what her heart was telling her. She had hoped for so long, but maybe her mind was playing tricks.

'After we had slept together at the hotel you only looked for me because you wanted me to make a statement to the press and deny the story they had published about us,' she reminded him.

'That's wasn't the only reason.' Sergio held her gaze. 'I wanted to see you again. The truth is I couldn't stay away from you, Krissie. But I admit that at that point I only hoped to persuade you to resume our affair. I didn't know…I didn't realize…' He hesitated, and in the silence Kristen was sure he must be able to hear the frantic thud of her heart.

'What didn't you realise?' she whispered.

'That I love you.'

Her heart stood still, but she was afraid to believe him. 'You were angry that I had hidden Nico from you.'

'At first, but I soon understood why you had decided to bring him up on your own. I had failed you when you had the miscarriage and let you think I did not want the baby we had lost. It wasn't surprising that you believed I would not want Nico. I was a coward then…and I am still acting like a coward now,' Sergio muttered.

'What do you mean?'

Instead of replying, he strode across the room and opened the drawer in his bedside table. 'I have something that I want to give you, something that might explain my feelings better than I seem to be doing with words.' He walked back to her, holding a small square box, and Kristen caught her breath when he opened the lid and revealed an exquisite oval sapphire surrounded by glittering diamonds.

'I…I don't understand.' The ring was clearly an engagement ring, but she didn't dare accept what her head and the expression in Sergio's eyes were telling her.

'It's very simple,' he said softly. 'I love you, Kristen. Four years ago I refused to admit that I felt anything for you and told myself I only wanted you as my mistress. But I never forgot you, and when I saw you at the Hotel Royale I knew I wanted you back in my life. But then I met Nico, and all my doubts returned. I reasoned that you would not have kept my son from me if you had cared for me.'

'I did care for you,' Kristen broke in, her voice cracking as a tear slid down her cheek. 'I loved you with all my heart. Last night I wanted to tell you…' Seeing him frown at her use of the past tense, she flung her arms around him and held him as though she would never ever let go. 'I wanted to tell you that I still love you and I never stopped. But I lost my nerve, and then…you were so cold.'

'Krissie…*tesoro*,' Sergio groaned. 'I was disappointed that you had only agreed to marry me because you wanted a brother or sister for Nico.'

'And I thought the only reason you asked me marry you was because you wanted your son.'

He shook his head and threaded his fingers through her hair. 'It was always you, my golden girl. Having Nico is a bonus. You are the love of my life—' his voice roughened '—but I was afraid to tell you and risk being rejected.'

As he had been rejected by his mother, and believed he had been rejected by his father, Kristen thought emotionally. 'You need to have a chat with Tito,' she murmured.

'What I need to do is make love to the woman who is very soon going to become my wife,' he said firmly, suddenly all dominant Sicilian male. But he kissed her with a tender passion that brought tears to Kristen's eyes, and her heart turned over when she saw that his lashes were wet.

'I will never stop loving you,' she said urgently, desperate to dispel the faint shadows still lingering in his eyes. 'You, me and Nico, and any other children we might have, we will be the family you never had. And, when we are old and grey, our grandchildren will hope that they find love as deep and long-lasting as the love we share for each other.'

Sergio did not reply. He could not when he was so choked with the emotions that he had held inside him for so long. But he told Kristen in myriad other ways how much he loved her. He claimed her lips in a sensuous kiss that made them both tremble. And when he undressed her and stroked his hands possessively over her breasts and stomach before moving lower to slip between her thighs, his gentle caresses spoke of a love that would last for all time.

'Ti amo,' he whispered against her lips as he made love to her with exquisite care. And the words healed him, completed him and left him with a deep sense of peace because he knew that Kristen loved him.

They married two weeks later in the little chapel on the Castellano estate. Kristen wore a simple white silk gown decorated with crystals on the bodice, and the garland of pink rosebuds in her hair matched the exquisite bouquet of roses that Sergio had placed on the bed on the morning of the wedding, while she had been getting dressed. The attached note simply read: *'I love you'* but those three words meant everything to Kristen. Sergio's unhappy childhood had made him suppress his emotions and he couldn't change overnight. But he was determined Kristen would never have reason to doubt that she was his sun and Nico was his moon. And knowing that his love was returned gave him the confidence to share his feelings.

Nico was an adorable pageboy and his cousin Rosa was a pretty flower-girl. The wedding was a glorious, happy occasion and even Salvatore, who had the role of Sergio's best man, gave one of his rare smiles when the groom kissed his bride in front of the congregation of family and friends in the chapel.

'I wish your brother could fall in love and be as happy as we are,' Kristen said to her new husband as they stood on the steps of the chapel for photographs.

'I wish so too. But I don't think any man could be as happy as I am,' Sergio told her in an unsteady voice. He drew her into his arms and looked into her eyes, which were as blue as the summer sky above them. 'You are my wife, my lover, my best friend and the love of my life, and I am the luckiest man in the world.'

Kristen blinked hard. 'I am the luckiest woman, and I'm so happy that I'm going to cry,' she said huskily.

'I love you, Krissie,' Sergio murmured against her cheek as he caught a tear on his lips. And then he kissed her with such tender passion, such love, that no words were needed.

* * * * *

HIS INSTANT HEIR

BY
KATHERINE GARBERA

Katherine Garbera is a *USA TODAY* bestselling author of more than forty books who has always believed in happy endings. She lives in England with her husband, children and their pampered pet, Godiva. Visit Katherine on the web at www.katherinegarbera.com, or catch up with her on Facebook and Twitter.

This book is dedicated to Rob Elser,
who makes me remember that it's not that
hard to live happily-ever-after if you have
someone next to you who wants to be there.

Acknowledgments

It's impossible for me to write a book about gaming and not thank my incredibly wonderful husband, Rob. He is responsible for me having a gamer account on Xbox 360 (RomWriter) and for my new skills as a first-person shooter—I'm a pretty good shot, BTW.

I'd also like to thank the very talented Nancy Robards Thompson, who introduced me to *Save the Cat!* and helped me jump-start my plotting when I was stuck.

Lastly, thanks to Charles for his insight and notes on the early stages—they were invaluable as always.

One

Cari Chandler paused in the doorway of the conference room. On the far wall was a portrait of her grandfather looking very young and very determined. Since he'd never been a "happy" man, she hardly noticed that he wasn't smiling. He certainly wouldn't be convivial at this moment when the grandson of his most-hated enemy was in his stronghold.

Since the late '70s the Chandlers and the Montroses had been feuding and trying to cut each other out of the video-game market. Her grandfather had won that long-ago skirmish by making a deal with a Japanese company, cutting Thomas Montrose out, but none of that mattered today as the Montrose heirs and their Playtone Games had just delivered the feud-ending blow with their hostile takeover of Infinity Games. And leaving Cari and her sisters, Emma and Jessi, to pick up the wreckage and try to forge some sort of deal that would save their jobs and their legacy.

But Cari as COO was the one who'd been chosen to deal with Declan Montrose. It made sense, since operations were her area, but the secret she'd been harboring for too long suddenly felt like it had a choke hold on her, and she wished she'd confided in her sisters so that maybe she wouldn't have to deal with Dec today.

The conference table was long and made of dark wood, and the chairs positioned around it were leather. She focused on the details of the room instead of the man she saw standing by the window. He hadn't changed much in the eighteen months since she'd last seen him.

From the back she could see his reddish-brown hair was a little longer than it had been before, but was still thick and curly where it hit his collar. His shoulders were still as broad, tapering to a narrow waist and that whipcord-lean frame that she'd remembered pressed against her as he'd held her. A shiver of sensual awareness coursed through her.

Don't. Don't think of any of that, she warned herself. Focus on the takeover. One problem at a time.

"Dec." She called his name. Her voice sounded strong, which pleased her since inside she was quaking. "I didn't think I'd see you again."

"I'm sure it's a pleasant surprise," he said with a sardonic grin as he left the window and walked over to stand not more than six inches from her.

The familiar smell of his spicy, outdoorsy aftershave surrounded her, and she closed her eyes as she remembered how strongly the scent had lingered on his skin right at the base of his neck. Then she forced herself to get it together, crossing her arms over her chest and remembering he was here for business. The knock at the door provided her with the distraction she needed.

"Come in," she called.

Ally, her assistant, entered with two Infinity Games logo mugs, handing one to Dec and giving the other to Cari. Cari walked around to the head of the table, already feeling more in control now that Dec was on the other side of it from her. She was aware of Ally asking if Dec needed anything in his coffee and him answering he took it black, and then Ally was gone.

"Please sit down," she invited, gesturing to the chair across from hers.

"I don't remember you being so formal," he said as he pulled out a chair and took his seat.

She ignored that remark. Really, what could she say? From the moment she'd first seen him she'd been attracted to him. Even after she'd learned he was a Montrose and technically her family's enemy, she'd still wanted him.

"I assume you're here to talk about moving assets around in my company," she said.

He nodded. "I'll be spending the next six weeks doing an assessment of the assets in the company and on this campus here. I understand you have three different gaming divisions?"

Wow. She should have been prepared for it, but he'd just completely shut off his emotions and switched to business. She wanted to be able to do the same, but she'd never been that good at hiding what she felt. Cyborg, she'd heard him called. He lived up to that moniker today.

He looked over at her and she realized she was just staring at him. This wasn't going to work. She'd call Emma, her oldest sister and the chief executive officer of Infinity, as soon as he left and tell her that she or Jessi would have to work with Dec. Though to be fair, as chief marketing officer, Jessi wasn't really the one who should be handling Dec.

"Cari?"

"Sorry. Yes, they all report to me—online, console and mobile."

"I will need to set up meetings with everyone in the company. The way this will work is that each person will be assessed and rated, and then I will give a presentation to our combined board of directors with my recommendations."

"No problem. Emma mentioned you wanted to talk to the staff. Do you think you'll just be here one or two days a week?" she asked, mentally crossing her fingers.

"No. I want to set up an office so I can be here in the thick of things," he said, leaning forward. "Is that going to be a problem?"

"Not at all," she said with the only smile she could muster. She'd rather not see him ever again, but that wasn't going to happen and she was mature so she could deal with it. She knew her smile must have looked forced when he laughed.

"You were never good at hiding your feelings," he said.

She shook her head. Though his statement was true, it wasn't something that he could know from personal experience. They'd had a one-night stand, not a relationship. "Don't say it like that. You don't know me at all. We only had one date and one night together."

"I think I got a fairly good impression of you," he said.

"Really?" she asked. She told herself to let it go and just concentrate on the business end of things, but that was going to be impossible. “Then why’d you leave me alone in that hotel room?”

He leaned back in his chair and took a long swallow of his coffee before standing up to pace around the room to her side of the table. He leaned back against the table and stared down at her, and she was tempted to stand up so he wasn’t towering over her. But she didn’t want him to think he intimated her.

“I’m not really a man for attachments,” he said at last. “And though you think I don’t know you, Cari Chandler, I’d have to be a blind fool not to see that you care too much.”

She wanted to deny it, but the truth was she was the bleeding heart of the Chandler family. She volunteered, donated time and money to charities and causes and she’d fallen for more than one sob story at work. Emma had been furious at first, until she realized it made their employees loyal because they felt that the executive management cared.

“I wasn’t going to cling to you and profess undying love, Dec,” she said. She barely knew him after one sex-filled night. She might have been interested in seeing him again and getting to know him better, but she’d learned all she needed to know when he’d left her. “It was only one night.”

“It was a fabulous night, Cari,” he said, putting his hand on the back of her chair and spinning her around to face him. “Maybe I should remind you of how good we are together.”

She pushed the chair back, standing up. It was time for her to take control of this meeting. “Not necessary. While I remember the details of the night, it’s really the morning after that stuck with me.”

"That's why I left," he said in that wry way of his. "I'm not good at dealing with the aftermath."

"Aftermath?" she asked.

"You know, the emotional stuff women usually bring up," he said. "The clingy things."

She shook her head. It was clear that a one-night stand was all that Dec intended for her to be. With her secret looming in her mind, she knew she had to say something about their night together, but for now she wasn't going to. She would focus on the business and try to figure out a way to save her family's legacy from being dismantled and destroyed.

Though she had to admit hearing Dec talk made her sad because she wanted better for herself. She had wanted to hear him say he wished he hadn't left and that he'd thought of her every day… Probably what he would term emotionally clingy stuff.

"Disappointed?" he asked.

"I guess I know why an eligible billionaire like you is still single," she said, trying not to be disenchanted that he was exactly like she'd thought he was. She'd hoped she'd just caught him on a bad day.

"Maybe the right girl just hasn't tried hard enough to change me," he said with a cocky half grin.

"Oh, you don't seem like the sort of man who can be changed," she said.

"Touché. I'm happy with my life. But that doesn't mean I don't know how to appreciate a woman like you when our paths cross."

She wanted to stay angry with him, but he was honest and she couldn't fault him there. Even though she'd hoped for longer with Dec, she'd known from the moment they'd gone to dinner that all he wanted was an affair.

"I think I'd have more luck changing the direction of the Santa Ana winds," she said.

"Have dinner with me and we can find out," he said.

"Would you be willing to discuss Playtone Games being a silent partner in Infinity?"

He laughed. "Not happening."

"Then neither is dinner." No matter how much he cajoled she needed distance and a chance to really think before she just jumped back into something foolish with him.

"We have to work together, so I don't think us spending time together outside the office would be wise," she said at last. She used to be more impulsive, but wasn't anymore. Her one-night stand with this man had reminded her there were consequences for acting without thinking.

"The Cari I know doesn't make decisions with only her head."

"I've changed," she said bluntly. Maybe if she hadn't fallen for his smooth-talking ways and blunt sexuality… What?

"I like it," he said slickly.

Cari knew she had to face facts that the man she'd had a one-night stand with was back in town. And it was becoming abundantly clear that a corporate takeover was the least of her problems. She was going to have to tell him about her son…his son.

Their son.

And she had no idea how to do that.

Cari had changed. That was easy to see even for a guy who'd spent only one night in her company. Dec knew things between them had always seemed complicated. Never more so than now. Their families were hated enemies of each other and his cousin, Keller Montrose, the CEO of Playtone Games, wasn't going to be happy unless Infinity was completely broken apart so that nothing of Gregory Chandler's legacy remained.

And this pretty blonde woman standing before him was going to be nothing more than collateral damage.

Dec had never been able to see her as his hated enemy. From the first moment he'd laid eyes on her he'd wanted to know more about her—and not so he could figure out how to use that information to take over her company.

Being adopted, Dec never truly felt like a real Montrose and was always striving to prove he was as loyal as both Kell and their other cousin, Allan McKinney.

Being back in California, conveniently with Cari, seemed his chance to do his job and continue to prove his worth to the Montrose family, as well as hopefully reconnect with the woman he hadn't been able to forget. With her thick blond hair that fell in smooth waves past her shoulders and her pretty cornflower-blue eyes, she'd haunted him. He couldn't forget the way she'd looked up at him as he'd held her in his arms.

Now that he had the chance to get a proper look at her, he could see the year and a half they'd been apart had added a quiet confidence to her. He started at her tiny feet in those pretty brown two-inch heels and moved upward. Her ankles were still trim, but her calves seemed more muscular. The hem of her skirt kept him from seeing any more of her legs but her hips seemed fuller…more pronounced. Her waist was still impossibly small, he noted, as the button on her jacket flaunted. Her breasts—whoa, they were a lot larger. She'd been slim and small but she was much—

"Eyes up here, buddy," she said, pointing to her baby blues.

He shrugged and then smiled at her. "I can see that you have changed a lot in the past year. Your figure is much fuller than before, but I like that."

He walked toward her with a long, languid stride and she backed up until there was nowhere for her to go. She put her hand up to stop him, keeping him an arm's length away. He stood there, staring down into her eyes, and had to admit there was something different about her. It was in her eyes. She watched him more closely than she had before.

She looked tired and he thought, well, duh, Playtone had finally gotten the upper hand on Infinity Games and she was more than likely worried about her job.

He backed away from her. "Sorry. I didn't mean to come on too strong. I'm sure losing your company to us was a shock."

"That's a bit of an understatement."

He smiled at the way she said it. "I'm a little jet-lagged still."

"Jet-lagged? I wasn't aware that there was a time zone between the Infinity Games campus and the Playtone offices," she said.

She gave up nothing. And he wondered how he could have missed this side to Cari eighteen months ago. But then he'd been in full-on lust and it was safe to say his brain hadn't been controlling him.

"I've been in Australia for a little over a year managing our takeover of Kanga Games."

"You let them keep their corporate identity," she said.

"They didn't screw our grandfather over."

"My sisters and I didn't either. We've always dealt with you and your cousins fairly."

"I'm afraid that doesn't matter when it comes to revenge," he said.

"Surely profit matters."

"It does."

She nodded and moved back to her chair. He sat down and so did she. She steepled her fingers together and he noticed she wore a ring on her right hand now that she hadn't before. It was a platinum band of hearts with a row of diamonds in the center. It seemed the kind of ring a lover would have given her. Was she involved with someone now?

Maybe that was where her new confidence stemmed from. She had a lover now. Well, he could be happy for her. Even though he regretted that he might not ever get to kiss her again.

"When did you get back from Australia?" she asked as she toyed with the ring. Those little gestures seemed to indicate her nervousness, though the rest of her body language didn't support that.

"Saturday, but I'm still adjusting. And seeing you again surprised me," he admitted, reaching for his briefcase, which he'd stowed next to his chair, and putting it on the table. He had his computer and the files he'd already started studying on the takeover.

"How did it surprise you? I knew you'd be here this morning," she said. "Didn't you know it would be me?"

"Yes, Emma informed me via email," he said. He wasn't about to tell her that he'd never expected to react so strongly to her presence. Not now. He'd thought since they'd slept together all the chemistry would be gone… but he'd been wrong.

The mystery of her body had been revealed to him. There wasn't an inch of it he didn't remember, though he realized now, with the flesh-and-blood woman standing before him, that those memories were a pale imitation of the real thing.

He wanted a chance to explore all of her curves and, more than that, he thought, to finally unlock the secrets she kept hidden deep inside. If he were busy dissecting her, maybe he would stop trying to get introspective in his own life.

In fact, the more he thought about it the more that Cari seemed the perfect distraction for whatever malaise had been affecting him lately.

He needed a distraction, and voilà, the universe had provided the one woman he'd hadn't been able to forget. He thought of his time frame for the takeover—six weeks. Surely that was long enough to satisfy his curiosity about her. Though being in the middle of a hostile takeover wasn't going to make seduction easy. In fact, if he were smart he'd forget about her personally and concentrate on business. But this was Cari, the woman whose image had haunted him throughout the past eighteen months, and now he wanted a chance to find out why. Was it just that he'd only had one night with her? Was there more between them?

"Then what's the problem?" she said with a half smile. She leaned boldly forward.

"There isn't a problem."

She stood up and put her hands on her hips. The movement pulled her suit jacket tight across her full breasts. She was a little bit flirty, which he liked. But also he sensed that it was a little forced this time.

"Are you sure? Doesn't it bother you that our families have been feuding forever?"

He'd like to say yes, but he suspected the problem was with him. He'd been traveling almost nonstop since he'd last seen her and he was a bit lonely for home. Not the Baglietto Bolaro yacht he kept at the yacht club in Marina del Rey that he'd christened *Big Spender.* Certainly not the Beverly Hills mansion that he'd inherited from his parents. He'd never had a place that he'd felt was home.

It had just started three months ago, that longing for something permanent. And he knew he had to get over it. It was out of character for him. Being adopted by the Montrose family was great, but being used as a pawn in his parents' messy divorce had taught him that he was meant to be alone. Then, at twenty-five, he'd lost his father in a freak skiing accident, and two years later his mother's liver had finally given out from all the drinks she'd used to medicate her life.

He shook himself out of his reverie to answer Cari's question. Was he bothered by the feud? Truthfully, it was something he'd grown up with, part of his family, and he knew it couldn't be ignored. Instead, he told Cari, "It should." Though he was going to be unbiased in his reviews, he knew Kell intended to fire all three of the Chandler women in revenge for what had been done to their grandfather all those years ago.

Starting an affair with Cari now had stupid written all over it. And he wasn't a stupid man. He'd have to work hard to keep reminding himself of that, because the way she was now smiling at him made him almost believe that an affair would work.

"I want a chance to convince you that Infinity should be kept in its entirety," she said.

He saw her sincerity. He groaned deep inside because that one statement gave him the excuse he needed to ask her out again. He could even tell himself it was purely business reasons why he wanted to go out with her, and maybe he'd be able to convince himself that it had nothing to do with wanting to kiss her again.

"Have dinner with me tonight," he said. If she were involved with another man, she'd say no. "You can tell me about how you've changed and I'll tell you all the reasons why I like it."

She blanched, bit her full lower lip and then looked away. "I'm not sure that's a good idea. The next few weeks are going to be very complicated."

Not exactly a no, he thought. He wasn't sure what that meant for the competition or for him. "They are, but I see no reason why we should deny that we are friendly. I'm not saying we'll go straight back to my place after dinner—"

"We won't. I'm a lot more cautious now," she said.

"See, that's something I want to know more about. And we're both going to be too busy at work. Besides, this isn't the place for anything personal." He wanted to know more about her. He didn't feel like he'd had enough time with her eighteen months ago. Now he had the time while he was assessing her company.

"I agree," she said with a cheeky smile that made him want to go over and kiss her.

"Great. What time shall I pick you up?"

"I was agreeing to your statement," she said.

But he noticed she didn't say no to dinner. Finally she sighed, pushed her chair back to the table and stared over at him, searching for something, he couldn't really say what. But then she seemed to reach a decision and nodded. "Tell me where and I'll meet you at seven. Meanwhile, I'll have Ally get an office set up for you, but until one can be made available, you can work out of this conference room."

He let her be in control for the moment and watched

her walk swiftly to the door, her hips swaying with each step. He followed a few steps behind. She'd clearly dismissed him, and for Dec, that wasn't acceptable.

No matter what she wanted to believe, he was in charge of this entire operation—the business one and the personal one. And she'd just dismissed him like a servant—something that wasn't acceptable to him at the best of times, much less when he was still jet-lagged.

She turned and gasped as she realized how close he was to her. Then she licked her lips and he saw her gather her composure around herself like a shield.

God, he'd never forgotten the taste of her or how her mouth felt under his, and in this moment he wanted nothing more than to taste her again. He'd never had a problem going after anything he wanted, and until she'd waltzed into the conference room looking calm, cool and confident, he hadn't realized exactly how much he wanted her.

"Was there anything else?" she asked.

"Just this," he said, lowering his head and taking the kiss he'd wanted since she'd walked into the conference room and made him regret leaving her all those months ago.

Two

Cari hadn't planned on Dec. Not at all. Not the way his lips moved over hers or the way he tasted so familiar to her. She'd missed this, she thought. Then chided herself. She hadn't missed anything. Dec had been nothing but a one-night stand. It didn't matter that she'd wanted him to be more. He'd only been interested in her because of this.

Sex.

She only wished she could be dispassionate in his arms, but she'd been alone, her feminine instincts directed toward mothering instead of being a woman. Dec was awakening something in her that she thought she'd lost. A wave of desire shot through her. Her blood felt like it was heavier in her veins and every nerve ending came awake.

She wrapped her arms around his shoulders, knowing this was the only embrace she could allow between them, so she was determined to enjoy every second of it. She tipped her head to the side, angling her mouth under his, and sucked his tongue. He groaned, and for the first time since she'd learned he was back in her life, she felt a measure of control.

But control was fleeting. When he put his hands on her hips and drew her in so that she felt his erection against her lower body, she felt her breasts respond.

Shocked and afraid he might notice, she lifted her head and looked up at him. His eyes were closed and there was a flush of desire on his skin.

He was a hard man, but his lips were always so soft on hers. She lifted her hand and rubbed her thumb over his lower lip. She paused a moment, hoping for something that would resolve the conflict inside her. But then his hands tightened on her hips and she knew this was only bringing more complications to the table.

She dropped her arms and pulled her blazer around her to ensure that he couldn't see the wetness that would be a sure giveaway that she had a baby.

She sighed. She wasn't ready for Dec to come back into her life. She'd just settled into her routine with her job and her son, and now Playtone Games and Dec were throwing her back into a tornado. She wanted to grab DJ and her staff and head for the cellar until this passed, but she knew she couldn't run away. She was the one in charge of everyday operations and the takeover meant she was the best person to advise Dec on her staff. It was up to her to somehow persuade Dec to keep as many employees as possible.

He laughed. "Was my kiss that bad?"

"That good," she said, opting for honesty. She'd always been a lousy liar. Something her sisters had twigged on to the first time she'd refused to name DJ's father. But it had been important to keep her secret from them given the bad blood between Dec's family and hers.

"Then why the sigh?" he asked, his fingers flexing and drawing her nearer to him.

She put her hand between them to preserve the distance and her illusion of control, because it was becoming startlingly obvious that she hadn't been in charge of anything from the moment she'd walked into this conference room. She stepped back and stumbled into the door.

He reached out to right her but she shook her head. "I can't do this, Dec. We need to talk and there are things—"

"I'm not doing this for revenge," he said.

"What?" she asked. She hadn't even considered that, but now that he'd mentioned it, wouldn't it be fitting for one of Thomas Montrose's grandsons to take sexual revenge on his sworn enemy's granddaughter?

"I just wanted you to know that what is between us has nothing to do with business or our families. This is you and me. Just us," he said.

"Ah, that's a nice thought," she said, thinking of her son and her sisters and the fact that no matter what he wanted to believe, they didn't live on an island. It would never be just them.

"It's my opinion. I'm not one to let my cousins dictate my personal life," he said, touching a strand of her hair, tucking it back behind her ear the way she normally wore it. "I had the impression that you were someone who made her own decisions, as well."

"Of course I am. Stop trying to shame me into—" She stopped. "What exactly is it that you want from me?"

She felt panicked and nervous, but not because of

him. It stemmed from herself and the fact that it would be easy to surrender and give him what he wanted. A casual affair. But that wasn't like her at all. Dec Montrose was danger, she thought. She had to remember that.

"I want a chance. I don't want you judging me based on my cousins or this takeover. That has nothing to do with what is between us. It didn't eighteen months ago and it still doesn't now," he said.

"I agreed to dinner," she said. She struggled to believe him. If she was a sap, she'd fall for his lines, but she wasn't. Was she?

She crossed her arms over her chest, not really caring that it was a defensive pose. She had to figure out how to manage Dec. But managing people wasn't always her best strength. She preferred to help people find their happiness. And Dec wanted two things that wouldn't leave her in a good place. He wanted her company and she was almost 100 percent certain once he knew about DJ he was going to want their son.

"I want more than dinner," he said.

"That was obvious," she said.

"I've never been subtle. Kell says with this mug I can't be," he said, gesturing to his face.

He wasn't classically handsome, but there was something about that strong determined jaw and those dark brown eyes that had made it hard for her to look away from him in the past, and now. "You use that to your advantage."

He shrugged. "I figured out early in life that I had to play to my strengths."

"Me, too," she said. "I was never going to be as strong as Emma or as rebellious as Jessi. I had to find my own way."

"You've done well from what I can see. Everyone I talked to about Infinity Games said you are the heart of the company."

She closed her eyes and wished her staff had said she was the ballbuster of the company. That would make it easier for her to deal with him. What could she say about that? She genuinely cared about her staff and had made it her purpose to make sure they all worked to their maximum. "You're the axman of Playtone Games."

"So I'm the Tin Man then and don't have a heart. Is that what you're saying?" he asked.

She caught her breath at the flash of pain in his eyes. Just as quickly it was gone, and back was the determined suitor. She still wasn't sure what he really wanted from her, but she was determined to know this man better. She had until dinner to figure out the best way to tell him about DJ. She had until tonight to figure out if there was a way to use him to save as many of her staff as she could. She had until tonight to find a way to handle everything he threw at her.

She had a bad feeling the latter was going to be much harder than any of the others.

Dec had always felt like he wasn't the same as everyone else. The adult in him knew it had everything to do with him being adopted. His mother had insisted he be treated like the other Montrose heirs, but inside Dec had always known he wasn't a true heir. And that had affected him.

Normally he didn't give a crap about that. He knew he'd been called a shark. Cold and heartless when it came to his approach to business. A man who coolly cut staff, sent them packing and didn't apologize for it. That was business. Usually the people who complained were the ones who didn't make the cut. But hearing Cari say he was heartless had given him pause.

"Tin Man, really?" he asked when he realized she wasn't going to respond to his comment.

Ah, hell, he thought, pushing his hands through his hair. "Well, Cari?"

"I didn't mean it that way," she said, but he noticed she bit her lower lip and didn't lower her arms. She in fact did mean it that way.

"I'm not here to hurt you or your company," he said. "In fact, as a shareholder I'd think you'd be happy about the takeover. Despite the enmity between our families, you are going to be a very rich woman when this is all over."

"Is money the most important thing to you, Tin Man?" she asked teasingly.

"I'm not a Tin Man."

"Sorry. I didn't say it to be rude," she said, then nibbled her bottom lip. "Well, maybe a little. I'm trying to figure you out."

It was there in her tone. She was hiding something, or maybe just hiding from him. Maybe she'd discovered that it was going to take more than one kiss to get over him. He sure as hell was winging from the embrace they'd just shared.

"Good luck with that," he said. "I have enough money to make life comfortable. It's a nice goal, though. Most people want more."

"That's true. Is that the reason most of our stockholders sold to you?"

"I didn't talk to them, so I can't say. But profit is why they invested in Infinity Games."

"I know. I just hate change."

Change didn't bother him and never really had. He

knew that life was one constant change. People who got comfortable in a situation found themselves… Well, like Cari right now. "I'm not heartless when it comes to staff. Is that your biggest concern?"

She shook her head and fiddled with the ring on her right hand. "Everything about you raises red flags, Dec. I wanted to be cool and sophisticated this morning. Instead I let you kiss my socks off and stumbled into a door."

"I like you the way you are," he said.

She gave him that half smile of hers that had originally drawn him across the Atlanta convention space to her booth. It was inviting and sweet and made a man want to do anything he could to keep her smiling.

"Good, because I'm too old to change."

He laughed. She was young enough and innocent, as well. Despite the fact that she was the spawn of his family's hated enemy, there was nothing malicious in Cari. "If you're old, I must seem ancient."

She tossed her hair and let her arms fall to her sides as she studied him. "Not old, but there is something ageless about you. I know you have work to do. My assistant will work for both of us…unless you have one who will be joining you here."

"No. I don't need an assistant and it's a cost savings to just utilize existing staff." He'd had an executive assistant a few years ago, but the man had become a liability when he'd started to get too chummy with the staff of the company they were dissolving. It hadn't been easy, but Dec had fired him. Not everyone was cut out to work in mergers and acquisitions. It required a person who could compartmentalize. And he was the king of that.

"Cost savings…is that how you always look at the business?" she asked.

Her tone said she didn't approve, but that didn't bother him at all. If she'd asked him something like this about their personal life, it might, but this was business. There was no place for emotions in the workplace. If something was losing money it had to be cut, and Infinity Games had made too many poor decisions. Perhaps leading with the heart instead of the wallet. It had left them vulnerable to a takeover and now Dec was here to clean it up. And he would.

"Yes, how else would I view it? It's all about the bottom line. That's how we were able to take over your company."

"I'm not a driven-by-the-bottom-line type of COO. I like to see my staff working and being productive."

"Maybe you should have been more focused on the bottom line," he suggested. She hadn't argued when he'd called her the heart of the company. In his experience, that meant the emotional one. He had the feeling that she had an open-door policy and never said no to any of her staff. He would love to be proved wrong, but he seldom was. That meant they were going to be at odds at work. Mentally, he shrugged.

What he wanted from Cari had nothing to do with business. He'd do his job and he intended to get to know her, as well. The two things were separate in his mind.

"I don't know. I mean of course I understand that profit has to be a driving force, but I always think about the people behind it. They need to feel safe to work at their best."

"It will be interesting working with you. I have the feeling I don't know you at all, Cari," he said.

"I'm sure you don't," she said. "Most men only see what they want to when it comes to women."

"Interesting thought," he said. "Whereas you see me as I really am?"

She flushed. "Sorry. I just hate the thought of you looking at a piece of paper and saying we need to cut head count when I know that head count means a person. A person who has a life that they are trying their best to balance."

"I'm not going to randomly reduce staff. We need to see where you are losing money, Cari. You have to know that your company isn't as profitable as it could be."

"Yes, I do. As you said, we'll have to work together to make it profitable again," she said. She reached for the door again and he had the feeling that she wanted to get away from him. Who could blame her? He'd given her two things to think about this morning.

"I'm sorry," he said quietly. Because he hadn't meant to reenter her life this way. Well, to be honest, he hadn't really meant to reenter it at all. She wasn't the kind of woman with whom he could have an affair. Even if there wasn't a decades-long feud between their families.

It wasn't just that she was the heart of the gaming company, she also was caring and compassionate and, he knew, worlds too soft for Beau and Helene Montrose's adopted son. The boy they'd fought over and eventually, when his mother had lost the argument, handed over to Thomas Montrose to be honed into a weapon to be used in this war against the Chandlers.

"This was never going to be easy," she said.

"How do you mean?"

"You left me without a backward glance, and probably thought our paths wouldn't cross again. Definitely like this. Now we have to work together and I'm going to try to save as much of my company as I can and you're going to—"

"Do what I do best."

"What's that?"

"Make this a profitable move for Playtone Games and somehow convince you that despite all of that I'm not really a Tin Man."

Cari entered her office and picked up the phone to call Emma. Then immediately put it down. The time to go running to her big sister had passed. She was a mom now, a decision maker. At work she didn't need Emma's advice and she'd made the difficult decision to stand on her own in her personal life, as well. She knew better than to backpedal now.

She couldn't help it, though. She felt scared and panicked at the thought of Dec just down the hall from her. And little DJ downstairs in the nursery. Two males who had the most influence in her life. One by her design, the other…by fate?

She shook her head. She wasn't going to figure this out right now and didn't want to try. She instant messaged her assistant.

Ally knocked on the door and popped her head around. "You wanted to see me?"

"Yes. I need you to draft a memo to the staff from me and my sisters letting them know that Playtone Games has taken over our company and we will be using the next six weeks to merge."

"Okay. Anything else?" Ally asked without hesitation or concern. Her assistant was thirty-two and had gotten married last summer, and Cari knew she'd just signed a mortgage on a new house. She had to be worried.

"Let them know that Dec Montrose is going to be

observing them for the next few weeks. Everyone who works to their full potential need not worry."

"Okay. I'll draft an email and send it to you for approval," Ally said.

"Thank you. Do you think we could get a temp in here to serve as my assistant?"

"Why?"

"Ally, I'm thinking of transferring you to finance. You have the skills to be in accounts receivable and that way you won't be attached to me," Cari said.

She wasn't sure how much any of the staff knew of the bad blood between her family and Dec's, but she didn't want to take any chances of Ally being a casualty of that old feud.

"That's not necessary."

"Being part of this office might be a liability," she warned.

"Like you said, if I do my job I'm fine. Besides, I'm not abandoning you," Ally said with a smile.

"Thanks. In that case, Dec and I will be sharing you as an assistant. Think of it as a dual-reporting relationship."

"Okay," Ally said.

As her assistant left, Cari leaned back in her chair and swiveled around to face the plate-glass windows that overlooked the Pacific Ocean. She took a deep breath, warned herself that if she didn't get her head together Dec was going to walk all over her. And she couldn't let that happen.

Her door opened loudly and she pivoted around to see Jessi standing there. She had thick black hair that she wore shoulder length with a thick fringe of bangs on her forehead. For shock value, she had a deep purple streak on the left side. On anyone else it might have looked frivolous but on Jessi it just added to her commanding presence.

"So, how's it look?" she asked, putting a Starbucks cup down in front of Cari before dropping down into one of her Louis XIV wing chairs. She wore a pair of skinny black trousers with a rhinestone top and an Armani tuxedo jacket. Cari loved her sister's bold style.

"Thanks for the skinny latte," she said, taking a sip.

"Figured you'd need it this morning, and with my cute little nephew you don't exactly have time to get one for yourself. So what'd he say?"

She didn't need to ask who she meant. She sighed. "Dec's here for blood. He pretty much said he's cutting the dead weight and going to find out where we are profitable."

Jessi propped one booted foot on her knee and leaned back, taking a sip of her own drink, which Cari knew was a mocha. Her sister was a rabid chocoholic. "Figured as much. Can you influence him at all? What do you think is the best approach?"

"Um..." That was a loaded question. Now that Dec was here and his family had the upper hand in business, Cari realized her sisters would be at a disadvantage once DJ's parentage became public knowledge.

"What? Did he threaten you?" Jessi said, jumping to her feet. "I've dealt with the Montrose clan before."

"You have?"

"Unfortunately. Allan McKinney was the best man at John and Patti McCoy's wedding."

Cari remembered Jessi being the maid of honor at her best friend Patti's wedding two years ago in Las Vegas. She recalled hearing nothing about Allan, however. "I didn't realize that," she said.

"Well, since we're feuding with his family I didn't

think I should talk about it. Besides Allan was a total jerk douche about a few things. I can see why there is bad blood between our families. Anyway, I spent the longest weekend of my life in Vegas thanks to him. If I need to go in there—"

"No. You don't need to do anything for me, Jess. Dec was fine," she said. Then she realized she needed to start laying the groundwork for Dec to be introduced as DJ's father. "In fact, we're having dinner tonight."

"You are? He must be nothing like Allan, who is an annoying jerk."

Cari laughed, and for the first time this morning she felt maybe it wasn't the end of the world. No matter what happened at Infinity Games, they'd be okay. They might be a bit worse for the wear, but her sisters and she would be fine.

Three

Dec rubbed the back of his neck as Ally escorted the lead programmer from the IOS team out of the conference room. He needed a long, stiff drink and an evening where he didn't have to think about staff reductions. It was clear to him that part of the problem with Infinity Games was the fact that Cari allowed her staff too much leeway. But that was neither here nor there. It was almost six and as he had a date for the first time in almost six months, he was leaving.

"Good evening, Mr. Montrose," the security guard said as he exited the elevator. The lobby of Infinity Games spoke of heritage. On the wall in large print was a list of accolades the company had garnered since its inception in the early '70s. Dec skimmed over the first one, which listed both Gregory Chandler and Thomas Montrose's names. The next accolade was a partnership with the Japanese video-game giants Mishukoshi, after which Thomas's name disappeared. And so began the family feud.

Dec looked at the guard. "Good evening. What was your name again?" he asked. He knew in takeovers it was important to have a face to go with every name on his list. Kell wanted this place gutted and soon there would be no need for two teams of security. And this man looked like a prime candidate for early retirement.

"Frank Jones," the older man said. His blue security uniform was neatly pressed, he presented himself in a well-groomed manner and despite his age, Frank was in good shape.

"Declan Montrose," he said, holding out his hand. The handshake was firm and strong. There might be some gray in his hair, but Frank's posture and attitude weren't as elderly as it had seemed from across the lobby.

"Who hired you?"

"Ms. Cari. She said we needed someone who took this job seriously and understood that security was the most important part of making a game," Frank said.

"And that convinced you to take the job?" Dec asked.

"That and her smile," Frank said.

"Her smile?"

"She has this way of making you feel like you're the only one for the job when she smiles at you. Makes me want to do my best," Frank said.

"She does have a way," Dec agreed. Suddenly he had an inkling of why Cari was so popular with her team. There was something to be said about being made to feel important. Obviously it was a skill that Cari had in spades.

His iPhone rang as soon as he was in his Maserati GranTurismo convertible. He glanced at the caller ID and wanted to toss the phone out of the car. He wasn't ready to download information to Kell, but as the man was his boss and not just his cousin, ignoring the call wasn't an option.

"Montrose here."

"Here, as well," Kell said. "Is it as bad as we feared?"

"Worse. The staff is really loyal. I think if we kick the Chandlers out we might have a mutiny. I've spent the better part of the day listening to how great they are."

"That doesn't concern me," Kell said. "We knew the takeover was going to be messy."

"And I'm mitigating the mess, but it's going to take some time."

Kell cursed under his breath. "You said six weeks."

"And that's still exactly how long I need. Calling and badgering me isn't going to speed it up."

"I know that. I was wondering how the Chandler girl was…Cari?"

She was nervous and sexy and sweet. But his cousin didn't need to know any of that. And if Dec had learned one thing from his socialite mother it was to keep some information to himself. "She's hiding something."

"What? There is no other investor in the wings," Kell said with surety.

"I'll find out what I can. But there is definitely something she's protecting. Maybe one of her sisters. From what I gather, the oldest one, Emma, is something of a barracuda. The staff spoke of her the way our team talks about you."

"I'll get in touch and see if I can find out what they are hiding. You keep working on Cari. I think that Allan's best friend is married to the middle Chandler girl's best friend."

"Why do you know this?" Dec asked. Kell just didn't

do personal stuff. If it didn't affect Playtone Games, usually Kell didn't bother with it.

"I had the misfortune to try to drink our cousin under the table last weekend and heard all about the girl."

So Allan knew the middle sister, and unless Dec was very much mistaken—and he was seldom wrong about anything—he himself was going to know the youngest sister very intimately. Again. And this time he was going to… What? He was the adopted son of the Montrose dynasty. He had been abandoned, adopted, pretty much left to his own devices again. He knew he wasn't a man for commitment. What could he do with Cari except have an elusive affair?

In fact the only thing he'd ever stuck with was his cousins and Playtone Games.

When he was in this twenties he'd tried to strike out on his own, but then Kell had called and the chance to be part of this new generation of game-making Montroses was too much of a lure. Dec still wanted to prove himself to a generation that was all but gone.

"You still there?" Kell asked.

"Yeah, but I've got to go. Dinner meeting tonight."

"With?" Kell asked. In the background Dec heard the sound of the evening financial news show that Kell watched religiously. He was a genius when it came to reading the market, which was in no small part the reason for their success.

Dec had always marveled that he and his cousins, Kell and Allan, each brought something unique to the table that no one else could. They made a very strong triumvirate, and though he knew he wasn't a blood Montrose, he was definitely a necessary part of Playtone Games.

"Cari," Dec said at last. "I'm having dinner with Cari."

"Good. I suspect that you will keep her off balance and maybe you'll be able to find out what she is hiding."

He intended to find out all of her secrets, he thought as he ended the call with his cousin. He wasn't as concerned that she was hiding something that would affect the takeover; frankly, at this point there was nothing else for the Chandlers to do to save Infinity Games.

He pulled into the parking lot at the Marina del Rey Yacht Club and parked his car. The Playtone offices were in Santa Monica just a few short miles from the Infinity Games offices. Something that Kell had done deliberately to make sure that every day when first old Gregory Chandler and now his heirs had gone to work they'd have to drive past the competition.

Tonight he wanted to see if there was anything real between him and Cari. There had to be a reason other than revenge that he was back in her life. He realized that he wanted to move Cari from competition to lover. His time in her bed had been too short and being this close to home always made him long for things he knew he didn't need and couldn't have. But for tonight he was planning to ignore all of that and just enjoy himself.

Cari stood in the foyer of her own house holding her son in one hand and her cell phone in the other. Canceling dinner wouldn't be construed as running away, she cajoled herself. But then DJ reached up and put his tiny hand on the collar of her shirt and made that sweet little sound. "Mamamama."

"Ugh," she said, tossing the phone on the hall table and walking back across the Spanish-tiled floor to the kitchen. She put DJ in his high chair and then leaned back against the cabinet. "What am I going to do?"

He just stared at her as she placed a teething biscuit on the tray in front of him. His eyes were brown. Not just any brown, but Dec brown. She knew that if she canceled this dinner, it would be solely due to cowardice. She knew that. Yet she was more afraid tonight than she had been this morning.

It had been one thing to see Dec in the office where she wore her business suit and had a certain air of authority, but this dinner—no matter how she tried to spin it—was more than business. He'd kissed her. And her body had almost betrayed her secret. She knew she had to tell him about DJ before he found out.

She touched her lips and remembered every sensation of his body pressed to hers. God, she thought, this was nuts. Just cancel and then run away.

Dec might be all into her at this moment, but their past told her that he moved on. His own words told her that he wasn't ready for commitment, and though a lot had changed in the eighteen months they'd been apart, she knew she couldn't just spring DJ on him. She owed herself, her son and even Dec more than that.

Some things once done couldn't be undone.

Her grandmother used to say that to her all the time when she'd been young and headstrong. Wanting to adopt a puppy or bring another cat or rabbit into the house. Grandma was always cautioning Cari to remember that when other lives were brought into the equation, it changed.

She gave herself one last look in the mirror. "Tell him tonight."

But the look in her own eyes and that feeling in her heart told her that telling him wasn't going to be easy.

But even though she wasn't a bossy woman like Emma or a badass rebel like Jessi, she'd never been a coward. And running away wasn't her style. Besides, she knew it was past time to tell Dec about his son. Until she did, he'd have one thing over her—guilt. She felt guilty about him not knowing about his son.

"I'm going," she said, smiling at DJ.

He clapped his hands and smiled back at her. She laughed at his toothless grin and drool-covered face. Truly he was the most adorable baby in the world. She scooped him up again and walked resolutely down the hall to her bedroom. She put his blanket in the middle of her bed and propped pillows around him to keep him in place.

He sat in the center, happily chewing on his biscuit while she puttered around getting ready for her date and awaiting Emma, who was going to babysit, along with her son, Sam.

The doorbell rang, and from the security monitor in her bedroom she saw not only Emma and Sam, but also Jessi. She wasn't ready for both of her sisters. Not tonight. She was so unsure, and hell, she had to admit, scared, that she was tempted to blurt out her secret to her big sister Emma. Then Emma would excuse her and—

Stop it.

She hated that she still sometimes wanted someone else to make decisions for her. She was a grown woman and a mom now. It didn't matter that it would be easier if she just gave up control of her life. She had to step up.

She pushed the intercom button. "Come in. I'm in the bedroom getting dressed."

She hurried into her closet and grabbed a retro-style cocktail dress that she'd gotten from ModCloth at a bargain. She didn't need to save money, but her mother had drilled into her that it was better in her pocket than in someone else's, and she'd always been frugal.

"Let's see what you are wearing," Jessi said as she led the way, ignoring DJ and coming into the closet to stand next to her. Her sister had an aversion for babies and was the first to admit she liked to keep her distance from children until they could walk, talk and order a drink.

She spun around so that Jess could see what she was wearing. The dress was slim-fitting, in a regal purple color that made her pale skin glow. It had a fitted bodice with thin spaghetti straps and a velvet ribbon that accentuated the slimness of her waist. She'd put on a strand of black pearls that their father had given their mother for a long-ago birthday and that Cari had inherited when her parents had died in a tragic boating accident, but she'd changed her mind at the last minute and now wore her usual charm necklace instead.

"Gorgeous, darling! Are you sure this is just a business dinner?" Jessi asked.

"Yes," she said, though the heat of her blush made her realize that she wasn't as confident in that answer as she should be. "What else could it be? He's a Montrose."

"Don't forget it," Jessi said as they both walked back into the bedroom.

Emma gave her the thumbs-up. "You look good," she said. "What are you not supposed to forget?"

"That Dec is essentially my enemy."

"Dec?"

"That's his name."

"His name is Declan, Cari. And you said it like…" Emma watched her shrewdly.

She didn't ask like what. Cari knew how she'd said his name. Like he was her salvation and her downfall.

And he was both. No matter how she tried to spin it. No matter what she wanted to pretend. No matter that he was a game changer and she had to decide how to proceed.

So far she'd let him get the upper hand at the office, and for her own sake and DJ's, she couldn't let that happen tonight. She had to be the one in control.

She glanced at both of her sisters as she sprayed perfume on her pulse points. They looked worried, and she just smiled at them as she adjusted the high ponytail she'd put her hair up in and fingered the bangs on her forehead.

Tonight she was going to be rebel, boss and angel all rolled into one. Tonight Declan Montrose wouldn't know what hit him. Tonight she would walk away victorious.

Dec was waiting in the bar for her when she arrived at the Chart House restaurant in Marina del Rey. He looked sexy and sophisticated dressed all in black. Pants, tie, shirt and jacket. On anyone else it would have looked like too much, but it suited him. He wasn't lighthearted at all and this dark attire reflected that.

But it also made him look devastatingly handsome. She noted that women sneaked covert looks at him as they sipped their drinks. She sighed and wondered if she was really up for this. Talking herself into being brave had been a daily ritual since she'd realized she was pregnant. She continued the practice now, put her shoulders back and walked over to him.

He turned just as she approached. And she arched one eyebrow at him in question.

"I saw you in the mirror," he explained, holding out a drink. "I recall you were a gin-and-tonic girl."

"Still am," she said. "But since I need my head about me tonight, I'll settle for just the tonic."

He smiled. "I'll get you a different drink."

He turned back in a second handing her a highball glass with a twist of lime in it. She took a sip of the refreshing drink and decided to stop her worrying for tonight. Somehow she'd figure out how to tell him he had a child.

"How was it today?" she asked.

"I don't want to talk shop tonight. I want to catch up on you," he said. "We've got fifteen minutes until our table will be ready."

He led the way through the semicrowded bar to a small intimate booth in the far corner and gestured for her to sit. She slid onto the seat and took an inordinate amount of time to straighten her dress about her legs.

"I make you nervous," he said when she looked up.

"Yes. You did when we first met, as well," she admitted.

"Why? Is it because I'm a Montrose?"

She thought about it. But really she didn't need the time to consider his question. She'd already spent a lot of time dwelling on Dec Montrose. "No. It's something about you. You seem so confident and determined… makes a girl feel like she needs all of her wits about her."

"You don't seem to have a problem with me," he said.

"There are one or two ways to keep you off balance," she said. "But I can't always count on being able to kiss you."

His surprised laugh made her smile. The black clothing wasn't a front where he was concerned. Dec was serious most of the time. So when he did smile or laugh it felt like a sort of gift.

"I'm willing to let you try it."

"I bet. Tell me about Australia," she said.

He shook his head. "That's business."

"You haven't done anything but work for eighteen months?" she asked. "I don't believe that. You seem a bit different than before."

He shrugged and took a swallow of his scotch on the rocks. "It might be the fact that after ten years of hard work Playtone Games has finally met our goal."

"Taking over Infinity Games?"

"Yep," he said. "Guess you don't want to talk about that."

"No, I don't. I should have thought harder about going to bed with someone who has a decades-old feud with me."

"I'm not feuding with you," he said.

"Really?"

"Not anymore. I've won the battle. Now it's simply a matter of cleaning up the mess and moving on. No conflict of interest between us anymore."

But there was a big conflict of interest, and for the first time since she'd given birth to DJ she realized that her son could be the leverage she needed to make Dec do what she wanted him to. As soon as the thought entered her mind, she shuddered with repugnance and pushed it aside. She'd never use her own son as leverage. That was despicable.

As was not telling him. Though she believed her reasons were valid. He hardly seemed like the kind of man who'd want a family or a son. But she owed it to him to let him make that choice now that he was back in her life.

"So, there's something I should tell you," she said, not sure how exactly to begin this conversation.

"Is it a secret?"

"Sort of," she said.

"Kell did want me to find out what you are hiding," Dec said.

"What?" How did his cousin know she was hiding something? Did he know that she'd had a baby with Dec?

"I told him I thought the day had gone well, except I felt there was something you weren't telling me."

"Oh." So he assumed it was something to do with the takeover. Why wouldn't it be? They'd had a one-night stand, not an affair or a fling. He'd never guess what she'd been keeping from him because his mind wasn't going along that path.

"Well, he'll be disappointed. I'm not keeping any business secrets," she said.

"I think you are. The security guard said that the staff would do anything if you smiled at them."

She blushed. He had to have been talking to Frank, who was like a Dutch uncle to her. "Frank exaggerates. Besides, what would I get them to do?"

"Mutiny," he said.

"You're not the captain of a ship," she said.

"But I am. I'm the one who's going to steer them through the shark-infested waters—"

"I thought you were the shark."

"Only in your eyes," he said.

But he wasn't a shark in her eyes. She reached over and took his hand and squeezed it in hers. "The acquisition isn't going to be easy, but I don't blame you for anything you have to do."

"What do you blame me for?" he asked.

"Leaving me." The words just slipped out. But now that they had been spoken she realized they were the truth.

"I'm back now."

"Yes, you are. For some reason, I'm not sure why you are here with me. You already satisfied your curiosity with me, right?"

"I'm nowhere near satisfied with you, Cari. I want more and I intend to get it."

Four

Dec couldn't relax. All he could do was stare at Cari and wonder why he hadn't seen this side of her eighteen months ago. There was a confidence in her that had been lacking before. Now she flirted and leaned in to make a point, whereas before she'd let him take the lead and set the pace.

A part of him acknowledged that if she'd been like this in the hotel in Atlanta, he would have had a harder time leaving her.

"Why are you staring at me like that?" she asked.

"You're a beautiful woman…you must be used to men staring," he said.

She shook her head and looked away from him. "Not for a while. I've been busy."

"Busy at work?" he asked. Given the state that Infinity Games was in, he highly doubted it.

"Not just work. My life is crazy right now," she said.

"What do you do outside of work? Charities?" he asked. It was what his mother had busied her time with and what his grandmother had, as well.

"You sound a bit disdainful," she said. "There is nothing wrong with charity work."

"I know. But the women I knew who spent all their time volunteering rarely had time for their families."

"Ah, your mom?"

"Mother," he said. "She didn't like the informal *mom*."

"Really? I don't know much about your past," she said.

"Why would you?"

"We're mortal enemies. I have done a few Google searches on you," she said with a sparkle in her eye. She took another sip of the water she'd ordered with her main course and smiled over at him. "But the internet was mainly just business-related articles, so tell me more, Dec. Let me know what your kryptonite is."

"Who says I have a weakness?" he asked.

"Everyone has one."

"Even lovely blondes?"

"I don't know about any other blonde, but I definitely have a weakness."

"Do tell," he invited.

"Forget it, buddy. We were talking about you," she said.

Knowing about his past wouldn't reveal any weakness. To be fair, he doubted he had one. He knew that only if he genuinely cared for something or feared losing it would he then be vulnerable. Therefore, he had nothing to lose.

"Well, my mother and father were very busy people. Mother had her charity work and Father was consumed with trying to please Grandfather on his quest for revenge against your family."

"Surely they must have made time for you," she said.

He could see this turning into a sob story if he wasn't careful, and a woman as softhearted as Cari would eat it up. For a minute he weighed using her emotions to his advantage, but discarded that thought. He didn't need to cheat or prey on her senses to win. "There were the usual family functions. But we all lived our own lives. It worked for us. Sorry I sounded bitter about charities."

"It's okay. I do give money to charities—more than I care to say—but I don't volunteer. I spend most of my free time at home or shopping on the internet."

"Truly? I thought you were more social than that," he said.

"I used to be, but lately, what with you and your cousins gunning for our business, I've had other things to concentrate on."

"I can't regret it," he said.

"The chance to finally get one up on my grandfather?" she asked.

Sort of, but for him it was more about winning than settling an old debt. "Not at all. I'm glad we won so that I can spend more time with you."

She rolled her eyes. "It's not like you were knocking on my door and I sent you away. Why this sudden interest in me?"

It was the one question he didn't know how to answer. Not even to himself. He could only say after being so long in Australia and away from everything in the U.S., he'd had a chance to realize that he didn't necessarily have the same agenda as he used to.

"Maybe it's you."

"Yeah, right. Excuse me if I don't buy that."

"Well, tonight it is. I intended to pump you for business info—"

"Liar. You said yourself no business."

"I meant originally, smarty-pants. But once I saw you tonight, I forgot about everything but our night together and regretted I didn't stay."

She tucked a tendril of hair behind her ear, where it simply curled back against her cheek again. She nibbled her lower lip and then sighed. "It would have been complicated."

"Definitely, but I'm very good at managing complications."

"Oh, I think this one would have thrown even you," she said.

"Which one?" he asked. He had the feeling sometimes that they were having two different conversations. Part of that he could easily attribute to the fact that she was a woman and he a man and they just communicated differently. But there was more to it than that. Maybe her secrets?

"Us staying together after our night," she said. "Wasn't that what you were talking about?"

"Yes, but I meant because my cousins wouldn't understand it."

"Fraternizing with the enemy," she said on a wistful sigh. "That always sounds so romantic until you have to answer to your sisters."

He laughed. "Yes, it would have been difficult. Maybe I did us a favor by leaving."

"There is no us," she reminded him gently. "This is dinner, not a romantic date."

"That kiss in the conference room says otherwise."

"It had been a while since I'd kissed a guy. Don't feel special," she said.

Too late, he thought. He already did. There was something about her and her damned smile and her kisses that made him feel like the only man in her world.

"I'm wounded."

"Ha," she said, taking another sip of her wine. "It will take a lot more than one comment to put a dent in that ego."

"Why do you think so?"

"You walk into my office building and my conference room bold as brass as if nothing had happened between us. You tell me how you are going to dismantle my staff, kiss my socks off and then tell me we are having dinner together. How is that anything other than colossal ego?"

He took another swallow of wine to keep her from seeing his smile. His father had always said that Dec had more confidence than smarts. "I can't say it's all ego. You are here with me tonight after all."

"Touché."

"Makes it hard for a man not to feel special," he said. He wasn't looking for anything permanent with Cari. He knew himself well enough to know that now was the only place he was comfortable living—he didn't dwell on the past or long for the future.

After they finished their meal, Cari excused herself to go to the ladies' room and called her sister to check on DJ. She knew that Jessi would have been long gone and Emma would be alone with Sammy and DJ. It was eight-thirty, which was the time she usually settled onto the couch with her iPad and online shopped while her baby slept in her arms. But she knew Emma wasn't going to hold DJ all night the way she did.

"How's he doing?"

"He's restless. He just keeps calling for you," Emma said. "I thought this was his usual bedtime."

"I hold him until he goes to sleep," Cari said.

"That's what I was afraid of. Sam's piled up some pillows on the nursery floor and is reading to him."

"I didn't know he could read," she said. Her nephew was only three.

"Well, he mostly just flips the pages of the book and makes up a story to go with the pictures. Right now *Green Eggs and Ham* involves a badly cooked breakfast."

Cari laughed and felt a little pang as she missed her own little guy and her nephew. "Sammy is so good to him."

"He's wanted a little brother for a while now," Emma said. "This was supposed to be the year for that."

"I'm sorry," Cari said. No one had expected Helio to die so young. His death had been a shock to everyone. And Emma had retreated into full corporate-executive mode. To be honest, most of the time the only one who saw the human side of her sister was Sam.

"It's okay. How's dinner? Did he let anything slip?"

"Dinner is fine. We're going to have a nightcap at the marina. Will you be okay to stay?"

"Yes. As a matter of fact, I think I'll take DJ to my place. Maybe the car drive will put him to sleep. You can either swing by and get him in the morning or I will bring him to the nursery at Infinity Games."

"Okay. I'll miss him tonight."

"You'll be fine. Concentrate on getting some answers from Dec about what he plans to do next."

"I will do my best," she said. "I might stop by tonight."

"Whatever you decide. Take care."

"You, too," she said. After disconnecting the call, she touched up her lipstick and fixed her hair before heading back to the table.

She noticed that Dec was on the phone as she approached and hesitated, but then remembered what Emma had said. She needed to find out what he was doing with the company. But to be honest, her heart wasn't in it. He said goodbye as she approached so she didn't get any information.

"Ready to go?" he asked.

She nodded as he got to his feet. He put his hand on the small of her back and guided her through the tables toward the front of the restaurant. She could obviously have walked through the place without his hand on her, but a part of her liked it. Liked the heat from his body that seeped through the fabric of her dress. Liked the sprawl of his fingers over her back. Liked…well, just liked the feel of his hands on her.

She shivered as he rubbed his forefinger back and forth over the zipper that went down the center of her back.

"Chilly?"

She shook her head. Then realized she should have said yes.

"I've missed touching you, Cari," he said, leaning close so that his words carried no further than her ears.

She'd missed it, too. She stopped walking and stepped away from his touch. "You didn't have to."

"I've apologized."

"I know, but that doesn't give you a clean slate. I should just go."

"I thought you wanted to talk," he said.

"I do. But I can't if you're going to touch me."

"I was being polite," he said.

She knew she was overreacting and it wasn't totally his fault. It had been too long since a man had touched her and she'd been hungry for it. She wasn't sure how much was her hormones and how much could be attributed to Dec.

"I know."

He gave his claim tag to the valet. "Is it still okay to take my car to the marina and come back for yours?"

"Yes," she said. She hoped while they were having a drink she'd be able to tell him about DJ. But she still wasn't sure how to say it. Also, a part of her didn't want to tell him. She still wasn't sure he was ready to be a father.

"Here's my car."

"A Maserati?"

"Yes, I like my cars fast and sexy."

"Why am I not surprised?" she asked. "Have you ever thought about what you'll do when you have a family?"

"I'm not planning on one," he said. As he glanced around and she met his calm brown gaze, she realized that he spoke the truth. She'd hoped to learn more about him as a man and all she'd learned was that his mom was a volunteer who hadn't made much time for him. Maybe that was why he didn't want a family.

"Oh," she said, knowing she sounded a little unsure. But really, what else could she say?

"I'm too much of a loner."

Well, there you go, she thought as she climbed into the car. What was she going to do now? No matter what he wanted or even what she desired, he had a son and she was the mother of that child. Whether he was ready to be a father or not. She owed it to him to let him know.

It was just that her fantasy of him suddenly falling

to his knees and making declarations of love for her and DJ were gone. She realized that this was real life, not some fantasy world where everything was going to work out simply because she dreamed it.

"You okay?" he asked.

"Yes," she said. The miles to the marina flew by and Cari leaned her head back against the seat as the bluesy beat of Stevie Ray Vaughan flowed through the car. Stevie sang of heartbreak, and even though Cari knew she didn't love Dec she couldn't help but feel like she was a little heartbroken, too. It was the first time she realized that dreams could be broken as easily as a heart.

Dec felt the mood change as soon as they got to the marina. He was a member here because he lived on a yacht that was moored here. He'd learned a long time ago that he didn't want a big house, but he suspected that was his way of keeping himself different from his parents. He liked to pretend that all the stuff he could buy meant nothing to him. He doubted that Cari would be agreeable to a drink on his yacht, the *Big Spender*. His cousin Allan had named it for him—a tongue-in-cheek reference to the fact that he liked expensive toys.

He led the way through the member's-only club to a table set on the balcony far away from the other diners. It was quiet this time of night. He signaled the waiter and when he arrived Cari ordered a decaf coffee and Dec did the same.

"I seem to have said something that upset you," he said.

"I have something to tell you," she said.

"Go ahead," he invited.

"Um...it's not as easy as I imagined it to be," she said.

Now she was starting to worry him. What could she possibly have to say to him that was so difficult?

"Are you married?" he asked.

"No. I wouldn't have come to dinner with you if I were involved with another man," she said. "Commitment means something to me."

"It means something to me, as well," he said. "That's why I avoid it."

"Really? Did something bad happen to you in the past?"

"Yes."

"Tell me about it," she said.

Their coffee was delivered and the waiter left. But he didn't start talking. He didn't like to think of his past. Didn't like to discuss the fact that he was an orphan and his adoptive parents had been in a facade of a marriage. He was just the final piece in their perfect little image of a family. But none of it had been real.

"I'm not interested in the past," he said at last.

"But without the past we have no way of measuring where we are going."

"I'm more of a live-in-the-now man."

"But you have to plan for the future," she said. "Just having business goals would necessitate that."

He shrugged. "I'm driven at work. But it's more because I don't like to fail."

She shook her head. "I don't know what else to say. Or really how to say this. Our one-night stand…"

"Yes? Has it lingered in your mind? I know it has mine."

"In a way," she said, twisting the charm on her necklace with her fingers and then patting it down.

He glanced at the piece of jewelry, for the first time

noticing that it was a charm with a small head on it and two initials. DJ.

DJ?

He was starting to put things together but what he was coming up with made no sense. Whatever it was she was trying so hard not to say to him…it couldn't be what was flirting around in the back of his mind.

She wouldn't have waited so long to get in touch with him. He had to believe that.

"What are you trying to tell me?"

She took another sip of her coffee and then put both hands on the table and leaned over toward him. Even in the dim lighting he could see the tension in her body and the nervousness in her eyes. He calmed himself the way he did when he had to fire someone. He pushed down all the emotions that had been swirling around him all night—even the lust that he'd hoped would lead to more than just a kiss.

"It might sound… That is to say after you left—Dammit, there is no way to say this nicely. I was pregnant, Dec. I had a baby nine months ago. A little boy," she said. Now that she'd started talking she couldn't seem to stop. "I know I should have called you or gotten in touch but at first I didn't—couldn't believe I was pregnant and then…well, your company was planning a hostile takeover of mine and…"

"I have a son?"

"Yes. He's nine months old," she said. She fumbled for her handbag and pulled out her cell phone.

He ignored her as the thoughts circled his mind. He never planned to have a kid because he didn't know how to be a father or really what it meant to be part of a family, and he knew from his own upbringing that a bad parent could be worse than no parent at all.

She was saying something else to him but he couldn't hear her words. All he knew was that the plans he'd made for his life had just disintegrated. He had to figure out what to do with this. A child. His child.

She handed him her phone. He glanced down at the screen and saw his son for the first time. His eyes were the same deep brown as Dec's were. His smile was small and toothless and his eyes wide. It was easy to see the baby was happy. And Dec felt his heart skip a beat and his stomach clench. This changed everything. It added a complication that even Dec couldn't navigate easily.

He stood up, knocking his chair over as he turned to face the glass and saw a reflection of himself. He'd never belonged to anyone, not really, and now Cari had told him he had a son. The first blood relative he'd ever known of.

"I have a son?"

Five

Cari knew she could have handled the announcement a little better, but at least it was out there, and a part of her felt relieved. She'd always told herself Dec had made his choice when he'd left and she'd made the best decision for herself—to have her son on her own. She'd felt bad about keeping DJ a secret from him, but she'd had no other choice.

Dec was quiet and those warm brown eyes of his were cold and hard. She knew she'd given him a shock and she wanted to just finish the conversation and get out of the marina bar. She'd never felt this unsure in her life. Except maybe that moment when she'd held her son in her arms for the first time and realized that she wanted to give him the world but had no idea how to take care of him.

"Given that you said you don't really want a family—"

He spoke without moving his eyes from the picture on her cell phone. “That was before I knew I had a son. He has my eyes.” There was a sense of awe and maybe a little nervousness in his voice. She’d never seen him like this before. This had shaken him.

Finally he put her cell phone back on the table and glared over at her. Aside from the occasional smile, this was the first real emotion she’d seen from him. He looked angry and, if she was being totally honest, scared. She had had months to get used to the fact that she was going to have a baby. And he’d grown inside of her, giving her a chance to adjust to the fact that he was real.

She felt a little guilty at how she’d sprung the announcement on Dec. He seemed shell-shocked. When he sat down again she reached for his hand, but he drew it away from her and stared stonily at her.

“I know he has your eyes,” she said at last. “Listen, we have a lot to talk about,” she added, taking control of the situation.

Once again she pretended she knew what she was doing, as she had every day since her son was born. It was important that Dec not doubt her. It was important that he thought she knew what she was doing. Because if she let her confidence slip for a second she knew he’d try to take over. “I didn’t try to contact you because there were all those months before I knew I was pregnant when you didn’t get in touch. It kind of seemed like you’d moved on and I had to move on, too.”

“You still should have—”

“What? Even today you’re not exactly warm and welcoming unless you count that kiss in the boardroom and frankly, I can’t. I don’t have the luxury of waiting around to see if you have changed. I'm a mother now, Dec. I have someone else counting on me."

He looked at her as if he'd never seen her before, and she just stared back at him. She'd spoken the truth. No one, not even this man, was going to protect her son the way she did. And she kept that in mind as she sat across from him now.

He sighed and tunneled his fingers through his thick hair, leaving it rumpled. His hands shook when he reached for his coffee and she wondered what was going on in his mind. But then she'd never really been good at guessing his motivations.

"Okay, let's stop the blame game," he said. "I behaved... Well, it doesn't matter. I used a condom."

She'd agonized over that moment a million times. He had used protection, and though she hadn't been on the pill, she'd thought they were safe. It was only when she'd started feeling queasy and then throwing up six weeks later that she'd thought... Well, she'd denied it could be anything but an upset stomach from spending too many months on the road at conferences. But when her stomach had started to grow and that little bump had appeared it had been impossible to deny the fact that somehow on that one night together she and Dec had made a baby.

"I know. I guess it must have not worked. Believe me, I went over that night in detail a million times. For a while before DJ was born I almost wished it had never happened. I'm never that impetuous."

"DJ?" he asked. He leaned forward, and some of the fear was leaving his eyes and she thought she saw him starting to plan.

She didn't want to give him too much time to think because Dec off his guard worked for her. Dec making plans and convincing her to go along with him… Well, let's just say that was what landed her in this position.

"Yes, I named him Declan Junior, but I've always called him DJ so no one in the family would suspect who his father was. Since this is California I didn't have to name a father on the birth certificate, and as far as my sisters are concerned, DJ's dad was a one-night stand. Someone whose last name I didn't get."

"I think they might put two and two together once I start—"

"No. You don't start anything. I'm telling you about him because you're here now and there might come a time when DJ wants to get to know you." She got that he had rights to his son but she'd seen so many fathers really screw up their kids—her own, for example. And she wasn't about to take a chance in letting DJ start to care and count on Dec just to have him bail when he was done with the merger.

She had no reason to believe he'd do anything else. Dec was essentially a stranger to her. If she could go back in time and tell herself anything, it would be to get to know this man before sleeping with him.

"I want to know my son," he said at last. He leaned forward and stared into her eyes. "I want to meet him and have a chance to be a father to him."

"Not even thirty minutes ago you said you didn't want a family," she reminded him, because the temptation was to believe him. She still had that vision in her head of the perfect little family. She still wanted a partner to help her raise DJ. But she just wasn't sure that Declan Montrose could be that man.

Dec was reeling. This was easily the biggest shock of his life. He had never thought of having kids because he knew how fragile life was. Knew how hard it was to be a great parent—he'd had two experiences of being essentially left alone as a child. First when his biological parents had put him up for adoption. And then when Helene and Beau Montrose had brought him into their Beverly Hills mansion. They'd both had very full lives and usually just trotted him out for family photos, leaving him feeling alone, more like a well-pampered pet than a son.

Having a kid... Having anyone rely on him outside of the office... Well, it wasn't something he'd been prepared for. He'd been leading Cari to seduction, but suddenly lust had taken a backseat. And that was what had him thinking that he needed to say and do the right thing here. He still wanted her, and the thought of a child with her wasn't sending him into full panic mode.

He'd always been a loner and he knew himself well enough to acknowledge that he probably was essentially the same sort of man that he'd always been. However, for the first time since he'd left his parents' home and their fortune behind, he felt charged with a sense of purpose.

He just wasn't sure what that purpose was.

A son. The thought still made his hands shake. He shoved aside his own nerves, put his hands on the table and leaned over toward her.

"I'd like to see my son," he said again. He was going to keep asking until he saw him. Until he held him in his arms. He couldn't believe he had a son.

She nodded. "It will be easier if you and I do this on our own. Once our families are involved it will get messy."

She had no idea how messy, Dec thought. Especially when Kell found out. Kell was a maniac when it came to the Chandler family, and given that he'd grown up with their grandfather and his mother hadn't brought in an influx of cash the way that Helene had, Kell had been bitter and focused all of his energy on revenge. His cousin, who was always looking for another way to bring the Chandlers to their knees, would use DJ as a pawn. He could easily imagine Kell urging Dec to be the sole guardian of the boy so he could be raised to hate the Chandlers the way Kell had been. Dec was sure of it.

In his mind he ordered the important events that had to take place. Order and planning were how he'd managed his life, and despite the fact that Cari was sitting across from him with those big blue eyes of hers and a determined stare, he planned to take charge. In the end she'd thank him.

"I will come to your house tomorrow and meet our son," he said emphatically.

"Just call him DJ."

"Why? He's my son."

"Yes, but you're not ready to be a father."

He arched one eyebrow at her, prepared to brazen out the fact that he could be an excellent dad. But then he thought of giving up his Maserati. Thought of the fact that a baby couldn't live on a yacht. Thought of all the things that he'd used to keep his life from having a real anchor and a real home. All of that would have to change….

"I am willing to try," he said.

She nibbled at her full pink lower lip and tipped her head to the side to study him. She was searching for something, and he tried to look earnest and not desperate, but he couldn't shake the fact that for the first time since he'd been brought into the Montrose family, he truly had flesh and blood of his own. He and his cousins were united in purpose, but they knew the same way Dec did that he wasn't really a Montrose. Now, though, he had a son. Someone who belonged to him. No one ever had before, and when he was alone he'd explore these unfamiliar feelings coursing through him for the first time.

The full importance of the moment hit him hard in the gut and he gripped the table to keep locked in this moment. He wasn't alone anymore. But this woman was the key to access to his son. He knew nothing about her except the sounds she'd made when she'd been in his arms.

"Trying is good," she said.

To be honest, he had no idea what she was talking about. Only knew that she was willing to give him a chance, and that was all he needed. "Okay, so I will come by your house tomorrow morning."

"I have to pick him up from Emma's first thing and then we can meet at the beach."

"Why the beach?" he asked.

"DJ likes it there. Plus my housekeeper will be at home and her sister is Emma's housekeeper. I want to keep this between you and me for right now. I don't want DJ to be part of what's been going on between our families."

"Agreed," he said. "When I said I wasn't ever having a family, that was just me trying to keep you from knowing that I wanted you."

She gave him a knowing look. "Yeah, right. That was you warning me that you weren't planning to stick around this time either."

That was exactly what it had been. And he was glad that she wasn't looking to him to be something he wasn't sure he could be. A part of him wanted to be upset with her for not instantly seeing him as part of her little family, but another part of him was relieved. Maybe he could be like a favored uncle to DJ?

But he knew that wouldn't satisfy him. Knowing he had a son was making him think of things that had never seemed important or that he'd never thought would be applicable to him. Suddenly he wanted to visit that mansion in Beverly Hills that he'd inherited when his mother had died eight years earlier. Suddenly he wanted to hold his son in his arms and show him how to be tough enough—no, to protect him so he didn't have to be tough enough to survive in the world. He knew that he wanted that little boy that he'd only seen on Cari's phone to grow up without the issues and fears that had dominated his own life.

"I'm sorry, Cari. You probably did the right thing by keeping our son a secret," he said.

"I did the only thing I could," she said.

"Now that we both know we have a son, I will be able to help you with the decisions," he said.

"I don't need help," she said.

"What do you need?" he asked, knowing he was going to have to be cooperative and to try to convince her he possessed whatever traits she deemed necessary for her son's father. Because the more he thought about DJ, the more he realized that for the first time since he'd left home and started helping Kell acquire and break businesses apart, he wanted to build something of his own. He wanted to build something that would last with his son. He wanted to build a family.

Cari wasn't too sure exactly what she needed except to get home and to get away from Dec. He was trying and that was one of the sweetest things she'd ever seen him do. Okay, it was definitely the sweetest. Dec wasn't a man who asked. He normally bullied and pushed until he got what he wanted.

She knew that she'd thrown him a curveball and she should probably get him to agree to as much as he would tonight. But she hadn't counted on it feeling like a curveball to her, too. She'd thought he'd deny the existence of a son. She'd feared he'd just shrug and walk away. But this reaction was the one she'd secretly hoped for.

In her mind's eye she could just imagine Jessi shaking her head and telling Cari to snap out of it. And Cari knew that Jess would be right to say those words. Dec was still the same man he'd been earlier. She had to remember that people didn't change in less than an hour.

Dec was a man who destroyed things. He was the axman for Playtone Games and there were probably hundreds of people whose lives he'd altered with the cold-blooded decisions he made every day. It was silly to think he wasn't going to apply those same principles to his personal life.

"I guess I should be going. If you don't want to take me back to the restaurant, I can catch a cab."

"Why would you say that?" he asked her.

"I figured you need some time to process everything I said tonight."

"I definitely do, but you're not catching a cab," he said. "We have to start getting to know each other."

She nodded. "That's why I came to dinner with you tonight."

"That, and guilt," he said.

She couldn't help but smile at the knowing way he'd said that. "Maybe."

She hadn't realized what a heavy emotional strain

keeping DJ a secret had been, but for the first time this evening she felt able to breathe and that knot of tension in her stomach had loosened.

"So tell me… Well, tell me about how you first took the news," he said. "It had to have been a shock."

She leaned back in her chair and she remembered she'd gone to the walk-in clinic in Vegas where she'd been for her last gaming trade show. The news that the doctor had delivered had been more of a confirmation of what she'd sort of already guessed. "Immediately I knew I couldn't tell anyone who you were."

"Why not?" he asked. "Are you close to your sisters?"

"We are sort of close. When our parents were alive, our dad was busy working and our mom had her moments when she was unavailable to us. So Emma and Jessi sort of looked out for me," she said. "I wanted to tell them, especially since Emma already had a son, but I was afraid and unsure. And I had this little baby inside of me and I knew that I was all he had."

She almost touched her stomach, remembering the very instant when she'd made the decision to keep the baby's father a secret from her sisters. Dec hadn't called and she'd felt like it was her and the baby together against the world. "I just knew that I had to protect him and keep him safe. From that moment forward I did everything for him."

He was watching her like he'd never seen her before, and she couldn't blame him. She didn't have to be a rocket scientist to know he'd wanted the evening to go in a different direction. And he was handling it as Dec handled everything.

"Does nothing throw you?" she asked.

"This did," he admitted. "I have always been so careful and never planned or anticipated a child."

She smiled. "DJ surprised us both. I said something similar to Jessi when I was decorating the nursery a few weeks before he was born and she said that maybe there was something in the universe that had a different plan for me."

"Do you believe that?" he asked.

"I can tell you don't. But a part of me would like to think that what happened between you and me was more than just hormones going crazy. That even though one night was all you really wanted from me there was something more going on there. I know I sound like a hopeless romantic," she said.

"I'm not romantic," he said. "I think the condom malfunctioned and we have a son. Nothing more was involved in it. But I do think what you and I do with him, how we raise him, how we treat each other, those are the things that will have a long-lasting effect on him."

"I agree," she said. "Which is why until I say otherwise, we're going to keep the fact that you are DJ's father a secret."

He didn't look too happy about her decision but she really didn't care. She wasn't about to risk her son or herself falling for a man who was used to leaving. Who was used to always having one foot out the door.

"Okay, but you and I will date."

"Why? Whatever for?"

"It's the only way to get our families used to the fact that we are together. And eventually they are going to learn about me and DJ. Don't you think it will be a lot better if we give them a chance to get used to me first?"

He had a point.

"I don't think so. We should keep this just between us."

But her sisters were going to give her the third degree. Even so, she was tired of keeping the secret of DJ's father. And it looked like she was going to have a chance at the family she'd always wanted with the only man who'd ever kissed her and made her forget everything but the way she felt in his arms.

Six

Dating. Dec wanted them to date and Cari had left him with a vague nod of the head, but had been careful not to agree to anything. There was no way that their families were ever going to accept them as a couple. Emma and Jessi would have a lot to say about her dating a Montrose.

Especially given the way that Dec had been sent to evaluate and chop up their company. No matter what spin he tried to put on it, everyone knew he was there to break up the company in payback for her grandfather cutting old Thomas Montrose out of Infinity all those years ago.

She rubbed her bleary eyes as she stared at the digital numbers of the clock. It was three-thirty and she doubted Emma would appreciate her showing up to pick up DJ. But she needed her son home in her arms.

She'd made a bad choice in allowing her sister to take him to her home.

Tonight she needed to hold his warm little body close and breathe in his sweet baby scent and remind herself that she could be strong. Instead she was lying in her big bed and dreaming of Dec. Was it any surprise?

She hadn't forgotten their one night together. Since then, no other man was interested in her. And to be honest she wasn't interested in any other man. Was she interested in Dec?

Attracted to him? Definitely. More than that? She just didn't know him well enough to be sure. The parts she'd seen had shown her a man who was ready for a good time and serious about business, but there wasn't much else she could say about him.

Perhaps his dating idea was a good suggestion. She'd have a chance to get to know him and see if he was really the right man to be a father to DJ. It didn't matter to her that he'd provided the sperm. In a very basic way she almost felt as if she'd gone to a sperm bank…. Why hadn't she thought of that lie to tell her sisters?

Jessi already suspected that DJ's father was someone they knew. She was always asking sly questions and trying to pry the name out of her. And if Cari hadn't been so determined to keep her secret she would have given Dec up long ago.

She rolled over and punched her pillow into shape, wrapping her arm around it and closing her eyes. It was only her inherent weakness where he was concerned that made her imagine she was curled against Dec with her arm around his chest.

She didn't even pretend she was thinking of any other man. There was only her in the bedroom and she wasn't about to lie to herself. She was weak where he was concerned and she really had to remember that he was just a man. And he was flawed.

He was a commitmentphobe. Sometimes she was frustrated with herself for never doing anything the easy way. It would have been so much better to fall for Jacob, who worked for the accounting firm that did the independent audit of their books each year and who was always asking her out and who, as he'd told her numerous times, wanted to start a family.

But she wasn't attracted to Jacob. He was safe and a little boring. To be fair, he was a lot like she was and she had always wanted someone a little dangerous. But danger didn't seem fun or exciting now as she lay alone in her bed and wondered how she was going to keep herself from painting Dec as the man she wanted him to be.

Even tonight when he'd said to stop the blame game, she had looked at him and seen guilt and maybe some pain. But as the man who drove a Maserati and told her he didn't want a family, he might not be thinking that he wished he'd known about his son sooner so he could have been with them.

She rubbed her head and tossed, turning over one more time. Biting back a scream of frustration at the way her own thoughts kept circling and making her crazy, she climbed out of bed and went into her home office. She turned on her Eiffel Tower desk lamp and sat down on her padded chaise before grabbing her iPad and pashmina. Time for a little retail therapy. Nothing cleared her mind like shopping did.

And right now she needed to get out of her own head.

But when she turned on her iPad she saw DJ's smiling little face. Those big brown eyes of his looked up at her and she wondered how she could hard-line Dec and keep him out of DJ's life if there was even the slightest chance that he could be the father she hoped he'd be.

She traced her finger over her son's face and knew that no matter what she had to protect him. The best thing to do with Dec and his dating plan was to keep it platonic.

But that wasn't going to be easy. It hadn't taken much for him to get her blood stirring and make her breasts heavy and full. She wanted Dec. Her body felt empty and aching. She wanted to just have more mindless sex with him, but she wasn't stupid. If the last time had had life-changing consequences, this time was even more dangerous.

She had to keep her head together. She opened the Safari web browser and saw the Mommy & Me class page was still open. She'd just signed herself and DJ up for swimming lessons. She leaned her head back against the wall and closed her eyes.

If anyone had told her that a man would have this much influence over her life she would have called him or her a liar. But even though he wasn't her boyfriend and hadn't been in her life for over eighteen months, Declan Montrose was surely the one who was driving every choice she made.

Dec waited at the entrance to the Santa Monica Pier where Cari had said she'd meet him. He'd grown up taking Saturday trips here with his nanny until he turned ten and his mother had decreed him too old for the amusements. Now as he stood in the mid-August sun on a weekday waiting to meet his own son for the first time, he wondered if he should just give Cari a check to help her out with any child-rearing expenses and walk away.

His mother should have done that. She just hadn't had it in her to be kind and caring, and she'd even told him when he'd asked her why she'd adopted a child that she'd done it so that Thomas Montrose couldn't get his hands on any of her fortune. She'd started to become bitter about being married for her money. He rubbed the back of his neck and shook his head.

"Dec?"

He turned and saw Cari standing a few feet from him. She was dressed for the office in slim-fitting black slacks that she'd paired with a sheer, flimsy-looking long-sleeved blouse. He could see the outline of her bra underneath it. But his eyes were focused on the baby in her arms.

She stood there sort of uncertain, and then she pushed her sunglasses up on her head and smiled at him.

"I knew you'd be here early," she said.

He realized she was nervous, and he thought back to that boy he'd been so long ago and how he'd never been sure around his parents. Never sure that they loved him and really wanted him. Then he looked at the baby in Cari's arms and felt a surge of love for him.

"This is DJ," she said when he walked over to stand next to her.

Dec looked down at his son and felt that strong surge of emotion again, and tears burned his eyes. He kept his head down so she wouldn't see. He'd never felt anything as powerful as he did at this moment. "Can I hold him?"

"Of course," she said. She turned the baby in her arms and handed him over to Dec.

Dec hesitated, feeling awkward and unsure, and the baby made a little noise as he took him into his arms. "Hey there, DJ."

"Mamamama," he said. But it wasn't clean or crisp.

His little mouth moved on the word and drew it out. His little hands reached up and Cari snatched Dec's sunglasses a second before DJ's hands got there.

"Sorry, he has a thing for sunglasses and I don't think you'd appreciate him chewing on these," she said.

"It's fine," he said. He was caught up in the fact that DJ was his. Of all the things he'd achieved in his life, this was the most unexpected.

"Want to walk up the pier?" she asked.

"Sure."

"You okay?" she asked when they started walking.

He nodded. He wasn't ready to talk about any of his emotions with Cari or anyone else.

DJ wore a one-piece romper-type suit made of cotton and he smelled like baby powder. His little hands moved on Dec's shoulder as he carried the baby so that they faced each other. Finally he just had to stop and look down at the boy who was muttering different little sounds.

He had a son.

Sure, he'd known that last night, but holding the boy in his arms today made it real. Until this moment he'd been able to think of the future and his own plans, but now he knew that he was going to have to consider this little boy and make sure he was safe and secure. Looking down into his face, he realized he wanted to be a better man.

He never thought or measured himself by anyone else's standards. He'd learned early on that he couldn't please others easily and settled for pleasing himself. Now, though, he wanted to make sure that in DJ's eyes he was always a hero.

The little boy stared up at him and one of his hands came up to touch the side of Dec's face, and he could only look down into that round sweet little face. His own son humbled him. Yet even as he was thinking about how DJ had his eyes, he saw Cari's little nose and that DJ's blond hair came from her, as well.

He glanced around and saw her standing a few feet away, taking a picture with her cell phone. She was giving him privacy to get to know his son and recording this moment for DJ, he guessed.

"Mamama…"

Dec turned to Cari.

"He sometimes means me, but usually he just mutters that a lot," she explained.

"Oh, so what does he do?"

"Mostly what you've observed. He talks and chews on his hand. He does get fussy but I just fed him and changed him so he'd look good for you," she said, coming over to them. "Wanted my little man to look his best when he met you for the first time. What do you think?"

He was humbled. "You did good, Cari."

She laughed. "I had a lot of drugs to help with the birth."

"Did you? I want to hear about that."

"Now?"

He shook his head. "Let's go get some breakfast and talk about what we're going to do now. I'm not sure what you're thinking but I would really like to be a part of his life."

"Okay, let's go talk," she said. She wasn't worried about her sisters seeing them since it was the middle of the morning on a workday.

He led the way to a coffee shop with outdoor seating and reluctantly gave DJ back to Cari to go order some coffee and muffins for them. He watched her through the glass and noticed that other men watched her, as well. She was very attractive, and even holding the baby wasn't a detriment to other men seeing her and wanting her. Dec had to fight against his own jealousy for the first time ever.

He wanted to walk out there and claim both the mother and child as his own. That scared him because he wasn't entirely sure he could have them both. Or what he'd do with them for the long haul. But he knew he had to find the answer to that soon.

Cari had seen a different side to Dec when he'd held DJ for the first time. She was trying hard to remember that right now he wanted everything to work out, but once life got back to normal he might not want anything long-term. He was thirty-five years old, enough to have settled down before this, but had never found a reason to. He was still a bachelor for a reason and she knew it was because he was, in his own words, a loner.

"Decaf latte," he said, placing it in front of her before he sat down across from her at one of those tiny tables that all coffee shops seemed to specialize in. His long legs stretched out on either side of her own as he tried to get comfortable.

Nearly impossible for a man as big as Dec. He was almost six-four. She wondered if DJ would be as tall one day.

"Thank you," she said.

"You're welcome." He took a sip of his drink, which looked like a double espresso.

"My thoughts are pretty straightforward on this," he said. "I want to start dating you and get to know you. I'd like to also spend time with DJ but not necessarily always with you. I want him to get used to me."

She narrowed her gaze on him. This was where she

had to be sure and remember she was DJ's mom. She couldn't give in the way she sometimes did at work. "Do you know anything about kids?"

"No," he said. "But I'm a quick learner."

"What I'm thinking is that you can come to our house and spend some time with DJ. That way I'm close by in case something goes wrong. Would you be agreeable to that?"

"At first, but I want him to get used to being at my place," Dec said.

"Where do you live?" she asked. "I have a place in Malibu."

"Right now I have my parents' mansion in Beverly Hills, but I usually stay on my yacht at the marina."

"I'm not sure—"

"I know a yacht isn't the right home for a baby. I'm meeting a Realtor after work to look at condos."

He was already changing, she thought. But having a baby wasn't always going to be like this. There were times when DJ started crying and nothing would soothe him. How would Dec react to that?

"We'll just play that part by ear," she said.

"Fine. But I'm letting you know that I want to have him at my place eventually."

She nodded. When he was thirty, DJ could go wherever he wanted.

"Now, about dating," he said matter-of-factly. "I don't want this to be a fake thing."

"Do you have a checklist?" she asked.

He scowled at her. "As a matter of fact I do. I've… This is the first time I've been around an actual blood relative," he said. "I don't want to screw it up."

She felt her heart melt. She wanted to be careful and

tried to picture him as the Tin Man again, but it was hard when he was earnest like this.

"Okay, what's next on your list?"

"I want to get to know you."

"I want that, too," she admitted.

"Good. There's more… I still want you." He reached out and touched the side of her face and she felt a shiver go through her.

"I had already figured that part out for myself," she said. It hadn't taken a brain surgeon to realize that the lust that originally brought them together was still sparking between them. "I want you, too, but I'm not sure if that's just because you're forbidden fruit."

"Forbidden?"

"Well, you are my family's enemy."

"Was that part of why you went out with me initially?" he asked.

"Uh, no. I didn't realize who you were until we were partway through dinner."

"What? How did you not know what I looked like? We grew up with flash cards of you guys," he said.

"Please tell me you are kidding," she said. "I'm picturing something akin to America's War on Terror cards."

"I am joking. But how did you not recognize me?"

"I just always pictured Thomas Montrose when I thought of your family. We have that portrait in our building."

"So after you realized it was me—your 'mortal enemy'—what did you think then?"

"Don't let this go to your head, but you can be very charming when you want something," she said.

"I know," he said with that arrogant grin of his. "So we'll date now and see where our relationship goes?"

"What if it doesn't work out?" she asked. "Will you still see DJ?"

"Yes," Dec said. "I'm not sure what kind of father I can be, but I want to try to be the best I can for him. He deserves to grow up knowing his dad wanted him."

"Being wanted is important to you?" she asked.

"You know I'm adopted, right?" he asked.

She nodded. They'd never talked about it and she wondered if he felt awkward about it.

"Well, I always knew my biological parents didn't want me."

"But your adoptive parents picked you," she said. She had a friend who'd adopted last year and Gail was always sure to let her toddler know that she loved her even more because she'd been chosen.

"I guess. But there is always that doubt that I'm good enough because my biological parents didn't want me."

She nodded; it explained a lot about how hard Dec worked and how he was always moving on to the next goal. She even thought that he might be a really good dad if it meant that he could keep DJ from feeling that way. But knowing that was what he wanted wasn't enough. He was going to have to prove himself with his actions before she'd really trust him.

"Okay. So this dating thing, how is it going to work?" she asked.

"As you know, this is a busy week at work for us. I believe you have a game that is supposed to be delivered," he said.

"Yes," she said. "Maybe we should wait until next week?"

"No, we can have a late dinner tonight. I'll stop by when I'm done for the day and see how your day is going," he said.

That he was willing to accommodate her schedule made her feel pretty good. "That would be nice."

"Where does DJ go during the day?"

"The nursery at Infinity. I usually bring him up to my office after hours and let him play in the corner while I finish working."

"I could pick him up," Dec said.

"No. My sisters would know you had and that would raise questions," she said.

"How would they know?"

"Emma has a three-year-old son who is in the day-care facility, as well," Cari said.

"Okay, then I will bring dinner to your office and we can all eat together," he said.

She wasn't sure how it had worked out that Dec had gotten everything he wanted from her. He had merely amped up the charm and she'd succumbed. In the future she had to be more careful. She wasn't going to make things too easy for him. After all, he was the guy who had wanted her for one night and then walked away. While she was the first to admit having a child changed people—it had changed her after all—she still didn't trust Dec.

She'd keep her eye on him and try to ensure that she didn't lose any more of herself than she already had. It would be a hell of a lot easier to manage if she didn't like him.

Seven

Cari tried to focus on work while she was at the office, but she had a steady stream of appointments from employees who all wanted to talk about Dec. Though they wanted to discuss the future and what Cari thought he was going to do with their roles in the company, she had no answers. She told Ally to hold her calls and escaped upstairs to the executive floor where Emma's office was.

The decision to move her office down onto the development floor had made sense when Cari had taken over the role of COO. She wanted to be where the staff saw her every day and where she could see what they were working on. The move had paid off and she and the staff had a good rapport.

"You look like you are on the run," Emma said when Cari got off the elevator. Her sister wore a severe-looking business suit and had her thick black hair pulled back in a bun. Her usual corporate look. Cari didn't envy Emma at all. As the oldest, the responsibility of keeping Infinity going had fallen to her.

"I am. Are you leaving?" she asked Emma.

"Yes. I have a lunch meeting across town," Emma said, glancing down at her watch. "Should I cancel? Do you need me?"

Cari remembered when she was seven and used to be scared at night. She'd creep down the long, dark hallway to Emma's room—her parents had a firm no-sleeping-in-our-room policy—and she'd stand in the doorway next to her sister's bed and whisper her name until Emma would roll over and lift the covers, inviting her into the bed with her. Emma had always been the one she ran to when she had a problem.

And it was so hard now to not tell her everything. Even harder than it had been before Dec had come back into her life. She wanted to lean on someone else, to unburden herself so that the responsibility of the decision wouldn't be hers. But she knew she couldn't do that. Inside she sighed, but outside she smiled at her sister.

"I'll always need my big sis, but I don't want you to cancel your lunch plans. The staff is in full panic mode. I just needed to escape where no one could find me," she admitted, which was partially the truth. She couldn't work with the steady stream of people coming to her office to ask questions every five minutes.

Since she'd worked her way up to COO she'd always had an open-door policy. She'd learned from her time at the different levels in the company that most of the staff needed to be heard more than they needed action.

"Well, you are welcome to use my office. I'm out until two," Emma said. "Sam wanted me to tell you that he's happy to babysit DJ whenever you need him to."

"Really?"

"Yes. He's trying to teach him to say 'what's up, dog?'"

"Why?"

"He thinks it will crack you up," Emma said. "He told me about you both doing hip-hop on 'Sing Star.'"

"That was supposed to be a secret," Cari said. But remembering playing the singing game with her nephew made her smile and she thought of all that Emma had been shouldering since her young husband had died. And Cari knew that if Emma could do it, so could she. Hiding out wasn't a Chandler trait. Cari knew that no matter how much she wanted distance, she could not run from Dec.

"Thanks, Em."

"You're welcome, sweetie. Are you sure you don't need me?"

Cari gathered her strength around her and stood taller. She was an adult, an executive, and she didn't need to rely on her sister anymore. She couldn't keep running away or hiding from the tough things in life. "Of course. Thanks for caring."

"Can't help myself since I'm always right. I like to show off," Emma said with a cheeky grin.

"As if," Cari said. "I think I just need a break. Thanks, sis. I'll ride down in the elevator with you."

The ride in the elevator was short, but when she got off Cari felt like a changed woman. So much had been out of her control since Dec had arrived, not only the takeover but her own personal life, though she realized that it was only her perception. She was still the confident woman she'd grown into since the birth of her son. Having Dec back here, just down the hall from her, changed nothing.

"I thought you were out of here," Ally said when she walked back into the office.

"I just needed a break," Cari said. She knew the takeover was hard enough on her staff without her running every time things got tough.

"Changed my mind," Cari said. "I think we need an all-staff meeting. Send a global email and tell them to meet in the cafeteria at two this afternoon. Get the cafeteria staff to set up cookies and sodas. I'm going to introduce Dec and talk about the takeover. I will take questions but only on general topics."

"Are you sure you want to do that? People are acting crazy," Ally said.

"I know. That's why we need to do this. Maybe if we get it all out in the open it will be better."

"All what?"

"That there will be staff reductions and the best way for them to save their jobs is to do them instead of coming to me," Cari said. "I'm going down to talk to Dec."

"I think Mr. McKinney is in there with him," Ally said.

"His cousin? Why is he here?" Cari asked.

"I don't know. Perhaps we should bug the conference room," Ally said with an arched eyebrow.

"I don't think that's a solution," Cari said.

"Well, it would make it easier to find out who is on the chopping block," Ally said.

"It's also illegal."

"Picky picky," Ally said.

She just smiled at her assistant as she went into her office to gather her thoughts before heading down to see Dec. She jotted down some business questions about reduction targets and the deadline to make all of them. But as she stared down at her own handwriting, she realized she had other questions. Maybe that was why she was so restless.

She wanted to know what he expected from dating her and if he'd be kissing her again. And as soon as she identified what her true worries were, she felt better. She wanted him, and this morning seeing him holding DJ had only made him more attractive to her. He didn't seem like a loner or a man who would abandon her a second time.

And that was very dangerous thinking.

Dec leaned back in the leather chair he'd had brought over from his office at Playtone and looked at his cousin, trying to gauge why he'd stopped by. Allan was thirty-five like Dec but was two inches shorter and looked a lot like the Montrose family with his thick dark hair and silver-colored eyes. He was an avid outdoorsman and always had a tan, not hard to achieve in California.

"Why are you here?" Dec said when they finished discussing the current lineup of the Lakers. The cousins had season tickets to floor seats and were anticipating a good year when the season started. "I doubt you came over here to discuss the Lakers."

"Too true. Kell thinks you're tired from Australia and don't have your head in the game," Allan said.

"Why does he think that? I've been sending him reports since I hit the ground. He's just anxious and acting like a maniac."

"I agree. But I told him I'd stop by and check it out."

"Well, you have, so I guess we're done."

"Not yet. The assistant to the COO practically glared a hole through me."

"It's safe to say the staff aren't happy that we've acquired them. Some of them are downright belligerent but I can handle it. Most of the companies we take over are the same," Dec said.

"But Kell feels so personal about this one," Allan said.

"I know," Dec said, pushing his chair back. "Do you? I know that I'm kind of not as involved in the rivalry as you both were. I mean, my mother could have cared less what happened to Gregory. She saw her money as the solution."

"It was a solution, but not the one Grandfather ultimately wanted," Allan said. "I think your dad was sick of the rivalry, too. That's why—"

"He married an heiress," Dec filled in. "I know it is. He said as much when he was drinking. Why couldn't the old man let it go?"

"He wasn't built that way," Allan said. "And neither is Kell."

"Well, he's going to have to give some ground on this. The days of coming in to a hostile takeover and firing everyone are gone. Especially in our industry. We'll end up alienating a lot of potential talent," Dec explained. "Some of the staff here are guys we want making games for us."

"I get it," Allan said. "I don't envy you this job. Why do you do it?"

"What do you mean?"

"We both know you don't have to work, you never have had to," Allan said.

Dec couldn't put it into words, but it made him feel like a real Montrose to be a part of the company. To do his part to help his cousins achieve their goal of revenge against the Chandlers. He'd always been on the outside until that day when he was twenty-three and Kell had called and asked him if he wanted to start a rival game company to beat Infinity in the marketplace. "I'm a Montrose."

"True dat," Allan said with a grin. "How's the Chandler girl you're dealing with?"

Incredible, Dec thought. There was no way he'd reveal to Allan his true feelings for Cari when he didn't even have a handle on them himself yet. But as an executive, she was actually doing a good job of giving him the space he needed to evaluate the staff. "She's good."

"I know the middle sister, Jessi."

"You do?" He remembered Kell mentioning a night of drinking and something about Allan and the middle sister. "Since when?"

"About two years now. Her best friend is married to my best friend," Allan said. "Every time they have a major event, there she is to annoy me."

"Is she serious about the rivalry?" he asked, because from what he could tell, Cari didn't really let it bother her too much.

"She's serious about being a pain in the ass. She had John investigated before the wedding."

"You're kidding. He comes from one of the oldest moneyed families in the country," Dec said. They were distantly related on his mother's side.

"I know, right? She said that money didn't make someone a good person," Allan said.

"Was she doing it just to needle you?" Dec asked.

"Probably. She gets under my skin."

"I know what you mean," Dec muttered under his breath.

"Woman troubles? I didn't even think you were dating anyone," Allan said.

"I might be dating," he said as the conference room door opened after a brief knock before he could say anything else. He glanced up to see Cari standing there. Her straight hair was pulled back in the high ponytail she habitually wore it in, with the fringe of bangs falling straight on her forehead. Her blue eyes looked quizzical.

"Sorry to interrupt, but I needed to talk to you about a staff meeting."

"Glad to have the interruption. Do you know my cousin Allan?"

"I do not," she said, stepping forward to shake Allan's hand.

"You seem less hostile than your sister," Allan said.

"I try," Cari said with a wry grin. "She's not overly fond of you either."

"I was totally aware of it, since she is usually scowling when I walk into a room." Allan let go of her hand. "You don't look anything like your sisters," he said.

"I know. They used to tell me I was adopted when we were little," she said.

"And I really was," Dec interjected. "We have so much in common."

Dec noticed Allan's glance flicking between him and Cari. "Interesting," his cousin commented.

"What's interesting?" Cari asked, looking slightly confused.

"Nothing," Allan said.

Dec stepped toward his cousin. "Allan, don't you have to leave?"

"Not yet," Allan said. "I'm here to observe, remember?"

The situation wasn't ideal in Dec's mind. He didn't want his cousin watching him and Cari together. But he knew there was no way he was getting Allan out of here short of throwing him out.

* * *

Cari had hoped not to see Dec's cousin, but it served to remind her of the other players in this game. It was hard not to look at the entire situation the way she did when they were building a game. It was easier to think of Allan as an adversary that had to either be swayed to join her team or destroyed.

In her mind she'd clothed herself in armor and a shield before coming down to the conference room and she was very glad she had. She realized that she had to keep the "dating" part of her life under very careful control. There was something about Dec and this entire thing that made her wish the timing was different.

Would she have been able to save Infinity if she'd sought Dec out when she'd first learned she was pregnant instead of waiting? She doubted it. Families didn't end feuds just because of marriages or heirs. World War I had certainly proved that, she thought.

"What can I help you with?" Dec asked Cari, breaking into her thoughts.

"It's the staff. They are all so anxious. I'm going to hold a general staff meeting this afternoon and I'd like to give them some information to ease their fears," she said.

"What are your ideas?" he asked.

"I'd like to have a hard target for your reduction. Just something like twenty percent of staff or thirty percent off the bottom line for expenses. Something concrete for the staff to know that if they work at it then they will be safe."

Allan leaned forward and looked up at her. "Sit down, Cari."

She sat down on the other side of the table from him.

"Do you really think knowing that will help the staff?" Allan asked.

"Yes. My group is really good at meeting financial targets. We all know reductions need to be made and by going to the staff in the past I've been able to achieve them. I want to make this transition easier on them. Right now if you looked at our efficiency, you'd see that in one day we're off track. They are all worried."

"Well, we don't have a hard target in reductions yet," Dec said. "I'm still gathering information to take back to Allan."

"I'm the CFO," Allan said.

"I know," Cari said. "We believe in knowing our enemy. And according to Jessi you have cloven hooves and a tail."

"She's the devilish one," Allan said.

Cari bit her lip to keep from smiling. Her sister and Allan didn't get along at all. "What kind of reductions in expense would make you comfortable?"

Dec glanced at Allan. There seemed to be some sort of unspoken communication going on between the men. She leaned back in her chair and noted that Dec was the more attractive of the two men. Sure, Allan had those California outdoorsy good looks, but he didn't affect her the way that Dec did. As she studied Dec, she noticed the tiny scar underneath his left eye that she hadn't noticed before.

And his mouth… Well, she'd done a lot of thinking about that full mouth and the way his lips felt pressed against hers. The way he opened his mouth and thrust his tongue into hers. From their very first kiss, she'd noted how he tasted good.

"Will that work, Cari?"

Damn. She'd been daydreaming and she'd missed

something important. So now she either had to pretend she agreed with whatever they'd just discussed or admit she wasn't paying attention. Being a blonde, she'd always felt at a disadvantage in discussions like this because people assumed she didn't get it. That she wasn't as smart as everyone else, and now she'd just acted like a fool and proved it.

"Let me see what you've worked out," she said.

Dec nodded and passed her the legal pad on which he and Allan had jotted some numbers down, and as she studied it she saw that if her division could move firmly into a 20 percent profit margin, then no one would have to be cut from the operational group.

"I can work with that," she said. It would mean long hours and getting their games in early. In fact, as she stared at the numbers she had an idea that might do more than save jobs. It might give Playtone a reason to keep Infinity in business.

"Glad to hear it. That's a very aggressive number," Allan said. "I don't know many divisions of any gaming company that could do it."

Dec spoke before Cari could reply. "Well, you haven't seen Cari in action. I've spent the past two days listening to every staff member tell me she's the best boss they've ever had. I think they'd kill themselves to please her."

Cari rolled her eyes. "He's exaggerating. It's just that I'm empathetic."

"It's more than that," Dec said. "There's something special about you."

She felt her cheeks heat up with a blush and shook her head. There was that glimmer in Dec's eyes that had nothing to do with her business acumen and everything to do with the bond between them. And whether it lasted or not, she realized there was always going to be that strong attraction between them.

"Well, I don't know about that. But I will do my best," she said, standing up to leave.

"I'll see you for dinner," Dec said.

"I'm looking forward to it," she said, smiling at him before turning and walking away.

She hoped that Allan would see a woman who was confident and knew what she was doing instead of a bundle of nerves who might have bitten off more than she could chew. Even the metaphorical armor she was mentally wearing felt tattered, but more from the inside than from any outer blows. It was going to be hard to keep these two parts of their lives separate.

Because she wasn't used to separating her emotions from any of her decisions. And Dec was certainly a man who made her feel emotional.

Eight

Dec ordered a dinner from his favorite restaurant for delivery at seven. Since the first evening they'd eaten together in Cari's office almost two weeks ago, it had become his favorite time of the day. Most of the staff was still present, but as he approached Cari's office he noted that her assistant was gone. He stood in the doorway watching her sitting on the floor with DJ.

DJ noticed him in the doorway, rolled onto all fours and crawled over to him.

"Uh, hello, Dec."

"What are you trying to teach him?" Dec asked, putting the take-out food on the credenza and reaching down to pick up his son. He felt that kick in the chest again from the thought that this was his progeny. He hugged DJ and the boy smiled up at him and made a grab for his nose. "Mamama."

"No," Dec said. "Dada."

"Mamama," DJ said.

"He's stubborn, must get that from—"

"Watch it, buddy," Cari said, getting to her feet.

"I was going to say me," Dec said, carrying DJ over to the desk where she had set his carrier. "Is he sitting here while we eat?"

"Yes. I have some yogurt in my fridge for him. Do you feel comfortable getting him settled?"

"Sure," Dec said. He might be new to this dad thing, but with Cari close by he figured he could handle it. Besides, there was little in his life that he hadn't been able to figure out. And this was no different. When he'd first struck out on his own he'd had nothing but his wits to guide him, having refused to touch the money his parents had wanted to give him, and his desire to prove himself. And he'd done a damned fine job of it.

"Do you need a hand?" she asked as she came back with the yogurt.

He'd been staring at the car seat instead of putting the baby in it. He got him in and fastened the straps before turning to the dinner he'd brought for them. "Mind if I close the door?"

"Not at all," Cari said.

She started spoon-feeding DJ mouthfuls of yogurt, and the little man didn't look too thrilled with that. "Are you sure that's good for him? He's a boy."

Cari rolled her eyes as she looked over at him. "I think I know what my son needs."

He held his hands up in a truce motion and went back to setting up their dinner. "I guess I'm a little jealous of all the bonding you've already done with our son and I hardly know anything about him. I didn't even know he'd like yogurt."

"Well, he loves chicken, too," Cari said. "I can see

you have a lot to catch up on. Are you sure you want to put in the effort?"

He looked at her and wondered what she was getting at. The first stirrings of anger moved through him, but then he looked down into her eyes and saw an emotion that looked like fear in them. He had to remember that he'd left her. After one night.

"What are you thinking?" she asked.

"That I wish you'd told me about him before he was born," Dec said with all the emotion he felt. "I feel like you cheated me."

"I know I did," she said. "I can't even say I'd do it differently now. Given that we had a one-night stand and you weren't easy to find…it just seemed like maybe I was meant to keep DJ for myself."

"I can understand that," he said, and that was a big part of why he was conflicted. He also felt that she was fully justified to have some doubts where he was concerned. "I do want to. I don't know if I'm changing or what this is, Cari, and you have every right to question me. Because every time you do it just reinforces my own desire to be here for my son."

She gave him a tentative smile. "Good. I intend to."

She wiped DJ's face and then went back to the refrigerator, heated the milk in the microwave and returned with a bottle.

"Is he on formula?" Dec asked.

"No. It's milk I expressed earlier," she said. "It's easier to keep to my work schedule if I do it this way."

She handed the bottle to DJ who took it and started sucking on it. A few minutes later his eyes started to drift shut. "He's like clockwork. After he eats he needs a nap."

"I guess that's a good thing for us tonight. Our dinner is ready," Dec said.

"Let me move his seat to the floor where I can keep an eye on him while we are eating," she said.

Dec watched as she got their son comfortable, putting a stuffed toy next to him and tucking a blanket around him. "I hate to leave him in the seat, but when I'm working late it's easier on him if he sleeps in here until I'm ready to go."

"Do you work late often?" Dec asked.

"Well, not to make you feel guilty—"

"You can't."

"I have only been working long hours since we got wind of the takeover," she continued as if he hadn't interrupted.

"I'm sorry you've had to. I could have warned you there was nothing that was going to keep Kell from his goal once he fixed on it."

"I'm not surprised. Stubbornness seems to be a Montrose trait."

"I'm a Montrose in name only."

"You were raised by them, Dec. Why do you always point out that you are different?" she asked.

"I've always felt different," he said. "It wasn't anything anyone said to me per se, just my own feeling that I had to work a lot harder to prove myself."

"Why? I've done some searching on your family and without your mom's money Thomas Montrose wouldn't have had any chance of reviving his game empire."

Dec looked over at her. It was odd to him, but it felt like she had just defended him and his right to be a Montrose. It wasn't like she'd said anything he hadn't already known, but hearing someone else with that opinion made the difference.

"That's all true, but I always felt like I didn't fit in," he said.

"I'm sorry," she said. "I didn't keep DJ from you because you didn't 'fit' my idea of a father. I just wasn't sure enough of myself to invite any other complications into the mix."

He nodded. He could see that. She was a good mom and her love for DJ was evident. He hoped someday that he'd be part of that circle of people she cared for.

Cari learned a lot about Dec as they dined after she'd taken DJ down to the nursery where the day-care staff were on extended hours. They had cribs and DJ was much more comfortable sleeping there than in his car seat. Plus she wanted a chance to have Dec to herself and figure out what she was going to do with him.

It was as if it were their first date. He didn't talk any more about his past. But she felt as if for the first time they were on the same track.

There was still an undercurrent of desire between them. Every time she looked over at him and caught him watching her she felt her blood flow a little heavier. And when their hands brushed, tingles ran up her arm and sent a delicious shiver through her entire body. But tonight was about more than sex. It was about getting to know each other. She wondered if perhaps it was fated that they do things out of order.

"What are you thinking?" he asked, breaking into her thoughts.

"That I'm finally getting to know the real guy you are," she said.

"That's not true. You've seen me naked. You know the real me," he said.

She shook her head. "You're wrong. Today I noticed this for the first time."

She reached over and ran her forefinger over the small scar under his left eye. "Where did you get that?"

He brought his hand up and caught hers, carrying it to his mouth for a brief kiss. "That scar is from when I was nine. It was the first time I went camping with my grandfather and Kell and Allan. They'd both been going with him since they were six, but Mother and Grandfather had been feuding so I hadn't been able to attend until that summer."

"What were they feuding about?" she asked. Seemed old Thomas had a beef with everyone.

"Her money," Dec said. "So when we got to Bear—"

"Big Bear?" she asked. "My maternal grandparents had a house up there."

"Yes, Big Bear," he said. "Am I going to be able to tell this story?"

"Sure, but with lots of interruptions," she said with a grin.

"So we got up there and my cousins were already expert snowboarders, but I had never been on one. I knew how to ski because my mother insisted I learn when we were in St. Moritz the previous winter. But Kell said skiing was for wimps so I asked for a snowboard and then proceeded to lose control and run into a tree. I had a lot of damage to the left side of my face and had emergency cosmetic surgery. This scar is all that's left."

She hadn't been expecting that. She reached over and took his hand in hers and rubbed her fingers over his knuckles. She felt for that little boy that Dec had been. Desperate to prove himself to the Montroses and find his place. "Can you snowboard now?"

"Nope. Just ski and I don't care if Kell thinks it's for wimps. He felt bad because he'd sort of dared me into taking the snowboard."

"You were just boys. Your grandfather should have stepped in."

"He thought that kind of thing was good for us. He said we should always stay hungry."

"Well, I don't agree with that. I'm not raising DJ that way."

"Good. I'm not complaining about the way I was raised, but I want DJ to have a more comfortable childhood than I did."

"Is that why you are trying to have a relationship with me?" she asked.

"Part of it. I don't want him to ever think that I didn't want him. I know how I felt knowing that my biological parents… Well, that's old news. What about you? Any scars?"

She didn't want to let the subject change. She wanted to know more about Dec and dig into his psyche, but she could tell he wasn't going to answer anything else about his past.

"I have one scar and if you guess where it is—"

"I get to kiss it," he said.

"Why would you want to?"

"So it's some place naughty?"

She just shook her head. "No."

"Ah, okay. And I can kiss it if I guess correctly?"

"Sure," she said. There was no way he'd guess it.

"Stand up," he said.

"Why?"

"So I can make a thorough examination of you. How am I going to make an informed decision without all the evidence?"

She rolled her eyes and realized that Dec wanted to keep things light between them tonight. So different from his usual serious and brooding manner. And so she pirouetted for him. That took a little of her joy from the evening. He was letting her see the parts of himself he deemed okay and keeping the real man hidden from her still.

And she was being her usual open book. She knew she had to change, but how? She wondered if there was a way she could learn from Dec. Maybe stop letting her heart be so open….

"The back of your knee," he said.

Her eyes widened and furrowed her brow as she looked at him. "Yes. How did you know that?"

"It was a guess."

"No way," she said, glancing down at her legs covered in trousers. "Confess."

"I'm guessing you're going to renege on the kiss," he said.

"No. We made a deal. I just want to know how you knew."

"I saw you naked, Cari," he said. "And I've revisited that night many times in my mind. Don't think for a minute that I didn't memorize every inch of your lovely body, from that scar on the back of your knee to that strawberry birthmark at the base of your spine."

She melted. That he'd remembered those details…it meant nothing. All it meant was that he was a thorough lover, which she already knew. But it felt like it meant something more to her tonight.

She looked at him and felt that sinking feeling in her stomach as she fought against doing something she shouldn't. Instead she lifted her hand and beckoned him to her with one crook of her finger.

He stood up and walked over to her slowly. She stopped him when he was a few inches from her with her hand on his chest. "I can't decide if you are a big flirt, a serious lover or the biggest mistake of my life."

"I am a big flirt and will always be serious about loving you. As for the other, this doesn't feel like a mistake to me," he said, pulling her into his arms and kissing her.

There was nothing light or tentative in the way that Dec's mouth moved over hers. His hand on the back of her neck was strong and he held her where he wanted her as he ravished her mouth. He was aggressive and strong, taking what he needed from her, giving her what she hadn't known she craved until this very second. Every move of his body seduced her into letting go of her own reservations and giving in to her need, as well. His tongue teased hers with a parry and retreat until he thrust it deeply into her mouth. His hands soothed their way down her back to her waist as he drew her in closer to him.

She felt the muscled strength of his chest and his pecs under the crispness of his dress shirt. She felt the tension in his fingers as he squeezed her waist and drew her up off her feet and against his body. She felt his hardening erection and knew that for tonight the games had ended.

There was no playing around with this kind of lust, and she didn't want to. She'd told him about his son, they were slowly working out how to deal with their companies and it had been a long eighteen months for her without sex. Without a man's hands on her body. Not just any man—this one.

She wrapped her arms around his shoulders and toyed with the hair at the back of his neck. He angled his head to the left to deepen their kiss and she knew she wanted more. She sucked on his tongue as he tried to withdraw it from her mouth. He smelled of man and musk and Dec. It was a scent she'd thought she'd never smell again and though she'd been trying so hard to pretend this was no big deal, she was so glad he was back in her life.

She tore her mouth from his, looking up to meet his dark brown gaze. His skin was flushed with arousal and the look in his eyes was so intense she shivered from it. He lowered his mouth again and this time the hungry kiss was slower, more sensual, deeper.

She stopped thinking, just let herself give in to the passion that he drew so easily from her. He lifted her again, his hands cupping her buttocks as he shifted his hips to grind his manhood against the apex of her thighs. He hit her in the perfect spot and she let her head fall back as his mouth moved down her neck.

"Wrap your legs around my waist," he said against her skin, his voice a gruff, husky sound that made her quiver.

She did as he asked and he carried her across the room to her walnut desk. He set her on the top of it. She kept her legs wrapped around his waist and lifted her hips against his erection, rubbing herself against him.

He put his hands on either side of the desk next to her hips. "Lean back."

She hesitated.

"Do it," he said.

She did, propping herself up on her elbows. He started to undo the tiny black buttons that lined the front of her blouse. Slowly he undid the first one and then leaned in and dropped a kiss on her exposed flesh. Then he moved to the next one and then the next. He stopped when her blouse fell open enough to reveal her bra.

"I seem to remember lace the last time," he said.

"My breasts are a lot bigger now."

"Yes, they are," he said, cupping the left one and stroking her nipple with the side of his forefinger.

Her breasts felt full and her nipple tightened and she felt a bit of wetness as a little milk came out. He rubbed his finger over it and then reached beneath the fabric of the bra to rub her naked flesh.

She wondered if that would shatter the mood. It didn't for her because she was on fire for him. And she needed him now. He lifted one hand to touch her almost reverently and she glanced up at his face. He still had that intense look of desire, but it was teamed with the softest expression she'd ever seen on his face.

"Not sexy at all," she said.

"Maybe not to another man, but it's a reminder to me of what we share," he said.

She wanted to ask him more about that but he leaned down and kissed her. This time wasn't as fierce as it had been earlier but it was just as intense. She was overwhelmed by an upsurge of tenderness from him as he drew her closer to him and continued to deepen the kiss.

"Sorry," she said, not sure how to stop her breast from doing that.

"Don't apologize," he said, continuing to unbutton her shirt.

She reached for his shoulders and drew him closer to her, wanting to embrace him so she wouldn't feel so vulnerable, but he kept the distance between them.

He looked deep into her eyes and asked, "Do you still want me?"

"Yes," she said, knowing she could hide nothing from this man. "Yes."

Nine

That was the response he'd been waiting for.

Growling her name, Dec reached between them for the fastening of her pants, undoing the button and then lowering the zipper. She shifted her hips as he pushed one hand into the opening. Then his mouth came back to hers.

Everything about Cari was more tonight. Her perfume lingered in his senses with each breath he inhaled. Her skin felt softer than before, and the new weight from carrying DJ filled out her curves. He loved every new thing he discovered about her.

He realized that no matter what it was he thought he knew about her, he hadn't really known her at all. The way he felt right now, like he was going to explode if he didn't get inside of her, made him regret that he'd put his business first. He should have stayed in her arms. He pushed should-haves out of his mind and concentrated on the way she tasted on his tongue.

He pushed his hand farther into her panties, letting one finger trace the humid warmth at the opening of her body. She said his name on a breathless sigh and he smiled down at her. She shifted against him, her hand finding first his thigh and then the hard length of his erection. She stroked him up and down through the fabric of his pants, holding on to him and rubbing her finger over the tip.

She fumbled for his zipper and he reached down and opened his pants, freeing his length. She gripped him and drew him closer to her, reaching lower between his legs to cup him.

He parted her with his fingers and she closed her hand tightly on his erection as her hips canted up toward him. This was a remembered pleasure. The way she responded to his touch. As lovers, they both heated up together, and he felt at this moment they were completely in sync.

He continued to explore her feminine secrets but was frustrated by the fabric of her pants, which trapped his hand. He used his free arm to lift her off the desk. "Shove your pants off."

She did as he asked and when they were on the tops of her thighs he set her back down on the desk and lowered her pants and panties to the floor, removing her shoes at the same time. He put his hands on her thighs and pushed her legs open, leaned down over her. He breathed in the feminine scent of her and then dropped nibbling kisses on the inside of her thigh, moving higher until he bit lightly at her hip bone.

She shifted and put one hand on his head and the other on her stomach. He saw that her belly had a slight curve to it now where before it had been flat, and he noticed the faint stretch marks on her skin. Every sign that she'd carried his baby just turned him on more and more. It enhanced his need to claim her again.

His child had left its sign on her and now he wanted to, as well. He lowered his head to bite the inside of her thigh and then he licked at the spot and kissed it gently before turning his head to her center. He'd not forgotten the intimate taste of her and he craved it again.

He parted her with his fingers and rubbed his tongue over the taut bud there. Then he suckled her gently into his mouth. She shifted under him, and he held her still as he continued to feast at her most intimate flesh and then slid his hand under her thigh to trace the opening of her body again. He entered her with just the tip of one finger, and her hips jerked against him until he slid it farther inside her and then brought it back out.

He moved his face lower and thrust his tongue deep inside of her. Her hands came to his head and held him to her as her hips canted upward toward him. He knew she was on the edge. Could taste it on her and feel it in the way her body was softening for him. He pulled back and pushed his finger in deep, and then up to find her G-spot.

She made a high-pitched keening sound as her hips thrust against him and he felt her body tighten around his finger. He kept his hand on her and in her, rocking it against her until she collapsed backward on the desk. He stood up, looking down at her, and smiled at her as she opened her dazed eyes.

"Thank you for that," she said.

"It was my pleasure," he said.

"No, it was mine. It feels like a lifetime since I've felt like that," she said to him.

"How long has it been?" he asked.

"Eighteen months," she said, looking up at him with

those clear blue eyes of hers. "I've been sort of busy, and most men aren't interested in a new mom."

"Good." He didn't want any other man in the picture. He felt possessive toward both her and DJ. They were his.

His.

Yes, he decided. She was his and he didn't have a clue about how to keep her or what he should do with her beyond sex, but he knew that he wasn't going to let her go. It didn't matter that she was way too innocent for a man like him. He had claimed her. Well, almost.

She reached for his manhood, which was still rock hard, and stroked him with her hand. As she leaned down toward him, he felt the brush of her breath against him and the touch of her tongue. Then, with a shiver down his spine, he felt a drop of his essence slip past his control. She licked it up and then took him into her mouth. He put his hand on the back of her head, stroking her blond hair.

He wanted to enjoy every second of her like this. He tried to pull back to warn her that she needed to stop, but she put her hands on his backside and kept him where he was. Her mouth moved over him until his hips jerked forward as his orgasm rocked through him.

She took him deeper into her mouth until he was totally spent. When he pulled back he didn't know what to say, but Cari didn't give him a chance. She just sat up, pulled him into her arms and rested her head right over his heart. And he held her in his arms, letting all the worries of whether he was the right man for this woman disappear. For tonight at least he wanted to enjoy just being in her arms.

* * *

Cari didn't have words right now or the strength to pretend like this was nothing more than sex. And she was so afraid that Dec would just leave her like he had the last time. She hadn't realized until this moment that the fear was still inside her, just under the surface of the confidence that she now recognized as bravado instead of strength.

She twisted her head and looked away, hoping to keep her emotions hidden from Dec. She saw DJ's car seat and it brought back the fact that the last time she'd been in this man's arms her entire life had changed. And though she was on the pill, she wasn't ready to risk another unplanned pregnancy.

She shifted away from him and hopped off the desk, gathering her underwear and slacks with as much dignity as she could muster.

"I'm going to pop into the bathroom. Be right back," she said, walking away before he had a chance to respond.

She closed the door to her private washroom and locked it before putting down the toilet seat and sitting down. A million different emotions roiled through her. Of course, pleasure still saturated every nerve of her body, but she had to keep blinking to stop the tears that burned her eyes from falling.

She wanted tonight to be real. Not just the sex but the dinner and the quiet conversation. She wanted it badly with every part of her being and it worried her that she might just be making it into something it wasn't.

What if she walked back out there and he was casual and blasé about what had just happened? How was she going to play it? She wasn't cool or sophisticated when it came to him. Any other man… Well, hell, any other man wouldn't have made her feel what Dec did. It was just him, and she was slowly coming to realize that she wanted more from him than she'd believed she could get.

He was trying.

But she needed more than trying if she felt this strongly. She needed him to be someone that she wasn't sure he could be. And she had the sinking feeling that she was setting herself up for heartache.

There was a knock on the door.

"You okay?"

"Yes, sorry. Just a few more minutes."

"I've got to go wash up. And then I'm going to go and get DJ from the nursery. That will give you some time to yourself."

"Okay."

She needed both the time and the continued privacy. She stood up, realizing she couldn't hide in here forever. She washed up, got dressed again. Her hair had slipped from her ponytail and she took it down and then slowly put it back up as she stared at herself in the mirror.

In movies and on TV people always seemed to convey conviction and determination with a look, but she couldn't. The more she tried, the more fearful she was that tonight had been a mistake.

It was too soon for things to be sexual between them. He was still adjusting to having a son and she was still adjusting to him being back in her life.

She opened the door and found the room empty. She cleaned up the dishes from their dinner and noted that Dec had left the baby carrier behind. She put it back up on the table and got all of her stuff together so she was ready to go home when they returned.

Her cell phone rang and she glanced at the caller ID to see that it was Emma. “Hey, Em.”

“Hello, am I interrupting anything important?”

“No. I just finished a late dinner and am getting ready to head home. What’s up?”

“I was thinking more about the idea you emailed me this afternoon, the one about getting a second game out in this quarter so that we can increase profit to meet the financial targets that Allan set.”

“I’ve been thinking about it, too,” she said. It had been playing second fiddle to Dec all afternoon and evening. And Emma’s call was just what she needed to get her mind back where it needed to be.

“Well, how do you feel about contacting Fiona? You know she was on that matchmaking show last year with Alex Cannon. You are still friends with her, right?”

Hardly, Cari thought. She’d met Fiona McCaw-Cannon at a UN summer camp when they were sixteen and for three years they had been pen pals. Not exactly the kind of relationship that warranted a call to ask her new husband to come bail them out with an award-winning game design. “I’ll see what I can do, but I’m not counting on that. I was thinking that we have our IOS team take our existing first-person-shooter game and turn it into a Christmas game for the iPad and Android tablets.”

“How will that work?” Emma asked.

“I thought we could change the target into a house or a tree and then have the game player decorate with a holiday gun? It’s just a first thought, but it would be a holiday game, and that is a lucrative market.”

“Yes, I like it. I’m going to send a meeting request to you and our project board. This sounds like the beginnings of just what we need. Use our existing assets.”

"It will save the bottom line, and I have to run it past finance, but I bet we wouldn't need to sell too many to make a profit."

"Good thinking. I can't wait to discuss this tomorrow. Thanks, Cari."

She said goodbye to her sister and leaned back in her office chair, wishing that she could solve the problem between her and Dec as easily. But games were much easier for her than real life because they were just that—games.

Tonight everything was going his way, Dec thought as he entered the nursery and retrieved his son from Rita, the day-care nurse who was on duty tonight. He carried the boy back toward Cari's office. DJ was chortling happily, making that "dada" noise again and Dec felt like he was king of his world. There hadn't been a lot of times when he'd been filled with… He didn't really know what this was. He wasn't a miserable son of a bitch generally, but he also wasn't happy. But tonight he felt the first seeds of what he might be.

It was scary, though, because when he'd held Cari in his arms he'd had that soul-deep fear that if he let go of her she might disappear. He knew she wasn't like him and wouldn't just walk away like he had, but another part of him feared she would. It would serve him right if she did, but he was praying that he could show her… What?

She was going to need more than sex from him, and he'd never been good at emotions. He hadn't been lying when he'd told her he'd left that morning after to avoid the messy stuff. Now here he was wanting it…almost. He'd seen the fear in her eyes as she'd dashed into her private washroom. Carrying DJ tucked against his chest and seeing those sleepy brown eyes watching him now, Dec felt the weight of his actions.

He almost wondered if he should propose to her. Get her to marry him. And then what? Being married wasn't going to be a solution to the problems that still existed between them. A marriage license hadn't been a magical cure-all for his parents' problems, and he knew better than to suggest that to Cari tonight.

He just had to find the right words to say. And the right way to say them. And then maybe they would be able to move on from here. What he really wanted was to take Cari and DJ to his yacht and then sail off for the horizon. But that was taking running away to the extreme and he couldn't do that. Not now when he was finally really part of the Montrose legacy.

He wasn't the outsider he'd always been. And Cari wouldn't leave her sisters now anyway. He knew that without even asking her.

He paused in the hallway that led to Cari's office. Saw the awards on the wall and the photos of the staff that were hung there. DJ reached out toward one framed picture and Dec realized it was of Cari, Emma and Jessi with their grandfather. This family was part of his son's heritage.

At that moment he realized how important it was that he save both hereditary lines for his son. And he had no idea how he was going to do that. Kell wasn't going to be satisfied if any part of Infinity Games still existed when the takeover was completed.

He shifted the boy to his shoulder and continued down the hall, stopping in the outer office when he heard Cari on the phone. Her exact words weren't clear.

He rapped on the door before pushing it open and noticed she sat behind her desk with her arms crossed over her chest. He remembered her nakedness and wanted her again. The orgasm he'd had was nice but he knew he wasn't going to be satisfied until he made her totally his again. Until he'd taken her and claimed her once again for himself.

He needed that. And he hadn't realized how much until this moment when he saw her defensive posture and realized that while tonight had eased some of his concerns, it had simply heightened hers.

"I guess you are ready to go home?"

"Yes. It's late and I have an early-morning meeting," she said. "Besides, DJ needs to be in bed, too."

"I think his nap helped him," Dec said.

"You're right," she said, reaching for the boy.

Dec dropped a kiss on his son's head before handing him over to her. "I know."

She moved around the office, busying herself with getting ready to leave. She slung her laptop case and the diaper bag over one shoulder and then balanced DJ on her hip while reaching for the car seat.

"I'll get that. In fact, I can carry your bags, too," he said reaching for them.

But she pushed his hand away. "It's okay. I can get it all. I'm used to doing it on my own."

The words weren't meant to be a jab at him, but he felt it all the same. She was used to doing it on her own because he'd left her. He wondered if her mood had anything to do with the fear that he might do it again. And what kind of reassurance could he give her? Just the fact that he still wanted her. That he had never felt this way before. That if he could, he'd stay with her forever. Even though he usually didn't think of himself in those terms—forever.

"I think we need to talk."

"Not tonight," she said.

"Yes, tonight," he countered. He reached past her, took the bags from her shoulder and placed them on the table. "I don't like the way you're acting."

"I'm sorry you don't. I'm not sure how to change it right now."

"I am," he said walking back to her.

But she put her hand up. "Stop. Sex isn't going to fix this."

"I didn't think it would. I was going to give you a hug, Cari. I thought you might need some reassurance that this isn't like the last time."

"I know it isn't, Dec. We have a son now."

Ten

"Yes, we do. I've been trying to ease my way into your life, but it's not enough, is it?" he asked. He had no idea how to build a relationship. Or anything for that matter. He was an expert on breaking up companies and parceling off different parts of them. He was an ace at walking away before things got too hot and heavy. And here he was trying to convince the one woman who knew him best that he wanted to change.

She shrugged, and it was like an arrow to his heart. He knew that he wasn't fooling her. There was not going to be an easy way for him to ease into this. Half-truths and grand gestures weren't going to win her over. He was going to have to convince her of his sincerity.

She nibbled at her lower lip as she shook her head. "I don't know. Tonight was nice and I really enjoyed it until that moment when—"

He didn't understand what she meant. He silently

cursed his adoptive parents, who'd shipped him away when he was old enough to start walking and talking. Even though they hadn't been close, it would have benefited him to have at least observed them interacting together. Maybe he would have gleaned something he could use now with Cari.

"What moment?" he asked.

She nervously pushed a strand of hair back behind her ear and then rubbed her cheek against DJ's head. Dec noticed that she held the baby closer and cuddled him like she drew strength from having their son in her arms.

"Cari?"

She sighed. "The moment that I realized I didn't know if you were going to stick around. Or if it was going to be like last time…and I know I told you I changed, and I have, but I also care about you, Dec. It's not love, I'm trying not to be too emotional or messy, but you're my baby's father and it's hard not to care."

Dec took a step back, not knowing what to say. He rubbed the back of his neck and cursed the wonderful legacy of his upbringing that had left him so hollow and empty inside that he ended up hurting this woman. He was trying to be what she needed, but he saw now that it was going to take a lot more than just trying to make her happy.

"I thought you knew that now I'm trying to find that bond with you," he said. He didn't want to have to talk about what he wanted. Or how a part of him wanted her to fill that emptiness that had been inside of him for too long.

"I don't know. All I know is that I didn't want to let you go, but I can't hold you either. I'm not sure if you're just enthralled with the newness of having a blood relative of your own or if this is something real."

She'd hit the nail on the head with that observation and he shouldn't be surprised. She was astute, and her staff had spent the better part of the week telling him she was empathetic. She'd want to ease his suffering to make this easier on him, but she had to keep her guard up because of who he was.

"I do want a bond with you, Cari. I can't make you promises because I know how easily they can be broken. But I'm trying. Can that be enough for you? For now?" he asked. He'd wanted so little in this life, nothing that had caused this ache inside him at the thought of losing her. Tonight when he was alone he needed to examine this new weakness. This kind of caring was a detriment to a man in the middle of taking over a company. This was the worst possible time for her to be making him suddenly feel emotions.

She tipped her head and studied him. Something he noticed she did when she was weighing options. He hoped he measured up, and did his best to look sincere. He thought he saw doubt and maybe some disappointment in her eyes, so he furrowed his brow as he looked over at her.

"You look like you might punch me if I don't say yes," she said at last with a sad little half smile.

"That was me being sincere," he said. He wasn't even good at that. How the hell did he think he was going to manage a commitment to her and to his son? He was going to have to be in touch with his feelings and express them. Or would he? His own father never had, and Dec had scarcely known the man. He'd wanted to have fun with him, to have a closer bond.

She shook her head and gave a little laugh. "You

shouldn't look so fierce if you want people to think you are sincere."

"I can't help it. Ever since you walked into the conference room I haven't felt blasé about a single thing. From the moment you came back in to my life nothing has been normal."

"Uh, thanks?"

"I meant it as a compliment, but it's clear to see you didn't take it that way. I'm not good at this type of conversation. Should I leave?"

She walked over to him, still holding little DJ on her hip, and put her hand on his chest over his heart, where her head had rested earlier. Even though he didn't know what he was doing, somehow he felt he was bumbling his way through this. He was doing what he needed for her to see that she was important to him.

"Don't leave. I'm so afraid that I'm giving you credit for trying harder than you really are. I don't want to be stupid where you are concerned again."

"Well, I don't want to go anywhere."

"Really?" she asked.

"Yes," he said.

She took a few tentative steps closer to him and he watched her trying hard to pretend that he hadn't just made a huge leap forward in her estimation.

The staff picnic at Infinity Games was held in mid-September. A lot of people weren't too happy with Dec because they'd had to work harder and longer than they ever had before. But everyone had heard the news, thanks to the figures she'd forwarded to the staff, that all their efforts were paying off and they were projected to be over their profit targets. So the mood on the campus at the barbecue tents was pretty upbeat.

"Davis actually smiled at me when he took his plate of food," Dec said to her with a wry grin as the last of the group of staff moved on.

"He doesn't like you, but he told me yesterday he understood that the bottom line was important," Cari said.

She and Dec had the first shift at the hot-food tent. It was a catered event but Infinity Games executive staff had always been the ones to serve the food. She had started the tradition.

It had been a little over two weeks since the night in her office, and they'd been on dates and really taken their time to get to know each other. She still felt there were times when Dec was keeping part of himself in reserve, but on the whole she was happy to have him in her life. Emma and Jessi had thought she was nuts to have gone out with Dec. But they'd both backed off when Cari had told them that he made her happy. Which was mostly true. He also made her scared and paranoid and neurotic. She didn't know why he was afraid of commitment and had done her level best to be cool and not too clingy. But each day, as she fell a little more in love with him, she had to fight her own instincts harder.

"So this is the famous cyborg of Playtone Games."

At the sound of her sister's voice, Cari looked up, sensing Dec tense beside her.

"I don't even need an introduction to know that you are Jessi Chandler," Dec said, turning to greet her sister, who looked funky in her minisundress that she'd teamed with a pair of combat boots.

"Jess, he prefers to go by Dec rather than cyborg," Cari said, going over to give her sister a hug and whisper in her ear, "Be nice."

Jessi just gave her a wink. "Ah, trying to blend in with the humans?"

"Indeed. Is there a point to all of this?" Dec asked Jessi.

"Just wanted you to remember that the staff are people with lives and jobs and had no part in anything that Gregory Chandler might have done to Thomas Montrose," Jessi said.

"He's a fair man, Ms. Jessi," Frank said, coming up to the serving line. "Good afternoon, Mr. Dec, Ms. Cari."

"Hello, Frank," Cari said, starting to make a plate of food for the security guard.

"Really?" Jessi asked Frank.

"Yes. I know most of the staff were a little scared when he first showed up, but he asks good questions, points out obvious improvements… I think most people are starting to like him."

Cari glanced over at Dec and saw that his skin was flushed and he looked distinctly uncomfortable. Jessi didn't look too pleased either and gave her a hard look that Cari couldn't really figure out.

"Thanks, Frank. Enjoy the picnic."

"I intend to," he said, walking away.

"You two are relieved from duty," Jessi said. She and her assistant Marcel walked behind the table and shooed Cari and Dec away.

Once they got out of earshot, Cari said, "Sorry about Jessi."

"It's okay. I get worse from Kell all the time. Want to grab a bite to eat before DJ gets here with your sister Emma?"

"Yes," she said. "You really made an impression on Frank."

Dec shrugged. "Six months ago I would have slated him for early retirement and given him a package of benefits, but when I talked to him I saw that he still had something to contribute here. The last thing he wants is to be retired."

"I agree. He's smart and surprisingly strong for his age," Cari said.

"How do you know that?"

"He's the one who carried my new Louis XIV side table upstairs. That thing is heavy."

Dec laughed. "Why do you like that frilly furniture so much? It's not very businesslike."

"Yes, it is. And people like it. Shows I have personality," she said. "That I'm not just another boring corporate drone."

"They don't need to see your office to know that," Dec said, glancing around them and then stealing a quick kiss. "Let's find a place to sit down."

She followed him to the picnic tables and as they approached, two of the game developers waved them over. She knew that Dec had been talking to her staff, but as she sat next to him at the table she realized he'd actually been integrating himself into the company. She didn't know if that was because he was trying to make the transition smoother or if he had another purpose.

But as she listened to the conversation flowing around her, she realized that he was a part of this group. Since observing him at the trade show a year and a half ago, she sensed that he'd changed. She wondered if it was a permanent change or if this was just his way with takeovers. She had no way of knowing for sure, she realized. She was just going to have to decide if she trusted him or not.

And as he reached under the table to squeeze her thigh, giving her an intimate smile, she knew that she already trusted him. She saw him now as a man who knew how to be a part of something bigger than himself. A man who understood that to have a successful future you had to build something, not just tear up what existed. A man whom she was glad to call her own.

Dec found a quiet spot out of the sun and away from the crowds at the picnic. Late afternoon was waning into evening and soon to come was a fireworks display and a band that would be performing as soon as dusk fell. He'd spent the day surrounded by the staff of Infinity Games. They'd all been friendly and made him feel like he was a part of the team.

He knew he wasn't. He knew that in just under two more weeks when he presented his findings to the board he was going to have to cut some of them. And the thing was, he had the feeling they knew it, too. He had never expected to care, he realized suddenly.

Takeovers weren't the place for someone who was empathetic and who couldn't keep his eye on the finances. Never before had he struggled with this, and he knew a certain blonde was to blame.

She kept expecting him to be better than he was and damn if he wasn't trying to live up to that.

But this wasn't him. He had made small talk all day long and smiled and played volleyball. And he had just reached the saturation point of being surrounded by people. He didn't want to feel vulnerable here. Business was the one place in his life where he'd always been so calm, so cool, able to keep moving forward.

But not now. Cari Chandler was changing him, and not just in his personal life.

"There you are," she said, coming up next to him.

"Mamamama," DJ said. The boy was dressed in a pair of khaki shorts and a blue Polo Ralph Lauren shirt.

"Hey there, buddy," Dec said, reaching out to his son. The boy leaned over and Cari handed him to Dec. He wished the boy would call him Dada, but he was learning that with babies and Cari everything happened in its own time.

As he cuddled his son close, some of the tension inside of him eased. "I just needed a break."

"I get that. These days can be so long. Wait until you go to the staff holiday party."

"Cari, about that," he said.

"Yes?" She looked over at him with those big blue eyes of hers and he felt a pain in his gut at the thought of saying what needed to be said.

Then he got disgusted with himself. "By Christmas, Infinity Games won't be like this."

"What do you mean?"

"You know I'm here to acquire your company. One of the things we're looking at is moving some of your staff to the Playtone campus."

She flushed and glared at him. "After today, you'd still do that?"

"Cari, that's my job."

"I thought you were starting to care."

"I am. I do care about you and about DJ."

"But not about his heritage."

Her words were quick and he understood where she was coming from. The past four-plus weeks had started a bond between them that he was reluctant to see broken, but he knew what he had to do. Kell wasn't going to give up on vengeance just because Dec had started to care about one of the Chandler sisters.

"The same could be said of you and your sisters," Dec pointed out. "The company was vulnerable. We weren't the only ones sniffing around at buying you out."

She shook her head. "We were having such a nice day. Why are you being like this?"

"Like what? This is who I am. It doesn't matter how much I like your staff. Some of them are still going to be cut. This is business."

She nodded. "I can't think like that."

"That's one of the things I really like about you," he said. "But that doesn't mean I can just give up sound fiscal thinking because I want to please you."

She crossed her arms over her chest and gave him a good hard glare. "I can't stay mad at you when you make actual sense."

He rolled his eyes. She couldn't stay mad at anyone. "That's because you're smarter than those blonde jokes you are always forwarding to me."

"They're funny," she said. "I'm sorry if it seemed I jumped on you. Is that why you are over here? Because it's hard to mingle and enjoy yourself with people you might have to let go?"

Dec didn't have the heart to tell her he just needed a break from all the people. He wasn't like Cari and wouldn't lose any sleep over the staff reductions that had to be made. The really good staff members had already proved themselves by stepping into the transition and taking the lead.

"I guess," he said.

"Sorry I wasn't more understanding," she said, giving him a quick hug.

"It's okay. Why were you looking for me?"

"To see if you'd watch DJ. My sisters and I have to introduce the entertainment and thank the staff for the work they've done this year," Cari said.

Dec realized that to her these people were extended family, and for the first time since he'd learned of the acquisition, he didn't feel good. He knew the top three names on the cut list all ended with Chandler. And as he watched this woman he was starting to care about, he realized the full impact of what that would mean to her.

"I'd be happy to watch him, but don't you think it might make people ask questions about why I am?" Dec asked.

"No one is going to be ballsy enough to question you," she said. "But if you wanted to keep hiding out..."

"I'm not hiding out, but I think staying over here out of the way of the staff is wise."

"Me, too. Thanks."

Cari leaned over and kissed DJ on the head before turning and walking away. Dec watched her make her way through the throngs of people and saw her stop and chat along the way. Though he knew they were different and he'd have no problem with losing staff, Cari was going to have a hard time when she was one of the staff who was cut.

He shifted DJ to his other arm and realized he wanted to find a way to keep her on. Because just like Frank, he didn't think Cari was going to enjoy not coming to Infinity Games every day.

Eleven

"We're here," Cari said as she parked her car in the big circle drive at the Chandler estate in Malibu.

Cari dreaded Sunday brunch with her sisters. She knew there was no way they could know what had happened in her office on her desk almost three weeks ago. They also didn't know about the dates she and Dec had been on or how without her meaning for it to happen she'd started to fall for him. But she felt like her emotions were transparent today. She adjusted the A-line slim-fitting skirt and the thick black belt at her waist as she got out of the car in front of Emma's house.

In theory they were all supposed to take turns hosting the weekly morning get-together but somehow they always ended up at Emma's. Cari liked to think it was because the house Emma lived in had been their grandparents' and of course Emma had a housekeeper who did all the cooking. But she had the feeling it was more than that.

Emma liked being the hostess. She liked being the one everyone came to. She was the oldest, and too bossy for her own good, so they let her get away with it.

She glanced at DJ, who was busy chewing on a small plastic boat that he called num-num. She got him out of the car and headed toward the house. She'd spent her weekends here as a child running on the marble floors and playing hide-and-seek in the landscaped gardens out back.

Now as she looked down at her son she smiled, thinking that he'd be doing the same thing soon. She gave him to Mrs. Hawkins, Emma's son's nanny, as soon as she entered the mansion.

She wondered what Dec's childhood home was like. He'd mentioned that he still owned it but that it stood empty. Did he have the kind of memories of his home that she did of this place?

"Sam will be glad to see this little one," Mrs. Hawkins said.

"DJ, as well. He likes playing with his cousin," Cari said.

She looked down at DJ. "You're going to see Sammy."

"Mamamama," he said up at her with that big grin of his.

She kissed his forehead just before Mrs. Hawkins scooped him up and turned to walk away. "Where are my sisters?"

"In your grandfather's den," Mrs. Hawkins said.

It didn't matter that Gregory Chandler had been dead for almost ten years now or that Emma had taken up residence here. That room would always be his.

Cari entered the heavily oak-paneled room that she

imagined still smelled of her grandfather's cigars. The large windows at the end of the room did their best to let in the sunlight but the room was still dark and felt very masculine. As a child Cari had never ventured in here as it was the domain of her stern grandfather.

"Hey, girls," Cari said. "I thought we were just having breakfast."

"We will," Emma said. Her oldest sister had thick wavy hair that she normally wore pulled back in a chignon because she said it made her look more professional. "Since Jessi is in charge of marketing I wanted to run your idea past her for the Christmas game."

"Now? I don't have any of the information with me and my staff is taking Sunday off," Cari said.

"It's fine. We'll just get a high-level rundown on it. I want to keep it a secret from Playtone until we have the finished product."

"I don't think that is going to work," Cari said. "Dec is in the office and I talked to Allan about the financial targets. If we don't show them our pro forma and some progress, I think we're in danger of losing everything."

"Why did you talk to Allan?" Jessi asked.

"He was in the office to see Dec," Cari explained. "What is it between the two of you?"

Jessi looked distinctly uncomfortable, which wasn't like her sister. "There's nothing between us. He got all protective and mad because I investigated John before Patti married him."

"Why did you do that?"

"They met in Vegas. I didn't know him, and Patti is a hot property with her business going international. He could have been a gold digger."

Cari reached over and patted her sister on the shoulder. Jessi really didn't trust anyone except those who'd proved themselves trustworthy. It made Cari a little sad because she could remember the sweet little girl that Jessi used to be before life had hardened her.

"Was he?"

"Would I have let her marry him if he was?" Jessi said, sounding disgusted. "Allan got all macho man and told me to back off."

"Just from having a private investigator look into John's past?"

"I may have also offered John a bribe to see if he'd take it and run," Jessi mumbled.

Cari shook her head and couldn't help laughing. "Oh, I'm sure that went over well."

"John forgave me, but Allan hasn't."

"Well, that doesn't matter," Emma said. "I want to know more about Cari and Dec. I know you went on one date with him the first night he showed up at the office, but scuttlebutt says you two are dating. That's not right, is it?" Emma asked.

Cari walked over to the large overstuffed leather sofa and plopped down on it. "Yes, it is right. We ended up talking about more than business at dinner and kind of hit it off."

"Hit it off?" Jessi said. "That doesn't sound like you."

"Well, it is me," she said. She didn't want to have this conversation, but realized it was exactly what she needed to do so that when she told them about Dec and DJ, it wouldn't give them both heart attacks. "I guess he just came along at the right time."

"I don't think dating him is a good idea," Emma said.

"Hell, I'm going to have him investigated," Jessi said. "Then we'll see if you can keep dating him."

"No," Cari said, standing up. "I'm sorry, but this is

my decision. I'm going to date him despite the fact that we have some history with his family."

"Does your family mean so little to you?" Emma asked.

"No, it's not like that. But men like Dec…"

"Men like Dec?" Jessi asked. "How well do you know him?"

"Not as well as you're implying, but I do sort of like him. And I haven't met that many men who I want to get to know better."

"Not since you realized you were pregnant," Jessi said.

"Yes. I don't want you two meddling in this. It's hard enough dealing with the takeover and starting to care for him. I know what I'm doing."

"I hope you do," Emma said. "Because he's not going to put you before Playtone Games. With the board meeting tomorrow morning I think it's safe to assume there isn't anything else you can do now. I just want you to be sure you know what you are doing."

Cari wasn't sure. She knew she was already putting Dec before her obligation to the company. In her mind there had to be a way for her to convince him to leave the company as it was and to keep him in her life. She wasn't going to be happy with anything less than that.

Cari believed she'd planted the seeds in his mind that he couldn't treat Infinity Games like just another business to be gobbled up. She hoped his feelings for her would lead him to the conclusion that she and her sisters and their company should stay intact.

Cari left her sister's house and drove up the Pacific Coast Highway with no real destination in mind. She had a Yo Gabba Gabba! CD on for DJ who seemed happy enough in his rear car seat.

There was no reason for the tension in her stomach. Right now she knew she was doing all she could to protect her staff from trouble at work. Right now she knew her sisters were safe and healthy. And right now she still believed that she and Dec were going to end up together and be happy.

But she knew that Jessi and Emma had planted a seed of doubt in her mind. There was no way she could just keep moving forward with Dec while not knowing what his plans were for her and her sisters and their jobs.

She knew that there was a chance—okay, more than a chance—that Dec was going to recommend that she and her sisters be cut from the head count. Everyone knew that they didn't need two sets of executives in one company who did the same thing.

But she had been hoping as the weeks had gone on that there would be a way to truly merge the different corporate entities. Today, though, she was going to have to face reality. There was no way that the Montrose heirs were going to let her and her sisters stay on.

Even worse, Cari understood where Dec and his cousins were coming from. She pulled her car onto a scenic overlook and sat there with the motor running as the truth of why her stomach hurt hit her.

She was afraid that even after he destroyed her family's heritage she'd still love him.

She hadn't wanted to admit that even to herself, but it was the truth. In fact, she loved him right now.

She glanced in the backseat at DJ and she realized that from the moment Dec had walked back into her life, she'd wanted this.

But she also wanted Dec to save her company, fall in

love with his son and love her back. She wanted him to change completely from the man she knew him to be.

And that wasn't realistic. She didn't need Jessi's P.I. to tell her that Dec didn't make business decisions from the heart. She'd called him a cyborg, and in truth that was what he was when it came to slashing the game-making companies that Playtone acquired.

She also knew that he had bonded with their son. She'd seen him on the floor playing with DJ. When he thought she wasn't looking, sometimes he held the boy close and kissed the top of his head. And she had seen that look in Dec's eyes. The one that showed how very much he cared for his son.

And he did like her. And lust after her. He made her feel like she was the only woman in the world. No matter that to him this might be something that only lasted six weeks.

She rubbed the back of her neck. In that moment she decided that she was just going to ask him flat out what his intentions were. There wasn't going to be any more guessing if he wanted her or if he was going to stay with her.

She reached into her huge handbag and took out her mobile phone, then dialed his number.

"Montrose here," Dec answered.

"It's Cari. Do you have a sec?"

"Just. I'm on my way out to play volleyball with my cousins. What's up?"

"Um…I'd like to invite you to come and have dinner with me tonight," she said. "My place six-thirty."

"I'd like that," he said. "I've got a few things I want to discuss with you."

"Me, too," she said.

"Not business," he added.

Perfect, she thought. She'd let Jessi and Emma rattle her, but she'd been spending a lot of time with Dec and her instincts where he was concerned were good. "Me, too. I'll see you later."

"I'm looking forward to it," he said, disconnecting the call.

The tension that had been in her stomach disappeared and she smiled to herself in the rear-view mirror. She needed to know where she and Dec stood and, it seemed, he wanted answers to the same questions.

The love she'd been afraid to admit to started bubbling up inside her and she had to sit in the car another minute before she started driving along. She wanted to enjoy this magical feeling inside her. Her sisters had warned her how impossible her dreams might be. Warned her that she couldn't have it all with Dec. But at this moment she realized she had to at least take a chance on him and see if her secret dreams could come true. The future she craved where she had her man, her company and the father of her son.

Dec wasn't sure how the tradition had started, but on Sunday afternoons if they were all in California, he, Kell, Allan and John, Allan's best friend, got together for a game of volleyball in Clover Park in Santa Monica. As it happened this Sunday, John was in town for the weekend. While Dec had been in Australia, John and his wife, Patti, had bought a B and B in the Outer Banks of North Carolina, after Patti had sold her interior design company for a small fortune. Dec had learned early on that it didn't matter who his biological parents were when it came to sports. No one cared as long as he was good at them. And he was. As a child, because he'd had a lot of excess energy, he'd always been signed up for something to keep his nanny from going crazy.

Kell was already there when Dec arrived wearing a sleeveless Sloppy Joe's T-shirt and a pair of board shorts. He waved when he saw Dec.

"How's it going, man?"

"Can't complain," Dec said. "It's been too long since I've done this."

"We should have come to see you in Australia," Kell said.

"Nah," Dec said with a shrug. They weren't that kind of family. "You were busy fulfilling Granddad's dream for you."

"I doubt he'd be pleased with me yet. The Chandlers are still running Infinity Games."

"Yeah, about that," Dec said. He had been slowly realizing there was no way he was going to be able to recommend that Cari lose her job. She was so much a part of the daily operation, he honestly—well, maybe his emotions were influencing him a little—thought she was necessary to the continued success of any division of Infinity.

"Yes?" Kell asked. Even though he kept his dark Ray-Bans on, Dec could feel the cold glare of his stare.

"It's just not going to be as easy as we'd hoped to separate the Chandlers from the operation."

"But you're a genius at this kind of thing. Don't sell yourself short, Dec. I'm sure you'll do what any Montrose would do," Kell said.

Dec nodded. *What any Montrose would do.* Those words haunted him. He knew how to prove to Kell he was a Montrose through and through, but he was also adopted and his mother's son. And she'd hated old Thomas Montrose more than anyone else.

Kell pulled his cell phone out. "Sorry, I've got to answer this email."

Dec moved away and let his oldest cousin get back to what he did best: business. It was clear to Dec that Kell wasn't interested in moving on from the past.

But he'd been raised by their grandfather in that old dilapidated house that Thomas had refused to move out of. His own father was the middle child and Dec had often noticed that his father never measured up. Kell's father had been killed in the first war in Iraq—Desert Storm. And there was no way Dec's dad could compete with a dead man even after he married an heiress and poured billions into the family coffers.

"Ready to get your butts handed to you, boys?" Allan called as he and John walked over to them.

"Has he been drinking already?" Dec asked as he shook John's hand.

"Just cocky as ever," John said. "Good to have you back in the country."

"Thanks," Dec said. "I've missed our Sunday games."

"You don't look like you've been sitting on your ass," Allan said.

"Not at all. I played squash in Sydney with a few boys from Kanga Games."

"Good to hear it," Allan said, reaching over to give him a slap on the shoulder. "John and I have been keeping our game strong. We're getting to be something of a legend around here."

John laughed and Kell put his cell phone away to come and join them. "Ready to do this?"

"Sure," Dec said.

A coin toss determined that Dec and Kell would serve first. Dec took the ball and went to the line. As the game progressed Dec and Kell held their own, but there was a marked difference in the two sides. John and Allan laughed and joked when they missed a shot and had the most ridiculous victory high five that Dec had ever seen.

He and Kell just got on with it and played. He wondered what made Allan so different from them. Was it the fact that his Montrose was a woman? And Grandfather Montrose had treated Aunt Becca like she was a princess instead of pitting her against her brothers?

He thought of his son and realized he wanted DJ to be more like Allan than he or Kell. He wanted his son to be happy and have friends that he laughed with.

He wanted a life of happiness, not bitterness, for the boy. And he knew that if he fired Cari there was no way DJ wouldn't someday be affected by it.

He'd never been so close to having full-blown acceptance in the Montrose family as he was at this moment, and he'd only just accepted the fact that to make his adopted family happy he was going to have to sacrifice the happiness of his own blood and his own future.

He didn't fool himself into thinking that Cari was going to stay with him if he followed the plan that would make Kell happy. And if he didn't follow it? How was he going to keep his place at Playtone?

He held a big-enough chunk of the shares to block Kell if it came down to it, thanks to his mother buying back some of the public stock, but he didn't want to make it about a power play. He wanted to find a way to make all sides realize that building the future involved a lot more than avenging the past.

And he had no idea how he was going to do it.

"Are you going to serve or just stare at the ball?" Kell asked him.

"Sorry. I just thought of something about the Infinity acquisition," Dec said.

"Don't apologize to me for thinking about crushing the Chandlers," Kell said. "That's all I do."

"All?"

"Well, I sleep, too," Kell said.

Dec felt a knot settle in his stomach. His cousins were like his brothers. The thought of hurting them was almost too much to contemplate, but he had a feeling Allan wouldn't be as upset about keeping one of the sisters on as Kell would. He was going to have to be very careful about how he managed this.

"We need to get you a hobby," Dec said.

"What do you call this?" Kell asked.

"Winning," Dec said, serving the ball and getting the last point.

"Great game," Allan said.

"Want to come back to my place for a beer?" Allan asked. "I've got some steaks and we can watch the NASCAR race."

"I can't," Dec said. "I've got a date."

"With?" Allan asked.

"If you must know, I'm going out with Cari."

"Cari Chandler?" Kell asked.

"Yes, we've been seeing each other."

"Is that smart?"

Dec just gave his cousin a hard look. "My personal life is personal. It's not going to affect our business."

"Unless you let it screw up your priorities," Kell said.

"Back off, man," Allan said while John took a few steps away and walked down toward the beach.

"My priorities are fine," Dec said.

"You say that now, but…we're so close to finally

fulfilling Grandfather's destiny for us. Why would you chance that for a woman?" Kell asked.

"She's not just a woman."

Kell looked like his head was going to explode. "Starting tomorrow, I will take over the transition."

"My report is finished. I have a few more notes to make but I'll be presenting it on Monday. You don't have to pull me out of my job."

"What are your findings?"

"I'd rather wait until Monday."

"I need to know that Gregory Chandler didn't pull another fast one on us in the form of his seductive granddaughter."

"She's not like that," Dec said.

"We will see," Kell said.

He walked away before Kell could say anything else, but in his heart he knew that he was going to have to choose between his past and his future. And for a man used to living in the now, that was a very uncomfortable place to be.

Twelve

Cari put DJ down for his afternoon nap at four. She'd tried to get him to sleep earlier so he'd be awake when Dec came, but he wouldn't cooperate with her. Now she was running behind on getting dinner ready.

She gave up her plans of making a roast and settled on pasta instead. It was quick and easy. Plus she knew that Dec wasn't going to suddenly realize he loved her simply because she'd made him dinner. She knew that when she was in her rational mind, but not when she was in that crazy gotta-make-him-love-me mind.

She had started an espresso granita for dessert, and since all it required was scraping the icy mixture once every thirty minutes, she was set. She rubbed the back of her neck and realized her hair was still down and probably looked a mess. She set the timer for the dessert and ran to her room.

Where was the time going? It was almost six. She

spent extra time on her hair and makeup and then got dressed in a simple sundress that showed off her arms and hid the tummy she had since she'd given birth. Pleased that she looked her best, she went back to the kitchen, but the doorbell rang before she could get there.

She took a deep breath and tried to relax. It wasn't like this one night was going to completely change her life. But she hoped it would. She'd never anticipated these feelings for Dec even two months ago. Somehow the man who'd abandoned her and left her with a child to raise had come through in a way she hadn't anticipated.

She walked to her front door to the staccato sound of her own heels and realized she hadn't put on any music. She opened the door and Dec stood there with his hair still damp at his collar, wearing a pair of khaki shorts and an open-necked shirt and deck shoes. He had on a pair of sunglasses, which he pushed up on the top of his head when she opened the door.

"Hello, gorgeous," he said. "It seems like forever since I've seen you."

"Me, too," she said with a blush. She stepped back so he could enter. He handed her a bouquet of multicolored flowers. The bouquet was large and she glanced down at it.

"Thank you."

"I didn't know which kind you liked so I settled on this bunch of gerbera daisies because they reminded me of you."

She looked down at the yellow, pink and orange petals with their large brown centers. This was such a warm bouquet of flowers. "How do these remind you of me?"

"They make me smile," he said.

She felt a giddy rush of joy shoot through her. She

wanted to be cautious, to tell herself to slow down and not take everything he said as an undeclared admission of love for her. But it was hard. She saw him now in the new light of her emotions.

"Why are you smiling at me like that?" he asked.

"You can be very nice sometimes, Dec."

"Sometimes? I thought I was nice all the time."

She just shook her head and leaned over to kiss him. She meant for it to be a light thank-you sort of buss on the lips, but instead it turned into something more. She wrapped her free arm around his shoulders and leaned up on her tiptoes to kiss him fully.

"Wow, if this is the reaction I get to a bunch of flowers, I'm going to give them to you every day," he said.

She stepped back. The thought of him being with her every day filled her with that same bubbly feeling. She truly felt like nothing could spoil this night and that everything in her adult life had been leading to this moment. The timer started going off in the kitchen and DJ started to cry at the same time.

"DJ or kitchen?" he asked. "I don't mind helping out with either."

"Would you mind getting DJ?" she asked. She thought he'd rather spend time with his son then try to figure out what she needed him to do in the kitchen. Besides, she wanted her dinner and dessert to be perfect.

"Not at all," he said with a grin. He seemed to smile more easily these days than he had six weeks ago, and she hoped that it was because of her.

"Do I need to do anything special to get DJ ready?"

"Um...change his diaper and I laid out a little outfit for him to wear. Can you get him dressed?"

Dec nodded. "I think I can manage."

He walked down the hall and she hurried into the

kitchen, setting the daisies on the counter while she opened the freezer to scrape her icy mixture. Then she got out a vase for the flowers and tried not to let the fact that he'd brought them to her mean as much as it did.

The fact was she didn't get flowers that often. Her sisters had sent her a bouquet after she'd given birth to DJ, but before that it had been years since she'd received them. She trimmed the stems and arranged the flowers in the vase before setting it in the middle of the island in her kitchen.

Then she went back to getting dinner ready. She had assembled the ingredients for a fresh and simple sauce for the pasta with basil, cherry tomatoes and some minced garlic. She filled a large pot with water and put it on to boil, and then turned her attention to making the garlic bread.

Since she was watching her weight since she'd given birth—it was a lot harder to take off the baby weight than she'd expected it to be—she was making a low-cal version of garlic bread with thinly sliced French bread that she'd rub a piece of garlic on when it was all toasted.

She realized she was nervous about the food and the table setting and everything else, but what she really wanted was for dinner to be over and for her to talk to Dec. He'd said he had something important to discuss, too, and she hoped that after the way he'd been at the door a few minutes ago he'd tell her he cared for her as much as she did for him.

She felt the first twinge of doubt in her stomach as she realized that she desperately wanted him to love her.

Dec would have laughed in the face of anyone who six weeks ago would have said he'd be changing a diaper and getting ready to spend the night at home. It just wasn't his scene—or it hadn't been. But tonight with the homey smell of dinner wafting through the house and his ten-month-old son chattering at him as he dressed him, Dec felt like he was in the only place he should be.

That feeling in his soul of the rightness of this moment was what convinced him that he wasn't going to abandon DJ or Cari again. And that scared him because he still hadn't figured out a way to save her job. But for tonight he didn't care about games or a generations-old feud. Tonight he wanted to simply enjoy the fact that for the first time in his life he felt like he was home.

It didn't matter that technically this was Cari's house or that he'd never even been here before. He had that feeling inside that he'd always been searching for and never truly experienced. That emptiness that had been a part of him all of his life no longer felt so cold and barren.

He sat DJ up and looked at the outfit he'd decided on. He had eschewed the romper that Cari had laid out in favor of a pair of elastic-waist khaki shorts and a little button-down shirt that matched his. He wanted Cari to see that he was a part of their lives now. It was important to him that he build as much of a connection between them before the board meeting tomorrow.

He lifted DJ off the changing table and the boy squirmed to get down. Since Cari lived in a one-story Mexican-style hacienda, there were no stairs to be a danger to him. He put him down and followed his son as he crawled through the house to the kitchen.

He thought of Allan and Kell and how his cousins were still untethered to anything but their jobs, and realized that he'd changed. He knew he was going to have to make a hard decision regarding Infinity and Playtone. He also knew that he might have to make a choice.

A choice that would have seemed so simple only six weeks ago, but no longer was.

As DJ crawled into the kitchen and Cari bent over to scoop up their son and then kiss him on the head, the decision seemed to make itself.

"Oh, I like your choice in outfit, sweetie," she said to DJ. "You and Daddy match." She looked over at him with so much caring in her gaze that he felt scared.

She'd turned on her iPod while he was gone and the speaker system on the countertop played "California Gurls" by Katy Perry.

He turned away and rubbed his hands together. She'd looked so vulnerable and probably wasn't aware of it. The burden of not hurting her again felt heavy on his shoulders. "I brought some wine and it's out in the car. I'll be right back."

He turned on his heel and hurried out of her house. As soon as he was outside, he stopped halfway between the house and his car. He was torn as he looked at the Maserati parked at the curb. A part of him wanted to get in there and drive away from this entire situation.

If he left, Kell would find a way to have his revenge and Cari would eventually find a way to move on with her life. And he wouldn't have to choose between his cousin and a lifetime goal—the very thing that had defined his past—and Cari and DJ, who he knew could be his future. But he knew he wasn't going to run off. He was no coward. It was hard for him to believe he'd left Cari in a hotel room all those months ago.

A slight breeze blew down the street in the older neighborhood where Cari lived. There were hibiscus plants growing in the front yard and large palms on either side of her driveway.

He had changed, he thought. Really changed, and it was almost as if he didn't want to accept it. The change was scary because he had something he didn't want to lose. Cari and DJ. He'd never thought he'd be as vulnerable as that, but the truth was there for him to see.

He grabbed the bottle of wine and headed back into the house. He found Cari in the kitchen dancing with DJ to Olly Murs's "Dance With Me Tonight." She glanced up at him and froze mid-gyration. Something moved between them and he knew that no matter what tomorrow held he'd cherish this night forever.

"Dance with me?" she asked.

He put the bottle of wine on the countertop and took both his woman and his son in his arms and danced them around the kitchen while the catchy pop ballad played in the background. DJ giggled and Cari hummed along a little out of tune.

Just like that, everything seemed so simple. They should be together. Though it was the solution he knew he'd been steering toward all afternoon, he was very glad to have his smart little son who saw things so clearly.

He didn't know how he was going to do it, but when the dust settled at the board meeting tomorrow he was walking out of there a Montrose with the respect of his cousins, but he was also leaving with Cari.

There hadn't been much chance to talk about anything serious over dinner what with DJ there and Dec in a contemplative mood. But once she put DJ to bed and went to find Dec sitting on one of the wooden loungers in her backyard, staring up at the night sky, Cari knew the time to talk was now.

She put the baby monitor on the table before she sat down on the double lounger next to him, and he reached over to take her hand in his. "Thank you."

She gave him a quizzical look. "For what? You already complimented me on dinner."

"Thank you for my son. I didn't realize until tonight how great a gift he is. You could have made a different choice, given that I wasn't in the picture. I wouldn't have blamed you at all," he said. "And I never would have known what was missing in my life."

She felt her throat close and tears burn the back of her eyes. He would never know how hard the decision had been, given that she had been on her own and that he was her family's sworn enemy. "I don't know what to say."

"You don't have to say anything." He pulled her into his arms so that her head was cuddled on his shoulder. Then he moved around so they were on their sides facing each other.

His hands swept down her side to her hip, his fingers flexing on her buttocks. He traced a pattern on her hip and she moved a little closer to him.

"Do you trust me now?" he asked. His voice was deep in the quiet of the night.

"Yes, Dec," she said. It was nothing less than the truth.

"Good. Will you let me make love to you?" he asked. "Since we were together, I've been limiting myself to good-night kisses since that night in your office to give us both a chance to really get to know each other, but I don't think I can wait any longer," he said. He rubbed his hips against hers and she felt his erection.

"Me either," she said. She'd been aware of the boundaries between them that she'd set that night in her office, but that had changed. She wanted to be in his arms again. To be honest, it was all she'd thought about for the past few weeks. As much as she hadn't been sure she could rely on him, she'd still wanted him. After the revelations she'd had this afternoon, nothing would make her happier than to make love with him tonight.

He lowered his mouth to hers, kissing her gently but thoroughly. With only the moonlight overhead and the fragrant blossoms in the backyard surrounding them, she felt like they were in paradise.

She put her hands between them and unbuttoned his shirt until she felt the springy hair of his chest under her fingers. She rubbed her hands over his hard pecs and traced the hair as it tapered down his stomach. His belly flinched as her fingers moved lower, and he put his hand over hers.

She pulled her mouth from his and looked up at him, but he lowered his head to her neck, dropping nibbling kisses down the length of it as his hands moved down her leg to the hem of her skirt and drew it up.

With long, languid strokes of his hand up and down, he caressed her thigh. She squirmed and reached again for his belt buckle. She undid it and then struggled with the button at his waist when his hand slipped under her panties and drew them down her legs.

He rolled her over onto her back and she stared up at him in the moonlight, and in his eyes she saw the emotions she'd craved. She saw the love and the caring that she felt for him reflected back in his eyes.

He nudged her knees apart with his and settled his hips overtop of hers. It was a shock to feel the warmth of his erection against her naked flesh. He shifted his hips, lightly rubbing his manhood over her center and she felt herself moisten as she got ready for him.

He pushed her thighs farther apart and held himself poised at the entrance of her, with only the tip of his erection inside her. She shifted under him, trying to force him inside of her, but he wouldn't be budged.

She looked up at him and he brought his mouth down on hers hard, thrusting his tongue deep inside her mouth as he finally entered her fully. Spasms of pleasure shook her as he continued to thrust deep inside of her. She wrapped her thighs around his waist and urged him to move faster, with her heels against the small of his back.

She tangled her tongue with his as she felt her orgasm wash over her. She tore her mouth from his and cried out his name as he thrust into her again and again, burying his face in her neck and suckling on the pulse point as he came with a final thrust and his entire body shuddered over hers.

She rocked her hips against his one more time. He settled over her for a moment and she thrilled to have his full weight on her. She wrapped her arms and legs around him and held him with all her strength. He kissed her lightly, and when she looked up at him he was staring at her with a look of tenderness she'd never seen in his eyes before.

He rolled them to their sides, cuddled her close and stroked his hand down her side and back. She tried to shift, afraid her weight might be too much for his arm, but he held her where she was and urged her to place her head on his chest, right over his heart.

She closed her eyes as she listened to the reassuring beat of it. Being in his arms made her think that she didn't have to worry about the issues Emma had raised this afternoon. Emma didn't know Dec like Cari did. Surely a man who held her this tenderly couldn't hurt her.

Thirteen

As night deepened around them, Dec held Cari in his arms. He wanted to make love to her again. In a proper bed instead of outside on the deck chair. But he didn't regret his actions. He had waited too long to have her in his arms again. He'd thought he'd explode if he hadn't gotten inside of her.

His determination to have her and to keep his Montrose cousins happy had set his mind to turning over what he was going to do next. It was hard to think when he had Cari in his arms. He fastened his pants, found her panties and put them in his pocket so that the housekeeper didn't find them later and then stood up and lifted her into his arms.

She stirred and smiled up at him.

"I feel asleep," she said.

"Yes, you did. Now I'm ready to sleep, too…with you in my arms. May I spend the night?"

"I was hoping you would. Just promise me if you do, you'll still be here when I wake up."

He hurt inside at the fact that she had to ask that. He didn't blame her for needing reassurances. He'd done that with own actions and he was going to keep reminding her that he was here to stay.

"Yes, I will be," he said.

She picked up the baby monitor before he carried her into the house and down the hall to her bedroom.

"How did you know where my bedroom was?"

"I checked it out earlier," he said.

He set her on her feet and she put the baby monitor on her nightstand. "I'm going to wash up for bed."

"Go ahead. I'll use the hall bathroom and meet you back here."

She gave him a tentative look as she entered the master bathroom, and he looked around her bedroom while he was in there alone. He'd noticed the baby pictures on her dresser earlier. Photos of DJ from the moment he'd arrived in the hospital being cradled in the arms of a very tired-looking Cari, all the way up to a photo of him from the Infinity Games company picnic two weeks ago.

She had chronicled her son's life, and he looked at the pictures from the nine months when he'd been absent in their lives and realized that DJ wouldn't have to know he'd been missing if he handled the next few days right.

But he knew that he was also going to have to be able to give Cari what she needed from him. And he suspected sex and a dinner companion weren't going to be enough. He shoved his hands through his hair and left her bedroom to wash up. He cleaned himself and came back into her bedroom to find Cari lying in her bed.

She was propped up with some pillows behind her

back and started when he opened the door. He stood there for a second and had no idea what to do next. Sure, he'd slept with women before—hell, he'd even slept with Cari—but it had been spontaneous and naturally flowed out of sex. This was different.

He was here because he wanted to be, and he felt a little vulnerable at that thought. It reminded him of his first night in his parents' mansion and how much he wanted to stay there forever. He'd gotten his wish, but it hadn't turned out exactly as he'd expected it to. But he'd been a kid with unrealistic dreams.

"Come to bed," she said, pulling back the covers and inviting him into the room. She'd left the nightstand light turned on and it cast a soft glow into the room. He wanted to believe he belonged in there with her, but he knew that he didn't. He was darkness and she was light.

He wanted to resist her. Despite what he'd been thinking all day, his gut instinct was to turn and run. Hadn't he learned that life was easier when he didn't rely on anyone? What kind of father could he be when he was still so afraid to stay in one place?

It didn't change his feelings for DJ. He felt so much love for his son; he wanted only the best for him. And he questioned whether or not he was actually the best for DJ and for Cari.

Despite the fact that she'd filled that emptiness inside of him, he still didn't know how to commit to her. He was still thinking of the gassed-up Maserati waiting outside and how he could be halfway to Canada before the sun rose if he wanted to be.

"Dec?"

He heard the quiver in her voice and knew she must be sensing what he was feeling. The trepidation after all these weeks of building up to tonight. Now that he was here, now that he'd gotten what he wanted, he was afraid to hold on to it. Hold on to her, he corrected himself.

Cari was different than anyone else he'd ever known, and that couldn't be clearer than it was at this moment. He took one step toward her and she smiled at him, but he saw a hint of sadness in it. He was so afraid that he couldn't be the man she needed him to be.

It wasn't just that emotions were foreign to him, it was that he had no way to balance the one thing he'd always wanted—Montrose acceptance—with the one thing he just realized he couldn't survive without. Her love.

Love was ephemeral and always just out of his grasp. She might be looking at him right now with love in her eyes, but how long could that last? Would she still feel that way when her sisters were out of a job and her family's legacy was in ruins around her?

He doubted it. How could he be enough to keep her happy? How could he be the one thing that gave her hope when he knew he wasn't lovable and had never been enough for anyone else?

Cari woke up early as she usually did and rolled over to look at Dec as he lay sleeping next to her. He'd woken her once in the night to make love and she'd enjoyed it and having him here. She didn't get a chance to tell him how she felt about him because she could tell that he was struggling.

If she had to guess, she'd say he wasn't sure how to handle his own feelings. From everything she knew of his childhood, she knew that he hadn't grown up in a loving home, and part of her wanted to just make up for every second of that. But she knew she couldn't.

She leaned over and touched the stubble on his cheek

with one finger. He didn't look so tough and ready to take on the world sleeping like this. It reminded her of how tender his face had looked after he'd made love to her outside.

It was hard for her to reconcile, but there was vulnerability in Dec that she hadn't realized was there. She rolled over before she did something silly, like drawing hearts on his chest with her finger and then waking him up to make love again.

She wanted to see what he was like this morning; if the gamble she was taking with her heart was going to pay off or if she was going to end up broken and alone again.

She shook her head as she got out of bed, grabbed her robe and left the room. There was a big board meeting this morning at the Playtone Games office building, where Dec would be giving his results to her and her sisters as well as the executive committee from Playtone. She and her sisters had a mock-up demo of their IOS Christmas game ready to show them and were hoping to use that as leverage to keep the Infinity brand alive.

She checked on DJ, who was awake and playing with his stuffed animal in his crib. "Morning, little man."

"Mama," he said. She got him out of the crib, changed his diaper and dressed him for the day before going into the kitchen to feed him. She heard the shower come on in her bathroom and knew that Dec was up.

She told herself it was silly to be nervous, yet the longer she sat there waiting for him the more that feeling grew. She finished with DJ and took the baby and her mug of coffee down the hall to the master bedroom. DJ squirmed to get down and she set him on the floor to go into her closet and get her clothes for the day. She heard the door open to the bathroom.

"Dada," DJ said.

Cari came out of the closet and looked over at Dec. In this moment, they felt like a real family. Except as he looked at her, she realized he didn't look restless at all. And she felt the tinge of doubt in her heart. She loved him; surely he felt the same way about her.

Why would he have stayed last night if he didn't?

She had no answers, and for the first time she recognized that love made her vulnerable. She needed something from Dec that he might not be able to give her. And it wasn't fair of her to ask for it. Love wasn't the sunshiny emotion she'd hoped it would be. And given the way that her relationship with Dec had developed, why was that a surprise?

"Morning," he said, his voice gruff with sleep. "I used your razor to shave. I hope that's okay."

"Yes, of course it is. Um…are you coming to my office this morning or just going straight to Playtone?"

"I have to go home and change first," he said. "But then I'll just go to Playtone. Cari, today is going to be a long day."

She saw the weight of the coming day on his shoulders. She took a deep breath. "I know it's going to be hard on everyone. But I've been working on those financial targets that Allan set. I think you might be surprised by some of the things I have to show you today."

He gave her a vague half smile. "That will be good. Do you need anything from me for your presentation?"

"No," she said. "Why would I?"

He shook his head. "Kell is going to be a tough customer, honey. Whatever presentation you make, it had better be solid and have documentation to back it up."

"It will," she said. "Do you think it's going to be bad news?"

"There are going to be reductions," he said. "But I can't say any more than that."

She nodded and she felt a knot of fear in her stomach. It didn't sound good for Infinity, but she was realistic. From the beginning she had the feeling that she and her sisters had been on the chopping block. She could only hope the new game and revenue stream she'd found would be enough to give them some more time in their jobs.

"Don't worry about it. I know you are just doing your job."

"Do you need me to watch DJ while you shower?" he asked.

"Do you have the time?" she asked. "Normally I bring him in with me, but I got him dressed to save time."

"I'll watch him," Dec said.

She started toward the bathroom, but then stopped and looked over at Dec. "I wish we could make the world go away."

"Me, too. But I think we both knew from the beginning that was never going to happen. Everything between us is going to be influenced by your sisters, my cousins and the feud our grandfathers started."

"I know. I was just wishing life would be simpler. When the dust settles from the meeting today, we have to talk. I meant to discuss something with you last night, but I got distracted."

"By me?" he asked, coming over and wrapping his arms around her waist and pulling her back against him. "Want to be distracted again?"

"I'd love to, but I think I'm going to need to be on time in order to impress the Playtone board."

"Yes, you are. Just relax when you get in there and

let them see how much you care about the company. And show off your smarts."

"How do I do that?" she asked, glancing over her shoulder at him.

"By being yourself."

"I'll try."

"You'll do it. I know you will," he said, giving her a tender kiss before nudging her toward the bathroom.

She had her shower and Dec left when she did. She headed toward the Infinity Games offices and he went home to change. She couldn't help but feel that even though he'd stayed the night with her, he'd pulled back from her a little bit.

Dec didn't head to the Playtone Games office building after he'd been to his yacht and gotten dressed for the day. Instead he detoured out of his way and went to the Beverly Hills mansion he'd grown up in. As he fumbled in the glove box for the remote control to the large gate that surrounded the place, he sat there remembering the first day he'd arrived here.

He'd been four, so his memories were hazy. He only knew that he had a new family, but he hadn't been told that they were wealthy, so the big house had been a bit of a shock. The wrought-iron gates with the ornate *L* on them for his mother's maiden name, Lingle, had opened just as slowly then as they did today. And as he gunned the powerful Maserati engine and shot up the driveway, he realized that no matter what happened today, he wasn't going to change inside.

He had never felt like a Montrose, partly because of the adoption, but as he got out of his car and walked to the front door of the mansion, he realized the other reason was his mother.

He'd asked her once when he was sixteen and she'd been railing against his dad why she'd married him, and Helene had said that she'd been fooled by love.

He opened the front door of the mansion. It was quiet with just the whir of the air-conditioning, and it smelled of fresh lemons. Though it sat empty, he paid a staff to clean it once a week.

With his mother's words echoing in his head, he wandered through the big house where he'd grown up and realized that part of his fear was that Cari was playing him. There had been something almost desperate in her tone when she'd asked about the meeting later in the day. They both knew that Infinity Games was history and soon there would be little left from Gregory Chandler's original company.

But beyond that, was there more to the two of them than a son? What was this emotion that kept making him want to give up sound business logic and do what his gut insisted and save Cari's job? Was it love? He didn't know. His mother had been unable or unwilling to describe what love was. All that Dec could remember was that he never wanted to feel the way his mother had felt. She'd lost herself in drink to numb the way she felt when she'd realized his father had married her for her money.

What if everything Cari had done had been to get him to try to betray his cousins and save her and her sisters?

He rubbed the back of his neck and knew there were no answers here in the past. He had to make a decision today. He had to trust Cari and the new life that she seemed to want to build with him.

That future shouldn't frighten him as much as it did, but he didn't know how to build a life with her. Or anyone. He didn't feel content or safe with the thought of having Cari by his side because he knew how fragile his hold on her was. He had no idea how to stay. Six weeks was one thing, but a lifetime? Could he do it?

Would she even want him for that long? He hated not knowing. This, he realized, was the worst part of falling for Cari—he didn't know how she really felt about him. Was it just that she wanted him to be a father to his child?

She'd said she wanted to talk tonight. What did that mean? After the meeting, if he saved her, would she tell him of her true feelings or would she move on?

He shook his head. He wasn't going to change his mind or his plan for Infinity because of her. He'd just have to hope that she was smart enough to get that even though he wanted to make a life with her he couldn't do something that made no business sense.

He left the house and hoped he wasn't doomed to follow in his parents' footsteps. They hadn't planned on being miserable all their lives and yet neither of them had ever found any real happiness. He finally realized that he'd spent a lifetime running and moving so he'd never be in the situation he was currently caught in.

He loved Cari Chandler and he knew without a doubt that he was going to disappoint her today. He hoped that it would be the only time he did it, but he wasn't sure that it would be. His relationship skills stunk and he believed that her sisters would never approve of him in his life.

He knew the kind of pressure that put on a couple. He had grown up in a house where two families had been in conflict. As he drove to the Playtone Games campus, he thought that maybe old Thomas Montrose was having his last laugh on Dec. The son of the son that

Thomas thought would never measure up was going to be the man who gave him the one thing that the rest of the Montroses couldn't. The real revenge that Thomas had wanted—bringing a Chandler to her knees not just in the boardroom but in life.

And Dec knew this because he was going to sacrifice his own chance at future happiness to save Cari from him. He knew he wasn't the right man for her and this morning had given him time to recognize that he had changed, but not enough to be able to tell her that he loved her. And she deserved a man who could do that easily and tell her that every single day of her life.

Fourteen

Emma and Jessi were depending on her to wow the board of Playtone Games when the meeting started, but Cari was nervous as they waited in the empty conference room.

"Did Dec tell you what was in his report?" Emma asked.

"No. He'd never do that," Cari said to her sister. "He's very loyal to his cousins. Just like I am to you both."

"We get it. How serious is this thing between you both?" Jessi asked. "Patti said that Kell wasn't too happy with Dec that he was dating you."

"How does Patti know that?" Cari asked, feeling a little of her confidence dip. She hoped that Dec would have found a way to save all the jobs at Infinity, but she was realizing that was just a silly dream. No matter how much revenue she found with new opportunities, jobs were going to have to be cut.

"John's out here for a visit. He played volleyball with Dec and Kell and Allan and apparently there was some discussion that involved you."

Cari wondered if he'd told his cousins about DJ. She could think of no other reason for the argument. She knew that Allan had already known they were dating, thanks to that conversation in her conference room.

She didn't have time to say anything else to her sisters as the door opened and in walked Kell Montrose. The first thing that Cari noticed about him was that his eyes were icy and hard. He looked over at the three of them with such disdain she felt a chill move over her. And Cari knew that this wasn't going to go the way she'd hoped it would.

Allan came in next, looking pensive and serious, and then came Dec. He didn't look at her or her sisters, and she nervously shuffled her presentation in front of her on the conference table.

Jessi reached underneath the table to pat her thigh and she squeezed her sister's hand before she cleared her throat.

"Before we get started, I'd like to tell you about some changes to our financial revenue streams," Cari said. "Would you allow me to do that?"

"We weren't expecting this," Kell said. "I doubt anything you could say at this point would change our plans."

"This is a significant addition to our bottom line and exceeds the targets I discussed with your CFO six weeks ago," Cari said. She might be a pushover where her staff was concerned, but she could be as tough as nails when it came to fighting for them.

Kell turned to Allan. "Did you give her financial targets?"

"Yes. They are aggressive and she wanted to figure out how to save more of her head count."

"We didn't discuss this," Kell said.

Cari was glad she wasn't Allan, as Kell looked like he wasn't too pleased with his cousin. "No offense, Cari, but I didn't think you had a chance of meeting them. I'd like to hear how you are going to do this."

Cari nodded to Jessi, who passed out the presentation that she'd prepared with the financial numbers. She led them through the financial statement, which showed a clear 25 percent increase in profit margin with the addition of a new game.

"But this is all theoretical," Kell said.

"No, it's practical," Cari retorted. "I have a demo of the game on my iPad if you'd like to play it."

"A playable demo?" Dec asked. "When did you have time to develop it?"

"We used an existing game skeleton and changed the assets to Christmas. I used the staff who were scheduled to develop a new game for the second quarter next year, as we aren't sure if we'll need a game then. They have really worked hard on it."

She handed the iPad over to Kell and all three of the men took a turn playing the demo before handing it back to Cari.

"I'm impressed. This is the kind of innovative thinking we reward at Playtone," Kell said.

"I'm glad to hear it," Cari said.

"Make sure that Dec has a list of everyone who was involved in this project," Kell said.

Cari nodded, and Dec smiled over at her. She felt good about the presentation, and she hoped it was enough to make Kell see that there was merit to this generation of Chandlers.

"Should we reconvene in a few weeks?" Emma asked. "Now that you've seen what else we are capable of?"

Kell shook his head. "No, this changes nothing of our current plans. Dec, please begin your presentation."

Emma paled and Cari felt a sinking feeling in her stomach as Dec stood up. "I've had copies of my report made and they will be available to you three after the meeting."

"Why not now?" Jessi asked.

"I don't want you reading ahead and reacting until I've had a chance to explain. The new revenue stream will be added to my revised report, but as Kell just said it really doesn't change much of what we already had planned.

"When I first came to Infinity Games I noticed there was a lot of redundancy between what we do here at Playtone and what you do. For example, we don't need two technical development directors, so that is one role I recommend we cut."

Cari felt the anger simmer inside her as Dec went on and on, talking about all the areas he thought should be cut. She heard him say that three-quarters of the staff should be kept on as they were hard workers and possessed "cutting-edge design knowledge." At least some of her people were going to make the cut.

"Finally, I'm sure it comes as no surprise that I am recommending we cut the executive staff of Infinity Games," Dec intoned in an emotionless voice. "Though Cari, Jessi and Emma all seem to work long hours and are viable in their roles, there is simply no need to keep them all on. Initially I was going to recommend cutting all three but over the past six weeks I've seen how much the staff at Infinity depends on Cari. She's their cheerleader, motivator and they all work harder when she asks them to. I think she's an asset as long as we keep the Infinity staff on and recommend keeping her in an operations-officer role."

Jessi jumped up and started talking but Cari didn't really hear a thing that her sister said. Instead she only heard what Dec said. Was he recommending keeping her because of their relationship? She couldn't keep her job if Emma and Jessi were both fired.

She stood up, pointed to Dec and motioned for him to step to the corner of the room. Her sisters were having a very heated discussion with Kell and Allan, but Cari was interested in only one person.

"What was that about?" she hissed when they were standing aside from the table.

"What do you mean?"

"Why keep me and not Jessi or Emma? We're all vital to the longevity of Infinity Games."

"You are because you're in the trenches with your staff. But the other two—"

"Stop it, Dec. The 'other two' are my sisters. We can't build a life together when you fired my sisters."

"We're not building a life together," Dec said.

"What have we been doing, then?"

"Hell, I didn't mean it like that," he said. "I couldn't save all three of you, Cari. Kell isn't happy that I recommended you stay on staff, but I told him that was the only option that I would agree to."

"I appreciate that. But you have no idea the kind of situation you've put me in," she said.

"It was always going to be impossible. I can't turn my back on my family," he said after a long minute had passed.

"I'm not asking you to. I'm asking you to think of our son."

"I am thinking of him, so don't try to blackmail me with that. He's on my mind as much as he's on yours."

"Yes, but your side of the family comes out looking like the victors. Do you think we can be happy when my sisters are angry? I'm mad, too."

"Be realistic. It's a better outcome than you could have hoped for."

"No," she said. "I showed you how we could keep working as we have been. I showed you how Infinity Games needs to stay as it is. I showed you everything I had and it seems to mean nothing to you."

"Infinity Games is no longer yours to decide. You're lucky we're even thinking of keeping any of the staff."

She shook her head as anger and hurt coalesced inside of her. "Of course you'd say that. You don't know how to stick around and see the devastation you leave behind you."

"I'm not running away this time," he said.

"Well, you might as well be," Cari said.

"Stop acting like this. It's business, not the end of the world. You can't operate a business based on emotion."

"You can't because you're the Tin Man and you have no heart. But I'm not like you, Dec. I love you. But I bet that doesn't even matter to you. You don't understand how love changes everything. How it makes you aware of all the people around you and the consequences of your actions. You said this won't affect me or DJ but it will.

"I've been a fool thinking you could change. I believed you were someone who would stay and build a future with me and our son, but I see now you were never interested in that. And as much as I appreciate you keeping my job, if my sisters go, then so do I."

She turned to step away from him and became aware of the others staring over at them. She saw the faces of her sisters, who had no doubt heard her talk about her son's parentage. Their eyes were wide, their mouths agape. She took a deep breath and blurted, "Yes, you heard right. Dec and I have a son together. Even though he abandoned us, I welcomed him back into our lives thinking he was a changed man, though I see now he is still consumed with an old family feud that has nothing to do with the present."

"I knew it," Jessi said.

"You knew it? Why didn't you say something?" Allan asked her. "Seems like that's the kind of information you'd run with."

"I just got the report from my P.I. this morning. I should have said I suspected it." She turned to Kell. "You can't fire your own nephew's aunts."

"The baby changes nothing," Kell said.

"It changes everything," Emma interjected. "We're all related now and we can't keep trying to tear each other apart. It's time to settle the feud."

"No," Kell said. "I'm not giving up on anything because Dec and Cari had a one-night stand. That's not a commitment. That's a mistake."

Cari cringed at his remark. "Was it a mistake, Dec?" Cari asked him.

Dec glanced at her, and the look in his eyes reminded her of an animal caught in a trap. He turned his back to her and faced his cousin. "Kell, enough of this nonsense."

"It's not nonsense. It's good business sense," Kell said.

"Good business sense doesn't rely on revenge,"

Emma said, walking over to Cari and putting her arm around her.

As her sisters led her out of the conference room, Cari looked back at Dec. He looked stone-cold, as if he didn't feel anything. So different from the man whose arms she'd slept in last night. She felt her heart breaking into a thousand pieces and knew this moment was the worst of her life.

She started to cry as they walked down the corridors of Playtone Games to the elevator, and she couldn't stop. She felt Jessi patting her shoulder and she knew she should try to compose herself, but it was impossible.

She'd let herself be fooled by Declan Montrose again. It was bad enough when he'd physically abandoned her after their night together, but nothing was as bad as this emotional abandonment. After he'd spent weeks pretending to care for her, letting her believe that there was some hope for them… Well, it was just cruel, and it cut her so deep she didn't feel like she'd ever recover from it.

The sun was a shocking glare when they got to the parking lot, and she stopped walking, unable to go any farther. Her sisters wrapped their arms around her and held her close, and she cried in a way she hadn't since her parents had died.

She felt as if all of the hopes and dreams she'd had for the future were gone and she wondered how she was going to pick up the pieces of this break and move on. She wanted more for DJ than the life she now knew he was going to have. But she knew there was no way that a man like Dec could be the father she wanted for her son when he couldn't be the man she needed him to be as her partner and lover.

* * *

Dec stood shell-shocked by Cari's words. He shouldn't be shocked, he told himself. He knew she loved him. She would never have let him back into her bed if she didn't love him. That much had been obvious to him from the beginning.

But hearing her say that she thought he was heartless and that he was still stuck in the past hurt him deeply. He'd done his best to walk the fine line between what he owed his family and what he wanted for himself.

"You have a son?" Allan asked, walking over to Dec.

"Yes. I didn't know about DJ until I got back here and saw Cari again," Dec said.

"You should have said something to us," Kell said.

"Why?" Dec asked. "It wouldn't have changed anything."

"You're right. We couldn't change the path we were on, but I would never have asked you to manage the takeover," Kell said.

Dec looked at his cousin for a minute before he shook his head. "I don't agree with everything that Cari said, but she does have a point that we can't move forward when we are still consumed with the past. This was never about Granddad for me. You know he and I weren't that close," he said.

"Then what was it about?" Kell asked.

"I liked the challenge, and you two are family. We're all each other has left—or *had* left until I found out about my son."

"Do you feel like that as well, Allan?" Kell asked.

"I'm not in this for revenge," Allan replied. "I mean, sure, Granddad got a raw shake—"

Kell interrupted his response. "Maybe you both don't remember that Gregory Chandler deliberately cut Thomas out of the business for his own personal gain. That's not a 'raw shake.'"

Obviously, Kell wasn't going to be reasonable about this, Dec thought. And the argument was heating up to be the same one he'd heard before. Countless times. Dec realized he didn't want to rehash any of this with Kell. He stepped toward the conference room door. "My mother never really wanted to be a part of this and I understand why now. I don't know what's going to happen with me and Cari, but I do know I'm going to go after her. She's the first person in my life that I truly love." He stopped and banged his fist against the door frame. "Dammit, I told you before I've had a chance to tell her."

"Go after her," Allan said, gesturing to the door. Allan had a sort of envious look on his face. "Kell and I will figure out a way to make this more of an acquisition and less of a demolition of Infinity Games."

"Speak for yourself, Allan," Kell said, his anger palpable in the room. Kell was never going to want to make peace with the Chandlers.

As far as Dec was concerned, he had lost two things today—his son and Cari—because he no longer wanted to be a Montrose and live under the mantle of hate that they'd all been raised under. He understood his mother so much better right now than he ever had before this moment.

As he stood in the doorway, he saw Allan get to his feet and stride around the table toward Kell.

"We're not kids anymore, Kell," Allan said in a soft but commanding voice. "You're the CEO because we voted you into that position. But remember who owns the majority of shares." He leaned down to his cousin. "You either back down on this and let us find something that will make the future better for all of us or you might find yourself defending your job at the next meeting."

Kell cursed savagely under his breath, balled his hands into fists and pounded the conference room table. "I can't do this right now." Then he stalked out of the conference room.

Dec just looked at Allan. "Why are you backing me? We're not blood."

Allan came over and squeezed his shoulder. "We are blood. And we always have been. Once Kell calms down, he'll realize that your son is the future of both of our game companies. That it's more than making sure that Thomas gets one up on Gregory. After all, his grandson is a Montrose."

Allan had a point. But Dec didn't really care about all that. He could only think of Cari. He had thought he would be able to appease her after the meeting, but he'd heard the heartache in her voice and he knew that there was no way he was going to be able to win her back easily.

Allan stepped out of the conference room to go find Kell and try to calm him down, but all Dec could do was sink into a chair and think about how much he loved Cari. Business, money and the Montrose name meant nothing to him if he didn't have her by his side.

He picked up his cell phone and saw on the screen the picture Cari had taken of him and DJ. She'd given him so much more than he could ever thank her for, and she deserved more from him. Something that would show her that he really had changed.

But grand gestures weren't his thing. He might be the man to force a change, but to woo someone he had no idea how to begin. He hoped that confessing his love for her would be a start, but he had a few other ideas, as well.

It would take some time to put his plan in motion, but that was okay; he wanted to leave nothing to chance. Last night when he'd held her and come up with his plan to save her job, he realized he'd been too narrow in his thinking. He and Cari were part of something bigger, and he knew that he was going to have to get her sisters on board before he went after her and won her back.

Fifteen

"Sorry about breaking down," Cari said later that night when she was ensconced on Emma's living room sofa. DJ and Sam were playing quietly on the floor and she felt a little more normal now that she'd had a pint of Ben & Jerry's One Sweet Whirled.

"You were entitled to," Jessi said. "I would have socked Dec if he'd done that to me."

Cari half smiled, but she didn't think that was amusing. "I don't want to talk about Dec. We should be thinking of a plan to ensure they have to keep the three of us on staff. I'm sure that if I have the finance department rework our new figures—"

"We don't want to talk business now," Jessi said, interrupting her. "We all heard you say that you loved Dec. What are you going to do about that now?"

"I don't know," she said. "I really thought he'd handle everything differently. I thought… Well, I guess that doesn't matter. I can't make him into any man other than the one he is. And I get why the takeover and being a Montrose is so important to him."

"Yeah," Jessi said. "He's adopted."

"How do you know?"

"I had him investigated. I sort of guessed that he was DJ's father, too."

"How?" Cari asked.

"The investigator talked to the staff at the Atlanta hotel where you stayed and found out that Dec had been there, too. The timeline worked out to make him the dad."

Cari nodded. She should have known Jessi would figure it out. She was like a dog with a bone when she got on something.

"I suspected that Dec might be DJ's father when you started dating him," Emma added. "You'd been so careful to keep every man away." She put her empty ice-cream pint on the coffee table next to Cari's and Jessi's.

"I wasn't planning to say anything about DJ to him," Cari said. From the moment she'd decided to have the baby, she'd realized she had only herself to depend on. And then Dec reappeared.

"What happened? You never really said too much about it," Jessi asked.

"It was just a crazy attraction and we ended up in bed. The next morning he was gone, and I felt stupid so I didn't try to get in touch with him. I mean, at first I didn't realize he was a Montrose," Cari said.

"So when you realized you were pregnant?" Emma asked. Her sisters were both watching her intently.

"He had been out of the picture for so long and I didn't really want him back in it. It was so overwhelming, you know?"

"If I had found out I was pregnant I'd be freaking out," Jessi said.

"So would I," Emma said with a wink.

"You should have told us, Cari. I would have been the one to liaise with Dec if I'd known."

"You couldn't have protected me from this, Em. No matter what we did in the office, once I heard his name I knew I had to tell him about DJ."

"Why?" Jessi asked. "He forfeited his rights when he walked away."

"Because he's DJ's father," Cari said. "And you know we love our parents no matter what. Remember how Dad was always trying to please Grandfather and Grandfather never had anything nice to say?"

"I sure do," Jessi said. "Okay, I see your point, but I think you should have let me go back in there and pop him one. He was definitely being an ass today."

"He was on the spot. His cousins wanted him to gut all of us and he must have felt torn. I should have gone easier on him," Cari said.

"No, you shouldn't have," Emma said. "It doesn't matter where he was coming from. He owed you the respect of talking to you before he went in there with his proposal. They have to worry about their bottom line, so I'm not saying he should have done anything differently as far as cutting Jess and me, but he shouldn't have sprung it on you the way he did."

She wasn't surprised to hear Emma defending both her and Dec. Emma had always been fair-minded and she understood the way that business worked. They all did. "I guess I was just hurt, and the anger from Kell was scary. I don't want my son to be related to them. They are all so hard."

"I agree," Jessi said. "Allan isn't as bad as Kell, but you could see that they were definitely all united."

Cari sighed. "I'm kind of mad at Grandfather for doing what he did—cutting Thomas Montrose out of the business. I wonder why he did it."

"I don't think we'll ever know. But you'll certainly have a good story for DJ when he's older about why we don't like his dad's family."

That made Cari sad. She knew she'd let anger get the better of her today and she wished now that she hadn't. She should never have stayed on in her role once Dec came into the picture. She was never going to be blasé where he was concerned. "I should have stepped aside."

"It's too late now. We just have to move on," Emma said. "I think the staff would go with us if we started a new company."

Cari shook her head. She didn't want to be part of a new feud with the Montrose cousins. One where she and her sisters were starting on the losing end. She'd sacrificed too much to the feud already and she was done with that.

"You don't think they would?" Emma asked. "Dang, I thought they were more loyal."

"They might, but then Playtone would come after us again. I don't want to keep fighting the same battle," Cari said. She looked over at her son and decided it was time to go home. She wanted to hold on to DJ and pretend that she hadn't stripped emotionally bare in front of Dec and he hadn't just left her standing there naked.

"I'm tired, girls. I think I'm going to head home. We can meet tomorrow to figure out our next moves."

"Are you okay to drive?" Jessi asked. There was concern in her voice and Cari wondered if her sister realized that a broken heart hurt worse than any other pain.

Then she remembered that despite that outer toughness Jessi had a really soft heart.

"Yes," Cari said. "I'll be fine."

She scooped DJ up off the floor and said good-night to her nephew. Once she was in her car and driving toward her home, she realized she didn't want to go back there tonight. She didn't want to sleep in a bed that smelled of Dec or walk through her own house that was now filled with memories of him.

She drove to the Ritz Carlton and checked in there, and as she lay in the king-size hotel bed, she thought about the last time Dec had left her and how long it had taken her to get over him. This time felt so much worse.

She ran a bath and then climbed in with her son; he played in the water and she realized that his little world hadn't changed. She envied him the fact that no matter what had happened today or in the past he wouldn't remember it.

It took Dec and Allan all afternoon to get Kell to agree to give Jessi and Emma a chance to prove their worth to the company.

"I'm not going to accept mediocrity from them," Kell warned.

"I don't care as long as they have a chance to prove themselves," Dec said. "It's really all we can do at this point." He looked at his cousins and let out a breath. "I'm going to need a few days off to win Cari back."

"She said she loved you, dude, I don't think it'll be that hard," Allan said.

"She said she felt like a fool for loving me," Dec reminded him. "I should never have let her walk out."

Kell got up, walked over to him and clapped his hand

on his shoulder. "You will win her back. What can we do to help?"

"You no longer care that she's a Chandler?"

"You have a son, Dec, and as you pointed out earlier, that changes everything."

Dec was glad to hear it. Kell might be stubborn, but eventually he'd acquiesced to what was right. "I want DJ to feel like a real Montrose."

"What does that mean?" Allan asked.

"Just that I never really felt like one. I was always aware I was adopted."

"To us you were always a Montrose. I don't want to hear you say that again," Kell said.

He was glad to hear that from his cousins; he felt the acceptance he'd always searched for was finally his. Now he needed to get Cari back, and then he'd be able to relax. There was only one way to do it. He had to prove to her he had roots.

He thought of his big mansion in Beverly Hills standing empty and he knew what he wanted to do. "I have to trade in the Maserati. Will you two do me a favor?"

"Why do you have to trade it in?"

"It's not a kid car," he said. Then he explained what he needed his cousins to help him do, and they were more than happy to do their part. He had the feeling that Kell still felt bad about his outburst of temper earlier. Dec wasn't too sure if they would succeed in doing everything that he asked, but he left them to go put his part of the plan in motion.

He went to the Porsche dealer and traded the Maserati in on a Cayenne and then drove to Cari's house as the sun was setting. He was surprised to find it empty. He called Cari's number, but the phone just went to voice mail. Damn. He didn't want to leave this rift between them any longer.

Now that he knew he loved her, he wanted his life with her to start right now. He finally called Allan and asked him to call John's wife and get Jessi's number. Thirty minutes later he had it. It was after nine, which was late, but not too late. Not when his future was at stake. He called the number.

"This is Dec. Can I speak to Cari?" he asked when Jessi answered the phone.

"She's not here. She went home, but I don't think she's in the mood to see you," Jessi said.

"I'm at her house and she's not here," Dec said, feeling a sense of real panic. What if she'd had an accident?

"What? Are you sure she's not just hiding from you?" Jessi asked.

"I'm positive. There is no one here and her car isn't in the driveway," Dec explained. He looked at that empty house and saw what he'd brought to her life. Maybe he should just respect her wishes and let her stay hidden from him. But he couldn't do that this time. The first time he could walk away because he hadn't let himself care, but this time he loved her too much. And he needed her back by his side.

"Let me see what I can find out," Jessi said after a long minute. "If I help you with this, you are going to owe me."

"Okay. I'll owe you a favor. But I can't do anything to stop the takeover," he warned her.

"That's okay. I'll think of something you can do for me. I'll call you back," she said.

"I'll be waiting."

Dec sat in the driveway of Cari's house for forty-five minutes before his phone finally rang.

"Yes?"

"She's at a hotel. She said she couldn't face sleeping in the bed she shared with you," Jessi said.

Her words cut him like a knife. He'd never meant to hurt her like that. "Where is she?"

"Why do you want to know?"

"Why do you think?"

"I think you want her back. That you realized that you screwed up. But I want to hear you say it," Jessi said.

"I screwed up," he admitted. "Now tell me where she is."

"Ritz Carlton in Marina del Rey. She checked in two hours ago. So she must have gone there straight from Emma's house," Jessi said.

"Thanks," he said, disconnecting the call. She was staying less than a mile from the yacht club where he lived. He wondered if she'd done it deliberately. But he was glad she was so close. He knew it was too late tonight to go to her room, but in the morning when she woke up… He finally had the right gesture to show her how much she meant to him.

He drove to the hotel and talked to the concierge. They wouldn't give him Cari's room number but they did agree to deliver his invitation to her. He went to the yacht but couldn't sleep, so he spent the night vacillating between excitement at seeing her in the morning and the very real fear that she might not accept his invitation or his apology.

The envelope sitting in front of her suite door was white and embossed with the Ritz Carlton seal, but when Cari looked at the front of the envelope she recognized the handwriting as Dec's. She slowly opened it and drew out the card inside.

> Please join me for breakfast on the *Big Spender* at slip number seven at the Marina del Rey Yacht Club this morning. I want a chance to apologize.
> Dec

It wasn't a wordy note, but she found she couldn't resist the chance to see him and hear what he wanted to say. To be honest, she'd had a miserable night and looked forward to a lifetime of lonely nights without Dec. If he wanted to apologize, then she wanted to hear it.

She got herself and DJ dressed after having the concierge send up outfits for them and drove over to the yacht club. She didn't need to ask directions to find Dec's yacht, as there was a trail of hearts with her name on them that led down the dock to the slip where she found the *Big Spender.* The gangplank was down and there were a trail of rose petals that led up to the deck, where they formed a huge heart.

"Hello?" she called out as she stepped on board.

"Hello," Dec said coming up the steps. He looked tired, as if he hadn't slept a wink the night before. He came over to her as soon as he saw her and took her into his arms. He kissed DJ on the head and then he kissed Cari on the lips.

"I love you," he said. The words hung in the air and he felt naked in front of her. For the first time he realized why Cari hadn't tried harder to contact him. She must have felt this fear when she thought of trying to get the man who'd fathered her son involved in her baby's life. The life of the child she loved so much.

She started to speak but he put his finger over her lips to keep her from saying anything. He couldn't let her tell him all the reasons why she didn't love him. He knew he'd screwed up yesterday and that it was going to take him forever to win her back. But he was okay with that.

"Yesterday morning when we left your place I knew it was going to be a difficult day. I also knew there was no way I could fire you and ask you to be my wife. And that's what I wanted, Cari. I don't know how things got so out of control."

"I think it was your cousin," Cari said. "He wants our blood. But it was also us. I wanted you to stop thinking like a businessman and just do what I wanted in my heart. And I made the meeting and the outcome into a big test."

"First, Kell did want your blood. But I said things to you I shouldn't have," he said. "You were right when you said that things are different now that we have a son. Everything changed for me the night you told me about DJ, and I was too afraid to admit it."

"I said things I shouldn't have, too. I was just so mad," she admitted.

She tipped her head to the side and stared up at him, and he saw tears in the corners of her eyes. "I love you, too. I want us to be a family, but I don't know how we can do that with the feud still going on."

"I agree," he said, cupping her face in his hands and using his thumbs to wipe away her tears. He hugged her close. "Business first so you can stop worrying about that. Kell, Allan and I have agreed to give your sisters a chance to prove they should keep their positions in the company. It's no guarantee for their jobs, but it's better than nothing. And Kell has agreed to be more civil from now on."

"That's a start," Cari said, wrapping her arms around his waist and resting her head on his chest. And finally he felt like there was a chance he might be able to really win her back.

"Did you mean it when you said you loved me?" she asked in a quiet voice.

"Yes, I did. I know you thought I didn't have a heart, and you're right. I don't have a heart because it belongs to you," he said.

"I love you, too, Dec. All those hearts that led the way to you…thank you for that," she said. "No one has ever done a big gesture like that for me. You make me feel special."

He leaned down and kissed her. "You are so special to me. I'm afraid to tell you how much you mean to me. I don't want you to have that kind of power over me, but no matter if I say the words or not, you still have it."

The tears were back in her eyes and she hugged him so fiercely that he felt the strength of her love.

"I want you to be my wife. I want to get married as soon as we can and start to live like a real family."

"I want that, too," she admitted. "It's the one thing I've wanted since we had dinner that first night you were back. I didn't want to believe that you could be the man of my dreams, but you are that and more."

"I hope I can live up to that, Cari," he said. "I'm going to make every effort to be that man. In fact, after we eat breakfast I have a surprise for you."

"Another one?"

"A few more," he said with a smile. He led the way to a table set up for breakfast for the three of them and when it was over he led them off the yacht to a Porsche

Cayenne—a family-style SUV that was the car of a man with a family, not a man who rode alone.

"This is my new car," he said, gesturing to the vehicle and the baby car seat in the rear bench. "I'm serious about sticking around and sharing my life with you."

She believed it. And she learned something else about the man she loved. When he made up his mind about something, he did it all the way. No half measures for Dec. He drove through the morning rush-hour traffic to Beverly Hills but wouldn't tell her where they were going. He stopped to send a text message, and they sat in the car holding hands while he waited to get a response. When it finally came he put the car in gear.

"Close your eyes," he said.

When she did as he'd asked, he turned the car down a residential street and a few minutes later he put the car in Park. "Don't open them yet."

She heard him get out of the car, come around to get DJ out of the backseat and then open her door.

He held her hand and helped her out of the car. "I've got DJ. You stay right here for a moment."

He left her standing in the midmorning sun; she thought she heard voices but couldn't identify them.

Dec was back by her side, alone, and he lifted her into his arms. He kissed her long and slow and when he lifted his head, he said, "Open your eyes."

She did, and saw a huge mansion with a banner tied to the front. For her and for all the world to see, it read: Cari, Please Help Me Fill This House with Love and Make It Our Home.

She hugged him close and buried her face in his neck, just breathing in the scent of this man she loved so very much.

"Yes, I will do that," she said.

"Good. I've already started by inviting our family over," he said.

Her eyes widened with surprise. She wasn't sure he'd really said what she thought she'd heard, but as he carried her over the threshold she saw that Kell, Allan, Emma, Sam and Jessi were all there, along with their son. Their families didn't look like bosom buddies, but they were all being civil.

DJ clapped his hands together. "Mama, Dada."

He crawled over to them as Dec put her on her feet. Cari bent down to pick up her son, knowing she'd gotten everything she could have wished for in love and life.

* * * * *

ONE NIGHT HEIR

BY
LUCY MONROE

Lucy Monroe started reading at the age of four. After going through the childrens' books at home, she was caught by her mother reading adult novels pilfered from the higher shelves on the bookcase... Alas, it was nine years before she got her hands on a Mills & Boon Romance her older sister had brought home. She loves to create the strong alpha males and independent women who people Mills & Boon books. When she's not immersed in a romance novel (whether reading or writing it), she enjoys travel with her family, having tea with the neighbours, gardening and visits from her numerous nieces and nephews.

Lucy loves to hear from her readers: e-mail LucyMonroe@LucyMonroe.com, or visit www.LucyMonroe.com

In sincerest gratitude to my readers, who have stuck with me through the droughts brought on by my mom's final illness and subsequent death, my own health issues and the many other challenges life offers us mortals. Your support and encouragement mean so very much to me and have blessed me truly beyond measure. Love and hugs to you all!

With particular thanks to Ms Gillian Wheatley of London for suggesting visual inspiration for my hero. XOXO

The necessary legal caveat: while Ms Wheatley shares a first name with the female protagonist in this book, Gillian Harris is not fashioned after her or based on Ms Wheatley in any way. Any similarities are purely coincidental and unintentional by the author.

CHAPTER ONE

FURY RIDING HIM like an angry stallion, Crown Prince Maksim of Volyarus let loose with a punch-cross-hook kickboxing combo against his cousin and sparring partner.

Demyan blocked, and the sound of flesh hitting pads mixed with his grunt of surprise. "Something the matter, your highness?"

Maks hated when his cousin, older by four years and raised as a brother with Maks in their family's palace, referred to him by his title.

Demyan was well aware, but the older man liked pushing buttons, especially during their workout sessions. He said it made the sparring more intense.

Today would have been sufficiently punishing without the added irritation. Not that Maks warned Demyan of that. His cousin deserved what he got.

"Nothing wiping the smug look off your face won't take care of." Maks danced back before driving forward with another fast-paced, grueling combo.

Well-matched in stature and strength, they both kept their six-feet-four-inch frames in top physical condition.

"I thought tonight was the big night with Gillian," Demyan said, scrambling in a way he rarely did during their sessions. "Don't tell me you think she's going to turn you down?"

"If I were going to ask, she'd say yes." And a day ago that certainty had given Maks a great deal of pleasure.

Now, it just taunted him with what he couldn't have. Namely, Gillian.

"So, what is the problem?" Demyan demanded as he went on the offensive, forcing Maks to defend against a barrage of punches and kicks.

"Her medical tests came back."

"She's not sick, is she?" Demyan asked, sounding sincerely concerned.

Coming from a man with a reputation for cold ruthlessness, it would have shocked anyone else.

But Maks knew how much Demyan cared about their family. And for the last eight months, the beautiful, sweet Gillian had been moving closer and closer to joining that group.

"She's perfectly fine." If you didn't count poorly functioning ovaries. "Now."

"What does that mean?"

"She had appendicitis when she was sixteen."

"That was ten years ago, what bearing does it have on her health now?"

"Fallopian tubes."

Demyan stopped and stared at Maks in confusion. "What?"

In no mood to give his cousin a break, Maks took

advantage of the other man's inattention and knocked him on his ass with a well-timed kick.

Demyan jumped to his feet, but he didn't come back for more like Maks expected. "Knock it off and explain what the hell appendicitis as a teenager has to do with an adult woman's fallopian tubes."

Demyan was no idiot. He knew Maks's interest in Gillian's reproductive system was of paramount importance to the House of Yurkovich, the royal family of Volyarus.

"She has a poorly functioning reproductive system." Maks adjusted his thin sparring gloves. "There is less than a thirty percent chance of pregnancy."

A lot less by some estimations, slightly more by others, according the specialist Maks had consulted.

Demyan shoved hair the same dark color as Maks's own off his forehead. "With fertility treatment?"

"I have no intention of becoming the next father of sextuplets."

"Don't be an ass."

"I'm not. You know I cannot marry a woman who won't be able to produce the next heir plus a spare."

Demyan didn't reply immediately. They were both too personally aware of the costs associated with those issues.

"You aren't your father. You don't have to marry a woman you don't love in order to provide an heir."

"I have no intention of doing so. Neither will I marry a woman I like whose only hope of providing that child would be via often painful and not always successful fertility treatments."

"You could adopt."

"Like my parents adopted you?"

"They didn't formally adopt me. I am still a Zaretsky. It was never your father's intention that I inherit the throne."

"You were just his spare," Maks muttered with some bitterness.

Demyan shrugged. "Duty is duty."

"And my duty precludes asking Gillian Harris to marry me." His personal sense of honor also dictated he break things off with her as soon as possible.

"You don't love her?" Demyan asked with only mild curiosity.

"You know better."

"Love only leads to pain," Demyan quoted one of Maks's mother's favorite refrains.

Maks added the rest. "And a compromise on duty."

Both men had reason to believe it, too.

"What are you going to do?" Demyan asked, dropping back into a sparring stance.

Maks executed a simple forward jab-left hook combo. "What do you think?"

"I'll miss her."

Maks didn't doubt it. One of the reasons he'd decided to ask Gillian to marry him was that despite her mostly small-town upbringing, she got along surprisingly well with his family and successfully navigated social situations many would find overwhelming.

The daughter of a renowned world news correspondent, Gillian had been attending events with the world's richest and most powerful since a young age.

Demyan blocked Maks's kick and returned one of his own. "Are you going to tell her tonight?"

"I may not need to." The lovely blue-eyed blonde would have gotten a copy of the results of her latest physical.

Gillian would know about the reasons behind her irregular menses now as well. She already knew the responsibilities associated with his position. She should be expecting the dissolution of their relationship.

A more practical woman than most, he had hopes there would be no awkward "breakup" scene.

"Yes, Nana, I think tonight's the night," Gillian said into the phone mashed to her ear with her shoulder as she hopped around the room trying to get her shoes on.

"Has he told you he loved you yet?" Evelyn Harris, Gillian's nana and the woman who had raised her, asked.

"No."

"Your grandfather has told me every night before we go to sleep for the last forty-eight years that he loves me."

"I know, Nana." But Maks was different.

He held his emotions in check like it was a royal imperative, and ever the dutiful prince, he obeyed. They came out when he was making love, though. After a fashion.

Maks made love with the single-minded intensity of a man who was thinking of nothing else but pleasing and getting lost in the woman who shared his bed.

For the past seven months, that woman had been Gillian.

They'd dated a month before he took her to bed the first time. She'd found that odd at the time, considering his reputation, but later she'd realized that, as unbelievable as it might seem, Maks was looking for more from her than a casual bed partner.

And while she'd been more thrilled than shocked, she'd been stunned all the same.

She didn't belong in his circle. She was not rich, famous, or powerful, but Gillian's father still liked to see her when he was in town. That inevitably meant going to some function or other on his arm. He couldn't dedicate time simply to visiting her, so he included Gillian in his schedule.

As the famous news correspondent's unremarkable daughter, Gillian had attended more than her fair share of diplomatic and high society events.

No one had been more shocked than she when it turned out that Crown Prince Maksim Yurkovich of Volyarus seemed to *like* unremarkable. Several comments made by him, and a couple by his mother on the few occasions Gillian had met the queen, had made it clear that royalty did not look for notoriety when choosing a mate.

Though regardless, she would have thought Maks would be looking for someone with more personal cache than Gillian to bring into the royal family. Apparently Volyarussians did not have the same requirements for pedigree in a mate than other royal families of the world.

And there couldn't be anyone less notorious than the small-town girl from Alaska who made her living as what her father termed a "chocolate-box" photographer.

There was nothing objectionable, or even questionable in Gillian's past. Her parents hadn't stayed together and neither had been interested in raising her, but they'd entered into a short businesslike marriage prior to her birth and hadn't filed for divorce until a year after.

"I may as well hang up now, your mind is clearly in the clouds again, child," Nana said over the phone line.

Gillian shoved her blond hair behind her ear and adjusted the phone. "I'm sorry, Nana. I didn't mean to—"

"I know. You get to thinking about Maks and the rest of your brain shuts off, especially the part attached to your ears."

"It's not that bad."

Her grandmother's snort said the older woman did not agree. "You make that boy tell you that he loves you before you agree to be his wife."

"He's hardly a boy, Nana." Gillian had made the same protest before, but to little effect.

"I'm seventy-five years old, Gillian. He's a boy to me."

"Some people never say those words," Gillian pointed out, returning to the subject she knew her grandmother considered most important.

"Some people have less sense than God gave a gnat then."

"Rich doesn't say it, but he loves me." Even as she said the words, Gillian knew she wasn't actually certain that they were *true*.

Her father wasn't an affectionate or demonstrative man. Rich Harris had made little more than a moderate effort to be part of her life, but he'd also been the one to make sure she had two people to raise her who loved and cared for her. The two dear people who had raised him.

"Your daddy is an idiot, no matter what those Pulitzer Prize people say."

Gillian laughed, knowing her grandmother didn't mean the words. Nana was hugely proud of her world famous son and still held out the hope that one day he would take on the role of Gillian's father.

That ship had sailed a long time ago, but Gillian would never say so to the older woman.

She owed too much to Nana to hurt her in any way. "Don't you let him hear you say that. He'll take back the motor home."

"I'd like to see him try. I still have a wooden spoon and I'm not afraid to use it."

Gillian couldn't help more laughter at that. Nana'd had the same fabled wooden spoon all the years of her growing up, too, but her backside had never felt the flat side of it.

"I swear, I don't know what makes that boy of mine think like he does."

"He's fine, Nana. His dreams didn't include having a family. That doesn't make him bad."

"Well, he has a daughter, whether he dreamed you up or not."

"I know." She'd spent her whole life knowing that while she had not been precisely wanted, both her parents had given her the gift of life and that was as far as the sacrifice was ever going to go.

"I don't like to see you settling," Nana said in that tone Gillian hated.

It was the I-worry-about-you-child-I-really-do tone and it came five minutes before Nana decided she needed to give up whatever adventure she and Papa were on to fly back to Seattle and check in on her granddaughter.

"I'm fine, Nana. Better than fine." She was on the verge of getting engaged to the man she loved with her whole heart. "I don't need the words."

And she didn't. She needed the actions. She needed Maks to put her first, to treat her like she mattered and he did that. His life was both high-profile and extremely busy, but Maks didn't cancel dates, he didn't show up late, and he didn't dismiss her interests or her career as a studio photographer.

"Hmmph."

That sound was almost as concerning as the older woman's tone earlier. It implied that Nana would be having a talk with Maks.

Gillian sighed. The man would have to be strong

enough to withstand a talking-to, or ten, if they were going to be married.

"Are you and Papa enjoying Vegas?" she asked, hoping to turn to the topic.

"He lost money at the blackjack tables, but I won on the slots." The glee in her grandmother's tone brought a smile to Gillian's face.

"Is Rich still meeting you two for dinner next week?"

"He hasn't *texted* us to cancel." Nana's lack of fondness for texting came through in the way she said the word.

"Good."

"I suppose we'll have good news to tell him."

"I think so." The doorbell rang. "That's him, I've got to go."

"You call us tomorrow, you hear?"

"Yes, Nana." With news.

Smiling, Gillian rushed to answer the door summons. Her gaze fell on the manila envelope with the results from her latest physical. She hadn't read it yet, but didn't expect anything surprising.

Gillian had her physical yearly, something her father had insisted on since she'd nearly died from appendicitis at the age of sixteen. She chose to see it as proof of affection he never gave voice to.

Maks looked serious and devastatingly attractive in his black Armani suit as Gillian pulled the door open.

She smiled up at all six feet four inches of muscular male towering confidently in her doorway. "You're early."

"And yet you are ready. You are no ordinary woman, Gillian Harris." He didn't return her smile, but his espresso-brown eyes traveled down her body like a caress.

He always did that, making her feel like all the super models in the world wouldn't take his attention from her decidedly normal blond hair, blue eyes, average height and curves.

She stepped back to let him in. "Nana didn't stand for tardiness."

"And here I believed you were so eager to see me, you could not wait to get dressed," he teased.

She grinned up at him. "That, too."

He lowered his head and kissed her, his lips brushing hers in polite greeting. She returned the kiss, letting her mouth open just slightly because she liked the feel of their breath mingling.

He made an inarticulate sound and deepened the kiss, pulling her body flush to his as he maneuvered them back into her apartment. As so often happened when they kissed, time stopped moving for her and the only thing her consciousness registered was the feel of his lips on hers and his hard body so close.

When he pulled back, they were both breathing a little heavily.

His dark gaze fell to the manila envelope by the door. She'd opened it, but the phone call had come in from Nana before she could skim the contents. She wasn't worried, though. At twenty-six, she was young. She lived a healthy lifestyle and showed no signs of illness.

Nana would chastise her nonetheless. It was a good thing the older woman was in Las Vegas.

"You got your results." There was a curiously flat quality to Maks's tone.

She nodded and led the way into the living room. "Would you like something to drink before we go?"

"I'll take a shot of Old Pulteney, if you have it."

"You know I do." She'd kept the twenty-one-year-old single malt whiskey on hand since he'd admitted to it being his drink of choice.

Gillian poured Maks two fingers in a rock glass, no ice, and handed it over.

"Thank you." He took a larger sip than usual.

She smiled, charmed by the evidence of nervousness in a man so completely self-assured.

"You never told me you had appendicitis when you were sixteen."

"You never asked." He'd seen the scar, faded and small though it was.

She was surprised it had been mentioned in her health report, though. His doctor had obviously done a much more thorough examination than her own GP for this physical. She wasn't surprised in the least that Maks had read the report with such attention to detail, though. That was very much like him.

Maks frowned and took a sip of his drink.

Not sure why having had appendicitis was worth a frown, Gillian poured club soda over ice and added a slice of lime, her drink of choice. Maybe Maks was like her father and responded strongly to the knowledge she'd almost died.

When Rich visited her in the hospital, it was the one and only time Gillian had seen overt concern for her on his movie star handsome face.

Her father never appreciated the reminder that he'd been vulnerable to worry for her and she assumed Maks would be the same, so she didn't comment on it, but asked instead, "Where are we going for dinner?"

He'd said he wanted to take her somewhere special. Combined with the fact he'd asked for the results of her yearly physical and that his own GP perform it, she was pretty confident that tonight was supposed to end in a proposal.

One she had no intention of turning down.

She loved him wholly and completely. She'd never told him, either. She hadn't admitted *that* to Nana, but the words had turned out surprisingly difficult for Gillian to utter.

"Chez Rennet."

It was the first restaurant he'd ever taken her to. No, he hadn't said the words, but Maks had a romantic streak he wasn't that great at hiding.

"Terrific. I love Rennet's food." The chef and owner had a soft spot for both her and Maks as well.

Dining in his restaurant was always pleasurable and Gillian took that as further evidence Maks wanted tonight to be special.

"I know you do." Again that serious look.

And it finally clicked. Tonight *was* a serious night,

an evening that would culminate in the kind of conversation she was sure Maks only planned to have once in his life.

She hadn't been nervous before, but knowing how important tonight was to him brought a flock of humming birds to take up residence inside Gillian.

She was getting engaged to a prince, and for the first time, she really thought about what it would be like to be a princess.

The prospect was more than a little daunting.

Nana had always said Gillian ignored what she did not want to deal with and she'd done a fair job of that while dating Maks, but his somber demeanor tonight forced her to evaluate what his proposal would mean to both of them.

Ultimately, however, it didn't matter.

She would have given up the creature comforts of civilization and moved to Antarctica to be with him.

Taking on the role of princess and living at least half the year in the Baltic island country of Volyarus would not be allowed to frighten her.

She loved him, Maks the man.

She could and would live with Maksim of the House of Yurkovich, Crown Prince of Volyarus.

CHAPTER TWO

DINNER WAS WONDERFUL. Although the solemn air never left Maks, he charmed Gillian with his usual urbanity.

There were several times he seemed on the verge of discussing something important, but he never followed through.

This further proof of a nervousness she never would have expected beguiled Gillian. She found herself falling just that much more in love with the man of her dreams as the evening wore on.

After dinner, he took her to listen to live jazz, one of her favorite things. The band was made up of musicians who had been around long enough they understood the music and how to live it, not just play it.

Relaxing, she was even relieved that the music prevented discussion, and the odd pressure she'd felt Maks was under seemed to lighten.

Afterward, she asked him back to her apartment and as expected, he accepted.

He'd taken her coat and laid it over the back of one of her club chairs, but stood as if not knowing what came next. It was so unlike him that she took pity and suggested another drink.

"I'd better not."

"You don't have to drive. Not if you don't want to." She offered her bed for the night in a similar oblique fashion to how she'd done on numerous occasions before.

He usually took her up on it, only refusing when he had early morning meetings or travel plans that would require him leaving in the wee hours and disturbing her rest.

So, it surprised her when he hesitated now. "Do you think that's a good idea?"

Did he think she wanted to spend less time with him with marriage in the offing? She wasn't going to pretend sexual innocence for the tabloids once their relationship went public. Though she appreciated the fact he'd kept it under wraps thus far, at some point in the very near future, everyone would know about them.

And she did not mind, but she would not pretend, either.

"Yes," she said firmly.

"We need to talk."

"After." Suddenly she knew she wanted words of love spoken between them, even if they only came from her before he proposed.

She would tell him while they made love. He could propose after.

Yearning she would not think of denying darkened his espresso gaze. "You are certain this is a good idea?"

"Yes." She wasn't sure where the need came from, but she could not bear the thought of agreeing to marry him without admitting her feelings for him.

If only with her body, then so be it, but she would express her love for him tonight and she had hope the words would make it past her lips as well.

Need did not make those three small words any easier to say. She could no more simply blurt them out than she could dance naked on a table at *Chez Rennet*.

While her grandparents had told Gillian they loved her and accepted the words in return, it wasn't daily like her nana claimed her papa did with her. And Gillian had only ever said the words to her own parents when she was younger.

Neither had ever returned them and she could not remember the last time she'd had the courage to speak her love for the absentee adults in her life. She'd never spoken them to another man, but then she'd never been in love before, either. Her heart wasn't so easy to reach.

With Maks, she had the option of showing him physically what she felt so strongly emotionally. He would *know* she loved him at the end of this night. One way or another.

He shook his head. "You are a very different sort of woman, aren't you?"

She didn't think so, but she liked the way he looked at her like she was something special, so she didn't deny it. And really, wasn't he supposed to think she was extraordinary? Their future would be rather grim if she was just like any other woman to him.

She certainly considered Maks a man above all others.

Maks took her hand and tugged her toward the hall that led to her bedroom. "Come. I have a mind to make love to you in comfort."

They'd been intimate in the living room many times, but she didn't mind him considering this time important and special. Maybe he found the words just as difficult to speak, but this was his way of showing how much he cared, too.

Regardless of his reasoning, her heart beat a rapid rhythm as she let him lead her into the darkened bedroom. Maks dropped her hand before crossing to the small table and turning on the lamp. Made of bronze and fashioned like a statue, the clump of three calla lilies had bulbs in each of the glass flowers that cast a soft golden glow over the room.

He'd given her the painting of a blonde woman standing with her head bowed in a field of the same blooms hanging on the wall above it. Maks had said it reminded him of her.

She thought the painting far too ethereal to have her likeness, but she loved it.

He turned to face her now, his chiseled features set in somber lines. "You give me a great gift." He sighed, releasing some great burden. "I needed this."

She smiled, her emotions choking her but still not rising to her lips to say aloud.

He seemed to understand because he came back to her and pulled her into a passionate kiss that let them both get lost for a little while. They were breathing heavily when their mouths separated and she was wrapped securely in his arms.

"You are a very good kisser."

"Or you are," he teased, more like his normal self.

"You're the one with all the experience." She hadn't been a virgin when they met, but she might as well have been for all her experience.

Two different fumbling attempts during her university days at intimacy that ended in dismal failure and none of the pleasure she found in his arms had left her with no real practical experience at pleasing a partner.

Maks had never minded and had always been extremely patient and *happy even* to teach her the joys of two bodies coming together when real attraction existed on both sides.

"We are good together like this." He sounded almost sad about that.

But he had nothing to be sad about, so she had to be misreading that tone in his voice. Or was he one of those men who believed that marriage meant sex went by the wayside?

She'd show him otherwise if he was.

She was a twenty-first-century woman who believed that not only were women *supposed* to enjoy sex, but that it belonged very firmly and frequently in the marriage bed.

She didn't say any of that, but concentrated on divesting him of his suit. He helped by toeing off his shoes and socks and yanking his dress shirt over his head once his tie had been loosened and the top few buttons undone.

"Eager, aren't you?" she teased.

"You have no idea." He nearly ripped her dress getting it off, her bra and panties disappearing with none of his usual finesse or time spent on visual appreciation for her preference for matching lace.

They were naked moments later. He looked at her then, his brown eyes eating her up with hot hunger.

She could feel her body's response to that look, her nipples tightening even more than they already were, her inner walls contracting with the need to be filled by his hard sex.

Heat suffused her from her toes all the way up her limbs, sending a blush of desire over her cheeks and shivers of emotionally laced physical need quaking through her.

They'd barely touched and she wanted sex with this man in this moment more than she'd ever wanted anything or another man, Maks included. Knowing this intimacy was the prelude of a lifetime together increased her passion in ways she would never have expected.

The expression in his eyes said he was similarly affected. Maks looked desperate with his need to be with her.

Without thought, she stepped into his arms and it felt so right when he lifted her like a bride and carried her to the bed. He managed to yank back the covers and top sheet without dropping her.

She helped by wrapping her arms around his neck.

Not so helpful were the small, exploratory kisses she placed along his jaw and down his neck. She stopped to inhale where his neck met his shoulder.

The subtle fragrance of his Armani cologne mixed with his own masculine scent triggering a reflexive response in Gillian's core that she could not stop, even if she had wanted to. And she didn't.

She loved the feel of her body preparing itself for his possession, reveled in the reaction that was primal and visceral to things like his smell and as simple a touch as his hand brushing down her hip as he laid her on the mattress.

"You are all that I want," he whispered in her ear. "If only..."

She didn't know if only what. In that moment, could not begin to care. His hands were moving over her, bringing her pleasure unlike anything she'd ever known.

Even at his touch.

There was such profundity in that moment, she did not see how their wedding night could possibly be any better or more special.

She touched him, too, mapping his body with her hands, loving the feel of his muscles, the tickle of his chest hair against her fingertips.

This amazing man, who was literally a prince and business tycoon rolled into one, belonged to her and as difficult as she might find that to believe, the proof was in her position. Naked, in bed with him, free to caress his masculine body as she liked.

"You and Demyan keep yourselves in amazing shape," she opined happily.

Maks's face twisted at the mention of his cousin's name. Another time she would have asked about that, but not tonight.

What they were doing was too important. What she was doing was life-altering, especially if she could force those three all-important words out of her voice box.

"Our sparring was rough today," Maks said, as if he realized she might wonder at his reaction.

She brushed her fingertip over a bruise she'd just noticed. "It looks like it."

"That is nothing," Maks said with his typical arrogance and pride that would never admit Demyan may have gotten the better of him in the sparring ring.

His cousin was hard to get to know, but the older man and Maks were close. She liked knowing he had a friend he could trust. Maks didn't live in a world where trust or even trustworthiness came in great supply. Gillian understood that world; she'd been on the edges of it because of her father for her whole life.

She leaned forward and kissed the discolored skin, then the area all around it.

Maks groaned. "I like."

She knew he did. He loved being pampered, even in bed. He gave as good as he got, though, so she never minded giving either.

He rolled her onto her back and came over her, his big body covering hers both sensually and protectively.

Maks looked down into her eyes, his own dark with emotion. "You are so perfect for me. Too perfect."

She just shook her head. Didn't he know there could be no too much about it?

He kissed her like he didn't want to discuss it. Like he couldn't bear not kissing her one more second. Like she belonged to him wholly and completely.

She kissed him back with her heart on her lips, because she did.

He pressed her into the mattress, the kiss going on and on and on, increasing intensity with every passing minute until the fire blazing between them was plasma hot.

All thought and feeling outside the pleasure their bodies brought to one another disintegrated in its path.

Wanting him inside her, *now,* Gillian spread her legs in invitation.

Instead of accepting, Maks moved back, breaking the kiss. "Not yet."

"Yes," she demanded.

But he shook his head, the expression in his eyes both feral and intense. He began to touch her again, this time with the clear and express purpose of driving her insane with delight.

He found the spot on her foot that made her shiver with need and the area of her inner thigh that made her ache to be filled. He caressed the curve of her waist and moved up to give careful attention to her breasts, licking and laving, kneading and playing until her nipples hurt with the need to be touched, too.

Only then did he put his mouth over one engorged tip and bite lightly.

She cried out, a mini orgasm going off inside her.

He let out a dark chuckle and sucked her nipple while her body writhed under him of its own volition. He pinched her other nipple between his thumb and fore-finger before brushing it featherlightly with his thumb. He did this over and over again as she moaned for more.

She was begging with her body and a few inarticulate "Pleases" by the time he pressed her thighs wide and surged inside her without a condom for the first time.

The thought they could be making a child increased her ecstasy to the point that her entire body convulsed with climax on his first initial thrust.

He didn't slow down and she didn't ask him to. He kept surging in and out of her, building pleasure that never actually slipped into lassitude until she came for the second time, her contractions so harsh, the rigidity of her body thrust him upward.

He never lost his position inside her, though, and shouted with pure male triumph when he came.

He looked down at her, his expression so intent, it sent aftershocks quivering through her. "Thank you."

She shook her head, no words coming out. Not even the three she wanted so badly to say, but then maybe they weren't necessary. After that, he had to know how she felt. She had no doubts about his feelings for her. A man could not make love to a woman with that level of passion and feel none of the finer emotions.

"I should have asked. About the condom."

"No. It's all right." They didn't need barriers between them.

He nodded, his expression somber as he moved to lie beside her. "I would like to spend the night. May I?"

"Yes." She wasn't sure why he felt the need to ask, but then maybe it was that kind of moment.

So much, it deserved proper consideration.

Gillian woke wrapped in Maks's strong arms. She could tell by his breathing that he was already awake.

Suddenly the words that had been impossible to utter were on the tip of her tongue. She sat up and looked at him in the morning light diffused by her bedroom curtains. "I love you, Maks."

How easy had that been? The words had practically said themselves, but she found she wasn't comfortable maintaining eye contact. Particularly when his were showing evidence of shock at her announcement.

How could he not have known? How could her words possibly come as a surprise to him after everything? Or was it her timing?

She'd never uttered those words to another man, didn't know if there were protocols in Maks's world that dictated they get said after morning greetings.

That sounded ridiculous, but it wouldn't be the first aspect to the life of a royal that she found so. It was a good thing she did love him, or she'd never consider spending her life in that kind of weirdly orchestrated fishbowl.

She tucked back down into bed, snuggling against him. “I could get used to this.”

“It is too bad we cannot.”

She heard the words, but they didn’t make sense, so they didn’t register.

Her mind was still on the night before and how unburdened she felt after making her confession this morning. Even if it had been awkwardly done.

At least he hadn’t laughed at her.

That was one of the nice things about Maks. He never mocked another person’s lack of aplomb, even though he never seemed short of suaveness.

“Last night was amazing,” she offered.

“Yes.” His tone was so serious and almost unhappy.

She didn’t understand why.

Maybe he was tired. He had been very energetic throughout the night. Honestly, she wasn’t sure she’d survive if every night was as passionate as the one before, wonderful as it had been.

They hadn’t gone to sleep after the first time making love, but had come together three more times throughout the night. Maks had never been so insatiable. She’d never felt such freedom to respond.

He’d been voracious, both for touching her and being inside of her. And she’d loved every second of it.

Her body twinged delightfully at the reminders of how hungry he had been.

“I am sorry.” If anything, Maks’s tone had grown heavier.

As much as she'd prefer to pretend she didn't know why he'd apologized, she could not.

But she *could* tell him that it didn't matter. She didn't need Maks to admit love for her so long as he needed her like he'd shown he did the night before.

"It's all right." Gingerly, keeping a lid on her own disappointment, Gillian sat up and met Maks's gaze.

His expression was stoic, like a man trying to pretend something didn't bother him. "No. Last night was a mistake, I think."

Then he winced as if he realized he should not have said that.

And well he might wince, the idiot. She wasn't going to demand words of love, but downplaying the night before wasn't going to fly with her, either.

Suddenly she had a thought that might explain his odd attitude. "You want to pretend we don't have sex?"

And did that bother him as much as she thought it did? As much as it absolutely appalled her?

"As wonderful as we are together, it will not be a pretense. It cannot. It would not be fair to you, or to me, if I am honest."

Her brows drew together. "I don't understand. You want to stop having sex?"

Until they were married? A royal wedding required at least a year, often two to prepare for. No wonder he'd been so hungry the night before.

But why forego condoms? Did he hope to have gotten her pregnant so they were forced to marry more quickly?

That just didn't seem like something Maks would do. He was not a master of passive aggressive. Full-on aggression was more his style.

"Continuing to have sex together will only make our eventual breakup all the harder, not to mention increasing the chances of the media picking up on our relationship. We've been lucky so far, they've left us alone."

Gillian thought that had something to do with her father's influence as much as how circumspect she and Maks had been. But that wasn't the most important thing right now.

"Break up?" she asked, completely at a loss. "Why would we break up?"

They were getting married. Weren't they? A cold spike of dread pierced her heart. *Weren't they?*

His expression was not hope producing. "A breakup between us is inevitable. Surely you understand this."

CHAPTER THREE

"NO. PRETEND MY IQ is in the low digits and explain it to me." Gillian's throat felt tight, the words hard to get out.

"I cannot marry a woman incapable of providing heirs to the throne. It's draconian, I know, but nevertheless, it is the way things must be."

"I can't provide heirs to the throne?" she asked, still very confused, but with a growing sense of apprehension that was making her current circumstances—naked and in bed with him—increasingly uncomfortable.

He frowned, sitting up, seemingly unconcerned by *his* nudity as he made no effort to cover himself. "You said you'd read the results of your physical."

"I said I'd received it. I had."

"I saw the envelope. It was opened."

"Nana called before I skimmed the results."

"One would think on something so important, one might do more than *skim*." His speech only grew so formal when he was very annoyed.

What did he have to be angry about?

"I've been healthy since my appendicitis at sixteen."

"The surgery to keep you alive left your fallopian

tubes compromised," Maks said with the air of a man who did not like having to explain himself.

Compromised fallopian tubes? What the heck did that mean?

Unable to stand the false sense of intimacy their situation provided once second longer, she jumped out of the bed. Grabbing her robe, she yanked it on so hard she wouldn't have been surprised if the sleeve ripped right off.

Gillian stepped back from the bed, putting as much distance as possible between herself and Maks while staying in the same room. "What are you talking about?"

Once again, Maks looked pained. "The likelihood of you getting pregnant is very low."

"What about fertility treatments?" Or had he not even considered them?

She was defective and therefore not worthy to be his bride. *Oh, God.* The silent prayer was filled with anguish, but received no heavenly reply.

Last night had not been about hunger or passion. It had been about saying good-bye. Everything she'd taken to mean they belonged together was in fact supposed to indicate the opposite.

"Fertility treatment could be an option for you with someone else," he said, like he was offering her good news.

"But not you."

"Marrying you knowing we would have to use them

would not be an intelligent or well thought out move on the part of our House."

"I would not be marrying your *House,*" she practically shouted.

She wouldn't be marrying anyone. Pain at that realization nearly took her to her knees.

What all this *talk* meant was that she was losing Maks.

"That is not true. I am a prince who will one day be king. I was born to a burden of duty none but elected officials in country can begin to understand. And even they live in their roles only temporarily whereas I will never know a day when my small country does not have to come first and foremost in my thinking."

She knew that. One of the few truly ruling monarchies left in the world, as Crown Prince of Volyarus, Maks's life was not his own. But his choices were.

"You do not love me." It was the only thing that really mattered and incidentally made absolute sense of his unwillingness to pursue fertility options.

He liked her, he desired her, he might even be as sad as he appeared at first over breaking up with her, but he *did not love her.*

"Love is not an emotion I have the freedom or inclination to pursue."

"Love either is, or *is not.* You don't have to pursue it." She'd learned as a small child, no matter how hard you *tried,* you could not make someone love you.

No. Love could not be forced. Nor could it be denied. Though she would give up her next visit with her grandparents and any hope of ever seeing either of her biological parents again if she could deny the tidal wave of emotions threatening to drown her now.

"You said you love me. I am sorry." Genuine regret reflected in the espresso depths of his eyes.

That regret hurt her as much as the words that came with it because the remorse proved their sincerity. Pain was a vise around her heart, radiating through her body in an unexpected and equally undeniable physical reaction to the emotional blow.

She could barely breathe for the agony. It was by sheer will she remained on her feet.

He was *sorry.*

She wanted to cry, felt like screaming, but she held it all in along with the pain building toward nuclear meltdown.

"Get out." She spoke quietly, but she knew he heard her.

"You are not thinking rationally."

"Since our first date, you've been very careful to keep us out of the eyes of the media."

"Yes."

She didn't ask, "Why?" Didn't really care about his reasoning anymore.

She just wanted him gone so she could let the pain out. *He* didn't get to see it.

"Do you think me calling the building's security to have you removed from my apartment would blow all those efforts to hell?"

His eyes widened at her oblique threat. "You're not going to call security."

He really didn't know her as well as he thought he did.

She spun around and pressed the panic button on her bedroom's security box.

"You have about a minute, maybe two, before they arrive. If you want to be caught here, by all means, stay." She didn't turn to face him as she spoke and she didn't raise her voice, either.

If she did, she'd end up screaming. She just knew it. And Gillian had never screamed a day in her life. She wasn't going to start now.

Not with him.

Not when the anguish inside her was already so close to imploding and taking her heart with it.

Ukrainian curses sounded along with the brush of clothing being yanked over naked limbs.

He paused at the doorway. She could sense it, though hadn't turned to watch his departure.

"I *am* sorry." Then he was gone.

And she was alone. Unable to stand under the onslaught of emotional agony ripping through her, Gillian sank to the floor.

Every dream she'd nursed in the past months shattered, every hope she'd let herself entertain despite her past and present life that in no way matched his for brilliance ripped violently from her still bleeding heart.

* * *

Nine weeks later, dazed and disbelieving, Gillian sat on the park bench outside her doctor's offices.

Utterly shattered by the news she'd received, she could do little more than stare at the tall buildings surrounding the small patch of nature.

Her doctor's words seemed impossible. *"You're pregnant."*

It was terribly improbable. And yet it was true.

She was pregnant. Exactly nine weeks along.

One night of unprotected sex with a man intent on evicting her from his life and they'd made a baby.

Emotions she had spent two months trying to contain and stifle were rioting through her. For the first time in her life, she was completely unable to ignore what she did not want to face.

Okay, maybe for the second.

Her grief over Maks's rejection had been so consuming, Gillian had no chance at ignoring it, either. Each day was a new reminder how much she'd loved, how much she'd lost and how much she missed the jerk.

But she'd worked toward some semblance of peace. She could almost sleep through the night without waking from a nightmare into the one of loss.

Pain at Maks's rejection had simply become such a part of her, she hardly noticed it anymore.

Or so she told herself.

It was the hope she couldn't stand. The need to feel anything at all, but most of all love for another human being, even a very tiny one.

Because unlike her parents, Gillian didn't care how her pregnancy had come to be. Planned or unplanned. With someone she wanted to share a life, or alone. None of it mattered.

She *would* love her child, already did, from the moment her doctor had uttered those impossible words, even before Gillian had been *sure.*

She had insisted they do the test again. Her doctor's PA had drawn Gillian's blood, but then she'd gone one step further while they waited for the in-office lab to run the results of the second test. She'd brought out a small device called a Doppler. A mini-ultrasound, the PA used the Doppler to find the baby's heartbeat.

Gillian had cried and nearly fainted when she heard the fast paced *swoosh-swoosh-swoosh* through the handheld device. There could be no denying another being was growing inside her womb. Her baby.

Maks's baby.

Unsurprisingly, at that point, the second test had come back just as conclusively positive as the first.

Gillian's pregnancy appeared perfectly viable, though her doctor wasn't particularly pleased about the fact she'd lost enough weight to hollow her cheeks. She'd been quick to assure Gillian this wasn't as uncommon as people might believe, however.

Many women lost weight in their first trimester.

Even so, miscarriage rates were higher than Gillian had ever expected. According to her doctor's PA, one in five pregnancies ended in miscarriage.

Wasn't that horrifically high for a country with such advanced medical knowledge and care?

Despite the early summer sun beating down, Gillian's hands were cold and clammy.

Pregnant. *Her.*

Part of her mind vaguely realized she was in shock. She probably should have stayed in the exam cubicle, but Gillian had needed to get out into the fresh air.

So, she'd told the doctor she was fine and the woman was busy enough to let her leave without pushing further.

Gillian shook her head, everything about the last hour incomprehensible.

She'd made an appointment to see her doctor at Nana's insistence. Gillian hadn't been all that concerned. She'd fought a serious case of depression since kicking Maks out of her apartment nine weeks before.

She loved him and saying the words had only made that knowledge more awful to bear when she'd realized there was no way he returned the feelings.

She'd *thought* she had a really persistent flu for the last few weeks, and frankly hadn't much cared. If her grandparents hadn't come into town for a visit, Gillian might well not have realized she was pregnant until she started showing.

But Nana had been very upset when she'd gotten Gillian to admit she had felt lethargic and nauseated for *weeks.* Though she'd only thrown up a few times.

According to Gillian's doctor, she was lucky in that.

The woman had also evinced surprise at Gillian not realizing there was even a possibility she was pregnant.

After all, she hadn't had a period in three months, but then Gillian's cycle had never been regular. Skipping a month was not unusual.

Compromised fallopian tubes, but they weren't compromised enough. Not only had Gillian managed to fall pregnant the one and only time she'd ever made love without a condom, but she'd been in the wrong part of her cycle for it to happen, too.

It was a miracle really.

She wondered if Maks would see the baby growing inside her that way? Most likely not. He'd walked away from her much too easily to be pleased when she popped up before him, carrying his child.

Would he even believe her that the baby was his? She wasn't risking miscarriage doing an amniocentesis for the DNA test.

No way was she.

If he had doubts about his fatherhood, he could wait until after the birth to assuage them.

As much as they would undoubtedly love the baby when it was born, Gillian's pregnancy wasn't going to make her grandparents happy. They firmly believed sex and pregnancy belonged within the bounds of marriage.

It only took a second to consider before she knew hiding her condition from them for the few days they were supposed to be in Seattle would be the best course of action.

There was a twenty percent chance this pregnancy

wouldn't make it past the first trimester. Gillian wasn't telling *anyone* about it until she'd made it past that important time marker.

Which meant she'd better turn in an Academy Award nominee worthy performance of a woman feeling one hundred percent better. Or her grandparents wouldn't be leaving town and heading for Canada the middle of next week as planned.

She would tell them her doctor said she was a little run down and needed to take better vitamins. It was the truth, if not the whole truth. Gillian's GP had prescribed gummy prenatal vitamins, which were supposed to be easier on her sensitive stomach, and folic acid for improved fetal development.

She'd also suggested an iron supplement because Gillian's levels were on the low end. That, at least, was a better explanation of her fatigue than the one she'd come up with on her own.

Missing Maks was exhausting.

Her grandparents would have no trouble accepting that Gillian wasn't feeling completely up to par in general. They believed the breakup had taken its toll on Gillian's health and hadn't hesitated to say so. Gillian had reminded them that most women had their heart broken at least once by the time they were her age.

Many had even been married and divorced by the age of twenty-six.

Nana had harrumphed and commented several times that she thought, "That young man had a lot to answer for."

It was a good thing Gillian's first appointment with her obstetrician wasn't until the following Friday, though. She didn't want to tell her grandparents another half-truth if she could help it.

Maks barked an answer into his phone and then cut the connection without saying goodbye.

"Idiots," he grumbled under his breath.

Demyan said from the doorway, "It seems everyone we do business with has lost IQ points in the last months."

Maks took a deep breath and consciously reined in his initial urge to snap at his cousin. "Did you need something, Demyan?"

"I have some information I believe you will find very interesting."

"We don't need another outlet for the rare minerals mines. We cannot keep up with demand as it is." Not and maintain environmental integrity.

A must for any energy or mineral extraction endeavor for Volyarus companies. Maks's father and grandfather before him had been well ahead of times in protecting the earth for future generations. No country on earth had stricter environmental regulations and policies than Volyarus.

And Yurkovich Tanner was ahead of any of the big ten oil companies in developing alternative energy sources as well.

As CEO, it was Maks's job to make sure that continued to be the case. "The last time I checked, our wind farm productions are all on schedule, too."

"It's not about business."

"I already know Father and the countess are on a *secret* getaway in the Cayman Islands." Maks made no effort to curb the bitter sarcasm lacing his voice. "Why do you think I'm returning to Volyarus tomorrow? I'll have to play *Head of State* for the month they are gone."

As if his job as CEO of Yurkovich Tanner wasn't enough.

But then his father had fulfilled both roles in the years between his own parents' deaths and when Maks took over as CEO of the company at the age of twenty-five. King Fedir could have hired someone else as CEO for Yurkovich Tanner, as Maks planned to do when he was made official Head of State, but his father insisted on running the company personally.

"Your mother will enjoy your company."

"More than my father's. I know." There was never anything as distasteful as a public row between his parents, but it was also no secret that they were not the best of friends.

His mother lived a completely separate life from his father except when their roles in the monarchy drew them together.

Demyan settled on the corner of Maks's large, antique executive desk. "I think you'll want to put off your flight at least a day."

"Why?" Maks all but growled.

He was looking forward to going back to his homeland and getting out of temptation's way. Nine weeks had not made staying away from Gillian any easier. He wanted her with a hunger he'd never had for another woman. It was inconvenient and frustrating.

Dating other women had only proved to him that when he could still remember driving a brand-new Mercedes sports class, he wasn't going to enjoy getting behind the wheel of a 1980s Volvo station wagon.

He hadn't had sex since his last night with Gillian.

"Ms. Harris made an appointment with a doctor."

Just the sound of her name made that desire in Maks he'd striven so hard to control thump inside him.

Using his formidable control, he evinced little interest in his cousin's words. "So?"

"An obstetrician."

"So, she's looking into fertility treatments." Maks's already dark mood took a turn for the worse. "Making plans for the future."

"Not exactly, no."

"What the hell are you talking about then?"

"According to our hacker, she's confirmed by two blood tests and the baby's heartbeat to be ten weeks' viably pregnant."

"What?" His cousin could not have said what Maks thought he'd heard. "We have a hacker on payroll?"

"Really? That's what you want to know?"

Maks glared at his cousin, his thoughts whirling and no clever retorts springing to mind for the first time in memory.

Demyan grimaced. "Your decision to go without a condom came with consequences."

Maks had never regretted sharing confidences with his older cousin, but he never would have told Demyan about that particular folly if he had not been paralytically drunk, either.

"Impossible!"

"Not so much, no."

"Damn it, Demyan, this is no topic for jokes."

"I am well aware." And Demyan had never looked more serious.

"Are you telling me that Gillian is pregnant with my child?"

"I am telling you that Ms. Harris was given a pregnancy test as part of a checkup for the flu and that test came back positive. A second test was administered. That test also came back positive. A Doppler ultrasound was performed and a baby's healthy heartbeat was recorded. Her file indicates the pregnancy is ten weeks old."

"She has the flu?"

Demyan just looked at him.

Shock had destroyed Maks's usual high level thinking processes. "What?"

"I imagine she went in for the flu and discovered it was morning sickness."

"Oh." Maks hadn't spent much time in the company of pregnant women, but even he knew about morning sickness. He should have realized immediately. "Is she all right?"

"I did not speak to your former girlfriend, Maks. I read a report from our investigative agency."

The reality of what Demyan was telling him, and all that it implied, finally and completely pierced his mind's stupor. Maks swore vehemently and at length in Ukrainian.

Demyan didn't flinch, though he understood the words as well as Maks. "You believe you are the father."

"Of course I'm the father. Gillian doesn't sleep around."

"She could have bedded another man in reaction to you dumping her."

The very thought infuriated Maks, but he kept all expression from his face. Even his cousin wasn't privy to Maks's innermost thoughts.

He didn't hide his displeasure at Demyan's description of the breakup however. "I didn't *dump* her. I was forced to end our relationship for the sake of the Crown."

"Because she could not give you children."

The irony was not lost on Maks. "Yes."

"What are you going to do?"

"What I planned to do before I found out her fallopian tubes are compromised. Marry her." There was no other option.

This child might well be their only child, but it would be *his* and that was a fact Maks would never dismiss.

CHAPTER FOUR

GILLIAN SHUT THE door behind her grandparents and sagged against it, free to do nothing to hide her fatigue and nausea for the first time in a week.

It had been touch and go for a while there, but Gillian had successfully hidden her pregnancy from the older couple. She had an entire lifetime's experience protecting them from truth that would hurt.

She had spent her childhood doing a very good job of keeping how devastating their beloved son's neglect of his only child had been to her emotions and ability to trust. Gillian had convinced them she did not mind only seeing her mother once a year, and that her father's more frequent but still sporadic and mostly impersonal visits were just fine.

To this day, neither of her grandparents knew how many nights she'd cried silently in her bed at night because neither of her parents would allow her to call them by anything but their first names. No mom or dad, or even mother and father.

Nothing to indicate that Gillian *belonged* to them.

She rubbed her hand over her still flat stomach. The

baby growing in her womb would never doubt its place in her life.

Unfortunately her own poor judgment meant she couldn't guarantee the same from her baby's father.

That knowledge, more than any other, caused her sleepless nights now.

Sighing, she moved into the bedroom. Time to get ready for work. She'd taken the week off to spend with her grandparents, but her boss and clients expected her in the studio later that morning.

Ten hours later, Gillian had put a full day in at the photography studio and stumbled into her apartment well after her usual dinner hour. Dragging with exhaustion, she popped some corn in the microwave for dinner.

Her plans for the evening included watching reruns of *Extreme Makeover—Home Edition* in her pajamas on the couch. She could do with some feel good, full on sap programming right now.

The door buzzer sounded and she had a terrible irrational thought that her grandparents had decided to stay in town for a while, but she dismissed it.

She'd gotten a quick call from Nana when they reached the Canadian border. They wouldn't have turned around without reason and she hadn't given them one.

It could possibly be her father. Rich was known to drop in without warning, but his unexpected visits were as infrequent as the planned ones.

She had friends, but one result of her upbringing and moving to the big city from a small Alaskan town was that she didn't invite many of them to her home. That had only gotten more acute the last year as she'd dated a man who could define circumspect with his social life.

Leaving the popcorn to finish, she crossed to the intercom box and pressed the communication button. "Yes."

"It is me, Gillian. Let me up."

Maks's voice.

Her fist came up to her chest, between her breasts, and she gulped in air. How could such a small thing wreak such devastation?

But his voice had the power to take her to her knees. Literally. It was only leaning onto the wall that kept her upright.

What was he doing here? In ten weeks, he hadn't so much as texted her to see if she was all right.

And now he showed up at her door?

"Gillian?" His voice sounded tinny through the intercom. "Are you there?"

"Yes," she croaked, her mouth and throat dry.

"You haven't pushed the release for the door."

And he was surprised?

She swallowed and took a breath, trying to ease the tightness in her chest. "What are you doing here?"

"We need to talk."

A week, or even two after he'd left, she would have welcomed those words. "It's been three months."

"Not quite. Ten weeks."

So, he'd tracked the time. It didn't mean anything. "What do you want, Maks?"

"Let me up and I will tell you."

"I don't want to see you." She'd just gotten to the point where she could go to sleep without a physical ache to be with him.

And that didn't happen every night.

"I will make it all right."

He didn't love her. Didn't want her. Thought she was defective. How did he make that okay? "No."

"Gillian."

A small voice laced with that horrible emotion hope whispered to her that at least he was here *now.* This was better than her approaching him with news of her pregnancy and facing "duty driven" Maks. Wasn't it?

There was only one way to find out.

It took more courage than she expected for her to give her tacit agreement to see him, but she was not weak.

She also wasn't overjoyed to have Maks seeking access to her apartment. "You'll have to keep it short, I'm tired."

He didn't reply and she didn't expect him to. It wasn't the empty admonishment it might have been before she rang security on him the last time he'd been to her apartment.

Gillian pressed the button to open the downstairs security door before very pointedly returning to the kitchen.

She'd showered after getting home from work and hadn't bothered to do anything but pull her hair into a ponytail and slip into her favorite pajamas since.

For the first time since meeting Maks, Gillian didn't care that she wasn't looking her best to see him. She wasn't about to go rushing around trying to look gorgeous for a man who had ejected her from his life with the efficiency and power of a missile launcher.

She was pouring the popcorn into a bowl when the doorbell rang.

Carrying the bowl, she made her way to the apartment's front door. She only had to take three deep breaths and give herself one very stern reminder she was in control here before opening it.

Maks looked a little less than his immaculate self, too. His almost black hair was messy, like he'd been running his fingers through it. He'd lost his tie between the office and her apartment and he'd skipped his second shave of the day, leaving the five o'clock shadow to darken his cheeks and jaw.

Ten weeks ago, she would have found that incredibly sexy. She also would have taken his state as proof he felt comfortable enough to be himself in her presence.

Now, it worried her a little.

Had their separation been hard on him, too? She had a very hard time believing he was here in hopes of getting back together. As far as he knew, nothing had changed.

She wasn't making any assumptions this time, one way or another, though. Whatever he wanted, whatever he was feeling, he'd have to come out and say it. In words that could not be mistaken to mean something else.

If he was looking for reconciliation, however, she had no idea how she would respond.

Things had changed for her, unequivocally, but one thing hadn't. He didn't love her.

Her stomach roiled with stress and she forced herself to take shallow breaths so she did not retch.

The one saving grace to this situation was that he didn't know she was pregnant. That, at least, wasn't on the table to complicate things further.

He reached out as if to touch her. "You're pale."

"I'm tired." She stepped back, not allowing that casual connection to happen.

It wouldn't be good for her campaign to get over him.

"So you said." He almost seemed lost for words.

"Come inside."

He nodded, the movement jerky, and followed her into the living room. She set the popcorn bowl on the table next to the glass of milk she'd poured herself earlier. "Would you like something to drink?"

He nodded and then shook his head. "You shouldn't be drinking."

"Because I'm tired?" She shrugged. "I'm not going to fall asleep on you. Besides, I'm drinking milk."

"Good. That's great."

She didn't respond. Seeing him was stirring memories and feelings that brought pain and hope, both in debilitating degrees.

The hope scared her the most. A lot of people didn't realize just how truly terrifying hope could be. Particularly for someone whose hopes had been dashed as many times as hers had been.

There was a cost for believing in someone bound to disappoint. Someone like her charismatic, famous and perennially distanced father.

Deciding a more relaxed Maks would be better for both of them, she crossed to her small bar and poured him a whiskey.

He was standing right behind her when she turned to hand it to him, making her jump back.

He reached out to grab her. "Careful!"

"Don't have a conniption." Once again, she jerked out of the path of his potential touch. "I wasn't going to fall and I wouldn't have been startled if you hadn't been hulking behind me. Take your drink and sit down."

He frowned, but then nodded almost meekly and did just that.

Gillian wasn't exactly sure what to do with an awkward, meek Maks. Maybe it was her pregnancy hormones, but she wasn't feeling any big urges to make him more comfortable, either.

She took her own seat, grabbing a handful of popcorn and starting to eat it one kernel at a time. Her stomach needed settling and she wasn't standing on ceremony to do it.

"Is that your dinner?" Maks asked, sounding truly appalled.

"Yes."

"But that is hardly adequate nourishment."

"It's fine."

"But…"

She rolled her eyes. "Did you come here to talk to me about my eating habits or something else? News of our former relationship hasn't leaked to the press, has it?" she asked, the prospect a truly dismaying one.

"No."

"Good."

"Yes, that would complicate matters in ways we do not need at the present."

"What matters? I'm not sure why you're here, Maks."

"Aren't you?"

She wanted to believe it was because the prince couldn't live without her, but somehow Gillian knew that particular fairy tale wasn't for her. "No."

"We have a very delicate situation and if we do not handle it correctly, it will blow up in our faces."

"The delicate situation of…"

"You can drop the pretense. I *know*."

"You know?" What did he know?

His gaze drifted to her stomach and then back to hers.

The dread of certainty filled her. But there was *no way* he could know she was pregnant. "Either tell me why you're here, or have your drink and leave."

"The baby."

"How?" she demanded as any hope she'd felt got crushed under the reality of truth. Again.

He wasn't here because he missed her too much to stay away. He wasn't here for *her* at all.

"Demyan."

"Demyan what? Bribed my doctor for information? But why would he?" None of this made any sense.

"He assigned typical post-relationship surveillance."

"You had me followed?" she asked, sick at the thought of strangers watching her.

She'd never foreseen this particular complication to dating a prince. Particularly when they'd taken such care to keep their relationship out of the eyes of the media. She'd never even considered *Maks* would be the source of such invasive actions.

She should have, but she'd been blind to a lot about her time with Maks.

"I did not, though I should have. When were you going to tell me? Or did you plan to get revenge by not telling me at all?"

"What a stupid question. At what point during our time together did I *ever* give you the impression I thought it was acceptable to make children pay for the poor choices of their parents?"

The question hung between them like a gauntlet thrown down and Maks knew he had no place picking it up.

She was right. This woman was not motivated by revenge or negative feelings.

The fact she had any sort of a relationship at all as an adult with parents who had shamefully neglected her as a child was testament to the fact Gillian's heart was more forgiving, not to mention tolerant, than most.

"I am sorry. That was uncalled for," he admitted,

though apologizing was not his forte and never had been. "When *were* you going to tell me?"

"Once I had gotten through the first trimester."

"Surely you realize the sooner I knew and appropriate action could be taken, the better."

"Appropriate action?" she asked, her expression completely closed to him for once.

"Marriage." What else could they do?

"I see."

She did not seem in the least excited at the prospect, though he was certain she had wanted nothing more than his proposal ten weeks ago.

Armed with the knowledge that she had *not* realized it was their last night together, he'd had time…much too much time…to go over that last night and the following morning in his head. The conclusions he had drawn were not all pleasant. Nor did they paint him in the best of lights from her perspective.

He comprehended that.

It almost made her action of calling for security that final morning understandable. Not entirely so, but almost. Such precipitous behavior would not be acceptable going forward, however.

No doubt his mother would explain things of that nature to a woman she would groom to take the position of queen one day.

At present, there was enough on the table for discussion without focusing on past behavior.

"You are taking a lot for granted, aren't you?" she

asked before he said anything else, or responded overtly to her noncommittal *I see.*

"My child will be heir to the throne of Volyarus." Surely she understood that.

Gillian's bright blue eyes lit with challenge. "Even a girl?"

"Yes. The monarchy passes to the oldest child of the monarch, male or female does not matter."

"How progressive."

"Not really. Many monarchies have no masculine stipulation for title bequeathal."

"Really? I didn't know." She dropped the popcorn she'd picked up back into the bowl and pushed her milk glass two inches to the right.

Maks admitted, "My father's generation could have stood to be more progressive."

"What do you mean?" Gillian asked.

"The business and political roles have always been shared amidst the siblings of the ruling family. My father was not open to having his sister's help in running Yurkovich Tanner."

"Oh." Clearly Gillian had expected him to say something else.

"His attitude toward provision of an heir is also archaic." His father had married his mother for the sole sake of children, because the woman he loved could not provide them.

They had ended up with a single child and no accord.

"Yes, it is."

Even though he'd voiced the criticism himself, having Gillian agree so quickly pricked at Maks's pride and sense of familial loyalty. However, he refrained from making excuses for his father.

"You look tired." She looked completely exhausted.

"I am."

"What is the matter?"

"Nothing. Apparently it's a normal part of pregnancy."

He did not like that answer at all. He needed information on pregnancy from someone with specialized knowledge. That was clear.

"There is as much as a twenty percent chance this pregnancy will not be viable." She spoke in a monotone, so at first her words did not sink in. "That number goes down to three percent once the baby makes it past twelve weeks."

The imperative to consult with an expert grew astronomically. "What? Why is the risk so high?"

"Apparently miscarriage is a lot more common than you'd expect." The casual tone of her words was belied by the tense line of Gillian's shoulders.

"My child will not miscarry."

Gillian shook her head, her expression mocking. "You don't have much to say about it."

"I do not believe that. There must be something we can do."

"*I'm* doing it. I take a highly soluble prenatal vitamin and folic acid. I've switched my exercise regime to one approved for pregnant women. I've given up caffeine and alcohol, though my doctor says I can indulge in both in small quantities. I do *nothing* to put undue stress on my womb." Determination darkened her blue eyes.

"You want this child." The jury was still very much out on whether or not she wanted *him,* but Maks had no doubts Gillian wanted their child.

"More than you could possibly understand. I plan to be an exemplary mother."

"Your grandmother set a high standard to follow." And Gillian's mother had shown his former lover just exactly what she did not want to be as a parent.

An almost smile curved Gillian's lips and she warmed infinitesimally toward him. "Yes, Nana did."

"She must be excited about the baby." It bothered him that someone else knew about their child before he had. He recognized the reaction as unreasonable, but that did not diminish his feeling of disappointment.

"I have not told her."

That shocked him. Gillian told her grandmother everything. She'd been willing to keep their dating out of the public eye, but not her family's. He had met her grandparents and gone through a grilling unlike anything he'd experienced before as a Crown Prince.

Neither of the older Harrises had treated him like royalty and he'd actually enjoyed it.

Gillian had even met his own mother on a few social occasions as well.

So, why keep the news of the baby from her grandmother? Because Gillian wasn't married?

"I don't think your grandmother would judge you for getting pregnant before the wedding, Gillian."

"She's more old-fashioned than you realize. Who do you think pushed the issue of my parents marrying to *legitimize* my birth?"

Which might well make her grandmother his best ally. He filed that bit of information away for later use if need be.

"I'm not telling *anyone* about the baby until I've made it past my twelfth week," Gillian offered in explanation.

She was taking the possibility of miscarriage very seriously. "You need to stop thinking in this negative way."

"I'm not thinking negatively. I'm being realistic."

He did not agree. "Realistic is you are pregnant and we must determine how best to react to that truth."

Gillian's general air of tired pessimism morphed into anger faster than he could track.

She glared fiercely. "I'm reacting to it just fine."

For the entire eight months they had dated, he'd been convinced of Gillian's practical nature. However, that final night had shown a romantic streak he should have guessed at from the beginning.

She earned her living predominately doing photography for the covers of romance novels. Gillian was far too good at it not to be at least a closet romantic, no matter how well she tried to hide it.

Maks knew he wasn't the most aware man on the planet when it came to interpersonal relationships, particularly those with women. He was a stellar diplomat and had no superior among his contemporaries in business savvy. However, past liaisons had proven those skills did not extend into the realm of lovers.

None of his former liaisons remained in the "friend" category, something Demyan found highly amusing.

And still, Maks had the unexpected and unquestionable revelation that only one thing would suffice in the present circumstances. It had precipitated making a stop at Tiffany's on the way to Gillian's apartment.

Pulling the pale aqua blue box from his pocket, he dropped to his knee in front of his pajama clad ex-lover. "Will you marry me, Gillian Harris?"

CHAPTER FIVE

SHE STARED AT him and then at the ring box like it might snap open at any moment to reveal angry wasps rather than a very expensive engagement ring worthy of not just any princess, but the woman who would bear that title for Volyarus.

"You brought a ring." She sounded dazed by the fact and not at all happy.

"You deserve all the trimmings, but you would not appreciate them after the way our last time together ended." Kneeling before her felt awkward; he was glad it was not a position he would be in again anytime soon.

What was romantic about this?

"You are right. The *trimmings* would be wasted after your *honesty* ten weeks ago."

There was no good response to that, so he didn't make one.

Opening the box, he revealed the large square cut diamond with yellow diamonds to either side of it. Set in platinum, all the stones were of unparalleled clarity. "Marry me, Gillian."

"It's a beautiful ring." She gave it a brief glance and then looked away, as if she could not bear to see it.

He did not understand why. Didn't women like jewelry? His mother certainly did. Though she insisted on nothing ostentatious, she expected significant gifts each year on the anniversary of her marriage to his father.

"You are a beautiful woman."

Her bow-shaped lips twisted in a moue of disagreement. "If I were one of the astonishingly beautiful people, you would not have been interested in me."

It was true. He might have bedded her, but he would not have *dated* Gillian if she was a woman who drew media attention merely from her looks alone. That did not mean, however, that she was not lovely.

"I have never missed a woman after our liaison ended." She deserved the admission, though he didn't like making it.

"You didn't do a lot of dating before me."

It was true, but he had been in two almost-serious relationships. Neither had ended well. Both had reinforced an important truth: love only compromised duty.

"I missed *you,*" he reiterated in case she missed the point the first time.

She tucked her body into the corner of the couch, her feet up on the cushions, her arms wrapped around her knees. "Am I supposed to be impressed? You dumped me."

It had been the expedient action, but if he reminded her of that salient fact, he did not think it would do him any favors in the present. "I have since regretted my decision."

"When you found out I am pregnant."

He could not deny it, so he remained silent. Though he had been unhappy about the decision before that, he had not allowed himself to regret it.

She sighed, glanced at the ring and then looked away again. "I'm not committing to anything until I've made it past my first trimester."

"That is not acceptable."

"Nine weeks ago, you made it very clear you did not want to marry me unless I could provide heirs for the throne. If I miscarry, the situation will be the same as before with the identical low chance of me conceiving again." The pain that knowledge caused her bled into her tone, but her expression showed none of it.

He had no way of knowing if that pain came from the knowledge conception was not a given for her, or that *they* would have little future if she could not do so.

Even so, his first instincts were to disagree with her dictate.

He moved to sit beside her on the sofa, acutely aware of the tiny move she made farther into her corner. "Every day we wait to announce our forthcoming marriage is a day in which someone in the press may stumble across your condition and then we'll be the center of a media storm."

"Unless they're also bribing doctors, no one is going to find out about my *condition,* Maks."

"Demyan did not bribe your doctor."

"Then how did he find out?"

"I don't think you really want to know."

"I do."

"A hacker."

"You had my medical records hacked?" she asked in shock-laced anger.

"Demyan—"

"Right, it was your cousin. Not you."

"Nevertheless, we would be foolish to assume no one else could find out. There are doctor's appointments—"

"I don't have another one until my twelve-week mark," she said, interrupting him a second time.

He just looked at her. She knew, maybe even better than him, how easily the press got hold of information people believed locked in the strongest vault.

"You work very hard to stay out of the limelight, don't you?"

"Volyarus is best served by its monarchy maintaining a low profile in the media."

"Why?"

"With the interest of the press comes the interest of the world, an interest that can quickly morph into political agendas and twisted perceptions. Volyarus has thrived as a little-known country with strategic location coupled with significant natural resources."

Some might think that because of the name, Volyarus was a country of Russian descent, but they would be wrong. Very wrong. Volyarus was a shortened version of a Ukrainian saying that meant freedom from Russia.

His antecedent had been a Hetman in Ukraine before Russia overtook the country. Seeing what the future held, he and a group of nobles and laborers had left Ukraine to settle on the island in the Baltic Sea that became Volyarus.

While Ukrainian was only spoken sporadically by the many living in Ukraine today, because of the Russian control for so many years, it was still the official and most prevalent language of Volyarus.

Citizens were required to be proficient in at least one other language before finishing the equivalent of high school in the U.S.A. Maks himself spoke four fluently and three additional languages with enough proficiency to travel without an interpreter.

And yet he found communicating with this woman an incredible challenge.

"Everything in your life is about Volyarus, isn't it?"

"Yes." He would not apologize for that fact, nor would he change it.

He was born to a duty few could comprehend, but a burden he had never resented. His place in the world was immutable, but then he'd never *wanted* to change it.

"Even more reason not to put the country in the limelight with a failed engagement landing on the tail of a miscarriage."

"I would not break our engagement if you miscarried." Though he should. It was the only course of action that made sense.

However, no one could deny the fact she'd gotten pregnant after *one* time making love without a condom.

They were clearly compatible chemically and even

if she were to lose this baby, though he was sure she was not going to, she *would* become pregnant again.

Besides, it wasn't an engagement they'd be breaking, but a marriage. The only politically expedient action in the circumstances was an elopement followed by a reception of extreme pomp.

His mother would be thrilled to plan it. She liked Gillian, had made her approval of the choice clear. She wouldn't be as happy about the timing of the pregnancy, but his mother was not the type of woman to bemoan what could not be changed.

The queen of Volyarus would expect an immediate elopement however.

He didn't bring any of this up, however. There would be time enough to convince Gillian to marry him *immediately* once she agreed to marry him at all.

"You're assuming I'll agree to marry you," she said as if reading his mind.

He dropped the ring in her lap and stood. "What choice do either of us have?"

"Lovely."

He didn't respond to her sarcasm. Perhaps it hadn't been elegantly phrased, but it was the truth.

"Even if I didn't want to marry you, I would." He gave gratitude that he did in fact like the idea of marriage to his lovely blonde.

"Even better."

He swore. He was usually much better at diplomacy, though once again his lack in the interpersonal arena was reaching out to bite him on the ass.

Maks prowled the room, stopping in front of the drinks cabinet. Not about to pour another whiskey when his first one remained practically untouched, he spun away. She could argue all she liked, the fact remained she carried the heir to the Volyarus throne. Gillian *had* to marry him.

"And you wouldn't be considering this course of action otherwise." No bitterness laced her tone. Just flat acceptance.

Still, he knew that fact did *not* make her happy.

He turned to face her. "Does it really matter? The baby you carry is nothing short of a miracle. Our miracle."

"Yes."

"So, you will marry me."

"Yes, the baby is a miracle, but yes, it matters," she clarified, her lovely features set in determined lines. "I'm not making any commitments for another two weeks. You can argue until your throat is raw with it, but I won't be changing my mind on that fact."

There was no give in her tone, no evidence of possible softness in her blue gaze. He was not used to seeing Gillian as the hardline taker, but there could be no question. This woman would *not* be moved.

"Then in two weeks' time we will be married."

"I'm not making any promises—"

"Until you've hit your second trimester. I heard you the first time."

"So, stop trying to push for a promise I'm not prepared to make."

"But you will make it."

"I don't know."

"You do." She must. "You made your choice."

"What do you mean?"

"You knew dating me came with different expectations than other men."

"I didn't sign my life over to you when I agreed to see you exclusively."

They'd never verbalized that agreement, but he took her point.

It just wasn't the salient one. "You did not know about your compromised fallopian tubes when you agreed to make love without a condom."

"We had sex and you made the same choice."

"I believed pregnancy was impossible, or at least extremely unlikely," he felt compelled to add.

"Unlucky you."

"That is *not* how I see it."

She frowned and then enlightenment dawned, but he held no confidence she'd seen light about the right thing. "No, I suppose you think me being pregnant with your child is lucky indeed. The heir is on the way."

"I will treasure our child, and not merely because he or she is the heir to the throne of Volyarus."

"Will you? Really?" she asked intently.

"Yes." There could be no doubt.

"That's something, I suppose."

"My parents were king and queen of a small but still demanding nation. Nevertheless, they were very good parents."

"Even though your father split his time between your family and his *friend* the countess?"

"No one's home life is ideal, but mine was good. Our child's will be better."

"That's what I want for my child. Better. I want her, or him, to know unconditional love."

"Like you did from your grandparents."

"Like I wanted from either or both of my parents."

She'd never voiced that desire before, though he could have guessed at it.

"We are not your parents."

"We aren't yours, either."

It was his turn to ask what she meant.

"If, and I do mean *if,* I agreed to marry you, there would be requirements."

"Like?"

"Like, no mistresses. I'm not your mother and I won't tolerate a long-standing or short-standing affair, or one-night stand for that matter. I would leave you and you'll sign a prenup giving me primary custody in the event of your infidelity."

"I am not my father." Maks was determined *not* to emulate the other man when it came to this area of his father's life. "The king's long-standing understanding with the countess is not something I will ever repeat."

"I'm the only one in your bed. Full stop. Period."

He hated she felt the need to make the stipulation because he knew this was about his father's choices not any Maks had made. He'd never cheated on a lover, even in his college days.

And he never considered his position made him immune to the rules of honor in regard to his future wife, either. "Again, I am not my father."

"You put Volyarus first, last and always."

"But my father does not."

"You don't mean that," she said in obvious shock.

Well, she might be. He didn't criticize his father often and he'd done so twice in one day to her. But if they were to be married, he would not pretend wholesale support of his father's decisions as he did for public consumption.

Like Demyan, Gillian would be privy to things Maks would never express elsewhere. "If my father put Volyarus first and in all ways, he would not continue a liaison that could explode in our faces at any time."

"Your outrage at your father's behavior is based on your concern for Volyarus, not your mother."

"My mother was well aware of the countess when she agreed to marry my father."

"If I am unable to conceive a second time, we will use a surrogate or pursue fertility measures. You will not leave me for a more fertile woman and that would be in any prenuptial between us."

"Fine." Though he didn't know how she planned to ensure that one.

"The prenuptial will include any future offspring in that custody agreement."

"You would have primary custody of any child I conceived with another woman?" He couldn't help the appreciation of her planning lacing his tone.

The woman was not only intelligent, but she knew how to be ruthless. He could appreciate that fact.

"Exactly."

"And if the mother doesn't agree?"

"She'll be forced to fight the Crown in a very messy custody battle right in the center of the media's eye."

"You will use your connections to your father to bring Volyarus into the public eye?"

"You have no idea how far I will go to protect my children's future and their happiness."

"I was raised by a woman willing to sacrifice anything for mine, I do know."

"Oh, no, your mother never fought the way I would fight. She's too wrapped up in the good of Volyarus to push as hard as I would."

That was true. "She is not weak."

He used to think otherwise, but had come to appreciate his mother's brand of strength.

"No, but she is too self-sacrificing. I won't be her."

"You won't be your parents, either. You'll never deny your child its birthright." The way she was talking made him realize just how much time Gillian had spent since discovering she was pregnant thinking about the scenario of a marriage between them.

There could be no doubt the prospect no longer thrilled her, but she clearly understood the importance of protecting their child and his birthright.

"I don't have to marry you for you to name our child as your heir."

"According to Volyarussian law, I can name any living relative as my successor, but the birth of a legitimate heir negates all previous claims to the throne."

"You're saying if you marry someone else and they have a child, that child inherits the throne?" she asked carefully and with clear thought.

"Exactly."

"Fine."

Shock coursed through him. "You would deny our child his place in life?"

In no scenario had Maks expected categorical denial.

"I'm not saying what I would do. You do not seem to be getting that. I'm acknowledging the consequences if I choose not to marry you."

"You cannot do that to our child!" She must realize that.

"You walked out on me ten weeks ago."

"And our child must pay because of it?"

"I have to make the best choice for this baby, one way or another. He or she deserves the best I can give. That may, or may not be, marriage to you."

"Damn it. Why?"

"You don't love me." She put her hand up when he made as if to speak. "In your mind, that doesn't matter. I know, but it matters to me and I have to decide if I can be the best mother possible married to a man who does not love me and who found it so easy to discard me."

"It was not easy."

He could see by the expression on her face that she considered his claim very much a situation of far too little, far too late.

And her words proved it. "It was easy enough. You wouldn't be here if you hadn't found out by nefarious means that I am pregnant."

"It was hardly nefarious means."

"You managed to get information in my confidential medical records. What would you call it?"

"Expedient."

She laughed, the sound both unexpected and welcome. "You're a piece of work, Maks, you know that?"

"I am a prince."

"Who thinks he has the right to put surveillance on an ex-girlfriend."

"I told you—"

"Demyan did it. I knew you two were like brothers. I didn't know that extended to finger pointing."

"He was doing what he thought best."

"Why? I wasn't going to go to the tabloids. You had to realize that."

"I told him about that night."

"What?"

"That we did not use condoms."

"Oh. You told him? Really?"

"Yes, really."

"Why?" She clearly could not see him sharing confidences.

"I was drunk."

"Oh." Her brows furrowed. "Why?"

"I missed you." Hadn't they already been over this?

"You said."

"I meant it."

"I guess you did."

"What? You thought I was lying."

"If it meant convincing me to your point of view? Yes."

"You do not trust me at all." That shocked him. He was eminently trustworthy.

"No, I don't."

"That is not acceptable."

"You say that a lot. You can't deny that it took finding out I was pregnant to bring you back here. What is there to trust in that?"

"You know why."

"I know I didn't rate even considering fertility treatments."

He had no answer for that. The truth was not always palatable.

"You never doubted the baby is yours?" she asked.

"No."

"Oh, right…you had me followed. You would have known I didn't so something crazy like sleep with a stranger to make myself feel better."

She sounded like that might have been in the offing and he did not like knowing that at all. "It never even crossed my mind you would have sex with another man."

"We weren't together. Why not?"

"You don't sleep around."

"People do crazy things when they're hurting."

He shrugged. He wouldn't know. Self-control had been drilled into him from the cradle. "You didn't."

"No, I didn't."

"Do not sound so miffed by that fact. I am very pleased about it."

"Did you?"

"Did I what?" And then he understood what she wanted. "No other women."

"Why?"

"I missed you." It didn't sound so naff now that he was trying to get her back with interest.

"I might just believe you."

CHAPTER SIX

GILLIAN FELT AS if the universe was conspiring with the Prince of Volyarus to keep him uppermost in her thoughts every second of every day.

As if it wasn't hard enough to get him out of her head as it was.

While photography for book covers comprised the majority of her work, it did not dominate it completely. Usually.

For three days running, every single shoot Gillian had done was for a *romance* cover. *Every single one.* And why all of the heroines were blonde she didn't know.

She often photographed brunette heroines, redheads, even one who had pinks streaks in her hair, but not for the past three days. All her female models were decidedly of the light haired variety.

And they'd all been paired with tall, handsome, dark haired love interests.

None of the men were a patch on Maks, though. They lacked the underlying steel in his character, that cold aloofness that had allowed him to walk away from her without a backward glance.

These models might be amazing men in their own right, but none were Maks. None made Gillian's heart stutter, her breath catch, or her body heat.

And their very differences made Maks even harder to forget.

He wasn't helping, either, not giving her a moment to collect her scattered thoughts.

Maks texted her several times a day. The bits of info on pregnancy were understandable, even charming. His short messages were geared as much toward her comfort as they were the baby's health. She appreciated him not making her feel like a brood mare.

But he acted as if they were still dating, wanting to go to dinner, take her to a show, asking if she was available to be his plus one at upcoming social events.

As if on cue, her phone announced in a snooty tone, "Your text has been served, madam."

The current pair of models both looked up from where they were getting into position for the first set of shots.

"Do you need to get that?" the dark haired not-Maks asked.

She shook her head. "It will keep."

"Don't worry on our account. Go ahead and check it," the blonde offered with a smile that encompassed both Gillian and the male model.

Oh. The woman was interested. The male cover

model wasn't married and Gillian had no intention of standing in the way of possible romance.

"Thanks." She grabbed the phone and clicked through to the text messages.

La Bayadére is playing. Do you want 2 go?

The fiend. He knew she loved the ballet!

She texted back. Too busy.

She wasn't getting sucked back in. Not until she knew what *she* wanted for the future.

R u sure? Great seats.

The temptation was strong, but she held out. Absolutely sure.

Silence. No reply text, no virtual butler giving her a little smile with his snooty tone.

Feeling unaccountably let down, she called the two models back to work.

Now her thoughts kept going back to the choice ahead of her. A choice that impacted the unborn child in her womb irrevocably.

Gillian would give thanks every single day of her life for her grandparents and their love, but they'd resisted her ever considering them full-on parents.

Maybe at first, they'd hoped her dad would take a more active role in her life. Later, it had been their way of maintaining the illusion that Rich Harris *was* her dad, when he'd never been more than a financially generous sperm donor.

He said so himself, laughing about it as if holding no particular affection for his only child was something funny rather than tragic.

That was not a destiny she was willing to write into the stardust of heaven for her own child.

Maks wasn't like Rich, though. The prince loved his own family, even if the words never passed his lips. It was in everything he did for them, the way he put the very select few ahead of his own wants and desires.

His parents. Demyan. They were all afforded the protection of Maks's considerable will and strength.

It was one of the first things she noticed about him; his commitment to family had given her false hope for their own relationship.

He didn't love *her,* but Maks would adore any child of his and that was a circumstance Gillian simply could not ignore.

Maks knocked on Gillian's door. He'd been texting and calling her since leaving her apartment—against his better judgment—the other night.

She replied to most of his texts and took some of his calls, though she never returned the ones she didn't. She'd put off seeing him on one pretext or another, even refusing his offer of *La Bayadère*.

It was very different than the way she'd behaved before, when her eagerness for his company had often caused him to smile on days otherwise very challenging.

He'd never expected Gillian to dig her heels in like she had. This streak of stubbornness was something he had to file away for future reference.

The woman could be supremely intransigent.

He was not used to being treated this way by women, and this woman particularly. He did not like it. He'd had enough.

He had to fly out to Volyarus in the early hours tomorrow and he wasn't leaving Seattle without settling some things between them.

The door flew open to reveal Gillian glaring at him in bad temper. "How did you get into my building?"

He shrugged. The hacker had upset her. Telling her he had sublet an apartment on the floor below hers he had never stepped inside so he would have open access to her building would not make her happy, either.

"You are too much."

"I am just enough."

She shook her head and turned toward the kitchen. "You may as well come in. The dinner you had delivered is clearly enough for two. I assume you intend to share it."

"You don't like it?" he asked.

"It's my favorite chicken Parmesan. From a restaurant that does not do takeout no less, though apparently they do for you. What's not to like?"

He didn't know. So, he said nothing. He'd read pregnant women could be emotionally unpredictable.

"I appreciate you sending me dinner the last few

nights." The words were grudging, her lovely face set in lines of annoyance rather than gratitude.

Her grandmother would be proud Gillian had remembered her manners when she so clearly would rather tell him to take a flying leap.

"You do not need to be cooking. It's clear you are tired." Too tired to be working full-time, he thought, but was smart enough not to say.

Right then. And though she hadn't allowed him to see her, he had done his best to care for her needs regardless.

"Pregnant women have been cooking their own dinners for millennia."

"This pregnant one does not have to." He laid his hand on her shoulder.

She jolted, like he'd touched her with live electricity, and stepped away from him with an alacrity that troubled him.

"You can no longer bear my touch?" He'd read that some pregnant women went right off sex, too.

He'd hoped Gillian would fall in the other category. The one where pregnancy drove their hormones in quite a different direction. The physicality between them had been something he'd missed sorely over the past months. And he'd hoped to use it to reestablish intimacy between them.

Gillian didn't answer him, but moved to where take-out containers sat open on the counter. With quick, economic movements, she plated the food in silence.

He took glassware and cutlery through to the small dining room.

"I'd prefer to eat on the sofa," she called from the kitchen, sounding every bit as cranky as she'd looked answering the door, not to mention as if she thought he should have known that already.

Not sure how she had expected him to read her mind, he made a quick change of direction, putting the glasses and cutlery down on the coffee table before returning to the kitchen. "What do you want to drink?"

"Milk." Her mouth turned down in obvious dissatisfaction. "It's good for the baby."

"There are many other calcium-rich foods you can eat. You don't have to drink milk if you'd prefer something else."

She used to like milk. Was this one of those pregnancy things?

She glowered at him. "Stop being so nice!"

"You would prefer I was dismissive of your desires?"

"Yes. It would make it easier."

"What?"

"You know what."

"This supposed choice you must make?"

"It's not supposed."

Annoyance rose to match hers, but he controlled it, allowing nothing but certainty to color his tone. "There *is* no choice when it comes to our child, Gillian. You know that, though you refuse to acknowledge it."

"Did your mother have a choice?"

What an odd question to ask, as if Gillian couldn't

imagine his mother marrying his father under any other circumstances. It pricked at Maks's pride.

Perhaps a little of his irritation came through when he said, "She was not pregnant when they married if that is what you mean. In fact, I did not arrive until two weeks after their first anniversary."

"Then *why* did she marry your father?"

Gillian made it sound as if marrying into his family was a fate worse than death. Forget small pricks at his pride, this was a fully realized blow.

"Many women would have been happy to receive my father's marital-minded intentions," he ground out.

Gillian's brow furrowed. "But she knew about the countess when she married him?"

Maks frowned at the mention of his father's *love* affair. Even though they'd discussed it before, he didn't like dwelling on something that had been a source of unpleasantness for his family his entire life. "Yes. Why?"

"I cannot imagine marrying a man who was in love with another woman."

"That is not something you have to worry about." Maks would never allow that particular emotion sway in his heart or his life.

Romantic love only caused pain and undermined duty and dedication.

"You could fall in love with someone else later." Gillian's tone wasn't at all certain.

Good. Even she realized how unlikely that was.

"If I were going to love anyone, I assure you, it would be you." Surely she realized this?

But then what Maks thought Gillian should know and what she actually accepted as truth were widely divergent, he'd come to appreciate.

She shook her head. "Do you have any idea how that sounds, what that does to my heart to hear?"

In truth, clearly he did not. He thought she would have liked knowing that. "You would prefer I withhold the truth?"

"I would prefer you loved me."

He wanted to turn away from the pain in her eyes, but he was not a weak man to refuse to face the consequences of his choices. "I am sorry."

"You said that before you left my apartment ten weeks ago."

"I meant it." He was not a monster.

She frowned and turned back to the plates, sprinkling the fresh Parmesan over the chicken instead of looking at him. "We're going to make a scandal, one way or another."

"Maybe a small one, but nothing truly damaging to the country if we take a proactive approach. My PR team is very good." It would cause some media furor.

His marriage couldn't help but do otherwise, but his PR team would make sure that furor died down quickly and remained mostly positive.

They wouldn't be able to do that if word of the breakup had gotten out before word of the baby and elopement, though.

"Is Demyan on it?"

He didn't understand the question. "You know he's Director of Operations for Yurkovich Tanner."

"I was being facetious. He's just Machiavellian enough to make a really good PR man."

"I'll tell him you said so."

"Do. And tell him it's not nice to hire hackers to break into confidential medical files."

"I will leave that admonishment to you." For his part, Maks was very grateful to his cousin's foresight.

"Don't think I won't say it to him. He might scare everyone in your company, but he doesn't scare me."

"He intimidates."

People said the same about Maks even though he'd played diplomat from the cradle, but Demyan had an edge to him unsmoothed by political expedience.

"He's a scary guy."

"But not to you." They'd had this conversation once before.

She'd finished it by reminding him that she had Maks's protection and that was all she needed to feel safe, no matter how intimidating a guy his cousin was.

The way Gillian's blue eyes flared now said she remembered that conversation, too. But she was clearly not going there with the conversational thread again.

Her lips set in a firm line and she picked up the plates to carry through to the living room.

He shook his head and approached the fridge. He found milk and cherry limeade. He took the juice with him to the living room.

She looked at the carton in his hand and though she tried to frown, he could see she was pleased.

"Your favorite."

"I've been craving it even more lately."

"Your body no doubt wants Vitamin A and C."

"Yes, Dr. Maks."

"I read that pregnancy cravings are often linked to things your body needs for the baby, or because the baby has depleted your stores already."

"I read that, too."

"So, you've been reading up on pregnancy?" She wasn't denying it just because she was cautiously approaching her second trimester. Good.

"Yes."

"According to my research, your chances of miscarriage are closer to ten percent than twenty." Though not all statistics agreed.

Many doctors still considered her chance of miscarriage at or above twenty percent until she hit the twelve-week mark.

It was the added stress she had to be under, pregnant to a man who was not only not yet her husband, but who would one day be king. Those added pressures and the tension between them increased her chances to miscarry.

He did not like it, but the stress of his position could not be avoided. And he did not see how to fix the other if she would not even entertain the idea of marriage until she'd reached that magical time marker in her head.

She looked at him curiously. "You think one in ten is good odds?"

"I do."

She sat down, but didn't argue. For which he was grateful. He didn't want her thinking negatively.

Thought was a powerful weapon.

They'd been eating for a few silent minutes when she turned to him. "Thank you for dinner. It's very good."

He didn't remind her she'd already thanked him. It was an overture.

He took it. "It is. There is no need to thank me. Your care is my responsibility. Thank you for allowing me to stay."

"We aren't together, Maks."

"The baby growing in your womb says otherwise."

"You're so stubborn."

"Have you looked in a mirror lately?"

He surprised her into a giggle and that made Maks smile.

"Nana always said I was sneaky that way. Everyone thinks I'm easygoing because I don't fight what doesn't matter to me."

He began to better understand this woman he had dated for months without realizing once she could be a rock when it came to doing things her own way. "However, what does matter to you, you fight to the last?"

"Something like that."

She hadn't fought for him, or *them* when he said they

had to end things. Despite her words of love Gillian had given in without a single volley to his side.

He felt pain in the center of his chest. Odd. This restaurant didn't usually cause heartburn.

CHAPTER SEVEN

"I HAVE BEEN thinking a wedding onboard a luxury cruise liner. A friend of mine owns a fleet that sails the inside passage to Alaska on one of its routes. Ariston will make certain word of our marriage does not leak out until after the event."

Gillian jumped, startled by Maks's comment. He'd been mostly silent since they began eating dinner.

"I thought you were mulling over business." She laughed more at herself than the situation. "I should have known better. You have a one-track mind."

A single-minded determination that had led him back to her.

Maybe Gillian would have gotten over Maks, eventually. She'd certainly been doing her best to master the unrequited love that tore at her decimated heart every day he'd been gone.

But one short visit had set her back to the beginning, her heart hurting so much it was almost numb with it.

She knew that at some point that numbness would have become a protective blanket over her emotions. Just like it had done sometime in her childhood.

Maks made it clear he wasn't going to let that happen.

"I assure you, my mind is capable of traveling multiple tracks at once."

"I used to think so."

"What has changed your mind?"

"It's either the baby, my pregnancy, or our upcoming marriage—which is not a done deal, no matter what you tell yourself—since you showed up here three days ago."

He settled back into the sofa, one long arm along its back, his left ankle crossed negligently over his right knee. "Those are three tracks."

"Ha, ha."

"I am not attempting humor, merely pointing out a fact. I have also in the last three days negotiated mineral rights for Yurkovich Tanner to a new rare minerals mine in Zimbabwe, overhauled and signed numerous contracts, avoided a political *situation* between Volyarus and Canada if you can believe it, interviewed several candidates for the position of Director of the Ministry for Education in Volyarus, mediated a labor dispute via teleconference in one of our currently operating mines, and finalized a new employee benefits package for the United States employees of Yurkovich Tanner."

Okay. So the man was a machine of efficiency in both the business and political realm. "And still, you've had time to text me several times a day and call me nearly as often."

"That should tell you where you sit in my priorities."

She opened her mouth to say something smart, but

closed it again without speaking. It was true. Maks had made time for her in a schedule that would defeat most men.

He always had.

"You don't love me." It wasn't an accusation, more a statement of confusion.

Why make her such a priority when his interest in her was more for the Crown's sake than his own emotions? But that was her answer, wasn't it?

No effort was too great on behalf of his country and its people. Including finding a wife and mother to the next royal generation.

"I do not believe in love as the all positive, powerful force everyone seems to think it is."

"How would you know?" He wasn't in love.

He'd shattered her scarred heart when he rejected her and let Gillian know in unequivocal terms that he did not love her.

Could she make that important in the face of her child's future, though?

That was the real question. How important was her pain in the balance of things? Both her parents had weighed their feelings, their desires, their careers, even their mildest convenience against their only child's happiness. Gillian had always lost.

She wasn't ever going to do that to her baby.

Maks lifted one dark brow in an unmistakably sardonic gesture challenging her question without words.

And then it clicked. She was being naive, not to mention somewhat myopic, wasn't she? He'd certainly experienced the negative side of love through his father's long-standing affair with the *love of his life*.

"Your father's love for the countess is not the problem, it's what he chose to do with that love."

"So you say."

"He had choices and he opted for the route most thinking people abandoned sometime in the Victorian era."

"Really? You are so sure about that?"

"No, but if the countess was like me, compromised in her reproductive abilities, he still could have married her. They could have used a surrogate."

"And risk having a woman make claims to the Volyarussian throne via her offspring? I do not think so."

"Baloney. There had to be a woman among your countrymen that he could have trusted to sacrifice for the good of the throne in this way."

"He approached my mother. Her dedication to Volyarus was a well-known circumstance."

"And she demanded marriage."

"She believed she would be a better queen than Countess Walek, a divorcée already with no children by her previous marriage."

Gillian couldn't help wondering if Queen Oxana had been in love with King Fedir back then, if her reason for demanding marriage had as much to do with affairs of the heart as the affairs of state.

Maybe like Leah in the Bible, she'd thought if she gave children to her husband she would earn his devotion. It hadn't worked that way for Leah and certainly hadn't for Queen Oxana.

"Your family is all kinds of dysfunctional, isn't it?"

"No more so than yours."

"Touché."

Maks's dark eyes studied Gillian with an expression she couldn't put a name to. "You said you *do* love me."

If she thought he was rubbing it in, she would dump the remainder of the pasta sauce pooled on her plate over his head. His tone was more clinical than gloating however, his expression still that enigmatic mask, but tinged with curiosity she could see.

"So?"

"Yet you did not fight for me."

"What? I fought for you."

"You evicted me from your apartment with haste."

She stared at him. "What did you expect? You'd just dumped me. I wasn't even worth looking into fertility treatments for."

"You could have argued, insisted on doing exactly that. If you wanted to be with me."

Like his mother had fought to be with his father? That had worked out well, hadn't it?

Shoving aside the sarcasm, she still couldn't believe he was trying to put it back on her.

Or was he? In his mind, he was only explaining his stance that love was not a positive, powerful force. And from his perspective, she had to think maybe she could understand why he'd come to that conclusion.

She tried to explain. "You admitted you don't love me."

"I never claimed to love you, but it had to be obvious I was considering marriage to you."

"It was." That was one of the reasons his rejection had hurt so much.

It had been such a shock in the face of what she'd thought were well-placed hopes. Hopes that had confounded her ten weeks ago and now, she still found inexplicable. "Why me? I'm not royal. I'm not anything special."

"That is not true. You are a woman of definite integrity."

"So are women a lot more politically connected than me."

"You have your own connections."

"You dated me because my father is a famous news correspondent?" It wouldn't be the first time, but it would be the first time finding out could hurt enough to make breathing difficult.

"No. I dated you because I was attracted to you. Full stop." His tone left no room for question. "Listen, Gillian, whatever you think of me, I did not want a marriage like my parents. I wanted to tie my life to a woman who would be my complement in every way. You handle yourself in diplomatic circles with an enviable aplomb."

"It's my shyness. I learned to use it to my advantage."

"You come off as reserved but kind. It's exactly what a monarchy like ours needs in its diplomats."

"I'm hardly a diplomat."

"But as princess of Volyarus, you would be."

"It's my mother's connections you find most appealing." That had never happened to her.

"She's a popular politician both in her own country of South Africa and on the international scene."

"Yes, she is." A stalwart feminist, Annalea Pitsu *would* not approve of Gillian marrying into a monarchy and taking a supporting role however. "She is not exactly political royalty, though."

Annalea was a mover and a shaker. Her disappointment with Gillian's choice of career was made clear at each annual visit.

Maks shrugged. "Marrying a woman from another monarchy, particularly a political one, comes with its own set of burdens. None of which have I ever wanted to negotiate."

"But...I don't know...wouldn't your people be happier if you married a Volyarussian?"

"If I had been drawn to a woman from my country as I was drawn to you, I would have pursued her."

"Oh." That told her.

In this, at least, Maks had no intention of being swayed by what the people of his country might prefer. Not the nobility, not the middle class.

There was no poverty class in Volyarus. It was too small and too well run for it.

Maks looked almost nonplussed. "That is all you have to say?"

"You've made it pretty clear you were sexually attracted to me." Not that she was some kind of vamp, or anything.

"I was also attracted to your personality, to the quirky way your mind works, and we have many interests in common."

"You thought I was your ideal woman."

"Yes."

"And then you found out I shouldn't have been able to conceive."

"Not easily, no."

"Were you upset?"

"You could not tell?"

"I thought..." She'd been very careful *not* to dwell on their last night together, but now, looking back, she realized he'd shown a near desperation for what he knew would be their last time together.

Looking at that night in light of what came later, she could see that he had indeed been really upset about breaking up with her.

She almost apologized, before she remembered the choice to walk away had been his. "You made the decision."

He nodded. "And you chose not to fight."

"That's ridiculous," she continued to argue.

What had there been to fight? By his own admission, he hadn't loved her.

What she had to decide now was: would their child be happy in a home where only one parent loved the other one?

Her gut told her, "Yes." In big, lead-heavy letters.

There was no particular pleasure in the knowledge, but there was a certain amount of relief. She could write her child's destiny with a very different brush than her parents had used on Gillian's.

If she had the courage.

If she trusted Maks to let her into that inner circle of his protection, even if he didn't love her.

"You knew I was considering making you the next queen of Volyarus."

"I didn't think of it in those terms, but yes."

"I *did* and you had to know that. Had to know that I was predisposed toward marriage to you, but still you let me go without any effort to convince me to stay."

She couldn't argue that particular point. From his perspective, he was right. "I didn't see any advantage in doing so."

"Did you not? Though you claim to love me."

Maybe she would have been able to convince him. Probably actually. From the way he was talking. That might have made Maks feel weak and even to question his own honor and dedication to duty.

Love ebbed and flowed in life, but Maks's sense of duty never would. If he felt it to her via their children, then it would never wane.

Would it be enough?

The one secret wish she'd cherished in her heart for her entire life was to be so special to just *one* person that they claimed her as irrevocably *theirs* and loved her more than their own convenience.

She'd never expected to come above everything in another person's life. Her aspirations had not been that lofty. And it was a good thing. Even if Maks loved her, he would never put her, or anyone, ahead of his duty to country.

But she'd wanted to be more. More than just the woman who got accidentally pregnant with his heir. More than the woman he could walk away from because her ovaries were flawed.

And if she could not be more, could she be happy?

Looking deep into her own heart, she thought maybe she could.

She stared at him, her heart squeezing in her chest.

No matter her arguments, she knew one thing was true, even if he didn't believe it. "Love is a very powerful force and I do love you."

"Even now?"

"Even now." Had all of this been to get her to admit it?

No. Again, the total lack of triumph on Maks's handsome features spoke for itself.

His strong jaw set in a frown, definitely no victory there. "And you are refusing to even consider marriage to me until you have hit your second trimester. Where is the *great* power of *love* in that?"

Once again, Gillian found herself opening and closing her mouth without the tiniest sound emerging.

He did look smug now, though it was tempered by something she wasn't sure she could name. If she wasn't so certain it was impossible, she'd almost call it vulnerability.

"Unrequited love hurts," she gritted out.

Didn't he realize that?

Sitting up, his agitation evident, he demanded, "In what way am I hurting you?"

"You don't want to be with me."

"I assure you, I do."

"Because of the baby."

"I wanted to ask you to marry me before I knew you were pregnant."

"But my supposed infertility stopped you."

"It is not supposed. It is a medical fact."

"Which means I may never be able to conceive again." He needed to acknowledge that fact and deal with it.

"Then we use a surrogate, or adopt."

"What about the potential problems with the surrogate or adoptive mother?"

"I do not share my father's fears, nor would I be open to my mother's type of ultimatum should my representative approach a likely candidate. I will already be married."

"With an airtight prenuptial agreement."

"Exactly."

She almost laughed, but shock was making her too breathless for that. He *wanted* the prenup. The cagey politician.

"You definitely want more than one child?" she asked.

His parents had stopped after him.

"Yes." Rock solid certainty in that single word.

"Even if it means using a surrogate, or adopting?"

"Yes."

"What about in vitro?" Her hand automatically went to her stomach as she thought of giving the child in her womb a brother or a sister.

"It depends how open you are to multiple attempts at the procedure. We will not risk your health by multiple births of more than twins."

That's what bothered him about in vitro? The risks to her health? "How many children do you want?"

"At least two, but I would like a house full."

She'd been raised an only child, but the mental image of her and Maks surrounded by a brood of children was incredibly appealing. "You live in a castle. That's a lot of children."

He laughed, tension leaving his body as he relaxed again in that wholly appealing pose she tried her best to ignore. "No more than four then."

"Four?" she asked faintly, her heart racing with emotions she didn't want to name.

"We will have help."

"I won't leave the raising of my children to strangers."

"Naturally not, but you will not be required to change every diaper."

She pulled a throw pillow into her lap, resting her arms on it as she tucked her legs up onto the couch. "And you won't change any, being a prince and all."

"I did not say that."

She shook her head. "Right."

"We have strayed from topic."

"What topic is that?"

"You claim loving me hurts you and therefore you cannot commit to marriage to me." Tension seeped subtly back into his frame with each word he uttered.

He did not like the concept at all, she could see that now.

But she wasn't going to lie to him to spare his feelings. He hadn't with hers. "You don't love me."

"So?"

"You aren't making this easy."

"I disagree."

She snorted. "Big surprise."

"You get sarcastic when you are tired, I have noticed."

"I'm not tired." But then she yawned, giving lie to her claim.

He smiled, the expression indulgent. "No, not tired at all."

"Okay, so maybe I am. What's your excuse?" It was getting harder and harder to maintain any level of annoyance with him, so her question came out more teasing than accusatory.

"For?"

"Your sarcasm."

"I'm a sardonic guy."

On that, at least, they could agree.

"You are saying that the mere fact that I do not love you causes you pain?" he asked.

Finally. He got it. "Yes."

"That makes no sense."

"You discarded me so easily because you don't love

me. If you had, you would not have let me go without a thought."

"Like you did me?" he asked, his brow raised in inquiry.

Or simple superiority.

She chose to believe it was the former, but in her heart of hearts she couldn't deny there was some truth to his comparison.

It ignored parts of reality she couldn't, though. "It wasn't without thought. I've missed you terribly."

Another admission she hadn't wanted to make, but had been compelled to because of his willful refusal to understand. Gillian glared at the culprit.

Maks did not appear fazed in the least by her small show of anger. "I missed you as well. I have said so."

"It was your idea to break up," she reminded him with some desperation as she felt the inexorable conclusion of this discussion growing closer and closer.

"I did not feel I had a choice."

Which was exactly why they had to wait to make plans for the future. Plans, she acknowledged, if only to herself, that would include marriage and the title princess in her future. "If I miscarry—"

"Stop talking like that immediately. You are not going to lose this child." His scowl seemed a lot more sincere than her glare had felt.

She didn't want to argue that particular point anyway. And every day closer to her twelve-week mark decreased her chances of losing the baby she'd already grown to love and felt such a fierce protectiveness toward.

"You might fall in love with someone else." She voiced her deepest fear, the one thing that no clause in a prenuptial agreement, no matter how carefully worded, could truly guard against.

No matter what he thought, love was an unstoppable force. He only had to look at his own father. There could be no doubt that Maks had come by his sense of duty and love of country naturally. And yet, the king had maintained a relationship for most of his adulthood that was not good for the Crown.

Because he loved the countess.

Maks looked supremely unconvinced. "That won't happen."

"Even you can't prevent it by sheer force of will."

"Of course I can. It is not merely a matter of will, but of actions. I can guarantee against it without doubt."

She did not share his confidence. "How?"

"Not allowing another woman close enough for a relationship to grow into intimacy that could lead to love, for a start," he said, like it should be obvious.

He had a lot of experience keeping people at bay, but proximity could undermine good intentions. "What if she works for you?"

"This is hypothetical as you well know. My personal office staff are all male, but if I thought a woman who worked for me was attracted to me, I would transfer her, or fire her, depending on how she revealed that attraction."

"You wouldn't be tempted?" Gillian had been to his company's headquarters.

And while his personal office staff might be male, there were still plenty of beautiful women working for Yurkovich Tanner, both in the U.S.A. and in Volyarus.

"No. *Would you?*"

"By another man? Of course not."

"But people in love cheat on each other all the time."

"Not all the time." But it did happen. "Most don't."

"Most? You are sure about that?"

What was she, Dr. Ruth? How should Gillian know? "Nana and Papa never have."

Maks nodded, conceding easily. "They are exemplary people, but they've also protected their marriage vows."

"Yes."

"As will I."

"You're so sure you can't fall in love with someone else."

"You're so sure I can?"

"No, but it's possible." Though the more they talked, the less likely she found it.

This man was determined *never* to be weakened by love. She couldn't believe she'd just realized that about him because, really? It should have been obvious from Day One.

She'd blinded herself to his disdain for the emotion, but it rang through clear when the subject of his father's "vacations" came up.

"And people *in love,* they never fall out of love and fall in love with someone else?" he pushed.

"You know it happens."

"Because they did not protect that love, nurture it, make it paramount."

"You sound like you understand love awfully well for a man who denies its reality."

"Oh, I admit love exists. I deny its all-strengthening positive power. Love undermines duty and makes strong men weak." That he believed every word he was saying could not be denied. It was in every line of his body, his tone and even the determination glowing in his brown eyes. "Insert relationship for love and you have my perspective on our marriage."

She swallowed, struck to the very core with his definition of how to handle marriage. "Our marriage would be that important to you?"

"It would come second to nothing."

He was delusional if he thought that. "That's not true."

"You accuse me of lying."

"About this? Definitely. Volyarus comes first, last and always with you. Our marriage won't trump that—it wouldn't even if you loved me."

"But our marriage is of paramount importance to our country's well-being. Stability in the monarchy has always marked stability for Volyarus."

They weren't talking about the same thing. "If it came between an important political event and our anniversary, the event would win."

"I am a better planner than that."

"Some things are unavoidable."

"Fewer than you might imagine."

Was he making a promise? The expression in his dark eyes said he was.

Against her better judgment, Gillian wanted to believe him. Her unique upbringing had taught her that even if a person didn't give the right name to it, they could have a necessary role in her life.

Like her grandparents, true mom and dad though they would never stand for being called that.

They had given her so much throughout her life, putting off their own dreams of early retirement and travel to see her raised.

Maks was offering her the same kind of commitment. It didn't come wrapped in the pretty bow of love, but it wasn't something to simply dismiss as unworthy, either.

No, Maks committed to her wasn't something to dismiss lightly at all.

"Why a cruise ship?" she couldn't help asking.

Now triumph flared in his espresso gaze. "Ariston can guarantee word of the wedding does not get out before we want it to."

"Ariston?"

"Spiridakous."

"The shipping magnate?" She wasn't in the least surprised Maks was friends with someone so wealthy and powerful.

The man would be king one day and was already

CEO of a company hugely competitive in the global market even though few people even realized it existed.

"His company is solidly diversified."

"With a cruise line?" It must be nice.

"Among other things."

"You only brought up the inside passage cruise because you know it's one I've wanted to go on." She'd mentioned it once.

Just *once,* but this man never forgot *anything* she was coming to realize.

"I will always try to meet your desires."

CHAPTER EIGHT

"ALWAYS?" SHE ASKED, feeling a sense of inevitability wash over her quickly followed by that irrepressible emotion: hope.

If she was burned by it again, she wasn't sure her heart would survive it. "We should wait until after the baby is born. To be sure."

"No. Stop. I have told you. No more of this negative thinking."

"I'm just trying to be realistic."

He laughed. Like she'd said something incredibly funny. "You are one of the worst pessimists I have ever known."

"I am not. I'm an optimist."

"In Eeyore's universe, maybe."

"You like Winnie the Pooh?"

"My mother read the books to me as a child, just like your grandmother did you. I was not raised on a different planet."

"No, I know. I just…" She wasn't sure what she wanted to say.

Telling him she didn't think he'd had anything that

normal in his childhood wouldn't go over well. And it wouldn't be true, either.

"If you are an optimist, then you will believe in our future and that of our child."

"Wow. You're so sure of yourself."

"I am not wrong."

"You are arrogant."

"Sometimes."

A lot more often than that, but saying so would just be querulous. And she didn't *want* to be argumentative. Not right now. She wanted to dive into his arms and have him tell her everything would be okay.

But she'd left those kinds of fairy tales in childhood.

The thought of approaching him for physical comfort sparked a strange sort of tension inside her as well.

Wanting a minute to regroup (as she was dangerously close to giving in), she stood and picked up the plates. "I'll just put these in the kitchen."

"Let me help." He jumped to his feet, quickly gathering the other detritus of their casual meal.

"I'm pregnant, not helpless."

"You didn't see me taking the plates right out of your hand, did you?" His smile was teasing, his expression unexpectedly lighthearted.

"No," she admitted grudgingly.

"There you have it. *Polite,* not overly protective."

Not entirely sure she minded overly protective or that he'd avoided it altogether, she found herself smiling back.

They fell into a surprisingly easy and natural rhythm

as the dishes were rinsed and put in the dishwasher. “You’re awfully domesticated for a prince.”

“So you’ve said before.”

“And you claim to have lived on your own for more than a decade.”

“I have.”

Right. “You have a housekeeper and a maid for a penthouse apartment in a posh building that comes with access to an onsite chef and laundry service.”

“So?”

She wiped down counters while he finished loading the dishwasher. “So, you’re a dab hand at rinsing dishes and you aren’t going to convince me the maid, much less the housekeeper, leaves them in the sink for you to deal with.”

“I went to university for four years here, as well as two additional to get my MBA.” He put a soap tab in the door and shut the appliance with practiced efficiency. “That is six years doing my own laundry and dishes.”

Leaning back against the counter by the sink, she asked, “You didn’t live on campus?”

“The first year, yes, and that only meant I didn’t have to do my own cooking. My second year, I moved into an apartment with Demyan.”

“And you didn’t have a housekeeper?” She couldn’t imagine Demyan doing anything for himself, either, honestly.

“We both wanted our privacy.”

Young college men, sowing their wild oats? That was more understandable than she wanted it to be.

"It was good for you."

"It was. Not everyone living in Volyarus is born in a palace. I need to understand the lives of my people if I am going to make decisions that best serve them." He shrugged out of his suit jacket, hanging it over the back of the kitchen chair.

"You think living without servants for six years helped you do that?"

His tie followed, draped neatly over the top. "That and the time I have spent living with different families throughout Volyarus in the summers, each one with a different job from a different walk of life."

"Wow. I wouldn't have guessed." Her voice went up an octave as he unbuttoned his shirt, exposing his snugly fitting undershirt. "I'm surprised your parents allowed it."

"They insisted on it. My father did the same and his father before him." He kept the shirt on, but there could be no question how he expected their evening to end.

She didn't call him on it because she wasn't entirely sure the confrontation would end up with a victory on her side.

So, she ignored his blatant gestures of intent. "That's kind of amazing."

"And may well be impossible for our own children. Security issues grow increasingly bleak."

"The world is too connected." In years past, a mostly unknown country and its monarchy would have found their first form of defense in their very anonymity.

The internet and a new level of paparazzi that catered to it ensured no one of *any* note remained entirely anonymous in today's world.

"For the freedom we once knew in Volyarus, yes it is." He leaned negligently against the wall beside the built-in desk where she paid her bills.

Feeling unsettled, she moved around the kitchen, rearranging things on the counter, checking the timer on the dishwasher, and avoiding his gaze if she could help it. "Now, you're forced to live the life of a royal because if you don't, you could be kidnapped."

It was a disturbing thought and quickly morphed to the realization her child would be facing the same risks in the future.

"Or assassinated."

A cold chill passed down her spine and Gillian stopped abruptly to face him. "Don't say that."

"Now you know how I feel when you make similar pronouncements about our baby."

"I didn't mean to upset you with the truth."

"Nor I you."

"Okay, fine. I get it. No more mentioning the possibility of miscarriage."

"And marriage?" he asked, with a hopeful charm she found utterly irresistible, but then what about this man wasn't to her?

"On a cruise ship?"

"If you don't like the idea, we can come up with another."

"No. I like it." Too much.

"Ariston will be pleased." Maks grinned, showing the man very pleased was himself.

"You've already approached him?"

"I'm an efficient man, Gillian. You know this."

"Yes, but..."

"Ariston has had his own marital challenges. He is only too happy to help."

Gillian wondered what a Greek shipping tycoon would consider "marital issues" but was too wrapped up in her own at the moment to ask.

"I want Nana and Papa there."

"Absolutely."

"The prenup isn't going to be pretty."

He tried to look all serious, but the grin lurking in his eyes and flirting with the corner of his lips was unmistakable. "Be aware that any assurances you ask for from me, I will demand from you as well."

"No problem."

He nodded, like he hadn't expected any other answer.

She took a deep breath and gave in to the inevitable. "I'll marry you."

Because when it came down to it, she would not deny their child its birthright. But also because she loved him. Because he was committed to making their marriage work in a way a lot of men in love weren't.

Because her future had too bleak a cast without him in it.

"Thank you." He reached into his pocket and pulled out the familiar blue box.

"You knew."

He flipped open the box, revealing the ring so perfect for her. “I hoped, but I had a backup plan.”

“What was it?” Seduction probably.

“My mother.”

Gillian felt her eyes widen. Some backup plan. That was a woman who could and had been ruthless for the sake of her family and country.

“I’m glad it didn’t come to that.”

Maks laughed as he removed the ring and set the small blue box aside. “She’s not that bad.”

“She’s a heck of a lot scarier than Demyan.”

“I do not think so.” He smiled and reached for Gillian, his intention to put the ring on her finger clear.

She flinched back without thought, the inexplicable urge to avoid him overwhelming.

Maks looked gobsmacked. “I cannot touch you?”

“I…” She didn’t know why she’d shied from him this time.

His eyes narrowed. “You are not adverse to my touch.”

“I don’t think I am.”

He began moving forward, his expression predatory. “You are not.”

“But—”

He put his finger on her lips, pressing with gentle firmness. “No. Our separation has caused you to withdraw from me. Now I will bring you back into the sun.”

“You are not the sun.”

“But you are a flower about to bloom again.” The

naughty look in his espresso dark eyes gave all sorts of connotations to his words.

"Stop trying to sound like a desert sheikh."

He laughed. "I assure you, I am very content to be Volyarussian."

Of that, she had absolutely no doubt.

No man was as proud of his heritage as Crown Prince Maksim of the House of Yurkovich. Part of her craved physical closeness with this dynamic man, and yet Gillian felt this inexplicable urge to push Maks away.

She tried to will her body to relax, but the muscles in her back and neck were rigid with no hope of releasing the tension.

Maks's eyes narrowed and his hands landed very deliberately on her shoulders. Her body tightened, her first instinct to jerk away from him again, but she managed not to give in to it.

He advanced and she backed up, could not help doing so, until she was up against the refrigerator.

Her breath came out in short, near-panicked pants.

He trailed one finger down her throat until it rested over her rapidly beating pulse. "This reaction is excessive, don't you think?"

"Yes." She did; she just didn't know how to fix it.

Their bodies were so close she could feel the heat coming off his. In the past, that heat had always excited or comforted her.

She'd loved it when he spent the night, thinking that he could have kept her warm on even the coldest nights in her Alaskan hometown.

Now, his hotter body temperature made her feel trapped, even marked by his nearness.

She did not understand it.

His fingertip brushed back and forth over her pulse point. "Your body shies from my touch and reacts with alarm to my nearness."

"I don't know why." Only maybe she did.

His leaving had devastated her, left her hurting in a way even her parents' ongoing rejections never had. Her atavistic reaction to him was that of one animal mauled by another.

Even if the mauling had been purely emotional and equally unintentional, she understood that now it had left her entire being wary of this man.

He could not guess at the depths of her pain because he did not truly understand the terrible power of her love. He was right about one thing, though, that power had not been a positive force in her life yet.

And only she could change that.

She'd thought it was all on him. His rejection. His lack of love for her.

But she should have fought for him. If she wanted him and she so did. Only she'd learned way too young that fighting for some things was futile.

"I tried. It didn't work."

"What did you try, *mýla moja?*"

The Ukrainian *my dear* touched her when she wasn't sure she was ready to be touched, reached her heart where she wasn't sure she was ready to be reached. "To get my parents to love me, to want me."

"Even if I refuse to give love room in my life, I want you, Gillian. I always will."

Could he promise that? His expression said he could and he would. She wasn't so sure, but she wanted to believe so much, that it was another, sharper pain to add to the dull ache that never left.

"You thought that by being as perfect as you could be, you would make them want to be with you," he guessed, his dark gaze filled with more understanding than he should be capable of.

"Yes, but it backfired. They thought I was well-adjusted without them. Even my grandparents never understood how painful Rich and Annalea's absence from my life was. Annalea even touts me as an example of what making rational choices can do for everyone involved."

"She believed it was best for all of you for her to abdicate her role as your mother."

"That's what she says."

His espresso gaze searched hers. "It would have been kinder to allow you to be adopted."

"Nana would not hear of it. She insisted on raising me. She and Papa love me, even if they won't claim me as their own."

"They have never denied you."

"Not as a granddaughter, no."

"But they do not consider you their daughter, though they raised you."

"They can't."

"It would mean admitting your father, the son they love, is not the man they choose to believe him to be."

His understanding shocked her until she realized that in Maks's family, he had plenty of experience with the exact same dilemma. "Yes."

"Even so, you are still a fighter."

She wanted to break eye contact, but couldn't. "About other things."

"Important things." There was a strange inflection in his voice when he said the word *important* she couldn't interpret.

"Important yes, but not *all*-important." Would he understand the distinction?

His dark brows drew together and she knew she'd have to spell it out for him. She didn't mind so much, now.

"I called in sick and cried continuously for three days after you left my apartment that morning." She managed to look away, not wanting to see his reaction to her admission. "I've had nightmares only to wake up and realize they were memories."

"That is..." His words trailed off as if this master communicator was at a loss for words.

"It's what people who have suffered a debilitating loss do."

"I did not die."

"Our relationship did." She looked back at him, needing him to see she spoke absolute truth. "I'd lost you. Had no hope of you returning."

"And yet you did not call me as soon as you realized you were pregnant." Confusion clouded his expression.

"I knew you'd insist on marriage and chances were, I would not be strong enough to say no."

"There is no weakness in doing what is best for our child despite what you believe it may cost you."

"The weakness comes in how much I want it," she admitted. "I didn't want to trap you."

"I do not feel trapped." He swallowed, his jaw taut with tension. "I never intended to hurt you that way."

"I believe you."

"Nevertheless, I did it."

"Yes." Because he didn't love her, he could not have guessed at what losing him would cost her.

"I will not leave you again." It was a vow, accompanied by the slipping of the ring on to her finger.

Even though it was prompted by her pregnancy and the fact she now carried the heir to the Volyarus throne, the promise in his voice poured over the jagged edges of her heart with soothing warmth. The small weight of the metal band and diamonds on her finger was a source of more comfort than she would ever have believed possible.

She was not sure her heart would ever be whole again, but it did not have to hurt like it had been for ten weeks.

"I won't leave you, either."

"I know." A small sound, almost a sigh, escaped his mouth. "Now we must convince your body that it still belongs to me."

"You have a very possessive side."

"This is nothing new."

"Actually, it kind of is." He'd shown indications of a possessive nature when they were dating, but he'd never been so primal about it before. "You're like a caveman."

His smile was predatory, his eyes burning with sensual intent. "You carry my child. It makes me feel *very* possessive, takes me back to the responses of my ancestors."

Air escaped her lungs in an unexpected *whoosh.* "Oh."

"I have read that some pregnant women desire sex more often than usual."

"I…" She wasn't sure what she felt in that department right now.

She always seemed to want him and could not imagine her hormones increasing that all too visceral need.

"However, I had not realized the pregnancy could impact the father in the same way." There was no mistaking his meaning.

Maks wanted her. And not in some casual, sex as physical exercise way. The expression in his dark eyes said he wanted to devour her, the mother of his child, sexually.

Gillian shivered in response to that look.

"Cold?" he purred, pushing even closer. "Let me warm you."

"I'm not co—" But she wasn't allowed to finish the thought.

His mouth covered hers in a kiss that demanded full submission and reciprocation.

Her body, the same body that had shied away from his every touch, now capitulated without a single conscious thought on her part. She sank into him while her mouth softened under his, allowing him immediate access to the interior.

Like the marauder his ancestors had been, he took advantage, his tongue seeking hers out with sensual intent. The hand on her throat slid down to her shoulder and then lower to cup her breast.

Sensitive from the hormones running rampant through her body, she felt that initial touch through her pajama top to the very core of her. Gasping against his lips, she pressed into his hand.

His triumphant growl was both animalistic and unbearably exciting.

This man might have all the urbanity expected of a prince on the outside, but underneath beat the heart of a ruthless Cossack. He wanted nothing less than *everything.*

She understood that finally, in absolute clarity. It wasn't enough for him to put a ring on her finger and name her his princess. No, this man would hold absolute possession of her body, would demand nothing less than complete loyalty of her mind and the heart he eschewed interest in.

And God help her, she'd promised to give it.

Not in so many words, but agreeing to marry him

carried with it all sorts of ramifications she hadn't even considered ten weeks ago.

Another shiver rolled through her and the hand still on her shoulder tightened before moving to her bottom. That big, masculine hand curved over her backside, squeezing, proclaiming ownership without a single word.

Then she was being tugged even closer, their bodies as intimate as they could get with clothes on.

His hardened sex pressed into her stomach, his thigh insinuated between her legs to press against her. Pleasure shot through her from the slight stimulation to her clitoris, the position that was both protective and undeniably sexual.

Her own hands found their way to his neck and into the silky, mahogany hair at the back of his head. She tugged on the strands, not to move his head away, but simply because she couldn't help herself.

He responded by deepening the kiss and flexing the leg between her thighs, using his hand on her bottom to maneuver her against his leg and increasing the stimulation to her clitoris almost unbearably.

She wanted to be naked, but couldn't stop kissing Maks long enough to tell him so.

His hand on her bottom kneaded the flesh there, moving inexorably toward her inner thigh and pulling her higher onto his leg at the same time.

Small bursts of pleasure exploded inside her with every small movement. She wasn't even sure she wouldn't climax before they ever got their clothes off.

He seemed intent on bringing her as much pleasure as possible in as short a time as he could. It was not his usual technique.

But then he'd said he was feeling desperate for her, hadn't he?

She didn't know if it was the pheromones coming off her body because of her pregnancy, or if he was simply feeling the separation of ten weeks and his celibacy over that time. And she didn't care.

This grittily passionate lovemaking was exactly what Gillian needed.

She needed him *not* to treat her like fragile glass because she carried his child. She needed to *feel* his desire for *her* to the deepest recesses of her soul.

CHAPTER NINE

GILLIAN HAD COMMITTED to a lifetime with this man without his love.

Knowing his passion for her was strong and imperative gave her hope for their future together.

His hand found its way under her sleeping T-shirt to the unfettered breast beneath. He brushed his fingers over her achingly hard nipple before cupping the flesh around it.

She moaned, no thought of hiding even a smidge of her reaction to him.

In this, at least, there was gut level honesty and an undeniable connection between them and she hoped always would be.

It wasn't love, but it wasn't merely lust, either. Not when her love was so consuming and his sense of possessive connection so overdeveloped.

He lightly pinched her nipple and she cried out against his marauding mouth.

He broke the kiss to laugh in triumph. "You are mine."

"You are even more arrogant than I knew."

Espresso eyes glittered down at her. "Admit it. This baby in your womb and the woman who carries it, you are both *mine*."

"Yes, we're yours, but you'd better remember that comes with a lot of responsibility for our welfare and I'm not talking about providing materially for us." She had a job and could support herself just fine.

"I know." His handsome face set in serious lines. "You believe I will hurt you as my father has my mother all these years, but it will not happen."

"Your father could never have hurt your mother like you can hurt me." Not even if his mother *had* felt some type of love for King Fedir when she demanded marriage in exchange for a child.

Maks's eyes flared in surprise and then narrowed in understanding. "Because you love me."

"Yes."

If Queen Oxana had loved King Fedir as much as Gillian loved Maks, she would not have forced him into the sordid life of a married man carrying on an affair with his one true love.

His happiness would have been paramount. Just as Maks's happiness was for Gillian.

If she thought marrying him would hurt him, she would refuse to do it. Of that she was absolutely certain. She knew her own heart and what it was capable of. She had a lifetime of testing and stretching it.

"You won't stop saying it because I do not return the sentiment?" Maks asked as his hands and hard thigh continued pushing so much pleasure into her body she thought she might explode with it.

"Do you care if I do?" she gasped out.

For a split second in time he went still, unmistakable vulnerability flashing before it disappeared. "I find that I do."

"I won't stop saying it." Who knew? One day, he might even truly understand what she meant when she did.

She could only hope he'd learn through feelings for her and not someone else.

"Stop it," he ordered, his voice harsh.

"What?"

"You are doing that thing again, that pessimistic thinking."

"How can you possibly know?"

"You get this look on your face, like all joy is in danger of being sucked from your life."

She dropped her gaze, not wanting the level of insight this man was capable of at that moment. "Don't be ridiculous."

He let out a frustrated sound and then his head lowered again, not to kiss her but to launch a sensual onslaught onto her vulnerable neck.

Delight spiraled through her as he reminded her he knew exactly how to bring her, Gillian Harris, the maximum sexual reaction.

And just like that, she was on the verge of climaxing again. This time, he didn't allow for conversation, or interruption, taking her up and over that pinnacle of pleasure without ever directly stimulating her clitoris.

She screamed out her pleasure, no hope of holding the sound in as her body shook in convulsions so powerful they should have been able to shatter bone.

Afterward, he stripped her naked, right there in the kitchen, and tore off his own clothes, before pushing her up against the wall. He lifted her legs, using the power of his muscular six-foot-four-inch frame to hold her in place as he spread her legs wide.

His erection pressed against her entrance, the bulbous tip spreading tender tissues for his invasion.

He paused there, the muscles of his neck corded with the strain of holding back. "You are the only woman I have ever had sex with without a condom between us."

"Even when you were young and stupid?" she gasped out as his erection pushed inside a single slow inch.

"I was young once, never that stupid."

"You never worried about diseases with me."

"I saw your medical records."

"Not stupid."

"Do you want honesty?"

"Always."

"It never entered my mind."

He hadn't even considered the possibility. That made her warm deep inside.

She smiled. "Good."

"Impractical."

"I won't tell."

He laughed, the sound strained. "I know. You would die of embarrassment."

"I'm not sure I can face Demyan as it is."

"You can." Then whatever restraint Maks had been under seemed to break and he pushed all the way inside with a single powerful thrust.

The sound of satisfaction that came from deep in his chest sent another wave of desire crashing over the first one caused by finally having the connection of full intercourse.

Whatever veneer of civility still intact over Maks's features and actions disintegrated in that moment and he began to make love to her with animalistic intensity. His powerful body pistoned in and out of hers, bringing intense pleasure with every potent thrust.

His breath came in harsh gasps, hers no better.

"Never again," he ground out between clenched teeth as he swiveled his hips on the next thrust, causing her clitoris to pulse with pleasure.

She agreed, not sure what she was agreeing to, but hearing the need for her accord in thought in the two words. "Never again."

"Ten weeks is too long."

Without sex. She understood and though she wished he needed her emotionally with the same intensity, his sexual need was its own type of relationship guarantee.

"Come for me again," he demanded as his body possessed hers so completely she would never again doubt who she belonged to.

Not that *she* had ever really been in doubt.

She said nothing, though, too intent on how her body seemed perfectly able to accede to his demand. The wonderful tension built inside, tightening, tightening, tightening…until it released with another life altering culmination.

This time, he came with her, his sex first swelling inside her, pushing her own pleasure toward the edge of unbearable before she felt the heat of his orgasm inside her.

He buried his face in the join of her neck and shoulder, his muscular chest rising and falling with harsh breaths as he repeated a single word over and over. "*Moja.*"

Mine.

And though there'd been nothing gentle about this coupling, the profundity she'd felt that night ten weeks ago washed over Gillian again, bringing tears to sting her eyes.

She did not know how he knew, but suddenly Maks's head came up and he searched her face, his own expression unreadable. "Too much?"

"No," she denied.

"Why the tears?"

"I can't explain."

"Pregnancy hormones."

"Maybe," she hedged.

His eyes narrowed. "I wonder."

He lifted her left hand to his lips, kissing right above the ring he'd placed there, the message of possession in his dark gaze unmistakable and undeniable.

Then the gentleness came. He withdrew from her body, carefully lowering her legs to the floor. But he did not leave her to stand on her own; he simply changed his hold and lifted her again.

This time he cradled her against his chest and carried her through to the bathroom. Nothing like the master bath in his penthouse, her bathtub was barely big enough for one. There was no hope of them bathing together unless they showered.

And somehow she knew that was not his plan.

But she didn't want to let go of the connection. She'd learned her lesson about clinging early in life, though, so she said nothing as he lowered her to the side of the tub.

He turned on the tap, adding her favorite bath salts. She watched the level rise, glad for his unconscious hand on her thigh as he swirled the salts so they melted into the hot water.

"The smell of rosemary reminds me of you."

"Isn't that the way it works? Rosemary for remembrance?"

"It's the scent of your bath salts. Rosemary and mint. I like it."

He'd said so before and she'd stopped buying other fragrances for her bath. She didn't admit that now, though. "I like it, too," was all she said.

He nodded before gently lifting her and placing her with what could be mistaken for tender care into the tub.

"I don't need this kind of help," she protested. "I'm pregnant, not helpless."

"We have just made the most passionate of love. I will see to your comfort if I like."

"You're kind of bossy."

"You're *very* independent."

"If you were looking for a leech, you shouldn't have dated me."

"I do not want a leech. A little clinging wouldn't hurt, though," he grumbled under his breath.

She couldn't believe her ears. "Men like you hate women who cling."

"I do not know where you come by your vast knowledge of men like me." He frowned down at her, even as he began to wash her body with a bar of glycerin soap and gentle caresses. "But *I* would enjoy *you* clinging."

"You wouldn't."

"Allow me to know my own mind."

"You get very formal in your speech when you are annoyed, did you know that?"

"It has been mentioned."

"Good, I wouldn't want you to be ignorant of a tell that could hinder your diplomatic or business negotiations."

"For my country they are often one and the same."

"For most countries, I think that's the case."

"You may well be right." He continued to wash her.

"You're still bossy."

"It is a trait you are more than capable of withstanding."

"You have a lot of faith in me."

"I chose you for my princess. Of course I do."

And though he'd rejected her it hadn't been for reasons to do with her character. "The world is very black and white for you, isn't it?"

"I know what I must do. I know what I want. I know how to go after both." He settled on the large fluffy rug she kept beside the bath and then continued to wash her as if every single toe and finger needed his undivided attention.

"Am I something you want as well as something you must do?" she asked, not sure she wanted the answer.

"You can ask that after what happened not ten minutes past?"

"This is me clinging."

Incredibly, he smiled. Lifting his head, so she could see the expression had reached his gorgeous eyes, he nodded once. "Good. Yes. I want you. Very much."

It wasn't love, but it was better than pure duty.

Maks held Gillian in his arms, her body lax in sleep, her features soft and vulnerable as they would not be awake.

The sun had risen thirty minutes ago and his schedule for the morning was tight, but he had not gotten up.

He could not help feeling like he'd narrowly averted disaster. Even more disconcerting was his inability to identify how he'd done it.

He did not know why Gillian had agreed to marry him.

No question, she'd taken their baby's welfare to heart. And she said she still loved Maks, but neither gelled in his mind as the reason for her reversal on her stance about agreeing to marry him before she hit her second trimester.

Was it the sex?

The physicality between them was explosive, but was it enough to push her over that mental precipice she'd been balancing on?

He was grateful she had agreed to marry him without doubt, but Maks did not like when the motives of others were cloudy to him. Perhaps it was the way he'd been raised, or his position, but it was never enough to simply know, he had to know *why.*

His life fit into neatly ordered compartments; it always had. The one where Gillian resided had been destroyed ten weeks ago when Maks read the results of her yearly medical examination. Her agreement to marry should have created a new compartment that he could understand and rely on.

It hadn't.

The compartment he had marked for his wife was no longer defined and measurable. And while that made him uncomfortable, he could not regret Gillian's willingness to align her life with his.

Though he found it hard to admit, even to himself, she filled empty places in his life he hadn't realized existed. He was not entirely convinced those places were not supposed to remain empty.

The last months had been hollow in a way his life never was before the recognition that his role and responsibilities might not be enough.

One night of incredible sex, a few days of *connection*

and that hollowness was gone. The possibility it could return made something tighten in his chest.

He was never letting this woman out of his life again.

She thought the prenuptial agreement was for her protection, but he was as eager to have her sign it as she was to take measures to protect the future of their family. Unlike his parents, or her own, theirs would be a real marriage for a lifetime.

Sliding his hand down her arm, he let it come to rest over hers, the large square-cut diamond of her engagement ring pressing into his palm, giving him a deep sense of satisfaction.

The expensive piece of jewelry marked her as his, but not as primally, and therefore satisfyingly as the passion mark he'd left on her breast, or the slight razor burn on her neck that evidenced his passion of the night before.

The desire to own and be owned surged through him.

Yes, he was a possessive guy. He would be king; absolute allegiance was something he'd been taught to give and expect.

What shocked him was the equally strong desire for others and Gillian herself to acknowledge that he was hers. Her fiancé, soon to be her husband.

The father of her child, the one and only man she would ever expend her passion on.

"What have you woken up thinking about?" she asked, her voice laced with amusement and sleepy desire.

"What do you mean?" he hedged.

She shifted slightly so his hardened sex rubbed against her hip. “What do you think I mean?”

“Oh, that.”

“Yes. *That.*” She laughed, the sound so pleasing his erection jumped against her hip.

“My desire for you is nothing new.”

“No, it isn’t.” She turned so her beautiful blue eyes could meet his. “I like it.”

“I also.”

“Want to do something about it?” she asked with a comical leer.

It was his turn to laugh, the sound going from his mouth to hers as he claimed her lips with a ferocity only this woman had ever sparked in him.

Their lovemaking was passionate and drawn out, Gillian giving as good as she got, and Maks had reason to appreciate her agreement to be his wife once again.

Afterward, she cuddled in his arms, clinging as she so rarely allowed herself to do and in a way he found himself craving more with each passing day.

As much as he enjoyed the moment, he could not prolong it. His day’s schedule had been set before he’d arrived at her apartment the night before and he would already have to cancel the phone conference he had planned for before his early morning flight.

With more regret than he wanted to admit to, even to himself, he pulled away to get out of the bed. “I have to fly to Volyarus this morning.”

It was not lost on him that she made no effort to hold him back. Gillian was no doubt correct that many men like him would find that reaction a relief from their lover. He would have been one with any other lover before her, but she was more than the woman who shared his bed.

Gillian Harris was the woman he had chosen to spend his life with.

For all her claims to love him, she did not act like a woman whose happiness depended on his presence. In any way.

He did not like the suspicion that he might find her presence in his life more necessary than she found his.

She sat up, pulling the sheet and comforter with her as she did so, maintaining a modesty unnecessary between them.

But strangely appealing nonetheless.

Was there *anything* about this woman he did not find attractive? Her lack of clinginess notwithstanding, he could not think of one.

"Okay." She tucked her blond hair behind her ear. "You'd better take a shower then."

"You could ask when I have to leave, or how long I plan to be gone." Did she not have even the most rudimentary interest in his plans?

Her brows furrowed and Gillian's head canted to one side. "You want me to quiz you on your schedule? Wouldn't it just be easier to sync our calendars?"

Annoyance surged through him. "You're very tech-oriented for an artist."

"What can I say? I love my smartphone, but you know that."

"Yes." He should have gotten her the newest one on the market instead of a ridiculously expensive ring from Tiffany's.

"Whatever you're thinking isn't very nice. I think you'd better keep it to yourself."

"You think you can read my mind?" he scoffed.

"Your expression isn't exactly stealthy right now."

Affronted, he drew himself to his full impressive height. "My ability to hide my thoughts is second to none."

He'd been training at it since birth.

"When you're making an effort, yes, it is."

"Perhaps I have allowed myself to become too relaxed around you."

"We're going to be married." Her brows furrowed and her lips formed a straight line. "I don't think I would like it if you hadn't."

"Oh." He had not considered that angle. "My parents are not trusted confidants to one another."

"We have already established that we are not going to emulate them in important ways."

"And this is one of those ways?"

"Absolutely."

He nodded, accepting that she expected a similar level of trust to what he gave his cousin.

Shockingly the prospect did not bother him. "I would like you to go with me."

"This morning?" she asked, her expression not promising.

"Yes."

"I have a full schedule today and tomorrow for that matter."

"You work too much."

"It would be pretty hard to pay the bills otherwise."

"You are no longer alone."

"What, we get engaged and suddenly I'm supposed to quit my job and let you *take care* of me?" The scathing tone left no doubt what she thought of that idea.

"Not quit, no, but cut back? I would prefer it. Wouldn't your doctor?"

"She made no stipulations about my work. It's not physical enough to be risky to my pregnancy."

"You are tired."

"Not right now." But her honest blue eyes told their own story.

"You would like to cut back your hours," he guessed.

"I'm not lazy."

"No, you are not."

"You don't expect me to quit?"

"No."

"Even after we are married?"

"Photography gives you a great deal of satisfaction. There is no reason you should give it up entirely."

"What part should I give up?" she asked in a wary tone he did not understand.

"I do not know. Whatever assignments are not as interesting to you?" Communication with women had always been like navigating a minefield for Maks.

He had hoped with Gillian agreeing to be his wife,

it would be more straightforward, less fraught with explosive traps.

"You don't have any particular ones in mind?"

"No."

"My father disparages my book covers and is barely more tolerant of my portraits, but they at least have some artistic merit in his eyes."

"I am not your father. And your portraits are pure and amazing art. I am no expert in the industry, but I like your book covers as well." Maks had seen Gillian's portfolio.

Her photographic portraiture was indeed unique. He was actually quite surprised it didn't dominate her work and had remarked on that fact in the past.

She'd told him her prices were very high for the portraits she did do and she was really picky about what clients she took on. She wasn't nearly as choosy about her book covers.

She brought other people's visions to life with them. For her, it was a different kind of art. Apparently equally satisfying, but different.

"You just want me to cut back my hours?" she asked cautiously.

"The life of a princess is not without its demands. Your body is already taxed with the pregnancy."

"How long do you plan to be in Volyarus?"

"Two weeks. I should have left several days ago."

"But then Demyan told you about our little problem."

"Our baby is not a problem."

"No, I didn't mean it that way."

"Good."

"You're awfully touchy."

"I am going to be late." He turned toward the bathroom. "Go back to sleep. It is still early."

CHAPTER TEN

"BOSSY," GILLIAN MUTTERED as Maks left the room.

She wasn't really sure why the conversation had ended so abruptly. He'd thrown his need to leave and desire for her to accompany him out there and barely given her a chance to respond before dismissing her and what they'd been talking about.

True, he hadn't left the apartment, but he'd effectively left the conversation, *with instructions for her to sleep.*

One thing Nana always said was that a woman who intended to enjoy her future had to begin as she meant to go on in any relationship. Whether of short or long duration, it was always worth setting expectations.

Their marriage would definitely fall under the long duration header.

Throwing back the covers, Gillian climbed out of the bed, glad the morning nausea that had plagued her seemed to be tapering off. She went to grab a robe, but then put it back deliberately. The water was already running for the shower.

He would just have to share.

It wouldn't be super comfortable, but they'd done it before.

The bathroom was already filling up with steam from the hot shower when she reached it.

"You're going to have to share the hot water," she announced as she pulled back the shower curtain far enough for her to step into the tub with him.

He turned around quickly, his expression reflecting surprise.

She barely refrained from rolling her eyes. "Did you really think you could just tell me to go back to sleep and I would do it?"

"You need your rest."

"We weren't done discussing the things you'd brought up."

"I thought we were."

"Really?"

"Yes." The exasperation in his tone would have been more impacting if his dark gaze wasn't devouring her nudity.

"We made love twice last night."

"So?"

"So, you look like you're thinking about doing it again."

"I am, but there isn't time." His tone was laden with unmistakable regret.

She laughed softly. "I don't remember you being this insatiable."

"Don't you?"

Actually, he'd never made his fascination with her

body a secret. "You're more primitive about it now. I feel like you have this need to mark me."

Incredibly, color washed across his cheekbones and then concern darkened his eyes. "Was I too rough?"

"No. Not at all. I like this less civilized side."

"That is good to know."

She put shower gel on a loofah and began washing him. "So, you want me to come to Volyarus."

"My mother will want to see you." He made a soft sound of pleasure in the back of his throat as she brushed the loofah over his chest.

"Will she be angry?"

"That you are not with me?"

She shook her head at this masculine inanity. "That we have to get married."

"She approved my choice ten months ago."

"Oh." Gillian hadn't realized it had gone as far as Maks talking his choice of a wife over with his mother. "My medical results certainly threw a spanner in the works for you."

"Temporarily."

She shook her head. "You really are an optimist, aren't you?"

"I think you need that."

"To counterbalance my so-called pessimism?" she asked sarcastically, her hands falling away from him.

His expression was entirely serious when he said, "Yes."

"I'm not a pessimist."

"Then you do a very good imitation of one."

"People say hope doesn't cost anything, but that's not true. When you hope for things and you are disappointed, it hurts. When it happens a lot, hope gets harder and harder to let in." She began washing herself, scrubbing with the loofah with jerky movements.

He reached to her, tugged the loofah from her hand and hung it from the hook on the enclosure wall, and then pulled her gently into his body. "I will do my best to fulfill the hopes you allow room in your heart."

"You're awfully poetic for a Cossack." Tears tightened her throat.

"I'm not a Cossack."

"Your ancestors were and sometimes genetics ring true."

"Do they? What hope does our child have then?" he teased.

Gillian opined firmly, "She will have the best of both of us."

"Was that optimism I heard?" He put his hand over his heart, feigning shock.

She smacked his chest, but gave a hiccupping laugh. "Yes."

"Will you be able to join me in Volyarus?" Tension she didn't understand after the humor and the charm came off him in waves.

"I think so. It will mean moving some things around and into the weekend, but then I can join you Monday and stay that week and through the weekend."

"You will do that?"

Gillian tilted her head back so their eyes met. This

needed to be said. He deserved to know she understood the differences that being his wife would make in her life. “Maks, I know that marrying you comes with a job title.”

“Princess.”

“It’s an honor.” That he’d wanted to give her ten weeks ago.

He grimaced. “But not one you aspired to.”

“No, but I always knew it would be necessary if I was to remain in your life permanently.”

“And did you have plans to do so, before?”

“You know I did.”

“You would have agreed to my proposal ten weeks ago.”

“If you’d made one, yes, I would have.” She wasn’t going to lie to him.

“But you had no intention of accepting my proposal when I made it four days ago.”

“You know why.”

He frowned, looking like he wanted to say no he didn’t, but was manfully refraining.

She couldn’t help laughing, though her humor might be more macabre than jolly. “I know. You don’t understand the fear that love might bring.”

“I thought the saying was perfect love casts out fear.”

“I’m not perfect and neither is my love.”

“On that we must disagree.”

“What?” Now *she* was totally confused.

He pulled her closer, their naked flesh fitting together so naturally under the cascading hot water that emotion choked her. "You are perfect for me."

"Because I carry your child."

"That's part of it, yes, but then even that only shows how insanely compatible we are. No one else could have gotten you pregnant in a single night without condoms."

"Conceited much?"

"No. This isn't about my prowess…it's about how we fit." He was very serious, his espresso eyes filled with sincerity.

To hear his words describing the feeling that had been washing over her touched something deep inside, something she thought would always hurt. Only right now, the pricks and stings were absent.

It was not love, but it was something.

She buried her face against his chest, needing a moment, but he refused to let her hide from him. Even for a second. He tilted her head up the same time he lowered his mouth to hers and pressed their lips together in the gentlest kiss.

Tenderness remained, but the gentleness quickly morphed into something else. A passion that coursed through her, making her heart beat so fast she could barely catch her breath.

They were both breathing heavily, the steam around them not as hot as their bodies had become when he moved to kiss down her throat.

"I thought we didn't have time," she gasped.

"I already missed one meeting." His hand slid down her backside and between her thighs, his fingertips playing over the slick flesh. "My pilot will have to wait as well."

She didn't argue, though she was sure it was more than his pilot that sex would put on hold. He knew it, too. And that just blew her away. Realizing Maks could be distracted from duty for the intimacy between them was more mind-altering than the pleasure they found in one another's bodies.

And that always left her feeling like she'd had an out-of-body experience, or rather a very intense in-body experience.

The need to show how very much that meant to her grew inside Gillian until she became determined to do something she'd never done before. Dropping to her knees, she nuzzled into his lower abdomen, her intentions clear.

Her wet hair brushed over his already hardened sex and he groaned, his hips canting for more contact. The man was insatiable and she was glad. Really, really glad.

No, it wasn't love, but it *was* something worth fighting for.

He sucked in air, another long, low groan pealing out of him as she turned and quite deliberately licked his length.

"What are you doing?" he croaked out.

"If you don't know, I am not doing it right."

"But you don't do this." He'd never asked it of her and she'd never offered.

"It isn't because I don't want to."

"Then why?"

She looked up; able to admit something she wouldn't have even twenty-four hours earlier. "I don't know how."

"You've *never* done it before." He sounded almost awed.

She shook her head. Gillian was determined to do it now, though, as much for herself as for him. She'd always wanted to—with him, but she'd lacked the confidence to try when his sexual history was so much richer than hers.

She didn't just want to try something new, she craved giving him pleasure like he'd never known.

Yesterday she would have doubted her ability to do that, but the day before Prince Maksim of the House of Yurkovich had not been so moved by his desire for Gillian Harris that he'd chosen to circumvent his own schedule.

While he did not make it a habit to cancel on her, he had *never* rearranged his schedule to spend time with her, either. Not once, not even pushing a meeting back by five minutes, much less rescheduling it altogether.

But not only was he purposefully giving up his takeoff slot at the airport, Maks had already missed a meeting to spend as much of the morning's early hours with her that he had.

Overwhelmed with a kind of giddy joy at the thought of it, Gillian kissed the weeping tip of his erection, lapping at the moisture. It was sweeter than she expected and she made a sound of approval.

His swollen hardness jumped against her lips. "Put it in your mouth. *Please.*"

"Yes." She took his head into her mouth and wondered how she was supposed to take more.

He wasn't small by any means and her mouth only stretched so wide.

Refusing to worry about the fact she couldn't take it all in, she swirled her tongue around the head, eliciting groans from Maks. He certainly didn't seem to mind she wasn't going to deep throat him like a porn star.

He fell back against the wall of the tub enclosure, his big body giving one long shudder. *"Feels so good."*

She curled both her hands around the wet shaft and began stroking him as she changed her licking to sucking.

He shouted, his hips surging forward as if he could not control the movement.

He penetrated her mouth farther, but her hands on his shaft prevented him from going too far.

"Sorry," he gritted out, making an obvious effort to remain still.

She felt like smiling, happy he'd lost control. It meant he didn't have all the power in their relationship.

Part of her had known that, because she carried his child, but part of her had felt helpless in the face of her own love.

She was feeling anything but helpless right now with his extreme response to her novice, but enthusiastic efforts. Increasing the speed of her caresses, she was surprised at how excited doing this for him made her.

She wanted to bring him off, but she ached with the desire to be filled, too.

She couldn't stop what she was doing to tell him. Didn't want to stop pleasuring him with her mouth. It was such an amazing feeling, to have him at her mercy and yet be so emotionally connected it was like a live current of electricity arced between them.

But he grabbed her head, pulling her back.

She frowned up at him.

His pupils were blown, his face dark with passion and he rasped out, "I'm about to climax."

"I want you to."

He let out a pained groan, his hips flexing. "No. You don't."

"I like the taste."

"Come is not as sweet as preejaculate, or so I've been told."

"Really?" Her frown turned to a glare, some of passion's haze dissipating.

He laughed, the sound almost tortured. "You have nothing to be jealous about. No other woman has ever affected me like you do. No other one ever will."

She believed him. Today. This morning, after he *chose* to miss his takeoff slot to be with her, she believed him.

He tugged gently on her head, both hands on either side of her face and she found herself rising to stand in front of him. "I want to be inside you."

"Y..." Her voice gave out, her own want was so deep. She cleared her throat. *"Yes."*

He kissed her, his mouth laying claim to hers without apology or hesitation.

She kissed him back, asserting her own claim, letting him know with the ferocity of her response that he belonged to her as well.

She didn't know which one of them broke the kiss, or how she ended up facing the far wall of the tub enclosure with her legs spread as much as they could go in the narrow space, her nipples aching in the moist air.

But she literally shook with the need for copulation.

His body blanketed hers, his sex aligned to the apex of her thighs. "Let me have you, *sérdeńko,* open yourself to me."

"Yes!" She threw her head back against his shoulder, a tiny part of her brain insisting she'd find out what *sérdeńko* meant later.

His erection pressed between her legs, zeroing in on the opening to her body and pressing inside in one smooth movement. He filled her, the stretch so perfect, so intense and the angle just right for hitting her G-spot, ecstasy sparked hot along each nerve ending.

One long fingered hand reached around and delved between her folds to tease her clitoris, the other slid up her stomach to play with her breasts. The multiple stimulations were body buzzing and mind numbing.

Her brain stopped making fully realized thoughts as he touched her in ways guaranteed to bring her the ultimate in pleasure and she offered her body to him without limits.

The water beat down on them; Maks moved with

passionate urgency, his sex caressing that sweet spot inside her, his fingertip rubbing circles of delight on her clitoris.

The pleasure spun higher and higher inside of Gillian, her body naturally arching up on her toes in response, her hands against the slick wall in no way holding her up. It was Maks's strength doing that, his big Cossack's body.

And then everything exploded in a starburst of color that rivaled the Northern Lights, her body convulsing around his sex, her womb contracting with ecstasy, her breath sawing in and out in passion-filled pants.

The scream of completion that ripped out of Gillian's throat mixed with Maks's feral shout as he climaxed, too, his body rigid behind her, their voices rising in a crescendo of delight.

As the pleasure ebbed, small aftershocks dwindling to an all over sense of perfect well-being and happiness, she became aware of the small kisses he was placing along her neck, cheek and temple. She turned her head and their lips met in a moment so laden with her love, it was a living blanket around them.

They shared kisses between drying each other off after finishing their shower in lukewarm water. Her apartment didn't have the unlimited hot water tank his swank penthouse suite enjoyed.

"What does *sérdeńko* mean?" she asked.

Maks stilled and then leaned forward to kiss the side of her face. "Heart. It means heart."

It was her turn to pause, everything inside her stilled in wonder. "Why?"

"You are the heart of this relationship."

It wasn't the words of love her soul longed to hear, but it was so much more than she'd expected after the way they'd broken up ten weeks ago, Gillian had to duck her head so he didn't see the moisture pooling in her eyes.

He knew, though. Maks always knew.

He pulled the towel from her unresisting fingers and pulled her into another full body hug. "It will be good between us, Gillian. Believe me."

"I do." For the first time since she was a tiny child, Gillian made no effort to temper the hope bubbling up inside her like the sweetest of champagnes.

CHAPTER ELEVEN

THE NEXT FOUR days were a blur of activity for Gillian as she worked to clear her schedule for the last-minute trip to Volyarus.

Maks video called her twice a day, once in the morning and before bed each night.

In between, he was back to texting her frequently and now she was getting all three meals delivered as well as snacks in between. Some came to her apartment, others her studio, but when the catered delivery showed up at an offsite shoot, she knew this was more than just a matter of Maks instructing someone to make sure she got fed.

He was taking care of her and she liked it. She liked it a lot.

The private jet Maks sent to bring Gillian to Volyarus was swank, every appointment on the luxury end of comfortable. It was also already occupied.

Gillian had only met the woman sitting primly in the leather seat facing the entry door a handful of times, but she would have recognized Queen Oxana even if she never had. The queen of Volyarus might be a lesser known royal in the world of monarchies, but her visage had been in enough magazines and newspaper articles to make her a recognizable figure.

"Good evening, Miss Harris."

Extremely grateful for all the awkward moments she'd spent at her father's side at social functions now, Gillian did a standing curtsy. "Your highness."

The queen rose from her chair, even that small movement graceful and elegant. "You may address me as Oxana. We are to be mother and daughter by marriage, I am told."

Gillian couldn't tell how the older woman felt about that fact from her perfectly smooth tone and politely inquiring features. Where the heck was Maks?

She couldn't believe this little tête-à-tête was his idea. Which meant it was the queen's. Oh, joy.

"Yes." Gillian swallowed, her mouth gone dry.

"You are pregnant with my son's child."

"He told you?" The adrenaline of shock lasted only a few seconds and then tiredness took over, the past weeks catching up to her in an inexorable wave of mental and physical exhaustion. Gillian sighed, putting her bag on the seat nearest her. "Of course he told you."

"Actually he did not."

"Demyan?" Gillian guessed.

"Yes."

"But why?"

"Apparently, unlike my son, he thought I should know the reason for Maksim's insistence on a rushed elopement followed by a State reception." The queen waved toward one of the cream leather seats, indicating Gillian should take it.

Knowing their takeoff slot was approaching quickly, Gillian put her seat belt on as soon as she'd lowered herself to the cushy leather. "Yes, of course. What I meant was why didn't Maks tell you?"

Perfectly tweezed and shaped eyebrows rose slightly. "He does not want me to believe you have trapped him into marriage."

"He's protecting me." Typical but not altogether welcome in this instance. Gillian would much rather Maks'd had this discussion with his mother. "The news was bound to come out."

Queen Oxana nodded as she returned to her own seat, leaving the belt undone. "Yes, it was. Sooner than later and if he was thinking with his usual clarity, he would have realized this."

"I haven't noticed any lack in his sharp brain processes."

"Haven't you?"

"No." Heat washed through Gillian, bringing with it a resurgence of the nausea she'd thought was gone for good.

Suddenly the queen was standing over Gillian, her hand on Gillian's forehead. "You feel a bit clammy. Are you nauseated?"

Gillian could only swallow and nod.

Moments later, Gillian had a glass of carbonated mineral water and soda crackers sitting in front of her.

The queen had returned to her seat, buckling her belt when the engines started warming up.

Gillian nibbled on the soda crackers while taking sips of the mineral water and tried to calm her inexplicably racing heart as the plane began its taxi toward takeoff. Or maybe not so hard to understand in the circumstances. She reacted to her own mother's presence this way.

Why not a queen's?

Queen Oxana spoke quietly to the flight attendant and then the man moved to the back of the cabin. Eyes so like her son's examined Gillian with probing dispassion. At least, it *looked* like a lack of feeling.

Gillian was fairly certain there was a cauldron of emotion under the placid royal exterior.

"Feeling better?" Queen Oxana asked.

"Yes. How did you know, that I wasn't feeling well, I mean?" Since she had been sitting down, there was no way the older woman could have seen how dizzy Gillian had become.

"Your face is quite expressive."

So her urge to throw up had been evident in her expression? How attractive. "I see."

"You will have to work on that."

If she was going to keep up with the queen and her son, Gillian certainly would. Thinking that went without saying and that Maks's mother didn't need Gillian's verbal agreement, she took a sip of her water and considered the next few hours in light of her company.

This led to another sip as her stomach roiled.

She was going to kill Maks. With his Machiavellian brain, he should have realized what Queen Oxana would do and circumvented it.

"I am not certain what that particular expression means, but it seems like someone might be in trouble."

"You could say that."

"My appearance surprised you."

"Yes." There was no point in trying to pretend otherwise. The way Gillian had nearly fainted in her seat was a dead giveaway.

"Maksim was born with duties and expectations few could understand, much less live up to."

Unsure where the queen was going with that statement, Gillian nodded.

"He has always accepted his role without regret or complaint."

"I know." Gillian wished she knew the script for this scenario. "He has a highly developed sense of responsibility."

"Some might even say *over*developed."

"Yes, but I would be surprised if you were one of them."

"I am not the starry-eyed idealist I was when I first became queen. As I have gotten older, I have come to realize that perhaps my son's happiness is as important as his duty to the throne."

Gillian could not stifle the gasp of shock that opinion elicited.

Queen Oxana smiled wryly. "Yes, I know, Maks and

his father both would find the idea bordering on the heretical."

"But…" Gillian realized she did not want to bring up the queen's own choices that precluded happiness for the sake of duty.

The woman might be a public figure, but that did not make her life an open book.

"I would like to ask you a question, and I would appreciate it very much if you would answer honestly. Though I have little confidence you could hide the truth with your open expressions," the queen mused, seemingly appreciative of that fact rather than disparaging.

"All right." Gillian took another careful sip of water, her nausea not noticeably improved yet.

Queen Oxana nodded, like she hadn't expected any other answer. "Did you get pregnant in order to trap my son into marriage?"

Water spewed as Gillian choked on the question and the beverage. The queen pressed a button and the flight attendant came bearing a linen napkin and a fresh glass of water. How he'd procured both so quickly, Gillian was content to leave a mystery.

He left, the damp napkin and her "compromised" glass of water in his capable hands.

"My question shocked you. It upset you as well, I think." Queen Oxana looked vaguely regretful.

Gillian took several deep breaths and frowned at the queen, not even a little appeased. "You think?"

"Sarcasm can be very unpredictable in its outcome when used in a diplomatic setting."

"So can inappropriately probing questions."

"Touché."

"I am not a gold digger."

"Many people find power far more seductive than money."

"The only thing seductive about Maks's life is the fact that he's in it," Gillian said with pure sincerity.

Queen Oxana's eyes widened infinitesimally, the only sign that she might be surprised by Gillian's viewpoint. "Demyan said you did not tell Maksim of your pregnancy."

"Demyan needs a hobby that *isn't* spying on me."

The queen's lips tilted in an almost smile, humor glinting briefly in her dark eyes. "He has not spied on you personally."

Gillian just looked at Queen Oxana, not willing to play a game of words right then. She was at enough of a disadvantage; she wasn't going to let the older woman lure her into engaging in a sparring match Gillian had little hope of winning.

Her experience with the rich and powerful had taught her the effectiveness of silence and reticence.

The queen nodded, as if Gillian had confirmed something though nothing had been said. "Tell me, why did you not inform my son of your pregnancy immediately?"

"I felt it was best to wait."

"Why? Did you hope the further along you were, the more desperate Maksim would be to give his child legitimate claim to its place in the House of Yurkovich?"

"No." What kind of manipulative, self-serving person did this woman think Gillian was?

Depressed emotion overwhelmed her. She'd been feeling so hopeful, but the queen's doubt and clear disapproval despite her calm air renewed Gillian's own worries about this marriage born of necessity, not love.

She kept telling herself that even though they didn't have love, they had something special. How long could the special part of it last though if his mother disapproved and sought to undermine Gillian's relationship with the future king?

Doing her best to swallow the emotion clawing at her, she said, "Eleven weeks ago, your son dumped me because my medical exam revealed that I have compromised fallopian tubes."

No shock showed on the queen's placid features. "Again, Maksim did not share this with me."

"But you knew anyway."

"Naturally. Demyan did not learn his habits from a stranger."

"Was that a joke?" If it was, Gillian wasn't laughing.

Queen Oxana flashed that barely there smile again. "Perhaps."

When Gillian made no effort to continue the conversation, the queen remarked, "I have yet to understand why you hesitated to tell my son of your condition."

"It's not a condition. It's a baby."

"I apologize. I did not intend to offend you."

No? Gillian just shook her head. "You and my birth mother would get along well."

"In that, I think you are mistaken." For a moment, unmistakable emotion clouded the queen's eyes and it wasn't humor.

There was no question that for some reason, the queen of Volyarus did not like the feminist politician from South Africa.

"If you say so."

"It truly was not my intention to offend."

"I find that hard to believe. Your diplomatic skills rival your son's, or so I've been led to believe."

"Perhaps my son is not the only one disturbed by recent events."

Well, that told Gillian where she and the baby in her womb stood in the queen's estimation. They were *disturbing.*

"I didn't tell Maks about our baby because my fallopian tubes are still compromised. If I miscarried, we were in the same place we had been ten weeks ago." Simply saying the words reminded Gillian what she was ignoring in order to marry Maks. "I would once again be the wrong person to be his princess."

"Maksim, in his usual optimistic fashion, ignored that possibility, did he not?"

"Yes."

Queen Oxana seemed to thaw slightly. "Why were you concerned about the viability of your pregnancy?"

"Rates for miscarriage are higher than most people are aware. Stress increases them."

"Having been abandoned by the man you loved would have caused enough of that commodity."

Gillian had never said so to Maks, but yes. She nodded.

"You felt like you were defective and worried that increased your chances of losing this miraculous baby."

Gillian had no idea how the queen came to that conclusion, but she could not deny it. "Yes."

"Maksim has no idea, does he?"

"Of course not. He wouldn't know how to feel defective."

"Thank you."

Gillian found a smile. "Nana would say you raised him right."

"Your grandmother is a very colorful character."

"She is that." Nana was going to add some interesting spice to royal gatherings in Volyarus.

"I, on the other hand, understand intimately that feeling of defectiveness." Sadness shone in Queen Oxana's dark gaze. "I lost three babies after Maksim's birth."

Gillian sucked in a breath. "I'm very sorry."

"Thank you. Some pain is so deep, it never leaves completely."

The fact the royal couple had married in order for Queen Oxana to provide heirs to the throne made the tragedies that much more poignant.

The queen looked out the oversize cabin windows into a rapidly darkening sky. "I would have enjoyed a houseful of children."

It was such an unexpected thing for a woman like the impeccable and controlled queen to say, Gillian gasped.

The older woman looked back at Gillian, meeting

her gaze with a troubled brown gaze. "You cannot picture it, can you?"

Gillian considered lying, but wouldn't disrespect the other woman with less than honesty. "Frankly, no."

"The miscarriages, the dissolution of my marriage in every way but on paper, it all changed me, but one thing I never lost was my desire for more children. I never resented Demyan's place in our lives. Far from it."

"Maks considered you a very good mother." No doubt Demyan had as well.

The man had picked up the queen's habits by her own admission.

"I am pleased to hear that, but I fear I did him a terrible disservice in raising him so focused on duty and with such a wariness toward love."

"You know he's only marrying me because of that deeply ingrained sense of duty, don't you?" Stupid tears Gillian blamed on pregnancy hormones burned her eyes. Understandably the queen regretted raising her son in a way that made the current situation possible. "I know it, too."

No matter how much Gillian might wish things were different.

"You do not believe my son would have married you without the baby to draw you together?"

"I know he wouldn't." Hadn't the older woman been listening when Gillian told her that Maks had broken up with her eleven weeks ago?

"Maksim has been very attentive the past days he has been in Volyarus for a man only doing his duty."

"He's a committed guy. I'm one of his responsibilities now." And she'd been an idiot to let herself begin to believe it might be something more.

If not love, something.

Right.

"Surely you do not begin to imagine my son does not care for you?"

She almost snarked back, *surely you don't imagine he does.* Only Maks did care, if only for the fact she was the mother of his unborn child. "Your son does not love me. He's been very clear on that point."

"Has he?" The queen almost looked guilty. "Has he explained why?"

"Can you explain why one person falls in love and another doesn't?" Gillian asked, trying to get hold of her emotions and knowing she hadn't succeeded when her voice came out shaky from the tears she refused to let fall.

"He is afraid to love. I made him that way."

Gillian wouldn't deny that his mother's views on the subject had influenced Maks, but ultimately the problem was with what he actually felt, not what he thought about feeling. "He doesn't believe in love and really, it's a moot point. If he loved me, he wouldn't be able to deny it."

"I think you underestimate my son's power of will."

Gillian shrugged, not agreeing but lacking the energy or will to argue the semantics of emotions with the queen.

She was sure the other woman had something else

of more importance—to her anyway—to discuss. “Is this where you try to buy me off, or something, your highness?”

“I must insist you address me as Oxana. We *will* be family.” For once all of the other woman’s emotions showed on her perfectly made up features. And every single one of them was horror. “As to your question, no. Absolutely not.”

“But you think I trapped your son into marriage.”

“No.”

“You asked…” Gillian let her voice trail off.

What did it matter? The queen…*Oxana* had only brought to the forefront what Gillian knew in her heart to be true. Maks had been coerced into marriage by his personal sense of honor and his very real concern for their baby. There was no getting around it.

They were both trapped and guilt was like a stone in Gillian’s heart because part of her was glad. That had to make her a very selfish person, even though she would never have intentionally pushed Maks into their current situation.

“I want you to marry my son,” Oxana said quite distinctly.

“I find that difficult to believe.”

“Again, I am sorry. I am not usually so inept at making my wishes known.”

Gillian had no trouble believing that.

“I did not like the idea you had tricked Maksim into marriage.”

“Like you did his father.”

The queen did not react angrily to the supposition, but she shook her head. "There was no trickery involved with Fedir. He wanted my womb. I wanted him."

"Maks believes you only wanted to be queen."

"Maksim sees the best in his parents. It is a child's prerogative."

"Yes, I suppose it is."

"Fedir never stopped loving that woman, even after Maksim was born."

"It didn't work for Leah, either."

For a moment Queen Oxana looked confused, but then her expression cleared. "From the Old Testament? No. I should be grateful that Bhodana never conceived, but I am not. Fedir would have enjoyed having more children."

"I thought the countess was infertile."

"No tests were done. It was her status as a divorcée that prevented her marriage to Fedir while his father still lived."

"And your presence as his wife after."

"He would not dissolve our marriage. He refused even when I offered."

"He and Maks have a warped sense of duty to Volyarus."

"Overdeveloped and maybe it is warped, but I never saw it that way."

"You shared it. After all, you stayed."

"Of course I stayed. My son was to be king one day. He needed me to guide him and Demyan's own parents abandoned him to our care for the sake of their own ambitions. He needed me as well."

"In the end, you're saying it was the children who came first."

"As it should be."

"I agree."

"That is why you are marrying Maksim?"

"Yes."

"You love him."

"With everything in me."

"And that is what makes this so difficult for you? That is what brings the grief and pain into your lovely blue eyes."

"He won't love me." The truth of that statement weighed like an anvil on Gillian's soul. "It's not an emotion that grows out of nothing."

"You have a child between you, common interests, shared experiences. That is not nothing."

"You had all those same things with King Fedir, but he never learned to love you."

"His love was already spoken for."

"It wouldn't have mattered."

"You don't think so? I am not so sure, but I suspect you are right. He cried out her name…the nights we tried for a baby."

It was such a startlingly intimate revelation, Gillian knew it was heartfelt and extemporaneous. "I'm sorry. If Maks did that, I'm not sure he'd leave the bed with his bits intact."

Incredibly Queen Oxana laughed. "As it should be.

Perhaps a good kick in certain regions would have knocked sense in the king."

"Maybe." Love wasn't the great bearer of rationality, though.

"I believe you are wrong."

"About what?"

"My son's feelings for you."

Gillian wished with all her heart she was, but she knew the truth. "No."

•

Gillian's first view of Volyarus was glittery lights in the extended blackness that was night in the Baltic Sea.

From research she'd done, Gillian knew that while the majority of the inhabitants of the small nation lived on the main island about the size of New Zealand, it was actually an archipelago with some of the most profitable mineral rights existing on the lesser inhabited, more barren islands.

The main island boasted a mountain whose snow peak never melted but at the base of which a thriving capital city was surrounded by extremely productive farm land.

The growing season was short, but the constant sunlight made for bumper crops.

Gillian couldn't see any of that as she stood on the top of the steps leading down from the jet's doorway.

The early summer darkness here was absolute, once the sun had set. Like it had been in Alaska growing up. The landing strip and its surroundings were lit, but the area beyond was nothing but inky blackness.

Three cars waited at the bottom of the stairs. Two SUVs with large unsmiling men standing beside them and an official-looking stretch limousine with the flags of Volyarus flying on either side of the hood. The driver stood by the open back door.

A silver Mercedes sports class, just like the black one Maks drove in Seattle, came screeching to a halt on the tarmac as Gillian reached the bottom of the steps shortly after the queen.

"Oh, dear," Oxana said. "It appears Maks has discovered my trip to meet you."

Gillian had no chance to answer before the driver's door slammed open and Maks sprang out. Moving forward with speed, his attention so completely on Gillian, he did not hear his mother's greeting as he walked right by her.

The queen smiled, surprising Gillian, turning to watch as Maks swept Gillian into his arms and kissed her until she was breathless.

Deciding he knew the protocols best, Gillian went with it and kissed him back, letting her body relax into the man she loved. Once again in his arms, her worries for their future dissipated.

Eventually he pulled back, though he kept her close, facing him, as Maks's dark eyes searched her own with an intense expression she didn't understand. "How was your flight?"

"Fine."

"I did not expect you to have company." He still hadn't acknowledged his mother's presence.

"Me, either."

"Is it all right? Did she..." Maks looked over at his mother, his expression one Gillian could live the rest of her life without having directed at her. "She did not attempt to turn you off marrying me."

There was no question that *if* Oxana had tried that route, it would have led to a near irreparable schism with her son.

"I did nothing, Maks, but get to know the lovely woman you intend to marry."

They actually had spent some time talking like two new friends, before the queen had insisted Gillian take a nap for the remainder of the flight. Oxana had kindly woken Gillian in time to brush her hair and teeth in the jet's lavatory before landing, so she didn't feel so rumpled meeting Maks.

"If she said anything to upset you..." Again that look.

And it made Gillian feel badly. Oxana loved her son deeply. "She only wants your happiness, Maks."

"I am happy to be marrying you."

"And to be a father, I am sure," Oxana said smoothly.

Maks jolted, as if it had not occurred to him that his mother would learn the truth before he told her. Which made no sense. How could Maks have believed that Demyan would keep something that elemental from the queen?

Oxana was right. Maks wasn't thinking with his usual clarity.

Gillian shook her head. "It's fine. She's happy about the baby, too. Okay?"

Maks again searched Gillian's features, as if he was not sure he believed her before turning to examine his mother with the same questioning intensity.

The older woman frowned. "How can you doubt it?"

He did not answer, but turned back to Gillian.

She looked up into brown eyes that caught at her heart.

"She did not upset you?"

"I was surprised when I found her on the plane," Gillian deflected.

Unmistakable worry washed over Maks's features. "But you are not upset."

Grateful he'd used the present tense rather than the past, she was able to answer without prevaricating. "No."

"Very well."

"Maksim. Really." The hurt outrage in Oxana's tone rang sincerely. "You will have Gillian believing I am a monster."

Maks sighed, his expression showing guilt only a loving mother could engender.

He turned his face toward Oxana, but he kept his body in a protective stance around Gillian. "Of course not."

Incredibly, Oxana laughed, the sound soft and free somehow. "Oh, Maksim, I was so afraid I'd ruined your ability to love."

Maks went rigid. "Love is—"

"A tremendous blessing when the one who loves

practices selflessness rather than selfishness," Oxana interrupted in a very unroyal way.

Maks opened his mouth to respond, but Oxana shook her head. "I fear that between your father and I, you have only ever seen the selfish side of romantic love. Perhaps if you'd spent any time with the countess, you would have seen what selfless love is like."

"How can you say that woman—"

Oxana put her hand up, interrupting again. "She is more than *that woman,* Maksim. She is *the* woman, the one woman who offered your father love without strings and he took it. Selfishly."

"Mother."

"Come, this is no place for a discussion about our family's brokenness."

Gillian thought perhaps both Maks and Oxana should have considered that reality before this moment; this entire night had been a strange one.

Maks frowned and insisted, "Our family is not broken."

The queen merely smiled that enigmatic smile and walked toward the limousine. "Come, Maksim. Ivan can drive your car back to the palace."

"I wanted…"

"Gillian is too fatigued for a nighttime tour of the capital city. Come, Gillian. Bring my son with you." The imperious tone wasn't one Gillian would think of dismissing.

Thankfully Maks showed he was smart enough not to, either.

Soon, they were all ensconced in the limo, Maks's car in Ivan's care. Despite the roomy compartment, Maks kept Gillian so close she was practically sitting on his lap.

She didn't mind. Not a bit. The closeness, his constant touching, it all helped overcome that sense of despondency she'd been feeling on the plane.

Laying her head on his chest, Gillian snuggled in as she wouldn't have dreamed she could do in front of his very proper royal mother.

Once the car was moving, Oxana said, "Maksim, I am very displeased."

"I'm sorry to hear that, Mother, but I will marry Gillian."

"Of course you will. She's the mother of your child."

"She is *sérce moje,*" he said with conviction.

"That is all well and good, Maksim, to say she is your heart. What she does not realize is that she *fills* your heart. Her reaction to my presence on her plane made that very clear."

"Mother," Maks warned.

Gillian didn't know what the queen was trying to prove, but whatever it was, Gillian was afraid it was going to end up breaking Gillian's heart all over again.

"Fine." Oxana crossed her arms in most unqueenly like fashion, a stubborn glint in her dark eyes. "You told me you love my son, Gillian."

"Yes," she croaked out.

Her feelings had been laid bare already. It shouldn't

hurt to have them dragged into the light right now, only it did. Very much.

And she really wasn't sure why.

Oxana nodded, like she expected nothing less than Gillian's agreement. Then she pressed, "Enough?"

"Yes." It didn't matter what Oxana meant, what Gillian loved Maks enough for.

She'd loved him enough *not* to go to him with news of her pregnancy to protect him and his freedom. She loved him enough for whatever it took to put his happiness above her own.

And then Gillian knew; this was the great power of love he could not understand.

But she knew it was there and would never again doubt the strength it could give her.

"Enough to give him his freedom after your child is born and a sufficient period of time has passed?" Oxana asked.

Gillian didn't hesitate. "Yes."

"No," Maks barked at the same time, his volume much higher than hers, his conviction laced with desperation she didn't understand.

If she did not know better, she would think he was the one unsure of *her* feelings for *him*.

He turned to her, his expression wounded in a way she'd never expected to see. "You will not leave me."

"She knows that you are better off without her if you do not love her." Oxana's eyes were filled with both certainty and compassion.

Maks sucked in a harsh breath. *"No."*

"Yes." Gillian felt the pain of that admission, but it wasn't greater than the strength of her love. "You deserve to find love, to live with the glorious knowledge that there is one person in this world whose happiness will always come ahead of your own."

"No. Damn it to hell! You are not leaving me." He turned a sulfuric glare on his mother. "If she leaves me, I will never forgive you."

The certainty in his tone left no room to question his absolute sincerity in the statement.

Oxana flinched, but she never looked away from her son's anger. "Why, Maksim? What would make you turn from your family so completely?"

"She is mine."

"And are you hers?" Oxana asked, her own voice sharp with pained censure.

Gillian understood only too well. King Fedir had never been hers, but Oxana had given the man her own heart and life.

He'd squandered both and never realized it, or if he had, did not care.

"Yes. I am hers." The ferocity in Maks's tone was matched by the way he pulled Gillian tighter into his body.

She squeaked.

He looked down at her, but did not relax his hold. "Are you all right?"

She nodded, completely lost for words in this conversation that seemed to be leading a direction she'd been absolutely sure no discussion between her and Maks could ever go.

The Rolls-Royce stopped and Oxana set a gimlet stare on her son. "You will give her the words. You will not hold *anything* back from a woman who loves you enough to give you your freedom for the sake of your happiness even knowing it will decimate her own heart finally and forever."

The queen got out of the car, walking toward the palace without looking back.

Tension vibrating off him like the aftershocks of an earthquake, Maks followed. Gillian went with them.

She had no choice. Maks had a hold of her and he wasn't letting go.

Full stop. Period.

Gillian barely noticed the austere beauty of the palace's architecture, or the opulence within. Her attention was fixed entirely on the man leading her across the massive foyer, up one side of a double marble staircase and down a long corridor.

He stopped when they'd gone into a room that could belong to no one but him with its masculine luxury.

He turned to face her. "Would you like a bath before bed?"

"Don't I have my own room?"

He shrugged. Like it didn't matter.

"I thought the idea wasn't to make a big splash in the media. Won't someone notice I'm sleeping in your room? That can't be appropriate, surely?"

"I am Crown Prince—no one will question me."

"The media don't have to question. They just have to report."

"Let them report it then."

"Maks! You're not thinking straight."

He stared down at her, his jaw taut with emotion she was beginning to think exceeded anything he'd ever admitted to. "I thought my mother would try to convince you to leave me."

"Why? You said she approved of me as your potential wife."

His paranoia was irrational, emotionally driven.

The concept blew her belief about their relationship straight into space. Because Maks claimed not to be motivated by emotion with her.

Had he been lying to himself and her?

"She went to meet you. She didn't tell me beforehand. That kind of subterfuge never ends well."

"She didn't do anything wrong, Maks."

"She suggested you leave me." The pained betrayal in his tone hurt Gillian's own heart.

But it made those champagne bubbles of hope start fizzing again too.

"Only after our child was guaranteed his or her place in the House of Yurkovich."

"Do you think that is all that matters to me?" he demanded, his eyes wounded. "Is it all that matters to you?"

"You know it isn't."

"Then why would you leave me?"

"So you can find love."

"I have already found love," he shouted, his entire body rigid with feeling he didn't seem able to keep inside anymore.

Emotion she had been utterly sure he didn't have inside of him. "You broke up with me."

"I should not have done."

Could it be that simple?

"You need heirs."

"I need you."

"You do?" she asked softly, her heart blossoming like a rose under the sun.

He stopped and stared at her. "*Koxána moja.* I live for you. My brain is clouded with thoughts of you. I forget my place in the middle of a meeting and find myself texting you while businessmen and politicians watch, believing I am contacting someone of more importance than them. It is the truth, but not in a way most would understand."

From his tone, it was obvious Maks wasn't truly understanding it himself.

"The prospect of you leaving me again fills me with dread." The intense feeling lacing his voice brought moisture stinging to her eyes. "What would you call it?"

"Love. I would call that love."

Could it be true?

He stared at her, his expression so dismayed it was almost comical. "I just called you my love."

"I didn't know that."

"I will teach you the words, so you can say them to our children."

"All right."

He dropped to his knees in front of her, his expression stricken. "I love you, more than duty, I love you. And I tried to deny it. There are no words for the depths of my sorrow at my own cowardice."

"You aren't a coward." Just a man who had been raised to believe that love was not meant for his future. "You didn't let your mind even consider the possibility."

And she'd refused to consider it, either. She'd been too afraid, too certain he couldn't love her.

But Oxana had known. Gillian shook her head at the inexplicable powers of loving mothers.

"No, do not shake your head. I *do* love you. I did not say it, but surely my actions pointed to it."

"I was shaking my head at your mother's intuition."

"My mother." Oh, the anger in his voice.

"She wanted you to admit your love—she never intended that I leave you."

"You are so sure."

"If you were feeling more rational, you would be, too."

"I am always rational."

"Except maybe when you are admitting for the first time that you are in love."

He opened his mouth, looked at her and then closed it again.

She smiled down at him. "I love you, with my whole heart."

"You loved me enough to let me go for my own benefit."

"Yes."

"Let us be clear on this. It will *never* be for my benefit for you to leave me."

"Okay."

He leaned down and kissed her stomach. "Our children will know nothing but the supreme power and joy of love."

"And making up, maybe." They were both too strong willed for them never to argue.

Maks gave her his most rakish grin. "I believe we have makeup sex to participate in now."

"We were arguing?" she asked.

"Oh, yes. You even threatened to leave me." His hands were already busy on her clothing, undoing a button here, sliding down a zipper there.

"Never again."

"Never again."

They made love for the first time with their love pouring between them in cascade after cascade of emotional bliss.

Later they cuddled in his huge bed and Maks whispered against her hair, "Say it again."

"I love you and I will never leave you."

"I love you, *sérce moje*."

She thought she just might be able to live the rest of her life as his heart, so long as she lived in it.

And now she knew she did.

EPILOGUE

THE WEDDING ABOARD the luxury cruise liner was both beautiful and intimate.

Maks made sure Gillian's grandparents were there as well as both the king and queen of Volyarus. His cousin Demyan was his best man and Gillian's grandmother stood at her side as her matron of honor, tears tracking down weathered cheeks.

The State reception that followed was indeed not even a nine days wonder; Gillian's giving birth only six months later causing only marginally more of a blip on the media's radar.

But then that might have been because of the sensational wedding between Demyan and the long-lost granddaughter of Bartholomew Tanner from the original Yurkovich Tanner partnership.

Gillian thought there was something squirrelly about that wedding, but she was so wrapped up in her new baby and incandescent happiness married to the love of her life, she let the thought float away on the breeze of her own joy.

* * * * *